I0725265

HONOR THY FATHER

By
ELLEN FANNON

Honor Thy Father follows one family through time, showing the story of how siblings become separated and how this turn of events affects each of them in a different way. When their biological father needs a bone marrow transplant, all of the scattered siblings will come together to get past old hurts and misunderstandings, and to solidify their faith and their love for each other. This cast of characters is fascinating and well-rounded, showing that in the end, family is everything. A saga that covers a lot of family woes. You'll like this one.

Lenora Worth, author of more than seventy novels (including ***The X-Mas Club***), Carol Award finalist, and a *New York Times, USA Today, and PW* best-selling author.

In ***Honor Thy Father***, Ellen Fannon weaves the multilayered story of a splintered family's journey toward restoration and redemption. Threading through this heart-tugging tale is the reassurance of God's amazing power to turn our tragedies into triumphs. Put this one on the top of your TBR pile!

Laurel Blount, Carol Award winning author of ***Shelter in the Storm***

Ellen Fannon's heartfelt story in ***Honor Thy Father*** shows how families can be torn apart by mistakes the characters make as well as the situations they find themselves in. Twenty-five years has passed since Adam Wallace has seen his children. Misunderstanding has turned them against each other, a situation they each deal with in various ways. But when Adam needs to connect with them to save his life, will they be able to reconcile? Fannon masterfully takes us through the characters' experience and emotions as they come to grips with what's most important. I highly recommend reading this book and seeing how time and error can be overcome to pull families back together.

Marilyn Turk, award winning author

Who hasn't experienced family misunderstandings and broken relationships? Few are left unscathed when it comes to the many branches of a family tree. Ellen Fannon artfully weaves the connected characters of ***Honor Thy Father*** to show the reader that God creates beauty from ashes, despite the choices and decisions we fallen humans make. Fannon gives us hope and reminders that restoration with our Heavenly Father is possible, along with renewed earthly relationships, too. Don't miss this one!

Julie Lavender, author of ***Children's Bible Stories for Bedtime*** and ***365 Ways to Love Your Child: Turning Little Moments into Lasting Memories.***

Honor Thy Father is an engaging story of a fractured family in crisis over the father's desperate need for a bone marrow transplant to save his life. It's an engrossing and very relatable book which is hard to put down. Highly recommend!

Cara James, author of several novels, including ***Love on a Dime***, and award-winning author from Romance Writers of America and the American Christian Fiction Writers.

ALSO BY ELLEN FANNON

Other People's Children
Save the Date
Don't Bite the Doctor

This book is dedicated to my husband, Doug, a true man of God, and a father worthy of honor.

Honour thy father and thy mother: that thy days may be long upon the land which the LORD thy God giveth thee.
Exodus 20:12 (KJV)

PROLOGUE

1989

CHAPTER ONE

CHARLOTTE

The letter that forever changed Charlotte's life arrived in the morning's mail. Charlotte, however, did not see it until eleven forty-five.

At exactly twenty minutes before twelve, after spending the morning in her little greenhouse, where she passed the hours repotting plants and clearing away accumulated debris, she walked into the kitchen, carefully wiping her feet on the mat just inside the door. A glance at the teapot-shaped wall clock told her she still had fifteen minutes to clean up and get lunch ready before Patrick arrived home from kindergarten. Enough time to sift through the mail which lay strewn by the front door under the mail slot. Perhaps today she would receive something from her publisher. No, she noted, with a tinge of disappointment, no familiar Greenleaf envelope.

But wait, what was this? As she picked up the letter, a strange sense of unease worked its way up Charlotte's spine. Although merely a simple white envelope, foreboding pressed in on her, causing her stomach to roil. The return address bore no name, only an unknown street in Los Angeles. The unfamiliar handwriting with Charlotte's name and address provided no clue as to the sender. With shaking hands, she tore open the envelope and removed the letter.

Dear Charlotte, it began. She skipped to the bottom. The signature read, *Your stepmother, Katrina Wallace.* Her heart fluttered erratically and seemed to drop to her stomach. Her stepmother? Who was this strange woman who presumed such a relationship? She hurriedly scanned the body of the letter.

I know this letter will come as a shock to you, and I deeply apologize for the disruption of your life. Your father does not know about this, or he would never have allowed me to contact you. But I have no other choice and I am desperate. Your father has been quite ill. He has a highly fatal form of leukemia. Although he is now in remission, the doctors have given him only a five percent chance of remaining there. His only hope at this point is to undergo whole body radiation and a bone marrow transplant from a close relative. It is risky for him, but there are no other alternatives.

Please help us, Charlotte. Your father desperately needs you. Even if you should not prove to be a suitable bone marrow donor for him, at least come and make peace with him. It means everything to both of us, and although you may not realize it, it is important for you, as well. All your expenses will be covered, of course.

I am praying for you and anxiously await your reply.

The same Los Angeles address and a phone number were underneath the signature.

In the short minute that followed the revelation contained within the words penned on paper, her routine day and her safe, carefully-constructed world spiraled out of its comfortable orbit.

Still unable to fathom the depth of this request, Charlotte stared at the letter in her hand with a sense of unreality as her brain struggled to process what she had just read. How could this be happening to her now? Hadn't she put her father out of her mind years ago? She had gone on, despite everything, and made a happy life with Jeff and Patrick. Why couldn't the past be left in the past?

She was jolted out of her reverie by the slamming of the front door.

"Mommy?" called a cheerful child's voice. Patrick's footsteps echoed on the hardwood floor of the foyer. He stopped in the living room. "Mommy? Where are you?"

"In here, Patrick." Her choked voice sounded foreign to her ears. "I'm in the kitchen, sweetheart."

The child appeared in the kitchen, his face flushed from having run all the way from the bus stop. With his violet-blue eyes and head full of curly, blond hair, he looked—even if he didn't always act—like a perfect angel. Although a bit small for his age, with delicate bone structure, what he lacked in size, he more than made up for in energy. Still, he was a good child, as five-year-olds went.

"I'm starving. Where's my lunch?"

Charlotte struggled to refocus her mind back to her son's lunch. But the numbness in her brain made it difficult to begin the simple chore of putting together a peanut butter and jelly sandwich.

She shook her head, as though that would dislodge the fog. "Oh, I'm sorry. I didn't realize what time it was."

Fortunately, her body knew the routine, because nothing had registered in her mind since reading the letter. She automatically reached into the cupboard for the peanut butter, then opened the refrigerator to find the jelly, fumbling with the jar on the shelf.

Patrick climbed onto the counter to watch. "I fell down on the playground today."

"Hmm?"

Charlotte's voice came out distant and distracted, her unblinking eyes on the bread she pulled from the bread box. Why couldn't she shake this crushing numbness and focus?

Patrick tilted his head. "I said I fell down on the playground today. I skinned my knee. Look."

He stuck out his bony leg for her to admire the Band-Aid applied by his teacher. "Mommy! What're you doing? You *know* I hate strawberry seeds!"

Charlotte stared at the piece of bread spread with strawberry jam she had grabbed by mistake.

"Oh, I'm sorry, honey." She returned the offensive strawberry jam to the refrigerator and pulled out the grape jelly. Then she wiped the butter knife with a paper towel and handed it to Patrick. "Here. You're a big boy, now. Why don't you make your own sandwich?"

"Mommy, are you okay?" Patrick's forehead wrinkled into a frown, as he held the knife with clumsy fingers.

"Yes, yes, I'm fine." By the look on his face, he didn't believe her. Not wanting to frighten him, she pasted on a smile. "Well, actually, I'm feeling a little tired from working in the greenhouse all morning. I think I'll go rest for a while. After you eat your lunch, I want you to go outside and play quietly. Would you do that for me?"

"Sure, Mommy," he uttered, eyes downcast.

Already peanut butter and jelly smeared across his hands and the front of his shirt. Maybe this wasn't such a good idea. She'd have more work to clean up after him. But right now, she wasn't certain she'd make it to the bedroom.

"Thanks, sweetie." Charlotte hugged him tightly. "I'm just going to take a little nap."

Brow pulled down and lips pursed, Patrick set about the serious job of completing the sandwich.

Charlotte retreated to the bedroom, closing the door behind her. Picking up the phone, she punched in the number of her husband's office, waiting for his secretary to answer.

"Hello, Tracy? It's Charlotte. May I speak to Jeff, please?"

"Oh, I'm sorry, Charlotte. He's in court today. Is there a message you want to leave for him?"

Charlotte sighed. "No, that's all right. I completely forgot his schedule. I'll talk to him later."

She replaced the receiver and eased across the bed, staring at the ceiling, her frozen brain attempting to sort out the news and the feelings the letter had stirred up—the ones she thought were long buried.

At the top of the list, her father—whom she hadn't seen since she was Patrick's age, who had walked out on their family, torn them apart, and ruined their lives—was still alive. In all those years, he never once tried to contact her, not even after her mother died. Now he was dying. Now he needed *her*! How ironic. Where was he when she needed *him?* How dare he seek out the child he abandoned and ignored for twenty-five years to make peace at the end?

It wasn't your father who sought you out. It was your stepmother.

The unwelcome thought wormed its way into her thoughts. She snorted a mirthless laugh. Out of the woodwork came a stepmother she hadn't known existed. She wondered how long they had been married. Had her father left her mother and two children for this woman? Did she know he deserted his first family? Did they have children? Did he love them more than he had loved her?

"But I really don't care!" She sat upright, punching savagely at her pillow. "I was forced to make a life without you, and I've done just fine. I don't need you to come back after all this time and stir up feelings and memories that are dead and buried. I don't owe you anything. What right do you have to do this to me, now?"

Her anger spent after her tirade, she sagged against the headboard. Unbidden tears stung her eyes, and she bowed her head. "Dear God."

She paused. *I can't even pray. I don't know what to say.*

"Mommy? Who are you talking to?" A little voice came from the other side of the door.

"I thought I asked you to go outside and play." Her words came out sharper than she'd intended.

The silence that ensued hurt her ears worse than if he'd slammed the door. A minute later, the swing in the backyard squealed, tearing an even deeper hole in her heart.

———— • ● • ————

Jeff found his son outside when he came home from work. It was growing dark and chilly. He crossed the yard and gathered Patrick into his arms.

"Hey, pal, what're you doing out here?"

"Something's wrong with Mommy." The boy sniffed. "She told me to stay outside."

"Oh?" That didn't sound like Charlotte. "Well, come along inside. It's cold out here and it's time for dinner."

Ushering the child in front of him, a prickle of alarm ratcheted his pulse when he found the house in darkness and no dinner started. Something was very wrong.

"Listen, you go turn on the television, and I'll order us a pizza after I go check on Mommy. Okay?"

"Okay, Daddy," replied the little boy, his voice dull.

Jeff followed his son into the living room, tucking an Afghan around him and handing him the remote control.

Then he strode down the hallway and opened the bedroom door. Charlotte whipped her head from the window and jumped.

"Oh, Jeff. You're home already? What time is it?"

"It's almost six, Charley. What's wrong, honey?"

"Six?" She hopped up. "Where's Patrick? Is he all right?"

"He's fine, Charley. Watching television." Jeff moved over to the chair by the window next to where Charlotte had been sitting. He took her hands and gently pushed her back down. "Honey, what's the matter?"

"I can't believe I've sat here all afternoon. I wasn't even aware of the time passing." She turned and peered into Jeff's eyes, a letter clutched in her hand. She handed the letter to him. "*This* is what's wrong."

Jeff quickly scanned the contents of the letter. Then he took her in his arms. "Oh, honey." He laid his chin on the top of her head. "What a shock this must be to you."

Charlotte shook her head. "I thought that part of my life was over. I never expected to see or hear from my father again." She pulled her face away from his shoulder and cried angrily, "How dare he do this to me now. He has no right."

Jeff smoothed her tangled hair away from her face. "Have you thought about what you're going to do?"

Charlotte's dark blue eyes flashed. "What *I'm* going to do? Why should I have to do anything? It's not my problem. Maybe I'll just pretend I never got this dreadful letter in the first place. Maybe I'll return it with 'no such person at this address.' Maybe . . ." She burst into tears. "How did he find me?"

"I don't know, honey. But if you want my honest opinion, I don't think you'll ever be at peace with this until you know everything."

Charlotte shook her head again. "How can I dredge up all that ugly past? I can't go through that again. After all those feelings I've buried? It's not fair."

Jeff continued to hold her close. Then he said hesitantly, "Have you prayed about this, Charley?"

She shook her head. "I tried, but I can't." A ragged sigh escaped her lips, and she hung her head. "I can't forgive him."

Not good. "You know what the Bible says about unforgiveness, but I'll go along with whatever you decide. I love you and I'll always be here for you, no matter what."

Charlotte managed a weak smile. "What would I do without you, Jeff?" She brushed her tears away. "I've got to pull myself together. Patrick's probably scared to death. I'll deal with this after I've had a little more time to think. I need to start dinner."

"I told Patrick I'd order a pizza. Let me go take care of him while you fix your face." He kissed the top of her head. "Come join us when you're ready."

For his son's sake, Jeff put on a cheerful face, although his heart felt like a lead weight pressing against his chest. "Okay, kid, what do you want on your pizza?"

Patrick looked up from the floor, where he was sprawled out watching cartoons. "Is Mommy sick, Daddy?"

"She's fine, son. She's feeling much better. Now, what do you want on your pizza?"

Patrick bit his lip and didn't answer right away. Finally, he said, "Pepperoni."

Jeff tickled him. "That's what you always want."

Too bad people rarely got what they wanted.

Or needed.

Particularly when others were in control of the situation.

——•●•——

After dinner, Charlotte curled up on the sofa, listening to and identifying the sounds of normality. Running water. Patrick's splashing in the tub. Jeff's soft voice reading a bedtime story. Then the click of Patrick's bedroom light.

Through dinner, she'd forced herself to appear as normal as possible for Patrick's sake, remembering only too well how upsetting changes in a parent's behavior were to a small child. But now, with Patrick safely in bed, she didn't have to pretend, finally able to return to the problem which sent her world into a nosedive in the span of a few seconds.

It had been years since she had allowed herself to think about when she was Patrick's age. After all, there wasn't any earthly reason to want to dwell on something so painful. But it was never really gone, was it? Deep down, she knew no matter how hard she had tried to forget, the pain always clung to her soul, lurking beneath the surface of her carefully created outer facade. No matter how far she had come, the past still had a stranglehold on her which couldn't be shaken off. Why had she so foolishly thought that she could? That she had?

Jeff joined her.

"Is Patrick asleep?"

"Almost. He knows something's going on, though."

"I'm sure he does." It suddenly occurred to her that Jeff had had a tough day, too. Pushing down her own distress, she said, "Oh, Jeff, I forgot to ask you how you did in court today."

Jeff shrugged. "We won. I was brilliant, as usual."

She hugged him. "Oh, I'm so proud of you, honey. I know this was an important case for you and I was so wrapped up in myself, it completely slipped my mind."

"All in a day's work," he murmured into her hair.

"Nonsense. You're the most talented lawyer in the firm. And if those old buzzards don't realize that and make you a partner soon—"

"Don't try to avoid the subject at hand by flattering me, no matter how well deserved. Have you decided what you're going to do?"

Charlotte sighed. "No. This whole thing is such a shock." She turned to him. "What do you think I should do?" She turned to him, her eyes begging him to make her decision for her.

Jeff put his arm around her. "Honey, it doesn't matter what I think. You're the one who has to deal with it. And like I said before, whatever you decide, I'll support you."

She pondered for a moment. "If I were to go to him—and that is a big *if*—would you go with me?"

"If you want."

"And what about Patrick?"

"Well, we could either take him along, or perhaps we could leave him with someone."

She shook her head. "No, I wouldn't want to do that. It would be too upsetting to him. I remember how frightened I was when . . . well, you know. Small children have such a fear of abandonment. And if we took him with us, we'd have to take him out of school. And you'd have to take time off work . . . no telling how long we'd be there." She paused as her mind raced ahead of her words. "If it were only summer it would be easier. But you're so busy right now and Patrick has school."

"It sounds as if you've made up your mind to go."

"I'm just considering the options." She sat back and frowned. "Oh, Jeff, why do I feel so guilty when I think about *not* going?"

"Is that how you feel?"

She shrugged. "I don't know how I feel." Her voice raised a notch. "But what do I owe these people, anyway? That man indirectly caused my mother's death by abandoning her and ruined my life. Why should I care if he's dying? Good riddance to him, I should say. For all I knew, he *was* dead for the last twenty-five years."

She began to cry again. "I just wish he had never found me. Then I would have never known. I wouldn't have to make this decision."

• ● •

Jeff held her close and let her cry until she was spent. He couldn't help in some ways agreeing with her. After all they had been through together, just the two of them against the world, why now? And they had made it, despite everything. But he knew Charlotte. She would have to see this through. He knew her decision even before she had completely admitted it to herself.

Her held her at arm's length. "Honey, have you considered that God may have a plan in all this?"

She reached for her soggy tissue and blew her nose. "I prayed for so many years for my dad to come back for me, but God wasn't listening, so I just gave up."

Her voice broke as the tears started again. Jeff just held her, letting her cry.

After a long time, the tears stopped. "It must be after midnight." She stood, touching his shoulder. "You've got to get up early."

"Never mind. I'll be all right."

"Let's go to bed. Maybe I'll wake up in the morning and find out this has all been a bad dream."

"Charley, you know that's not going—"

"I know." She sighed. "First thing in the morning, I'll sit down and write that woman a reply. I don't think I can handle calling her. Then I'll make arrangements to fly out there. But that's all I'm going to commit to, even if I do turn out to be a suitable donor. I could be putting myself at risk. And I have you and Patrick to think of."

Jeff kissed her lightly. "I love you, Charley. Everything will work out."

———•●•———

Later, as Charlotte lay in bed, listening to Jeff's even breathing, another thought occurred to her.

She wondered if that woman had managed to find her baby sister.

CHAPTER TWO
DANA

D ana DeVoux had just returned to her Fifth Avenue apartment from her early morning rehearsal at Carnegie Hall where she was to give a concert that night. At twenty-five, she was one of the country's youngest concert pianists in the performing circuit—as well as one of the most praised pianists to come along in years.

However, despite her success, a black mood hovered over her as she dropped her purse onto the caramel-colored leather sofa. The rehearsal had not gone according to her exacting standards. The Steinway concert grand piano had not been tuned to her satisfaction. She couldn't imagine such an oversight. Someone had really dropped the ball. Or perhaps the lazy stage manager thought he could get away with not having the piano tuned and she wouldn't notice. But her perfectly trained ear immediately picked up that the higher registers were just a hair flat. Perhaps nobody else had noticed, but she'd torn a strip up one side of him and down the other. The stage manager assured her it would be taken care of immediately, and heads would roll. She didn't care if heads rolled or not. She just wanted that blasted piano tuned by tonight.

Then the incompetent lighting crew could not get the lighting effects the way she wanted. How difficult could it be? She had requested an ethereal effect for her Debussy pieces, a concept the dolts simply could not comprehend. Their limited imaginative ideas for the effect she wanted consisted of either casting a blue spotlight on her, or plunging her into a shadow. She'd laid into them, too, after she finished with the incompetent stage manager.

"That's *not* the way I want it!" she had shrieked. "Do I look like a Smurf to you? I want *ethereal.* Can't you understand that? Or maybe you're too stupid to know what the word means." She projected her anger at them, wishing her words were arrows. Or machetes. In a voice dripping with disdain, she enlightened them. "It means `light, airy, heavenly, intangible.' Listen to the music. Then maybe you'll understand the effect I want."

She stomped away toward her dressing room, her heels tapping a staccato on the backstage floor. Then, hearing the stagehands' voices echoing through the empty hall, she stopped in her tracks and edged back to where she could see and hear them better.

"What does she want from us, anyway?" grumbled Frank Taylor, the head of the crew. "Ethereal, for Pete's sakes. How the heck do you light `ethereal'?"

Reuben, who had just transferred from Off-Broadway productions, wrapped an extension cord around his hand and elbow. "Maybe we could bring in some dry ice and blow it across the stage, like a mist. That's what they did for *Phantom of the Opera* when the fog machine malfunctioned."

Frank snorted. "Too bad Carnegie Hall doesn't have a fog machine. But the Debussy numbers are at the end. I'm not sure dry ice will keep that long under these hot lights. Even with a cooler."

Tim, the third member of the crew teetered on the top step of a ladder as he screwed in a burnt-out bulb. "With the Ice Princess? It'll be freezing up there."

Dana, having heard enough of their insolence, edged back to the stage without making a sound. Standing behind them, she said, in a caustic voice, "I like the dry ice effect. Figure out a way to keep it cold. Surely you can handle that."

She derived a small measure of satisfaction from startling them and making them jump. Then she spun on her heel, again intending to retreat to her dressing room. But just off-stage, she paused once more, as their hushed words reached her ears. Idiots. Didn't they realize even soft sounds carried in this cavernous hall?

"Oops," muttered Tim. "I've put my foot in it this time."

"Do you think someone like her cares what we think?" asked Frank. "To her, we're just the peon working people. She's so high up on her pedestal nothing we think could even phase her."

She closed her eyes and took a calming breath through her nose. They were wrong. It galled Dana more than she would ever admit that what those dim-witted jerks said behind her back bothered her. But as a perfectionist, she had come to expect a certain lack of understanding by those who were clearly beneath her. Sometimes she felt so alone. So few people understood her efforts, let alone appreciated them. But to have to suffer the indignities of the stagehands, of all people, insulting her was too much. She would see to it they were all fired.

Spying her mail which had been laid on the hall table by the cleaning lady, she sifted through the pile. Typical junk mail, requests for charities, bills . . . What was this? A personal letter with a handwritten address from someone in Los Angeles whose handwriting she didn't recognize. A little curious, although still out of sorts, she tore open the envelope and proceeded to read. Not understanding, and feeling perhaps she hadn't been concentrating hard enough, she reread it. Then she looked at the envelope again. There was no mistake. It was addressed to Miss Dana DeVoux from a supposed stepmother. How bizarre.

"This is either a mistake or someone's idea of a stupid joke," she grumbled as she tossed it aside.

She had to rest for her performance tonight. She had no time for stupid mistakes or fools.

A cup of herbal tea sounded good and might help lift her spirits.

As she was putting on the kettle, she heard the doorbell, followed immediately by the sound of her front door opening. Dana swore under her breath. "I wish she wouldn't do that."

"Are you home, darling?" called her mother.

"In the kitchen, Mother. I do wish you'd wait for me to answer the door before you use your key."

"Only trying to save you some steps, darling."

"Right. Only trying to give yourself a few more seconds to snoop," Dana mumbled.

"What was that, dear?"

Of course her mother had heard the comment. She had ears

like radar. "I said would you like some tea?"

"Love some. How did rehearsal go?" Her mother continued to call from the foyer.

Drat the woman. Why didn't she come into the kitchen so they wouldn't have to continue this shouting match? Wiping her hands on the kitchen towel, Dana left the kettle to boil and made her way to the front hall. "Awful. You just wouldn't believe . . . Mother, really? You're reading my mail?"

Caught in the act, Andrea DeVoux dropped the letter she had been holding. Her face had gone ashen.

Dana snatched up the mystery letter. "Honestly, Mother, you can be so—"

Her mother's strangled voice came out in a whisper. "What is this letter, Dana?"

Dana's annoyance at her mother's snooping had made her momentarily forget the strange letter.

"This?" She tossed it aside again. "I have no idea. Somebody's idea of a joke, I suppose. Or the wrong person. My name is rather common, you know." She huffed out a mirthless laugh, the implications of which were clear. Everyone in the world was incompetent and therefore it was not surprising everything was always fouled up. "I think I hear the kettle."

Retreating to the kitchen, she fumed over her mother's complete disregard for her privacy. She returned to the living room holding a tray with two steaming mugs of tea and a plate of cookies to find Andrea looking as if she had seen a ghost. She stood clutching the letter again.

"Mother, what on earth is the matter with you? And didn't I ask you not to read my mail?" Dana set the tray on the lacquered coffee table and looked up at her mother, her lips flattened in annoyance.

A growing sense of unease began working its way through her gut. Was her mother ill? She had never seen Andrea like this.

Dana sank down next to her mother on the sofa. "Mother, what is it?" she asked, softening her tone. She took her mother's hand. It was ice cold.

Andrea sat still, staring out the window, yet not seeing the magnificent view of Central Park.

Dana's done quite well for herself. And it's because of Charles and me. Nobody else. Nobody else helped make her who she is. How could this happen now after all these years? How did they find her?

Andrea drew a long, shaky breath. Then she turned to face her daughter. *Her* daughter. With the flashing, angry blue eyes so unlike hers and Charles' brown eyes. With the pale blonde hair, so unlike hers and Charles' dark brown hair. With her tall, slim features, so unlike hers and . . . Hadn't the child ever noticed? They should have told her. But there had been absolutely no way for her to ever find out. She and Charles had discussed it over and over. And in the end, they had decided to leave things alone. Dana was too special to go off on some tangent about finding her roots and ruining her life. She was famous, she was talented.

Maybe she shouldn't tell her. Dana didn't realize what that letter was. But it wouldn't stop with one letter, would it? Those people were clearly desperate. They would send more letters or worse yet, send somebody to enlighten Dana. And then how would Dana feel about having been deceived all these years? She would despise them. They might lose her, forever.

"Darling, I've got to tell you something," Andrea began, her voice quivering.

"What, Mother?"

Andrea's soft brown eyes brimmed with tears as she registered the intensity of her daughter's eyes searching hers.

"I don't know quite where to start. You may hate me when I tell you."

Dana reached for her mother's purse on the coffee table and fished for a handkerchief. "Hate you? Oh, Mother, you know I could never do that." She gently pressed the handkerchief into her mother's hand.

Andrea took another deep breath and dabbed her eyes.

"You see, darling, your father and I should have told you long ago. But we didn't want you to stop thinking of us as your real parents."

Dana gasped. "Are you trying to tell me I'm adopted?"

Andrea nodded, unable to speak. Tears trickled down her cheeks.

"I see," Dana said, her voice calmer than Andrea would have imagined from her volatile daughter at the stunning revelation. "I should have guessed. There are so many things. I mean I don't look like either one of you, do I?"

She took her mother's cold hand again. "I'm not angry, Mother, just confused. Why didn't you ever tell me?"

"Well," Andrea stopped, blew her nose, then continued, the story rushing out quickly before she lost her nerve. "At the time, we didn't see any reason to tell you. You were just under a year old when you came to us, so you didn't have any memories. Your biological mother died and nobody knew where your biological father was. We were told he abandoned you. Charles and I had tried for so long to have children and we were getting older, and . . ." She stopped to blot her eyes. "Anyway, Charles had a friend who was a judge at that time, and he suggested we consider adopting a child."

"But I still don't understand why you never told me."

Andrea hesitated. She knew she had to tell it all. "Well, you see, by the time we got through all the adoption formalities, we were told we were too old to adopt a baby. We were both in our early forties at the time. So this friend of Charles' arranged for a private adoption. He knew a lawyer who made the arrangements. However, the lawyer thought it best if we agreed to move out of the state so no questions would be asked. It was all legal, mind you, but we did not go through normal channels."

"Mother, how legal could this be if you had to move out of the state to avoid questions? It sounds like black-marketing babies to me."

Andrea hung her head as the ugly truth of what she had never allowed herself to acknowledge sliced through her soul like a hot knife.

"I never let myself believe it," she whispered. "I knew things weren't quite right, but your father and I wanted a baby so badly. I let him convince me everything was all right."

"Oh, Mother." Dana breathed out a sigh and closed her eyes. "Then what happened?"

"Well, we took you and moved to New York. The family was cautioned about mentioning anything for fear of causing trouble for Charles' judge friend."

Dana's jaw dropped. "Mother, then you *knew* the adoption wasn't legal." She massaged her forehead, where a steady throbbing had begun.

Andrea bit her trembling lip and raised her eyes to her daughter's. "Oh, darling. Like I said, I wanted you so badly, I made myself believe it was legal. Charles took care of everything. Not that I'm shifting the blame onto him, mind you, but it was just easier for me to live with if I didn't admit it."

Tears coursed down Andrea's cheeks. Dana hugged her to her shoulder, rocking her like a small child.

"Do you hate me?" Andrea sobbed.

"Of course not," Dana assured her. "But this does put us in a mess, doesn't it?"

Andrea pulled back, searching her daughter's face through the blur of her tears. "What do you mean?"

"Well, here I am now with a dying biological father whom I never knew existed until a few minutes ago. And I may be the only one in the world who can help him."

"What?" Andrea cried. "You can't be serious. That man, whoever he is, may have fathered you, but that doesn't make him a father. Charles is your father. That man never cared about you until now, when he needs something from you. He probably found out you are famous and wants to exploit you."

"Oh, Mother, I doubt that. He could have found me a long time ago if that's what he wanted. I think he must not have any other options. And actually, he didn't write the letter. His wife did."

"For him. He was probably too ashamed to contact you himself. As well he should be. Any parent who abandons a child should have no future claim on that child, no matter what happens."

"But, Mother, he's dying. Don't you think I owe it to him—"

"No!" cried Andrea, sharply. "I don't. Where was he when you needed him?"

Dana shook her head. "I don't know. Perhaps there were circumstances beyond his control. Or maybe he is just a selfish jerk. But either way, I may be his only living blood relative. And he needs my help."

Andrea clutched at her daughter. "Dana, no. Darling, please consider your career. You're due to go on tour week after next. You can't throw all that away."

Dana moved away from her mother's reach. "The tour can wait. I'll take a leave of absence."

Andrea moved toward her again. "Darling, please don't do this. You don't know these people. And what things they'll fill your head with once they get you in their sympathy. And this donor thing. It could be dangerous. What if something should go wrong?"

Dana disengaged herself from Andrea's grasp and stood.

Andrea's face crumpled, and she held out her hands to her daughter.

"Dana, please. I beg of you. Don't do this."

Dana's shoulders slumped. "Mother, I understand how you feel. Really, I do. But try to understand how *I* feel. Believe me, having this news thrown into my lap just a few hours before my concert is unnerving. But in all fairness, I should have been told years ago."

"Yes, yes," agreed Andrea. "And I'm sorry about that, darling."

"It doesn't matter now. What matters is that I have an obligation to another person. Not an obligation I particularly want, but nevertheless, one I have to meet. Can you understand that?"

Andrea began to cry again. "I knew this would happen. I just knew it."

"Mother, this has nothing to do with my finding my roots, as you put it. In fact, if I had known before, I seriously doubt I would have cared. But I didn't seek him out. He sought me because he needs my help."

"But he's not your concern," Andrea pleaded. "Your father and I need you, too."

"Oh, Mother, you're not going to lose me. You are and always will be my real parents."

The lump in Andrea's throat grew larger as she came to the sinking realization that nothing she could say would dissuade Dana. With difficulty, she swallowed, and in a raspy voice, tried one more time. "Darling, I wish you'd think this over before you make a dreadful mistake. At least do that much."

"I don't have to think about it. I know what I have to do." The tea, untouched, had grown cold. "Shall I warm up your tea?"

"No, thank you," Andrea answered, the defeat evident in her voice. "I'd better go home and let you get some rest for tonight." She struggled to her feet, kissed Dana on the cheek, and without another word, took her leave.

———•●•———

Dana sat thinking for a long time after Andrea left. What a fine thing to be told on the afternoon before her performance. How was she supposed to concentrate on her playing? If she made it through this night, she would take some time off. The aggravations of the morning's rehearsal suddenly seemed far away and insignificant.

———•●•———

A few blocks away, a tearful Andrea spilled her heart out to her husband. "We've lost her, Charles. We've lost her forever, just like we were afraid of."

Charles attempted to comfort her. "Nonsense, dear. She'll be back. Nothing will change. You'll see." But as he murmured reassurances to his wife, his own mind was full of the same doubts and fears.

CHAPTER THREE
SCOTT

————•●•————

On the other side of the continent, in a dirty little apartment in an undesirable section of San Francisco, Scott Wallace was just waking up. For a moment, his fuzzy brain registered nothing. Where was he? What time was it? Rolling over onto his side, he found he lay on the living room floor, fully clothed. And he had a massive headache. He looked at his watch and groaned. One o'clock. Brooke would be home any minute now, and she wouldn't be pleased.

Scott struggled to sit up. With his head pounding, he surveyed the damage to the room from the night before. Scattered beer bottles and ashtrays took up every surface, as well as the floor. A few joints smoked down to the butts cluttered the ashtrays . . . and a few had been left wherever they happened to land. The lingering, sickly-sweet odor of marijuana hung like a heavy cloud in the airless room. Brooke would have a fit. He really shouldn't have popped those pills with all the booze. He had been out cold for hours. The place could have burned down or been robbed for all he knew. Before he passed out, he had a vague recollection of several people still in the room.

Staggering to his feet, he inched his way to the bathroom, avoiding the obstacle course of last night's litter. He surveyed his puffy, sallow face in the mirror.

"Scott, you are really going to have to stop doing this to yourself, old buddy," he told his reflection. Opening the medicine cabinet, he groped around until he found the aspirin, then downed four of them with a glass of water. His stomach recoiled in nauseous rebellion.

Today he'd had an interview scheduled for nine o'clock with Hanson Construction. Brooke had had to pull a few strings to get him that interview after what had happened on his last job.

He'd blown it. It was already one o'clock. Maybe he could call and explain . . . what? He had gotten so drunk and so stoned last night that he'd passed out? Hardly. He'd have to think of something.

Should he jump in the shower first or try to clean up the mess before Brooke came home? As his foggy brain wrestled with the seemingly overwhelming decision, he heard the door slam. Uh, oh. Too late for either.

"Scott? How did the interview . . . *what the* . . .?" She had obviously caught sight of the living room. "Scott!"

Angry footsteps sought him out. The bathroom door banged open, and an irate woman stood in the doorway.

Scott knew the double shift she had just finished at the hospital on top of coming home to the remnants of last night's party would not help her mood. He grinned sheepishly.

"I'm sorry, babe. I'll clean everything up. Just let me get a shower to get me started."

Her dark eyes blazed with fury. "What went on here last night?"

"Just a little party. No big deal."

"With drugs!" she spat. "How many times do I have to tell you what will happen to me if drugs are found in my apartment? I'll lose my job at the hospital. Even *you* should know that."

They had been through this lecture before. Brooke could really be a drag, sometimes, but for free room and board, Scott figured he could put up with her occasional tirades.

She placed her hands on her hips. "And you obviously missed your interview."

"I'll call them and set up another one. I can tell them I got sick or something."

Her nostrils flared. "You idiot. That interview wasn't easy for me to set up. You're history now, as far as they're concerned."

"So, who needs their stupid job, anyway? I'll find something else." Scott thrust out his jaw and matched his tone to hers.

Brooke narrowed her eyes and flattened her lips. Her long black hair had begun to escape the hairpins hours ago when the exhaustion of the double shift had begun to take its toll. This was the last straw. Hungry, tired, and coming home to her trashed living room pushed her over the edge. She had loved the guy once, although only God knew why. She was going to "reform" him, help him change his ways, help him beat his drug and alcohol habit. What a fool she was. Scott didn't want her help. He just wanted to use her.

Her voice softened. "I hope you can find something else, Scott. Because I want you out of here. Today."

She could tell by the pitiful, helpless little boy face he donned that he knew he had gone too far. He held his hands out to her. She had seen it all before.

"Brooke," he pleaded, "you don't mean that. You're just tired and angry with me, which you have every right to be."

She remained silent.

"Please, babe, give me another chance. I'll change. You know I can do it. I swear, no more drugs, no more booze. I'll get a job, I promise. Then we can find us a nice place somewhere and make a real go of our lives. I'm sorry I let you down again, but that's over. I swear."

He took a step toward her but she backed up. His eyes locked on hers. "I know everything is my fault. From now on, I'll be straight. I'd do anything for you. You know I love you, babe."

How many times had she heard this speech? And how many times had she let him con his way back into her heart only to be let down again? She almost let his words and the earnest look in his eyes work on her fragile emotions again, as her heart struggled with what her head was telling her. It was all an act.

Taking a deep breath, she forced herself to say the words before she changed her mind. "Scott, you need more help than I can give you. And if I'm always here to take care of you, you're never going to get that help. This is hard for me, Scott, but I meant what I said. I want you out. Today."

—— • ● • ——

Whoa! This was serious. His pulse began thrumming in his ears and he felt a trickle of sweat on his brow as the initial twinge of panic set in.

Come on, Brooke, I really don't need this right now. Not with this headache. I've got to do something to change her mind.

He walked toward her again, intending to take her in his arms.

She stiffened her arm and blocked his advance.

"Today, Scott. I'm going to bed. When I get up, I don't want to see you here."

She turned, and with her head held high, walked into the bedroom, closing the door and locking it behind her.

Scott stared at the closed door for a minute.

Better not push her right now.

But what was he supposed to do with no place to go and no money? He wandered back into the living room, stepping over the debris, and sank onto the sofa.

Got to think.

But his head hurt too badly. Spying the stack of mail Brooke had dropped, he moved to gather it up. Maybe there was something. He didn't know what.

Suddenly, the past leapt out at him. A letter from his mother. He hadn't seen his parents in almost eighteen months, although his mother occasionally wrote to him—but she never sent the requested money. Still, he hadn't received a letter from her in quite a while. Maybe they were finally sorry for kicking him out and wanted to make amends. That might be a solution to his immediate predicament.

Yeah, maybe I could go home for a while.

He ripped open the envelope and pulled out the letter with Mom's familiar handwriting. But he was unprepared for what he read.

My dear son,

You have no idea how difficult this letter is for me to write. When we asked you to leave a year and a half ago, we told you not to come home until you straightened your life out. I hope and pray you have. That was the hardest decision we've ever had to make, but we did it as much for you, Scott, as for ourselves.

Did it for me? Right.

He continued reading.

What I'm writing about, though, has nothing to do with your problems. I'm writing because of your father. He's terminally ill with leukemia. The doctors say he has only a few months at the most unless he has a bone marrow transplant from a close relative. That procedure, in itself, is risky, but it's his only hope. I'm not asking you to be a donor—I know your blood types are incompatible, so it wouldn't work. However, there are some other routes I am pursuing at the moment. But I want to ask you to come home and make peace with your father. Regardless of how you feel, you owe him that much. You may never have another chance, Scott. I pray you will take this opportunity to put things right between you and your father. I anxiously await to hear from you.

Your loving mother

Scott couldn't believe it. After the way they treated him, his parents had the gall to beg him to come home and play out some morbid deathbed scene like a bad movie? No way. Let the old man die with the guilt on his conscience of kicking out his only child.

"Serves him right," Scott muttered. Nothing against the old lady—she had to go along with the old man, but she had a lot of nerve sending him this tear-jerker letter. As if he cared about setting things right. Nothing could be set right. They were responsible for his lousy, messed up life. He owed them nothing.

The letter had not been the apology he hoped for. If only he had somewhere else to go.

"Scott, come home and make peace with your father," he mumbled, in a sarcastic falsetto.

He wadded up the letter and threw it among the rest of the trash on the floor. Why did everyone want something from him? Why couldn't they just leave him alone? If only he had some money. If only he had another option. He was sick of Brooke's nagging, but he didn't want to go home under these conditions.

He sat for hours pondering what to do. It always came back to the same two choices—either get Brooke to change her mind or go home. Great. He hadn't realized how long he sat there until he heard the bedroom door open. Maybe Brooke would be in a better mood after her nap.

He waited, listening to her bare feet padding down the hall. She stopped abruptly at the sight of him. He had to admit she looked rather inviting in her over-sized T-shirt and mussed hair.

"I thought I told you to get out!" she screeched.

Scratch option number one. "I'm going!" he shouted back. "I had to wait for you to get up so I could get my things from the bedroom."

"Then get them and get out."

As he sauntered to the bedroom, he heard her groaning over the mess in the living room.

"Let her clean it up," he muttered under his breath. "It's her apartment." Like she didn't remind him of that fact constantly.

He threw his few belongings into a duffel bag and meandered back into the living room. Perhaps at the sight of him actually leaving, she would change her mind. Brooke had pulled the trash can into the living room. The clunk of beer bottles hitting the side of the can caused the throbbing in his head to ramp up with a vengeance. She didn't look up when he came in.

"I'm going now," he announced.

"Goodbye, Scott," she said, her tone flat. "Have a nice life." She swiped at a stray tear on her cheek.

"Yeah. You, too."

So that was that. The end. He picked up the duffel bag and walked out the door.

He only had one option now, much as he hated to have to use it.

"But, that's one more than you had a few hours ago, buddy," he told himself. "Cheer up. Things will get better. Maybe the old man will die happy and leave you a fortune."

He walked the few blocks to the bus terminal. Spotting a pay phone, he placed a collect call to Los Angeles. His mother answered the phone.

"Scott!" she cried. "Is it really you?"

"Yeah, Mom, it's me."

He could tell she was crying. "Are you all right?"

"Yeah, I'm fine, Mom. I got your letter. I'm coming home."

"Oh, thank God. When are you getting here?"

"Around midnight, Mom, if you can spring for a bus ticket."

"Of course. I will call the bus station and arrange for a ticket. I love you."

Yeah, right.

He hung up.

CHAPTER FOUR
ADAM

———— • ● • ————

Katrina replaced the receiver. Tears spilled down her cheeks. "That was Scott."

The thin, pale man to whom she spoke made no comment. His head, with its sparse, fuzzy hair—the casualty of numerous chemotherapy treatments—resembled that of a worn teddy bear. His face wore a scowl.

"He's coming home, Adam."

Adam let out a long sigh. "Is he straightened out?"

"I don't know. I didn't ask. It doesn't matter. All that matters is they are all coming."

He sighed again. "Doesn't matter? Just what we need, our junkie son in the house again. As if we haven't got enough trouble. A sick man can't even die in peace."

"Don't you talk like that, Adam," she warned, her voice taut. "Both the girls are coming. One of them will surely be able to help."

"You shouldn't have done it, Kate," he snapped. "You had no right going behind my back and interfering in their lives."

"I had *every* right!" she snapped back. "I'd do anything to save your life."

"They have their own lives without me. It wasn't fair to them, Kate, and when they arrive, I'm telling them to go back home."

"You'll do no such thing. I went to a great deal of trouble to find those girls. You know I wouldn't have done it if I'd had any other choice." She raised her chin and thrust out her jaw. "But what's done is done. They're coming and that's all I care about. Besides, you owe them an explanation from your own lips. And they owe you something. You *are* their father."

"They don't owe me a blasted thing. Do you hear me?" he bellowed.

She folded her arms across her chest. "Then why are they coming?"

"Maybe they want to tell me to my face to drop dead—which I will be doing shortly."

Katrina's mouth flattened. She took a deep breath and blew it out through her nose. "You listen to me, Adam Wallace. I will not have any more of that talk. Do you hear me?"

He didn't answer. He turned away, certain that his wife's meddling was going to bring heartache for everyone. But he was too tired to fight any more.

PART 1
A TRAGEDY OF ERRORS
1963

CHAPTER FIVE
ADAM

It was a beautiful April morning, and not just because of the glorious cobalt sky filled with wispy white clouds or the radiant sun which had begun to warm away the chill of the early day. Adam had another reason to feel as if he were walking on air. As he practically bounced to his car, humming cheerfully to himself, he drank in the clean spring air and thought about the changes that were going to give him a second chance in life.

Too excited to complete his calls for the day, he had telephoned each of his clients and explained he would be unable to stop by today, promising to catch them next week. Then he had tried to call Connie to share his news. But there was no answer. Disappointed at first, he later decided it might be better to just head home and surprise her. Connie was going to be so excited.

As he pulled out of the motel parking lot and automatically headed for the interstate, he allowed his thoughts to drift back to last night's regional meeting of Fenner Pharmaceuticals. Normally, the Thursday night meetings constituted a necessary bore, a ritual to be endured once a week. But not last night. He'd had no inkling of what was to come.

After the usual new product introductions and production reports, Earl Creary, the regional manager, asked Adam to remain after the meeting. With feelings of anticipation mixed with curiosity and just a twinge of trepidation, Adam fidgeted in his chair until the last of the sales representatives finally finished their after-meeting small talk and went their various ways. Earl rose and closed the door after them.

"Adam," he began, without preamble, "I know you've not been completely happy being on the road."

Not knowing where Earl was going with this observation, Adam didn't know whether to agree or protest. "I've no complaints, Earl," he replied.

"Oh, no, my boy, you've never complained. And you're one of the finest sales reps we've ever had. You're dependable, productive, and the clients like you." Earl paused for an agonizing moment while Adam waited for the "but."

When it appeared Earl might have completely lost his train of thought, Adam prompted, "But?"

Clearing his throat, Earl went on. "I know despite your apparent contentment with your job and your obvious ability, you're still not totally happy. Am I right?" He stopped and pinned Adam with sharp eyes.

Adam hesitated. "Well, like I said. I can't complain. The money's good and I like what I'm doing, but . . . well, it's really harder on Connie than me, being alone all week with Charlotte, and now, of course, with the baby . . . well, it's not easy."

He didn't elaborate. To say it was hard on Connie was an understatement. She had been miserable ever since he had taken this job. And she never failed to remind him how unhappy she was. But he didn't say this to Earl.

"It's a hard life for a family man," agreed Earl. "But I think I have an interesting proposition for you."

"Oh?" Earl definitely had his attention now.

Earl didn't answer immediately. Instead, he seemed to be intent on prolonging Adam's agony. Finally, after much throat clearing, he proceeded. "I know you lack one year of getting your pharmacy degree, Adam. Darn shame, too. You're bright. You're wasting your time and your potential being a sales rep." He paused, letting his words sink in.

However, Adam was only too acutely aware of his missed opportunities.

"If I'm not mistaken, your goal at one time was pharmaceutical research."

Adam nodded. His dream, yes, but that plan had derailed.

"Here's the situation. Fenner recently opened a new plant in Atlanta. We need to bring in some fresh, young blood and new ideas."

Adam's heart began to beat faster.

"What we propose is to send you back to school to finish your degree and then put you to work in our research facility. While you're finishing your degree, we'd like you to assist Dr. Rothchild. You're familiar with Rothchild?"

Familiar? Who in the pharmaceutical world hadn't heard of the great Dr. Robert Rothchild? The man was single-handedly responsible for a number of ground-breaking drugs. Too dumbfounded to speak, all Adam could do was nod. He silently willed the older man to hurry and get to the end.

"The fact is, as you well know, we could hire a hundred kids fresh out of pharmacy school, right now, for half the salary we're proposing to offer you. But you've got something that ninety-nine percent of them don't have." Earl stabbed the air next to Adam's chest with his finger. "You've got brains *and* common sense. That's a rarity. And you've got ambition, as well as almost five years of experience in the real world. That's something most of these wet-behind-the-ears newbies know nothing about. They don't realize that once you create the drugs, you have to market them in order to make money."

Adam grinned. He refrained from interrupting, but his restraint hung by a thread while waiting for Earl to continue.

After another lengthy pause, Earl said, "It won't be easy for you, my boy. You'll have to dig out those old notes and catch up. You'll be in school all day and in the lab all weekend. You'll probably see less of the wife and kids than you do now. But I guarantee if you stick out this year, you'll go far with Fenner. Because you've got what it takes."

Adam wasn't sure whether Earl was finished or not, but he could restrain himself no longer. Jumping out of his seat, he grabbed Earl's hand.

"I accept!" he cried, pumping the older man's hand. "I can't thank you enough, Earl. I know you recommended me for this opportunity, and I really appreciate your confidence in me. I won't let you down."

Earl's face flushed. Clearing his throat again, he replied, "I'm sure you won't, Adam." Then he extracted his hand from Adam's and wiggled his fingers. "Well, it's settled then. Congratulations, my boy." He slapped Adam's shoulder. "I'll be in touch over the weekend on the exact details. Hope you like Atlanta."

Adam floated back to his motel room. Still giddy with excitement, he reached for the telephone to share his news with Connie. Then, looking at the time, he replaced the receiver. It was after eleven. Charlotte would be asleep, and if he woke the baby, Connie might have a hard time getting her back to sleep. With a tinge of disappointment, he decided to wait until morning.

When the first morning rays of sun began to filter through the pre-dawn gray sky, Adam realized, after a sleepless night, he was too wound up to finish his calls. He would stop in next week, he promised his clients. Chances were he would have a new man with him on the route to break in, anyway. The only thing that mattered now was getting home to his wife and kids.

He smiled as he anticipated Connie's relief at finally having her husband home and working regular hours. At last, he would get to spend more time with his children. Charlotte changed so much from week to week, and he had been on the road for most of the important milestones that had marked her five-and-a-half years. And the baby, Diana, was almost six months old, just learning to sit up on her own. He had missed so much. But he was going to make up for lost time. He would make up a lot of things to Connie, too. Maybe now they could have a real go at their marriage. It had been hard enough on both of them, but perhaps now, they could put the tough times behind them and start building a stronger relationship with each other. They could be a real family.

A little pang of guilt tugged at Adam's gut when he thought of Connie and how they had been forced to abandon their young dreams because of the unplanned pregnancy. His thoughts drifted back to the beginning of their relationship. How pretty Connie had been when he first met her on campus. With her bouncy blonde curls and dark blue, almost violet eyes—just like Charlotte's—she had been young and full of life. He was older, a second-year pharmacy student, and Connie, having come to the big city university from a strict, small town, had been awed by his maturity. She was impressionable and sweetly naïve, and it had not taken much to seduce her.

He knew it was wrong. He knew what the Bible taught, and he knew how he had been raised. But he had been so attracted to her he couldn't help himself—not that he tried all that hard. For Connie's part, free and on her own for the first time, she had been eager and willing to learn. Adam was wildly infatuated with her, although if he were totally honest, he hadn't been in love with her. Then, toward the end of his third year in pharmacy school, she came to him in tears saying she was pregnant.

Adam sat down with his parents to give them the news.

"Son, we are deeply disappointed in you," his father said. Silent tears streamed down his mother's face. "You know sex outside of marriage is wrong. There are good reasons for that, this situation being one of them."

Adam nodded, too ashamed to meet his father's eyes.

"There are always consequences when we insist on doing things our way instead of God's way. You know what you have to do."

Adam nodded again. "We'll get married."

"You realize you can't be married and live on campus. And you may lose your scholarship, too."

"I know." Adam hung his head.

"I wish your mother and I were in a position to help you financially, but we're just not able to right now."

"I understand, sir." Adam briefly met his father's eyes before looking down again. "I'm going to take responsibility for my actions. We'll get married and I'll get a night job. Connie will work until the baby comes. It'll be a tough year, but we'll make it." He drew in a ragged breath. "I'm sorry I let you down."

His father crossed the room and wrapped him in a comforting hug. "Son, we all make mistakes, but it's how we handle those mistakes that count. We love you and we're here for you."

Tragically, however, both Adam's parents died in a car accident shortly after the quick wedding in the judge's chambers.

Connie's parents, upon hearing the news, had immediately disowned her for having brought disgrace upon the family.

"This is what happens when children go off from their respectable upbringing to some big city college," her father declared to her mother, as if the young couple hadn't been standing in the same room. "You wanted Constance to be the first in the family to get an education. Well, it's some education your daughter got." He stormed out of the room, his angry footsteps vibrating the squeaky floorboards.

The couple turned to Connie's mother, who so far hadn't opened her mouth. Without looking at them, she spit out, "You've made your bed. Now you'll have to lie in it. But don't expect no help from us. 'Cause you ain't our daughter no more."

Adam thought Connie's parents would change their attitudes after the baby came, even though Connie assured him it wouldn't happen. She turned out to be right. Her parents stubbornly refused to have anything more to do with her, grandchild or not.

For a while, the young couple tried to balance school with work. But Connie's pregnancy made her so sick that she couldn't hold a job, and after a few weeks of trying to work and go to school full time, Adam found that not only couldn't he make ends meet financially, but he was falling hopelessly behind in his classes. With a heavy heart, he had to admit defeat. His school advisor, who tried unsuccessfully to secure a student loan for him, managed to find him a job with a pharmaceutical company as a traveling sales representative. "Perhaps it will be a stepping stone to your future," he told Adam.

Adam covered several hundred miles each week, meeting with doctors, hospital administrators, and pharmacists, informing them about new drugs and offering his company's specials of the month. Although the pay and benefits were good, it meant being away from home, Monday morning until Friday evening—a difficult way to begin married life for a young couple with a baby on the way.

Connie seemed to grow older and more unhappy each week. Instead of the perky, sweet coed she had been when Adam met her, she rapidly transformed into a dull, whining, apathetic old woman. Although she never said so, Adam sensed she blamed him for her lost opportunities and for trapping her in this hopeless situation.

Motherhood hadn't altered her outlook. If anything, she grew more resentful at having to care for a persistently demanding little creature who stole every minute of her time. With Adam away all week, Connie had no respite from the ever-increasing needs of her dependent child. And with no marketable job skills, she couldn't afford to pay a babysitter while she took a minimum wage job.

Adam watched helplessly as his wife sank into depression, becoming bitter and sullen. When the weekends came, she dumped everything on Adam, claiming it was his turn. Often this meant Adam spent the weekend with Charlotte, while Connie ignored both of them. Although Adam loved spending one-on-one time with his precious daughter, he longed for Connie's desire to be more involved with their family.

Finally, with Charlotte due to enter kindergarten the next year, things began to look up. They even discussed the possibility of Connie getting a part-time job, when to her dismay, she discovered she was pregnant again. And they had been so careful. She became inconsolable. Adam had grown alarmed, his fears intensified by the fact that he was unable to be with her most of the time.

Then, a few months after the birth of Diana, Connie suddenly became more serene, as if the dark cloud had finally lifted from her. Although still not exactly happy, she seemed to be more at peace. Adam didn't know why. They certainly never talked about such matters. But he was immensely relieved.

Adam checked his watch as he drove, pleased to see he was making good time. He could be home in another hour. His reflections continued as he drove.

The hard times are almost behind us. After this next year, maybe Connie can even go back to school and get her degree.

It had once been so important to her—to be the first person in her family to go to college.

Although their marriage had been conceived in necessity, rather than love, perhaps with time and less pressure, they could finally be a happy family. He still had affection for Connie, even though she had not exactly turned out to be the wife of his dreams. But he took a good deal of the blame for that. After all, he robbed her of her youth and her ambition. But they were still young. There was still time.

His thoughts turned to his daughters, and his heart swelled with the warmth of his overflowing love and surge of supernatural protectiveness. Little Charlotte, a carbon copy of her mother, with her curly blonde hair and deep blue eyes, seemed to worship him as if he were some sort of distant god whom she rarely saw—which, to his chagrin, was largely true. And precious little Diana, who looked exactly like Charlotte had as a baby, changed so much from week to week. No more. From now on he would be there to share in both their daily lives. He would see to it his daughters grew up surrounded by his love and guided by his wisdom. Well, perhaps not wisdom. Maybe experience was a better word. He would teach them by example that even when life looked hopeless, one must continually have hope. God was good.

Such was Adam's optimistic outlook as he drove toward home. The interstate had never seemed so long. He felt ready to burst with having to hold in his news. He played and replayed the scene in his mind when he would finally walk through the door and a surprised Connie would ask him what he was doing home so early, and he would tell her the wonderful news. The urge to drastically exceed the speed limit and risk getting a ticket became more and more tempting. He hadn't even stopped to eat, and his stomach rumbled in protest, reminding him of this fact. But he just wanted to get home to his family.

Finally, after what seemed like an agonizing eternity, he headed toward the exit ramp, his excitement becoming unbearable. He cursed his luck at getting stuck at the long red light at the bottom of the ramp. As the interminable light switched to green, his foot hit the accelerator and stayed there for the next two blocks. Looking quickly around to see if anyone were watching, he even ran the last stop sign on the corner before his building.

At last! He was home. His car squealed into its assigned parking space. Before completely shutting off the engine, he threw open the door, leaving his overnight bag and sample case behind. Without taking the time to collect them, he raced into the building, almost colliding with old Mrs. Flemming in the corridor.

"My, aren't *we* in a hurry," she chided.

"Sorry," he called over his shoulder, without pausing to see if she were okay.

"Could've knocked me down and broken my neck," she grumbled.

What was the old crone babbling about? Her words registered as nothing more than irritating noise in his distracted brain. But he wasn't going to stop and ask. He fumbled for his key, dropping the whole key ring in the process. The loud clang of the metal against the tile floor jarred his already overwrought nerves. Muttering a word he rarely said under his breath, he retrieved the keys from the floor and finally managed to insert the proper key into the lock. He threw open the door with a bang and shouted, "Connie! Connie, come here. I've got great news."

The apartment was strangely quiet. No sign of the girls anywhere. He caught a faint whiff of what smelled like cigarette smoke, then dismissed it as being his imagination. Connie didn't smoke.

"Shoot, I hope they're home," he said aloud, disappointment flooding through him. He hadn't anticipated the possibility they might be out.

"Connie?" he called again, this time methodically poking his head into each room to be sure she wasn't hiding somewhere.

He found her. In the bedroom with a man he didn't know.

"Adam?" She spoke his name like a question, as if she weren't quite sure who he was. Hastily, she gathered the sheet around herself.

For a long moment, nobody said or did anything. At first, Adam's shocked brain refused to accept the fact that his eyes were not lying. His insides clenched and his heart plunged heavily into his stomach. Surely this wasn't really happening.

As he tried to resolve the conflict between his eyes and brain, the other man took the opportunity to quickly pull on his clothes. The sudden movement caught Adam's eye.

"Get out of my home!" he shouted.

Keeping his eyes glued on Adam, the man finished dressing without actually watching what he was doing, tripping over his trouser legs. The results might have been comical under different circumstances.

But there was no humor in the situation. Adam realized he stood in the way of the only door through which the unfortunate fellow would have to exit, but he didn't step aside. The other man, still keeping his eyes on Adam, managed to slide around him without actually touching him. It took every ounce of restraint for Adam not to knock the man through the opposite wall. As the man safely reached the other side of the door, he turned, almost as an afterthought, and said, "I'm sorry."

The sound of the man's voice forced Adam from his inertia and triggered a violent burning deep in his gut. Fueled by blinding rage, he lunged at the other man, but the guy was faster. He escaped, just barely, out of Adam's reach. Adam's fist connected in a sickening crack with the wall where the man had been standing only a split second before.

Adam ignored the sharp burst of pain extending from his hand all the way up his arm, as he turned back to his wife. She had taken advantage of the momentary distraction to throw on her clothes, and now sat warily on the edge of the bed, obviously waiting for him to make the first move. Neither said anything for a long time.

Finally, Adam spoke around the dry thickness in his throat, his voice bordering on hysteria, "Do you want to tell me what's going on here?"

Connie's initial panic seemed to subside a little. "Really, Adam," she replied, a half smirk on her face. "I think that's fairly obvious."

Adam's shock and disbelief gave way to anger at her intentional impudence. Without even realizing what he was doing, he crossed the room in two swift strides and slapped her hard across the face. "You *tramp*!" he bellowed. "I want an explanation. *Now*!"

Connie's hand flew to her quickly reddening cheek. Sobbing, she curled into a tight ball against the headboard, her keening high-pitched and distressed like that of a wounded animal.

Adam stepped back, staring at his hand in horror. Had he actually struck her? Adam had never, ever hit her. He would have never thought himself capable of such a thing.

"I hate you!" she shrieked, through her weeping.

Adam's body began to tremble uncontrollably. Did she really mean that?

"I … I'm sorry, Connie," he said, his voice shaking. He moved a step closer, but stopped when she recoiled. "There was no excuse for that."

He tried to advance toward her again, but she shrank further away from him. He collapsed on the foot of the bed, the mattress creaking in protest under his weight, and placed his head in his hands. Connie remained curled up at the head of the bed, sobbing.

Finally, after a long silence, he whispered, "Do you really hate me, Connie? Did you mean what you said?"

The noisy weeping subsided a bit. She didn't meet his eyes. "Sometimes."

He digested her answer for a minute. He felt like an outsider watching his body playing out some tragic scene in a movie.

Then he heard himself plead, "Why? Why do you hate me?" His voice sounded hollow and far away.

She sniffed and barked out a bitter laugh. "Look at me. You've ruined my life."

He turned toward her, extending his arms, begging her. "Connie, I know things have been hard for us. I know I'm mostly to blame for that. But this isn't the answer."

"It is for me, Adam. You're never here for me." She took a deep breath. "I'm tired of being alone." She paused, then added in a faltering voice, "I … I want a divorce."

He felt the wetness of tears he hadn't noticed until that moment rolling down his cheeks. His heart squeezed as though strangled by a parasitic vine. "Then you don't love me at all?"

She shot him a timid glance before looking away again. "I'm not happy, Adam. You know the only reason we got married was because we had to. I … I want a divorce," she repeated, nodding as if to convince herself as much as him.

How was it possible that so much had changed in such a short span of time? Wasn't it just a few minutes ago he had been on top of the world? Now that world was crashing around his feet, shattering into a million pieces.

"What about the girls? Does Charlotte know about this man who's been here in my absence?"

"Of course not. What do you think I am, anyway?" she huffed.

Adam raised an eyebrow. He wanted to laugh but it hurt too much.

Connie pursed her lips. "I don't care what you think of me. And I'm not sorry for what I've done. At least Stephen is here for me." She tossed her head.

"So, you want to throw away our lives together, just like that?" He forced his words out around the tightness in his throat.

"Our lives together?" Her voice dripped with scorn. "When did we ever have a life together?"

"It hasn't been easy for me, either, you know," he replied, resentment coloring his tone. "I never intended to be a traveling salesman, but I did the best I could. I tried to make things work."

She remained silent, her tear-filled, shimmering eyes downcast.

"This isn't the way I want things to be, Connie."

She still didn't say anything.

Adam stood, her silence fueling his anger. "Fine! Go off with Stephen if you think he'll make you happy. But you're not taking my daughters with you."

She jerked her head as if he'd struck her again. "What do you mean?"

"I want custody of the girls."

"Don't be ridiculous. Fathers don't get custody of children." There was just the slightest tremor in her lower lip.

"Tramps don't either!" he snapped. "If you fight me on this, I'll drag you through an ugly court battle. You and your boyfriend."

Connie hesitated for a moment. Then she replied, "I wouldn't, if I were you. They're not your daughters."

With that, she stood, picked up her purse, and walked out the door, before a stunned Adam could respond.

CHAPTER SIX
CONNIE

———•●•———

Connie walked to her car, her outward calm belying her inner hysteria. What had she just done? If only Adam hadn't slapped her. He had made her say those awful things. She'd wanted to hurt him back in the only way she knew how. Now she regretted her words. But it was too late. As she pulled onto the road, with no idea where she was headed, she tried to sort through the nightmare that had just occurred. It was Adam's fault. He had put her on the defensive. Then she wearily admitted it wasn't his fault. She was the stupid one. What was she supposed to do now?

She drove aimlessly trying to figure out what to do. Going home wasn't an option. She had burned that bridge. Adam would never take her back after the things she had said and done, and the sudden realization that she couldn't make it on her own enveloped her in panic. With her heart hammering in an erratic cadence, her thoughts turned to Stephen. But her conscience whispered the unwelcome truth that she didn't love Stephen any more than she had loved Adam when they married—assuming Stephen would even have her. Would she be trading one unhappy life for another?

She thought back to the night when Stephen had come into her life—the night when Diana had fallen from the bed and split her chin open. Connie turned her back for just a second to grab another diaper when, without warning, Diana rolled onto the tile floor, hitting her chin with a sickening crack. Connie panicked at the inch-long gash in the baby's chin and the rapidly pooling crimson puddle staining the white tile. Snatching the screaming child, she rushed into the emergency room at St. Andrews Hospital, where calm, compassionate Dr. Stephen Gates took control of the situation. He stitched up the wound, assured her there would be no scar, and then, as he was just going off duty, insisted on escorting the obviously distraught and beautiful young mother home. One thing led to another. Connie was lonely and Stephen had been there.

She had never stopped to consider what she was doing was wrong. After all, Adam had his life, but what did she have? Adam had taken everything from her. First her parents, who disowned her when Adam had gotten her pregnant, then her college degree which she had longed for all her life, and along with it, her future, fabulous career. And now he threatened to take away her children. Not that she was all that crazy about her daughters, but they were the only things she had left. She wasn't about to let Adam make her into a failure at motherhood, as well.

She knew, however, with a sinking heart, she couldn't manage alone. She had no choice but to go to Stephen and ask him for help. He had said he loved her. Maybe a marriage to Stephen could work out. After all, he had enough money to provide for childcare, so maybe she could go back to school or get a job—anything to get her out of her unwanted role as housewife. Her stomach in knots, she realized she would just have to get up her nerve to confront Stephen.

With shaking hands and a racing heart, she drove to his house. It suddenly occurred to her that he had never taken her to his house before, although he had told her where he lived. Why was that? An ominous feeling began to wrap around her, as icy tendrils of fear deadened her extremities and worked their way inward. She had never stopped to consider the obvious. But she refused to consider it now. He had to take her in or she was in serious trouble.

She tried to shake off her apprehension as she pulled up in front of Stephen's home. The house was much more than she expected. She knew Stephen was well off financially, but she hadn't imagined *this*. The white, two-story colonial home sat majestically back from a perfectly manicured, sprawling lawn, shaded by enormous magnolia trees, their waxy leaves forming a peaceful canopy against the harsh sun. A winding drive, edged on both sides with colorful perennials, curved around to the massive oak front door.

Her eyes took in the beauty of the surroundings. *I could be happy here.* Taking a deep breath, she descended down the slight incline of the driveway and stopped the car opposite the home's entrance.

On trembling legs, she forced herself to exit the car and walk to the front door. She closed her eyes briefly, then took hold of the large brass door knocker and rapped loudly. The sharp sound jarred her already taut nerves.

The door opened almost immediately, and Stephen stood in the doorway. The color drained from his face when he saw her.

"Connie?" he cried, looking past her as if afraid Adam might spring from the bushes behind her and attack him. "Wh . . . what are you doing here?"

"I've left him, Stephen," she announced, with a quivering voice. "I've left Adam."

Stephen regarded her with a blank expression. It was hardly the response she had hoped for. Quickly looking around again, he ushered her inside and shut the door. He didn't ask her to sit. They stood awkwardly in the foyer, the stunning opulence of which would have awed her under other circumstances.

"What do you mean you've left him?"

Connie's frazzled nerves unraveled. "What do you mean, 'what do I mean'?" she snapped. "I *am* speaking English. I've left Adam."

Stephen ran his hand through his short, sandy hair. "What is it you want from me, Connie?" He sighed and turned away from her.

Connie's jaw dropped. Grabbing his arm, she forced him to turn around and look at her. "Stephen, correct me if I'm wrong, but haven't we been lovers for the past several weeks? And didn't you say you loved me?"

He averted his eyes from her penetrating glare. "Yes," he admitted, "but—"

"But what? I thought this was what you wanted."

"Now, Connie, be fair. I never said . . ." He hung his head as his voice trailed off.

She released his arm. Her heart began to flip-flop against her ribs and a stabbing pain throbbed between her eyebrows. Could this possibly be the same man who had been so supportive, so understanding, so loving to her these past few weeks? She hardly recognized him now.

"Stephen," she whispered, her voice breaking. "I thought you wanted me." She chewed on her lower lip.

He breathed in slowly through his nose and raised his head. Taking her hands in both of his, his pleading eyes gazed into hers.

"Sweetheart, I do love you. I did want you. But I didn't mean for you to leave your husband."

"Well, it's too late. I didn't exactly plan for things to work out like this, but after what happened this afternoon . . . well, maybe it's for the best."

Stephen didn't reply.

Her heart beat faster, feeling as though it might burst through her chest. "Stephen, I don't have anywhere else to go." Tears welled up in her eyes.

He dropped her hands and thrust his hands deep into his pockets, once again refusing to meet her eyes.

"I'm sorry, Connie, but you can't stay here. Beverly's due home tonight."

She felt the room closing in around her. "Beverly?"

"My wife."

The air rushed out of her lungs leaving her light-headed. Suddenly, she couldn't seem to remember how to breathe. For a terrifying moment, everything became black, and she sank down to the floor. She could hear Stephen's voice, but it sounded distorted and far away.

"Wife?" The word came out hollow.

Stephen knelt beside her, steadying her. "Connie, I didn't mean to mislead you. And I never intended for us to become so involved." His disembodied voice seemed to float through the air. "It just kind of happened."

The blackness gave way to white hot fury as her vision cleared. "And in all the time we were together, the conversation never got around to the fact you were married."

He hung his head. "Beverly and I have been having problems. She's been in Europe for the past four months."

"I don't care about your marital problems." She shoved him away and climbed awkwardly to her feet. "You used me. I left my husband for you. What am I supposed to do now?"

"Look, if you need some money to tide you over . . ."

She drew back her arm and delivered a vicious slap to his cheek, the sound echoing in the high-ceilinged room.

"Curse you and your money. Unless you intend to leave your wife for me, as I left my husband for you, you can . . ." she bit off her angry retort, as her jumbled brain couldn't think of anything bad enough. Hot tears ran down her face.

His eyes beseeched her. "Connie, I can't do that. You don't understand how it is."

"I understand." Her words rose in hysteria. "You're a lying, cheating monster who preys on vulnerable women for your ego trips. You've destroyed my life and my family for your fling. I'll hate you 'til I die."

She turned and tugged open the heavy oak door. Stumbling out the door, she looked back over her shoulder and met his guilty eyes.

"I pity your wife." Then, blinded by tears, she ran to her car on rubbery legs, climbed inside, and peeled out, leaving a trail of tire marks in his perfect driveway.

How could she have been such a fool? After escaping Stephen's street, she pulled over to the curb until the cascade of tears ran dry. Her mind churned with mixed emotions—hate, anger, despair, and humiliation. She had to clear her mind and think.

After wiping her eyes, she started the car again, and searched for a phone booth. While placing her call to Mrs. McCarthy, she spied a liquor store across the street.

Why not? I need something to help me get through this nightmare.

She purchased two liters of vodka. The clerk looked with curiosity at her swollen, red eyes and tear-stained face. "Are you all right, ma'am?"

"Wonderful!" she snapped, as she snatched up her purchase and stomped out the door. Meddling old fool. What did he think he could do to help her?

She drove to a nearby park, locked her car doors, and took out her bottles. The burning liquid seemed to ease the pain and the confusion, as it settled warmly in her tight stomach.

CHAPTER SEVEN
CHARLOTTE

Charlotte loved staying with Mrs. McCarthy, a plump, jolly, grandmotherly woman, who baked homemade cookies and allowed Charlotte to climb onto her ample lap for stories. Since Charlotte didn't know either of her real grandmothers, she thought Mrs. McCarthy was probably the next best thing. When Charlotte had first stayed with the kind, older woman, Connie had asked Mrs. McCarthy what she wanted Charlotte to call her.

The woman had thought for a moment, and then replied, "Well, Mrs. McCarthy is kind of a mouthful for a little one, isn't it? Why doesn't she just call me Grandma?"

Charlotte pondered this. But it wasn't really proper because Mrs. McCarthy was not really her grandma. After considering the impropriety of addressing the lady as "Grandma," Charlotte announced, "No, that wouldn't be right because you're not my real grandma. I'll call you Mrs. Grandma."

Mrs. McCarthy laughed. "That would be perfect, dear."

Her mother had begun bringing Charlotte and the baby to Mrs. McCarthy's home a few months earlier, shortly after Diana was born. Sometimes they stayed only a couple hours, other times, the whole day. Charlotte never knew when they were going to visit the older lady, for there was no set pattern. So, it was always an unexpected treat when Connie said, "How would you like to go to Mrs. Grandma's today?"

Mrs. McCarthy didn't treat Charlotte like a child, as most adults did. Charlotte could sit for hours just talking to the old lady. Mrs. McCarthy often joked to Connie that she should pay *her* for letting Charlotte visit because it was like having another little old lady around to gossip with. Mrs. McCarthy always had time to listen to her.

On this particular day, Connie had dropped them off right after lunch. With Diana napping most of the afternoon, Charlotte helped Mrs. Grandma bake a cherry pie. She let Charlotte roll out her own little crust and then helped her lay it in a pot pie pan and fill it with cherry compote. The pies were almost ready to come out of the oven when the phone rang. Leaving Charlotte to watch the oven timer, Mrs. Grandma scurried into the living room to answer the telephone. She came back into the kitchen, shortly before the buzzer sounded.

"That was your mother," she told Charlotte. "Guess what? You and Diana are going to be spending the night with me. Won't that fun?"

"Oh, yes." Charlotte's blonde curls bobbed eagerly in anticipation of spending the whole night with her friend.

"I'll tell you what we'll do tonight. We'll have our cherry pie for dessert, and then, after Diana's asleep, you and I will stay up and watch a late movie and make popcorn. Would you like that?"

What an adventure. Charlotte had never been allowed to stay up and watch a late movie. This was going to be fun. But something just out of reach in her consciousness dampened her eagerness. What was it? She struggled to grasp the elusive, troubling thought. Of course. It was Friday. Daddy came home on Friday night. She always looked forward to her daddy coming home on the weekends.

"What about my daddy?" she asked. "He's s'posed to come home tonight. It's Friday."

Mrs. McCarthy shrugged. "I don't know, dear. Your mother didn't say anything about it." Then she winked at the child. "Maybe they want to be alone."

Charlotte cocked her head and wrinkled her nose. "Why would they want that?"

Mrs. McCarthy chuckled. "Well, sometimes mommies and daddies need some time to themselves, dear."

Charlotte had never really thought about her mommy and daddy wanting to be alone together, but she couldn't believe that was the reason for the change in plans. Something just wasn't right, but she didn't know how to express her concern to her substitute grandmother.

"Oh, there's the buzzer. Hand me the potholders, Charlotte, and let's see how our pies look."

The pies came out the oven smelling heavenly—a delightful mixture of cinnamon and tart cherry—their hot golden crusts slightly sticky with the bubbled over fruit. Charlotte pushed her nagging worry to the back of her mind, dismissing it with her usual disdain at the adult belief that children didn't need to know everything. There was an explanation for this turn of events, of course, but they hadn't felt it necessary to let her in on it. Although still a little miffed, she wasn't going to let it spoil her unexpected adventure with Mrs. McCarthy.

"Oh, I think I hear the baby. Charlotte, go see if she's awake."

Charlotte ran into the spare bedroom where Diana lay in her bassinet, cooing happily. The infant's face broke into a broad smile when Charlotte looked down at her.

"Yes, Mrs. Grandma," Charlotte reported, racing back into the kitchen. "But she's not crying."

Mrs. McCarthy wiped her hands on her apron. "Well, she's going to want a diaper change and a bottle, I imagine. Come along and help me, Charlotte."

Charlotte felt very important being allowed to help. Her mother was usually too impatient to let her help with anything. Charlotte trailed after the older woman, almost, but not quite, wishing she could stay with her all week and just go home when Daddy came home on the weekends.

"Get me a diaper from the diaper bag," Mrs. McCarthy said, as she lifted the gurgling baby from her bassinet. "Aha. I thought so. You do need a clean diaper."

Charlotte noted that Mrs. Grandma even talked grown-up to Diana. The older woman patiently demonstrated the art of changing a diaper, while Charlotte absorbed the information like a hungry little sponge. That was one of the things Charlotte liked so much about her. Mrs. Grandma seemed to make every small task a learning opportunity.

Another thing she liked about Mrs. Grandma was the way she always talked aloud to God, as if He were right there in the room with them. They could be cooking dinner and she might say, "Now, Lord, where did I put my glasses? You know I can't read these directions in this tiny little print," or "Lord, what a silly old woman I am to forget they were on top of my head." And she always pointed out the beauty of simple things such as flowers, rainbows, or sunsets, telling Charlotte that God was certainly good to give them such a blessing.

"There. That's better. Now, come along, Charlotte, I want you to sit in the kitchen chair and hold your sister while I warm her bottle."

Connie usually didn't allow Charlotte to hold the baby. Feeling very responsible, indeed, Charlotte did as she was told, holding the infant securely.

"You'll make a good mother someday," observed Mrs. McCarthy. "You have a natural touch with babies."

Charlotte's head swelled with pride. "I want six children," she announced. Then a thought occurred to her. "How many children do you have, Mrs. Grandma?"

"Oh, the Lord blessed Mr. McCarthy and me with two," she answered, her tone becoming wistful. "But they're far away. My daughter lives in California and my son lives in Washington, D.C."

Charlotte wasn't exactly sure where those places were, but she knew they were a long way from Biloxi.

"And I have three beautiful grandchildren. But I don't get to see them very often." Then, with a kind smile, she added, "That's why you and Diana are so special. I like to think of you as my adopted granddaughters."

Charlotte cocked her head. "What's 'dopted?"

"Well," the older woman began, as she handed Charlotte the bottle and helped her hold it upright, "it's when people take in someone else's children to raise. They aren't the birth parents, but they take care of the children just as if they were. Do you understand?"

"Sort of." Charlotte bit her lip in concentration as she held the warm bottle properly so no air got into Diana's stomach. "But why would anyone do that?"

"Well, say, for example, your parents couldn't take care of you anymore. Then some other man and woman might take you into their home to take care of you. They would love you all the more because they picked you out special."

Charlotte frowned and nodded, in serious contemplation. "But it couldn't be you, could it? Because you don't have a husband."

Mrs. Grandma blinked back a tear. "No, I don't have a husband. My dear Walter died five years ago."

"What's 'died' mean?"

"Well, it means a person isn't alive anymore. Do you understand?"

Charlotte shook her head. Then, as though a lightbulb had come on inside her brain, she asked, "Is that like when you go to heaven?"

Mrs. McCarthy nodded. "Yes, that's exactly what it is."

"Then you shouldn't be sad when someone dies because they're in heaven."

"Yes, that's true," admitted the older woman, "but the people left behind are sad because they miss their loved one. You would be very sad if your mommy or daddy went to heaven and you didn't get to see them anymore, now, wouldn't you?"

Charlotte had never thought of that. "Oh yes."

"Well, that's not going to happen for a long, long time. So don't you worry about it now." Then, changing the subject to something less morbid, she exclaimed, "Oh, look. Diana's almost finished her bottle. My, she was hungry."

Charlotte handed the nearly empty bottle back to her substitute grandmother. "Now she needs burped."

"Yes, she does." Mrs. Grandma smiled. "You remember me telling you that before, don't you? Do you remember what to do?"

Charlotte nodded. She allowed Mrs. McCarthy to turn Diana over so Charlotte could pat her back. The baby let out a noisy belch and Charlotte giggled. Mommy would fuss at her if *she* burped out loud like that.

"There. She should feel much better now. Why don't we put her in her playpen, and you can draw me some pictures while I work on my knitting."

———— • ● • ————

They retired to the living room, where slivers of late afternoon sun streaked across the dark wood floor. Charlotte amused herself by drawing pictures and making up stories to go with them. Mrs. McCarthy eavesdropped a little, always amazed at how intelligent and creative the little girl was. She would go far one of these days. If only her mother spent a little more time teaching her. The older woman clucked, subconsciously. Charlotte was such a bright child who needed so little encouragement. But unfortunately, Connie wasn't much more than a child herself—a rather selfish child, at that. A small, nagging worry for the family lodged in her mind, but for the life of her she didn't know why. She had never met the father. But Charlotte seemed to dote on him.

The afternoon passed peacefully. Mrs. McCarthy let Charlotte help her with dinner preparations. It was nice having someone else in the house to cook for again. After dinner, they ate their cherry pie, and then curled up on the big, overstuffed couch for stories. First, Mrs. McCarthy read Charlotte a story, then Charlotte told her the stories she had made up that afternoon. Then they fed and changed Diana and put her down for the night.

"Oh, dear," observed Mrs. McCarthy. "You don't have any night clothes with you. I didn't even think about that when your mother called."

She thought for a moment. "I know. You can wear one of my old blouses."

She rummaged through her cramped closet, finally emerging with a pullover top. It dwarfed little Charlotte, but it was better than nothing. "We'll just have to make do for tonight. We'd better hurry and make our popcorn. The movie's about to start."

— • ● • —

Charlotte helped her melt butter into a large pan and pour in the popcorn kernels, then watched as she shook the handle vigorously over the burner. The smell of hot butter and sweet popcorn filled the small kitchen with a comforting aroma as the kernels exploded in staccato bursts into fluffy white puffs.

Charlotte didn't particularly care for the movie. She didn't really understand what was going on, but she didn't mind. Sitting next to her adopted grandmother, staying up late and eating popcorn, filled her small soul with an overwhelming sensation of peace and comfort. If she had only known it would be the last happy moment she remembered for a long time, she might have savored it more.

CHAPTER EIGHT
ADAM

I didn't even have a chance to tell Connie my news.

Adam's thoughts swirled through his still shocked brain. He moved into the living room and stared out the open window, where a lethargic breeze faintly ruffled the beige cotton curtains. The sun cast warm, amber streaks across the hardwood floor. Cheerful birds sang in the trees just outside the window, and the sound of happy children playing in the balmy spring afternoon drifted into the stuffy room. But he hardly noticed the joyousness of the beautiful day.

Where was Connie? Had she gone to Stephen? Were they really in love? Or was their affair just a by-product of Connie's intense loneliness and unhappiness? Had she really meant those things she'd said? Did she really hate him? The jumbled questions stumbled over each other as they raced through Adam's troubled mind. The last thing she'd said—about his daughters not being his—he refused to think about. It couldn't possibly be true.

She would have to come back to the apartment sooner or later. Everything she owned was here. Then perhaps they could talk. Maybe she had said those horrible things because of the horrible things *he* had said—and done. He winced at the reality of having slapped her, and remorse squeezed his heart.

Where were the girls? Who would she have left them with? He longed to see them, to hold them. There was no way those two little girls were not his daughters. And if Connie was truly serious about a divorce, he was not going to give them up without a fight. Connie's adulterous behavior should be a pretty good reason for a judge to award him custody, even if he were a man. Times were changing. Mothers didn't always get custody. But even as he tried to convince himself, he didn't feel very confident that he would win.

The shrill ringing of the phone startled him. He snatched up the receiver and cried, "Connie?"

"Uh, no, Adam, it's Earl."

"Oh." Adam hoped his disappointment didn't carry through the phone.

"Is everything all right, Adam? You sound strange."

"What? Oh, sure. I was . . . napping."

"Oh. Sorry to wake you. Listen, I hope you've had a chance to spring your news on your family. We need you in Atlanta as soon as possible. Rothchild's assistant was taken to the emergency room this afternoon with a massive coronary. Rothchild's right in the middle of a big research project that can't be put on hold. He needs help right away."

Adam's fuzzy brain refused to register this information. What did this possibly have to do with him? Earl's words buzzed like meaningless noise in his ears.

"He needs you there as soon as possible. If you could be there, say, day after tomorrow, we can move the family later."

"But, Earl," Adam protested. "I don't know anything about Rothchild's research."

"For Pete's sakes, man," exploded Earl. "Are you sure you're all right? Where's your head, anyway?"

Adam wasn't sure. He shook his head to try to clear it. "Um, sorry, Earl. I'm not fully awake yet. Please . . . run this by me again."

Earl gave an exasperated sigh. "Rothchild needs you in Atlanta A.S.A.P. He's got a research project that can't wait and no assistant. He doesn't want to break someone else in and then have to start all over again with you. Don't blow this, Adam. If you're not there in two days, you'll probably ruin your chance for this opportunity. Now do you understand?"

Adam ran a weary hand over his face. "Yes, perfectly."

"All right, then. Throw some clothes into a bag and get to Atlanta. We'll make arrangements to get you settled later."

"Okay, Earl. I'll be there no later than Sunday. Thank you."

Earl's exasperation seemed to dissolve a little. A touch more gently, he asked, again, "Are you sure you're okay, Adam? You sound kind of . . . pre-occupied."

"No, no, I'm fine. Thanks for everything, Earl."

Adam replaced the receiver and sank onto the sofa to think. Surely, Connie would be home soon. He had to tell her about the new job before he left. Maybe that would change things.

But by ten o'clock, she still hadn't returned. If only he knew where she was. If only he could talk to her calmly, without the ugly fighting and accusations they'd had this afternoon. He didn't want to leave without seeing her, but he would have to leave by tomorrow to make it to Atlanta. And he desperately wanted to see his girls before he left. Midnight came and went. His insides clenched. She was probably with Stephen and wouldn't come home until morning. But where were the children?

Unable to sleep and full of nervous energy, Adam dug out his suitcases and began to pack.

Might as well take everything, just in case I won't be back here again.

Afterward, just before daybreak, he lay on the couch, exhausted. The emotional turmoil, coupled with the two nights without sleep, were beginning to take their toll. He would have to leave by noon, at the latest.

Please, God, let her come home before then.

He awoke with a start. "Connie?" he called out.

What had awakened him so abruptly? Rubbing his grainy eyes, he rose and peered out the window.

"Just some kids playing," he muttered, as a stab of pain for his own children blindsided him with its intensity.

Straggling into the kitchen, he assembled the coffee pot and sat at the table, his head in his hands, waiting for it to perk. The clock said eleven-thirty. His stomach, although knotted into a tight ball, reminded him noisily that he hadn't eaten anything yesterday. He couldn't start on a long journey like this without some food in his belly. So, with the expertise he had acquired during his weekends of cooking breakfast for the family, he whipped up a huge platter of scrambled eggs and cinnamon toast, and although his head said he wasn't hungry, he devoured the whole thing.

By the time he finished eating and had loaded the car with his clothes and books, it was twelve-thirty. Still no Connie or the children. He couldn't wait any longer—he had to leave.

With a heavy heart, he wrote her a short note, saying he had to go to Atlanta, and he would call later to explain everything. He ended with "I love you, Connie," and propped it up on the desk just inside the door, where she would be sure to see it.

The note was thrown away later, when the apartment was cleaned out, having fallen behind the desk when a gust of wind from the open window across the room swept it to the floor.

CHAPTER NINE
CONNIE

onnie awoke stiff and foggy headed. Where was she anyway? As she opened her eyes to the harsh glare of sunlight bombarding the windshield, the unrealities of the previous day suddenly became very real. She looked with revulsion at the empty vodka bottle on the front seat. Had she really gotten drunk and passed out in her car in the middle of a public park? The lingering stench of the alcohol in the close confine of the station wagon confirmed her fear. She couldn't believe she had sunk so low. She was no better than some wino in the gutter. As she attempted to shift her cramped position, she became acutely aware of an intense throbbing in her head and queasiness in her stomach. Flinging open the car door, she looked hurriedly around for a restroom.

After becoming violently sick to her stomach, she forced her wobbly legs to convey her shaking body to the restroom mirror. Her own reflection shocked her. A pale, bloated face surrounded by limp, tangled hair stared back at her with bloodshot, puffy eyes.

"You're a disgusting, worthless, pig," she hissed at the woman in the mirror. She dug her comb out of her purse and attempted to unsnarl her matted curls. Sparing herself no mercy, Connie yanked furiously at any strand of hair that gave her resistance. Then she splashed cold water on her face with a vicious delight at the chilly assault against her skin.

When she was finished, she stood back and appraised the

results. "You still look like a train wreck."

At that moment, a mother with a young child entered the restroom, casting a curious look at her. Embarrassed at being caught talking to herself in a public restroom, Connie fled to a picnic table overlooking a duck pond.

"First you're a slut, then a drunk, and now a lunatic who talks to herself," she whispered. "Now what are you going to do? You've driven away Adam and you never had Stephen to begin with."

She sat in the warm sun, letting it soothe her aching mind and body. Unwanted thoughts invaded her attempts at peace. Why had she been so awful to Adam? He had always been a good husband to her and a good father to the girls. She could blame his job for her unhappiness, but she knew that wasn't the real reason. He'd given up as much, perhaps even more, to marry her. Nobody had forced him. He had done it voluntarily, for her, and he had taken the best paying job that he could to provide for them. He hadn't complained. No, it had always been she who grumbled about everything, making his life miserable. Maybe she had never really forgiven him for the unwanted pregnancy, which she had always perceived as entirely his fault. After all, he was six years older and supposed to know better about taking certain precautions. But, she sadly admitted to herself, she should have known better, too. And having gotten into trouble, she should have made the best of things, as Adam had tried to do, instead of constantly lamenting over her lost opportunities. What if he had refused to marry her? Then where would she be?

Right where I am now.

But this time, it was entirely her own doing.

There was only one thing to do—crawl back to Adam and beg his forgiveness. And if he did forgive her and take her back, she promised herself she would spend the rest of her life making it up to him. She was going to be the best wife and mother who ever was. She would learn to be happy with the life she had and make her family happy, too.

As if awakened to a great spiritual revelation, Connie felt refreshed, alive. Why had she had to hit bottom before she could appreciate what she had? Although she didn't much think about God, other than as a judgmental tyrant, maybe it was His way of getting His message across to her to straighten up.

She walked back to her car with a new sense of purpose. In

disgust, she hurled the liquor bottles, one of which was almost full, into a nearby trash container, wincing at the loud crash of the shattering glass against the metal bin. Then she headed home, with an excitement that burned to the depths of her very soul. Things were going to be all right, now.

As she neared the apartment building, a vague feeling of fear washed over her.

"Please, God," she prayed, "let Adam forgive me." Although not a religious woman, Connie vowed that if God would just grant her this one thing, she would make up for all her past sins.

She pulled into her parking spot and threw open the car door. She had to get to him as quickly as possible. By the time she reached her door, she was out of breath. She paused for just a split second to work up her courage, then, with her head held high, rammed her key into the lock and thrust open the door.

"Adam?" she called, in a quivering voice.

There was no answer. The lingering aroma of Adam's breakfast hung in the air. Entering the kitchen, she found a frying pan and plate in the dish rack. The coffee pot was still warm. The kitchen clock read one-o'clock. She couldn't have missed him by much. With a feeling of disappointment, she guessed she would just have to wait for him to come back. She wondered, fleetingly, where he had gone.

Wandering back into the living room, she thought to check the usual place to see if he had, by chance, left a note. But before she got to the desk, something else caught her eye. The bookcase was completely empty. With a rising sense of panic, Connie ran into the bedroom. The bed was still in its state of disarray from yesterday afternoon, and the closet door stood open. Without even looking inside, she knew his clothes weren't there. But she had to be sure. Tentatively, as if she could change the outcome by how quickly she moved, she stepped gingerly into the closet. A half-empty rack with a few straggling hangers greeted her.

"No!" she cried. "Oh, no."

Although, by that point, she knew what she would find, she rushed into the bathroom to look for his razor and toiletries, which weren't there. Then, realizing that truly everything of Adam's was gone, she sunk to the floor and began to sob.

"Oh, Adam," she wailed. "What have I done?"

CHAPTER TEN
CHARLOTTE

———·●·———

It was late afternoon when her mother finally picked them up from Mrs. Grandma's house. Although she loved being with Mrs. Grandma, Charlotte had begun to worry when her mother hadn't come for them in the morning. As the day wore on, Charlotte knew something was wrong. She could tell that even Mrs. Grandma was having difficulty concealing her anxiety from Charlotte. When at last her mother appeared, she looked terrible.

"Connie," said Mrs. McCarthy. "I've been so worried about you. Are you all right?"

To Charlotte, it was obvious just from looking at her mother that she wasn't. Although the sky was overcast, she wore large, dark sunglasses that hid a good portion of her face. Once inside, she didn't take them off.

"Yes, I'm fine," her mother replied, her voice soft and thick. "I'm terribly sorry I didn't call you. There were some unforeseen . . . circumstances. If you'll tell me what I owe you, I'll get the girls and leave you to your peace."

Charlotte was dying to know where her daddy was, but something restrained her from asking.

Mrs. McCarthy hesitated. "Dear, if you need some more time, I don't mind keeping the girls another night."

"No, no. I've troubled you enough." Then, directing her attention to Charlotte, she said, "Run and get your things together,

Charlotte. We must be going."

Without arguing, Charlotte did as she was told. Then, even though she hadn't been asked to, she collected Diana's diaper bag and bottles, and lugged everything out to the car. Her mother was just folding up the portable playpen and stuffing it in the trunk when Charlotte appeared, spying the luggage jammed everywhere. Hastily, she closed the trunk.

"Get in the car, Charlotte," she ordered, "and wait for me while I get Diana." She started walking back toward the house.

"But …"

She stopped and whirled around to face Charlotte, removing her large sunglasses. The look on her face frightened Charlotte, even more than her ominous tone of voice.

"Do as I say."

Tendrils of fear wrapped around Charlotte's heart. She had never seen her mother like this before. Bad-tempered, yes, but this was more than just a bad mood. Charlotte curled up in the back seat, feeling small and vulnerable.

Her mother returned with the baby and buckled her into her car seat. Charlotte peered out the window at Mrs. McCarthy standing on her porch watching the car, her brows furrowed. As their eyes met, the older woman smiled and waved at Charlotte, but Charlotte was not deceived by her false cheerfulness.

They rode in silence for several minutes. Charlotte noticed they weren't going in the direction of home, but she was afraid to ask where they were going.

When they pulled onto the interstate, her mother finally told Charlotte in a flat voice, "We're going on a little trip, Charlotte, to see your grandparents. You've never met them, so this will be a treat for you."

Although Charlotte had always been curious about her real grandparents, her parents had been vague and dismissive when she asked about them. She had the feeling this trip was not going to be a treat. Something was not right. Why were they going to her grandparents *now*, out of the blue, when they had never been there before?

"I want you to be on your best behavior. Do you understand?"

"Yes, Mommy," she answered, in a small voice. Then, her curiosity overcoming her gnawing fear, she asked, "Is Daddy coming with us?"

"No," her mother replied, her tone flat. She didn't say anything further.

Charlotte's tiny heart began to flutter in alarm. Why was her mother acting so strangely? And where was her daddy?

They rode in silence. After a while, they left the interstate and traveled along a two-lane road. Ordinarily, Charlotte would have had her nose pressed to the glass, taking in everything she could from the passing scenery. There were many interesting sights to see as they made their way past farmhouses, fields of grazing cattle, fruit orchards with colorful spring blossoms, and acres of soil ready for planting. But today, Charlotte's mounting apprehension prevented her from appreciating any of it.

The road became progressively rougher until eventually it turned into dirt and gravel. Her mother reduced her speed as the car bounced along the uneven path. The setting sun, glowing in a magnificent red-orange blaze, came into view at the top of the next hill, briefly streaking the sky with a majestic splash of color before quickly sinking below the horizon.

They stopped at a fork in the road. A wooden hand-painted sign with words Charlotte couldn't read pointed toward the left. The sudden stop woke Diana, and she began to fuss.

"Find her pacifier, Charlotte."

Charlotte rummaged through the diaper bag, located the pacifier, and jammed it into the infant's mouth. The baby promptly spit it out and continued to whine.

"We're almost there. Try to keep her quiet for a few more minutes. Jingle her keys or something."

Charlotte searched again through the diaper bag until she found the plastic key ring, as her mother turned the car toward the left fork. The bad road grew worse, rocking the car from side to side, throwing them off balance. Their speed reduced to a crawl. Diana, clearly not enjoying the bumpy ride, began to howl. Charlotte tried numerous methods of calming her, but nothing worked.

Finally, they pulled up in front of a small run-down looking wood-frame house. Old car parts, rusted machinery, and other assorted junk littered the front yard. A clothesline hung in the side yard, drooping under the weight of wet laundry. A grim-faced couple stood on the sagging front porch, dressed in old, faded apparel. They made no move to come out and greet the car.

"Those are your grandparents, Charlotte," her mother said in a cheerful voice, but Charlotte knew the cheerfulness was forced. Reaching over to remove the screaming baby from the car seat, her mother said, "Come on, get out of the car."

With a leaden feeling in her heart, Charlotte appraised the couple. They didn't look like grandparents to her. She hung back a little behind her mother as they approached the creaking porch steps.

"So, Constance, your chickens have come home to roost," said the older woman, tartly. The man said nothing.

Her mother sighed. "It's nice to see you again, too, Mama." Then drawing Charlotte out from behind her, she introduced them. "Mama, Papa, this is your granddaughter, Charlotte. Charlotte, these are your grandparents."

The couple gave Charlotte a curt nod. Charlotte stared at them, wide-eyed. The woman wore a dirty apron over a faded gingham dress. Her hair, blonde streaked with silver was drawn back severely into a bun at the base of her neck. Her eyes were blue—not the deep, violet-blue of her daughter and granddaughter, but a piercing, steel blue that seemed to penetrate right through to the soul. The man, tall and slender, with thinning light brown hair, had the same cold steel-blue eyes. He wore a patched cotton shirt and bibbed overalls. Neither offered to help unload the car.

"Come on in," said the woman, although her tone didn't sound very inviting.

They stepped into a dreary living room with a slanting wood floor, over which a threadbare, braided rug had been thrown. A sagging sofa sat against the far wall. Dingy wallpaper peeled in the corners of the room.

"I see everything's still the same, Mama."

As if reading her mind, her father replied sharply, "The coveting of material possessions is a sin against the Lord."

Her mother closed her eyes and nodded. "Look, I'm sorry to impose, but Charlotte hasn't had any supper. And I need to warm up a bottle for the baby." Then she added, as if the couple had failed to notice the wailing infant, "This is your other granddaughter, Diana."

Her grandmother pursed her lips and frowned. "We finished supper and cleaned up the kitchen an hour ago." Then, as if reconsidering forcing a small child to go hungry, she said, "There's some leftover stew you can heat up for the child. Help yourself to some, too."

"Thank you, Mama, but I'm not very hungry." She shifted Diana onto her other hip and went into the kitchen, Charlotte trailing closely behind.

After her mother prepared Diana's bottle, she heated up a bowl of leftover stew and placed it before Charlotte. "Now you stay in here and eat while I unload the car."

Charlotte sat forlornly, taking in her surroundings. The kitchen table with its chipped Formica top balanced on wobbly, rusted metal legs. The chairs also rested on wobbly metal legs, and the cushions were cracked, red vinyl with dirty white stuffing poking through. Two brightly colored braided rugs, lying on top of the yellowed linoleum, added the only bright accents to the otherwise dreary room. A massive, stained porcelain sink with old-fashioned faucets sat under the curtainless windowsill, across from the stove and refrigerator. Charlotte had never seen a stove that had legs. Despite the gloominess, however, the room smelled clean, with the strong odor of pine oil.

Having long since finished her tasteless stew and feeling very alone, Charlotte wandered into the living room, where Connie sat in a stiff wooden chair feeding Diana, and her grandparents—it felt odd to think of these strange people by a name that sounded so warm and affectionate—sat unsmiling across the room on the sunken sofa.

"Can I watch T.V.?" she asked.

"We don't have no T.V.," the older man replied, as if she had insulted him. "The T.V.'s nothin' but an instrument of the devil."

"Charlotte, I think it's time for bed." Her mother rose and placed a hand on her shoulder.

"You will be going to church with us in the morning?" Although phrased as a question, the older woman's statement sounded more like an order.

Charlotte brightened. She loved church. Usually her daddy took her, as her mommy didn't like to go all that much. Charlotte mostly went to the children's church service, where they sang songs, had Bible stories, and made little projects, but sometimes Daddy took her into the big sanctuary, with its thick, wine-colored carpet and padded pews. She was awed by the huge pipe organ, which emitted a resplendent sound that seemed to come down from heaven, itself. Although she didn't understand a lot of what Reverend Aaronson talked about in his lengthy sermons, he was always friendly, and teased her after the service.

She broke away from her mother's prodding hand and ran back into the living room, her temporary excitement overcoming her shyness of the two older people. "I just *love* going to church!"

Her grandparents exchanged surprised glances. The woman's face almost softened a little. "Do you, child? You do go to church, then?"

"Oh, yes," Charlotte cried. "Daddy takes me almost every Sunday."

The almost-smile disappeared, and her grandmother's lips flattened. "I see. Your daddy takes you." Then looking over Charlotte's head, she added, "I see *you've* not changed, either, Constance."

Her mother averted her eyes. "I go sometimes, Mama."

"The Lord don't cotton to part-time Christians," grumbled the old man.

"Come along to bed, Charlotte."

Bewildered, Charlotte had thought she'd found some common ground for breaking the ice with these people. But all she'd done was cause more tension in the already strained house.

Her mother led her down the dark hall to a small room at the back of the house. "This used to be my room when I was a little girl," she told her, brightly.

It was, by far, the most attractive room Charlotte had seen in this dismal house. There was a double bed with a colorful patchwork quilt, lacy pink cotton curtains at the windows, and a large woven beige rug on the polished wood floor. A shelf loaded with several dolls hung on the wall facing the bed, and underneath the shelf sat an old wooden toy box.

"Mommy, are those your dolls?"

She nodded and smiled. "Yes, those were mine when I was a little girl. I can't believe they kept them. You can play with them tomorrow. But now you need to get some sleep. You've had a long day." She began to help Charlotte undress.

"Mommy?"

"What?"

"Why don't Grandmother and Grandfather like me?"

Her mother stopped trying to wrestle Charlotte out of her clothes and sat on the edge of the bed. "Oh, honey, they do like you. It just takes time to get to know some people."

Charlotte considered this. "How come they act so mad?"

Her mother's eyes took on a faraway look. "They haven't always been that way, honey. When I was a little girl, they were very happy." She finished removing Charlotte's clothes, pulled her nightgown over her head, and tucked her in, lingering a minute, as if debating whether or not to continue. "I'm going to tell you something that might help you understand why they seem to be so unhappy. You may not be old enough to understand, but I'm going to tell you, anyway. Only you have to promise never to repeat what I tell you, especially to your grandparents. All right?"

Charlotte nodded, feeling important to be privy to this secret.

———•●•———

"You see, they always wanted a son. And when I was twelve years old and still had no brothers or sisters, they thought they couldn't have any more children. Then I had a baby brother. They were so excited. But the baby was born sick. They were very worried and in desperation, they turned to a preacher." Connie gave an involuntary shudder, remembering the big, intimidating man who had changed their lives forever and condemned everything they did, causing her to distance herself from the church. "He was supposed to be a faith healer."

"What's a faith healer?"

"Someone who is supposed to be able to heal sick people in the name of God. But he was nothing but a . . ." She broke off, biting her lip. Taking a deep breath, she continued, "He told them it was their sin that caused the baby to be sick, that their faith was not strong enough."

Connie knew the concept of sin was a little much for her young daughter, but she didn't stop to explain. Her eyes glazed with the memories. "The baby died a few weeks after he was born. The preacher told them God was punishing them for their sin, just like he punished King David by taking away his baby when he sinned."

"Why would God do that?"

Connie hesitated. "Well, nobody knows for sure why God does some things. God's ways are not always our ways. But this preacher convinced them it was their fault because they had not lived their lives the way God wanted them to. So they became disciples, or students of this pastor and did everything he told them. They became very strict. He told them that by denying themselves a lot of worldly things and giving most of their money to the church they could be closer to God."

She paused and looked at her wide-eyed daughter. "Oh, Charlotte, I'm afraid this is too much for you to understand. But all I'm trying to tell you is to be patient with them and be on your best behavior. Everything will be all right." Then she kissed her. "I'll be sleeping with you tonight. I'll come to bed in a little while."

—•●•—

Charlotte lay for a long time thinking about the strange day she had had. Her mother had never confided anything to her before. Whatever sin was, it must be something really bad. But the baby was in heaven, right? So that was good. Charlotte was still a little apprehensive about her grandparents, but maybe, like her mother said, they weren't really so bad once you got to know them. But the most nagging question of all was where was her daddy? And why had Mommy brought them here?

CHAPTER ELEVEN
ADAM

———•◦•———

Adam arrived in Atlanta physically and mentally exhausted. It was late. He needed to find a motel and get some rest before meeting Dr. Rothchild in the morning. Spying a neon sign just up the road, he silently thanked God that he wasn't going to have to drive around for another half-hour looking for a place to stay.

The room wasn't much, but he didn't care, as he lay down, completely drained, on the lumpy bed. He sadly noted there was no phone in the room. Even though it was late, he had planned to call Connie. But she was probably with Stephen, anyway, he thought, miserably. What did he have to look forward to now? Without his family, especially his girls, why go on living? Nothing would matter anymore, anyway.

"Stop it," he told himself, aloud. "Pull yourself together. As soon as I get settled here, I'm going to get my daughters back." But, even if he did get custody of his girls, how was he going to take care of them by himself? When he started back to school, it would be impossible. Could he afford a full-time housekeeper? He would have to look into it. He wasn't going to give up.

He should have been excited at the tremendous career opportunity that had fallen into his lap, but right now, he just felt empty. Tomorrow he would have to go to the Atlanta plant and pretend to be enthusiastic about the chance to work with Dr.

Rothchild, as anyone with half a brain would be. But it was going to be difficult. He hoped he could fake his way through the next few days until he could sort out his personal life. What a way to start a new job!

Despite the fact he was sure he wouldn't sleep, Adam drifted off with no trouble. The raucous buzzing of his travel alarm jolted him from a sound, dreamless sleep at eight o'clock. For the first brief moment upon wakening, he lay in a sleep-laden, blissful state of unawareness. Then all the unwelcome reality came flooding back. He sighed. How nice it had been to forget everything for a few hours in sleep.

After a quick shower, shave, and change of clothes, he looked, even if he didn't feel better. There was a small coffee shop across the street, where he grabbed a quick cup of coffee and a roll. Then he tried to call Connie from the pay phone outside the restaurant. No answer. It figured. Why had he dared to think she might have changed her mind and come back to him? He cursed himself for not having told her about the new job. Maybe it would have made a difference. He walked back to his motel and checked out.

The Fenner Pharmaceutical plant sat on the east side of town. Fortunately, Adam had a good sense of direction, partly natural and partly from necessity in his years of travel. He found it without difficulty. The outside of the plant was impressive. The building, itself, took up a good city block, with a multi-level parking garage attached to the north wing. Although he had visited the Fenner plants in several other cities, this was by far the largest. Two wings jutted off at ninety-degree angles from the main section. A landscaper's delight occupied the center, with an almost too green, manicured lawn, two perfectly parallel walks edged with low hedges, and colorful flower beds, also perfectly shaped and designed. Several benches sat strategically placed under picturesque weeping willows. Factory workers in their regulation baggy green scrubs and plastic hair bonnets were taking advantage of the pleasant surroundings as they enjoyed their coffee breaks. He was a little surprised to see the factory operating on Sunday.

He lingered for a moment, enjoying the peaceful atmosphere. Someone had put a lot of thought into this arrangement, anticipating the positive effects on the workers who had to endure the drudgery of the assembly line for eight hours a day. A whistle blew, as if calling children in from recess, and the workers filed back into the building, chattering among themselves.

Adam followed them into the main corridor and located the reception area. A pretty, young girl, with long auburn hair and sparkling green eyes looked up from her paperwork and asked, "May I help you?"

"Yes. I'm Adam Wallace, Dr. Rothchild's new assistant. I understand he's expecting me today."

"Oh, Mr. Wallace," she cried, as if he had just made her day. "I'm so glad to meet you. But I'm afraid Dr. Rothchild isn't in yet. He never gets in before noon on Sundays. However, if you'd like, I can show you around the plant while you're waiting."

"I hate to take you away from your desk," Adam protested.

"Oh, no trouble at all. It's usually quiet around here on the weekends. I'll just leave a sign on the desk for visitors to check in with the business office up the hall." With that, she quickly pulled out a small piece of laminated cardboard with an arrow pointing to the right and taped it to the front of her desk. "There, now, we're all set. My name's Katrina Graham, by the way." She flashed him a radiant smile and stuck out her hand.

"Well, it's nice to meet you, too, Miss Graham," Adam responded, taking her hand, and finding himself relaxing in her bubbling presence.

"Oh, please. Call me Katrina."

"Very well, then, Katrina. Where shall we start?"

"I'll take you over to the south wing, which is mostly quality control, then downstairs, where they do the actual compounding of the drugs, and then we'll work our way around to the inspection areas, the assembly lines, the packing rooms, shipping department, business offices, and end up in the research facilities in the north wing."

"Sounds good. Have you been here long, Katrina?"

"I started here when the new plant opened last month. But I've been with Fenner Pharmaceuticals a long time. I love it here. I've learned so much already." She was walking swiftly toward a bank of elevators, her heels echoing loudly in the mostly empty, tiled corridor.

"Quality control is on the third floor." She pressed the button and smiled at him as they waited.

"I'm surprised to see factory workers on Sunday," Adam commented.

"Oh, they had to put in some overtime. There were some start-up problems, initially, and some of our orders were late in getting met. We've just about ironed those issues out, now. But believe me, most of the factory workers don't mind Sundays at double time."

The elevator arrived, and they stepped inside. "This is an experimental plant. It's the only one of the Fenner Pharmaceuticals plants that has everything from start to finish under one roof. We have everything from the scientists upstairs discovering the drugs to the guys on the loading dock shipping them out." She paused and smiled. "Well, it's not quite that simple, as you know, with the years required to get FDA approval on new products."

"A necessary evil," agreed Adam.

They arrived on the third floor, and Katrina took off to the right. "Quality control is in this wing," she announced over her shoulder. "Oh, sorry. Am I walking too fast for you? Force of habit."

"You seem like a young woman who knows where she's going," Adam said.

Katrina blushed. "Right through this door."

They stepped into an enormous laboratory, full of equipment, some of which Adam had never seen before. "Impressive," he said.

"Each day, representative samples are collected from the floor, broken down, and chemically analyzed to be sure they are pure and of the correct potency. If there is even a minor discrepancy, the whole batch is discarded. The chemists are not told what compounds they're testing for. That way there can be no question as to whether someone actually did his job. Also, each chemist only performs certain steps in the analysis, so to identify the compound requires the work of three or four people. Then finally, the computerized printouts are kept on permanent file for each day. Fenner is one of the strictest companies in terms of assuring its products' quality."

"Yes, I know."

"Oh. Of course, you do. You've been telling your customers that for years, haven't you? But now you can actually see with your own eyes that it's true, not just propaganda."

She led him to the far side of the room. "Over here are our gas spectrometers, the very latest in state-of-the-art chemical analysis."

She demonstrated the principal involved by injecting a small amount of a colorless liquid into the receptacle and flipping some switches on the machine's console. After a brief warm-up, they watched as the liquid was sucked into the mysterious internal mechanism. Then the mechanical arm began to move up and down, creating a graph. She pulled the sheet of paper out of the printer and handed it to Adam.

"Ta-da!" she sang.

Adam looked at the graph of peaks and valleys. "Wonderful. What is it?"

She took it back, studied it for a moment, and then said casually, "Offhand, I would say it's salicylic acid. Aspirin."

He laughed. "That's amazing. How did you know that? Or do you perform the same trick every time?"

It was her turn to laugh. "No, actually, I'm finishing up my master's in biochemical engineering. This," she waved her hand nonchalantly, "is really very basic stuff."

Adam's jaw dropped. "You're kidding me. Then what are you doing at a reception desk?"

"Learning the business from the ground up. My father, the senior vice-president of Fenner Pharmaceuticals, Mr. Trenton Graham," she said the name with mock formality, "thought it would be good experience for me. And, to be honest, it has been."

"That's incredible."

"I have worked at various Fenner plants doing everything from manning the assembly lines to developing a synthetic penicillin." She hastily added, "It's still in the field trial stage."

"I'm totally amazed. *You* should be Dr. Rothchild's assistant, not me."

"Come June, I will have my own lab, assuming my master's thesis is approved. Then I'll start on my PhD."

"I don't know what to say. I took you for a recent high school graduate who was working her way up to a secretarial position. My apologies."

"Oh, please, don't apologize. I have also been a secretary." She laughed, again, and Adam noted how delightful and breezy her laugh sounded.

She continued with their tour, showing and explaining everything with a first-hand working knowledge. As the morning progressed, Adam found he was actually enjoying himself, temporarily pushing his problems to the farthest corner of his mind. The girl seemed to know everything! Each time she revealed another amazing fact, he became awestruck all over again. At last they ended up in the research wing.

"Dr. Rothchild should be along any time, now. I would show you some of his work, but I don't want to steal his thunder. So, I shall wait and let him do the honors."

Adam was sorry to see the pleasant and enlightening morning come to an end. "Perhaps you would let me buy you lunch for all your trouble?"

"Oh, thank you, anyway, but I've got a ton of paperwork to get back to. Maybe some other time." She flashed him her merry smile that she had bestowed upon him several times in the past couple of hours. "But we will be seeing a lot of each other after the next couple months. Then no more playing receptionist for me."

"I look forward to it."

"Me, too. Oh. Here comes Dr. Rothchild now," she cried, as if thoroughly thrilled.

Adam strained his eyes to get his first glimpse of his future mentor. Robert Rothchild was a tall, imposing figure, of indeterminate age, with thinning, unruly black hair and large, thick-lensed glasses that magnified his myopic crystal-blue eyes. His clothes were wrinkled, as if he had slept in them. He looked just like the stereotype of the mad scientist. It was all Adam could do to suppress a chuckle.

Katrina picked up on his repressed laughter. "I know what you're thinking," she whispered, "but the man is brilliant. He can afford to be eccentric."

By then the great scientist had reached the lab, where they stood in anticipation. "Miss Graham," he greeted. "How nice to see you."

"Dr. Rothchild. I want to introduce you to Adam Wallace, your new assistant."

Dr. Rothchild turned to look at Adam as if he had previously been unaware of anyone standing there. "Ah! Adam!" he exclaimed. "I appreciate your getting here so quickly. You heard about our unfortunate Mr. Pesco." Without waiting for a reply, he shook his head sadly and hurried on, "Terrible thing! He'll be gone for quite a while, that is assuming his doctors let him return to work at all.

Triple bypass. But I was always on him about his weight and his smoking. You don't smoke, do you, my boy?"

"No sir."

"Good! Good! Filthy, nasty habit."

"I've given Adam the grand tour," interrupted Katrina. "All except your lab."

"Excellent. Did Miss Graham tell you she is after my job? Brilliant woman. Absolutely brilliant. Wouldn't doubt she'll get it, too. Twenty-three years old and already getting her master's in biochemical engineering. Can you imagine?" Again, he didn't wait for a comment, but plunged on, "Of course, her idiot father has her doing all kinds of menial work that's totally beneath her. Terrible waste of her talents." He made a clucking noise with his tongue.

Katrina laughed. "I think I've gotten a very good education. At least I know what goes on in this plant outside of the third-floor research lab."

"Bah. Who cares? That is for the working class." His voice held a touch of disdain as he made a majestic sweep of his hand. "But unfortunately, with her exposure to the common working world, she'll probably end up marrying some smooth-talking man who sweeps her off her feet and give all this up to have babies and fight wax build-up on her kitchen floor."

"Hardly. I haven't met a man yet who I didn't scare off. Or if not me, my father. No, I'm afraid I'm destined to be an old maid." Then she waved good-bye and set off down the hall.

"I must admit," said Adam, "I feel a little overwhelmed in the presence of two such geniuses."

"Nonsense! I hear you're a fast learner. And I am a good teacher. You'll soon find that we're all a bunch of old windbags anyway." Chuckling at his own little joke, he put his arm around Adam's shoulders, like a father figure. "Come, my boy, I'll show you what they pay us the big bucks to do. Of course, since none of *them* can understand our work, they figure we're a lot smarter than we are." He cut loose with a booming laugh as he propelled Adam through the doorway.

CHAPTER TWELVE
CHARLOTTE

She didn't remember falling asleep. The night before, her small head had been so full of questions that she didn't think she would ever go to sleep. But suddenly, it was morning, and her mother was shaking her awake.

"Hurry and get dressed, Charlotte. Breakfast is almost ready." Her mother hurriedly assisted Charlotte into her church dress and rushed her into the kitchen. Her grandparents were already seated at the table, and they didn't look any happier than they had the evening before.

"In this house, we're on time for meals," stated her grandfather. This morning, he wore a starched white shirt with a stiff collar and a dark blue tie. His neck looked terribly uncomfortable, as if it were incapable of bending.

"I'm sorry, Papa. Charlotte is a heavy sleeper, and she was tired after the trip yesterday."

Her grandfather glared at her. "Laziness is a sin. She should have been up hours ago."

"I'm sure she'll adjust, Papa."

"We've waited long enough. Let's say grace before our meal gets cold." With that, he launched into a lengthy prayer that assured a cold breakfast, even if Charlotte's transgression of having overslept had not.

Breakfast consisted of lumpy oatmeal and toast with no jelly.

Charlotte hated oatmeal, but made an attempt to force down the tasteless food lest she further invoke the wrath of her grandfather. She didn't dare ask for sugar or jam. The meal proceeded in an uncomfortable silence. After eating as much of the unappetizing gruel as she could, Charlotte waited quietly for the adults to finish. Her grandmother's sharp eyes did not miss the half-full bowl.

"The child doesn't eat much," she complained. "With all the hungry people in the world, you'd think she'd be more appreciative for the food the Lord provides."

"Charlotte doesn't have much of an appetite in the morning."

Charlotte didn't correct the lie, as she thought about the big Sunday breakfasts her daddy liked to concoct, with pancakes or omelets. Even without the look her mother shot her, she knew to keep quiet.

"Well, we'd best be off or we'll be late for services." Her mother and grandmother carried the dishes to the sink and left them to soak in the sudsy water.

They all squeezed into the cab of the older couple's pick-up truck and bounced along the rough dirt road, pulling up in front of a tiny white church a few blocks away. The little church was surrounded by huge oak trees, in an almost cathedral-like setting, with beams of sunlight filtering through the leaves.

"The church we go to is much bigger," observed Charlotte.

"The Lord isn't impressed with big, fancy buildings," snapped her grandfather.

Charlotte bit her lip. It seemed she was always saying or doing the wrong thing without knowing why.

They were greeted somberly by a few other people as they made their way down the cracked walk leading to the entrance. Charlotte thought her church was much friendlier, too, but refrained from saying so. At the door, stood a tall, emaciated-looking man, with a shock of white hair and bushy white eyebrows. His skeletal, lined face and naturally down-turned mouth gave him the impression of being rather fearsome. As they approached, he appraised them with a penetrating stare.

Her grandparents nodded to him, the corners of her grandmother's lips curling up in a slight smile. "Reverend Harmon, you remember our daughter, Constance. And these are her daughters, Charlotte and Diana."

Charlotte noticed she didn't say, "our granddaughters."

Reverend Harmon fixed his unblinking, black, beady eyes on her mother. "Ah, yes, Constance." He said nothing else, but his burning gaze sent a shiver down Charlotte's spine.

Her mother returned his stare. "Reverend," she greeted, unsmiling, holding her chin up.

Charlotte sensed a tension between the two, but didn't understand why.

There were more people coming in behind them, so thankfully, they were forced to move along inside. Charlotte took an immediate dislike to the church. The air was hot and stuffy. As they walked down the dusty, hardwood aisle to an uncomfortable, hard, wooden pew, Charlotte noticed that nobody was smiling, nobody was talking, and there was no heavenly organ music. She nudged her mother. "Where's the organ?"

Her grandfather turned around, angrily. "God don't need no fancy organ to entertain Him. He needs for people to fear Him."

"Just keep quiet," her mother whispered to her.

They sat silently while the rest of the people filed in. Then the frightening-looking Reverend Harmon appeared, as if by magic, in the front of the church, holding a big black, leather-bound Bible. Charlotte wanted to ask how he had gotten from the back door to the front of the church without coming down the aisle, but she decided against it. There was no pulpit, only a small wooden platform for him to stand on. He ascended to his pedestal, looking even more intimidating by virtue of his height.

"Woe unto ye who sin against the Lord!" he boomed. Without looking at the big open Bible he held in one hand, the other hand outstretched, he continued by rote: "For the wicked shall be revealed, whom the Lord shall consume with the spirit of his mouth and shall destroy with the brightness of his coming!"

Charlotte shrank back at the ferocity of the delivery. Reverend Aaronson never began a church service like this.

Reverend Harmon fixed his eyes on her mother. "Ye ask, and receive not, because ye ask amiss, that ye may consume it upon your lusts. Ye adulterers and adulteresses, know ye not that the friendship of the world is enmity with God? Whosoever therefore will be a friend of the world is the enemy of God."

His voice became louder and more urgent. "In flaming fire

shall the Lord take vengeance on them that know not God, who shall be punished with everlasting destruction from the presence of the Lord and from the glory of his power."

Charlotte felt several pairs of eyes on her and her mother. Her mother shifted on the hard bench, jostling Diana, and Charlotte secretly hoped she would cry so they would have to take her out. Her grandparents sat nodding, in grim agreement. The preacher continued with increasing frenzy.

"The Lord is known by the judgement which he executeth; the wicked is snared in the works of his own hands. The wicked shall be turned into hell, and all the nations that forget God."

Charlotte cowered in the corner of the pew. She didn't understand the words, but they frightened her. Her mother began to squirm in her seat. Her grandparents shifted their eyes toward her, without actually moving their heads.

The preacher began to wave his arms frantically, lifting his head to the rafters, as if to call down the wrath of God upon the hapless congregation.

"They that plow iniquity and sow wickedness, reap the same. By the blast of God they perish, and by the breath of his nostrils are they consumed. Oh let the wickedness of the wicked come to an end!"

He paused. The abrupt silence jolted many from their trance-like state. Then, very deliberately, he stepped down from the platform, pointing his finger directly at her mother and said in an ominously, quiet voice, "Repent therefore of this thy wickedness, and pray God, if perhaps the thought of thine heart may be forgiven thee. For I perceive that thou art in the gall of bitterness, and in the bond of iniquity."

He stopped, looming over her like a large bird of prey, still pointing his finger. Her mother's face, which had initially gone pale, began to flood with color.

She jumped to her feet, startling the sleeping baby, who began to fuss.

"How dare you judge me!" she hissed. "Where is the grace and the mercy? Where is the love?" She looked around at the stunned congregation. "You deceive innocent people. You're worse than Satan, himself." Then, taking hold of Charlotte's trembling hand, she marched out of the church, amid the shocked gasps and murmurs.

Charlotte allowed herself to be pulled after her mother, grateful to escape the terrifying atmosphere in the stifling, little church. Once they were safely free of the building, she looked up, in horror, to see tears running down her mother's cheeks.

Although her grandparents' house was several blocks away, her mother walked with long strides, seemingly unhindered by the heavy baby in her right arm, dragging Charlotte behind. She had to run to keep up, but she still lagged behind her mother. The bright sun had disappeared behind a large, dark cloud as if to accentuate the menacing overtones of the minister's frightening words.

When they reached the house, both mother and daughter were panting for breath, but her mother seemed unaware of the physical discomfort. Without stopping, she banged open the front door and hurried into the bedroom. Finally, after laying Diana in her bassinet, she turned to Charlotte.

"Charlotte, I need you to listen to me," she gasped. She paused for a minute, catching her breath.

An alarm sounded in Charlotte's brain, and she knew her mother was about to say something she didn't want to hear. She stood, quietly waiting, her little chest still heaving from exertion.

"It was a mistake for me to come back here. I should have known it wouldn't work. Now I need you to be very brave for me." She knelt down and took Charlotte's arms. "Can you do that?"

Charlotte nodded, biting her lip. She wanted so hard to be brave, but she was terrified she wouldn't be able to.

"We can't stay here. I'm going to have to find a job and a new place for us to live. But I'm going to have to leave you and Diana with your grandparents for a little while until I can get us settled."

Charlotte's heart began pounding with dread. She started to shake her head, but her mother put up her hand, forbidding her to argue. Tears rolled down her cheeks.

"I don't have any choice, Charlotte. I don't have anywhere else to leave you for now."

"Mrs. Grandma," blubbered Charlotte. "Please . . ."

"I can't afford to pay her to keep you full-time right now. We need all the money we can save. Now listen, Charlotte. Your grandparents really are good people." The helpless look on her mother's face frightened Charlotte even more, and she shook her head in denial. "They'll be good to you. But you've got to try to be good, too. Please, honey, it will only be for a little while."

Just then they heard the sound of the screen door opening, and the older couple came storming into the bedroom.

"I hope you're pleased with yourself," hissed her grandmother. "Your papa and me won't never be able to show our faces in church again after that little stunt you pulled."

"You shamed us in this town years ago. But that weren't nothing compared to what you done said to the reverend this morning. And him a man of the Lord," added her grandfather.

Her mother whirled to face the couple. "*Him*? What about what he did to *me*? Humiliating me in public."

"The man was trying to get you to see your wicked ways and repent before it's too late."

"He doesn't know anything about my ways!" she shouted. They glared at each other for a moment before her mother averted her eyes. Then, with resignation in her voice, she said, "Anyway, I'm leaving. I can see it was a mistake to come home." She took a slow breath through her nose and exhaled slowly. "If you would just be so kind as to keep the children for me until I can get settled, I would deeply appreciate it. I won't burden you with them for long, I promise."

"No!" cried Charlotte.

Both grandparents turned to scowl at her.

"Please, don't take your feelings for me out on the children. They're innocent."

"The sins of the father are visited upon the children," declared her grandfather.

"Since you're so good at quoting Scripture to me, perhaps you should read Luke 15. It's the story of the prodigal son!" her mother spat at them, then picked up her suitcase and began to move toward the door.

"There's a difference in being sorry for your sins and being sorry your sins have found you out!" her grandfather yelled after her.

Her mother stopped in her tracks and turned to face him. Her voice choked with tears, she replied, "Oh, I am sorry for my sins, Papa. I've lived with the consequences of my sins every day for the past six years." She paused briefly, then looked him in the eye and said, "But I've asked forgiveness for my sins and God has forgiven me. Why can't you?"

The grandparents exchanged wide-eyed glances with each other, but said nothing.

Her mother turned back toward the door.

Charlotte watched in panic, as her mother moved farther and farther away. She *couldn't* stay here with these awful people. She just couldn't.

"Mommy!" she wailed. "Don't leave me!" She shoved her way past her grandparents and rushed to her mother. "Please, Mommy, please take me with you."

Her mother stopped and knelt by her. "Charlotte, I've already explained to you why I can't take you with me now. You promised to be a brave girl for me, remember?"

"I *can't*!" Charlotte sobbed. "I want to go with you. I'll be good. I promise. *Please*!" She clung to her mother's skirt.

"Stop it, Charlotte." Her mother reached down to break Charlotte's clinging grasp and proceeded quickly out the front door.

"No!" screamed Charlotte. She watched in horror as her mother continued down the front steps. Then she bolted out the door after her.

———•●•———

As Connie reached the car, she felt the full impact of her daughter's body thrown against her. "Don't leave me, Mommy," she begged, her little face distorted in terror.

Connie fought to release the child's ferocious grip from around her waist. Reasoning with Charlotte was doing no good. She would just have to leave. Charlotte would calm down after she was gone. But the emotional turmoil of the past two days was becoming more than she could bear. She opened the trunk, threw her suitcase inside, and ran around to the other side of the car, quickly climbing behind the wheel and starting the engine.

"I want my daddy! I want my daddy!" screamed the hysterical child. "I *hate* you." Charlotte ran into the road, shouting into the car window as Connie backed out. "I want my daddy! Take me to my daddy!"

At that point, Connie's nerves, stretched to their limit, snapped. "I can't take you to your daddy!" she shouted back. "Your daddy's abandoned us. He doesn't love us anymore." Then she drove off, leaving the child standing in the dusty street.

The words stunned Charlotte so badly that her tears just stopped, as if she had turned off a faucet.

"You get in this house a'fore I give you something to cry about," threatened her grandfather from the front porch.

Numb, she turned around and went inside.

CHAPTER THIRTEEN
ADAM

Adam's eyes were dazzled by the most spectacular lab he had ever seen. Spotless lab benches extended three-quarters of the way around the room, with stainless-steel sinks and gas jets interspersed. Massive glass-doored cupboards jammed with various equipment filled the space above the benches to the ceiling. In the far corner of the room stood a large, ventilated hood, with eye protectors, rubber gloves, and aprons hanging neatly to one side. A floor-to-ceiling incubator took up another half-wall. Several microscopes, protected with plastic covers sat at the ends of each lab bench. Titration equipment filled the corner opposite the hood. The only sound in the empty room came from the humming of the incubator. A strong odor of disinfectant hung in the air.

"Wow," exclaimed Adam. "What a set-up."

"Oh, this," poohed Dr. Rothchild. "This is just the basic stuff. But wait until you see the next room. I finally talked them into an electron microscope." He sounded as excited as a little child on Christmas morning. Proudly, he ushered Adam into a smaller room, obviously awaiting Adam's response to his newest acquisition.

"I'm astounded," Adam admitted, as he stared at all the buttons and dials. "I've never seen one of these. I can see I have a lot to learn."

Rothchild chuckled. "All in due time, my boy."

Then, seemingly reluctant to leave this room, he continued

with the tour. They went through a door into another small room. "Radioactive area," explained the scientist.

Adam examined the special coveralls, boots, goggles, and hazardous waste disposal bins. "Of course, it goes without saying that nothing leaves this room," Rothchild told him. "We follow strict procedure. By the book in here."

Adam nodded. They proceeded out into the main corridor. "The lab animal facility is at the other end of the hall." Rothchild made a wry face. "Odors, you know. Come."

Adam followed the scientist down the hall and through a heavy swinging door. They stepped into a large anteroom, through which the sounds of barking, chattering, and other animal noises could be heard. The anteroom contained two big refrigerators, four carts, a broad kitchen counter, and several metal bins. "Food preparation area."

As they spoke, a tall, thin young man came through the door pushing an empty cart. "Oh, hello, Dr. Rothchild," he greeted.

"Hello, Gary. This is my new assistant, Adam Wallace."

"Nice to meet you, Mr. Wallace," the young man said, extending his hand, then withdrawing it. "Sorry, I'm rather dirty. Cleaning time at the zoo, you know."

"Why don't you show Adam through the animal facilities, Gary?" urged Rothchild. Then, aside to Adam, "I can't stand seeing all those little brown eyes. Unfortunately, I'm a real animal lover at heart. But all in the name of science, you know."

"Sure, Dr. Rothchild. Come with me, Mr. Wallace." Gary motioned for Adam to follow him.

Adam looked back at Dr. Rothchild.

"Oh, I'll just wait here for you."

Adam trailed Gary into the first room.

"Really, Mr. Wallace, the animals are all treated humanely. Dr. Rothchild is rather a paradox. He wants to develop new drugs, but he can't stand the animal control studies necessary to get FDA approval. He always leaves that part to his assistants, which will probably mean you. But, as you'll see, we don't do any unnecessary testing."

They stopped in front of a bank of cages containing rhesus monkeys. "This is our primate area." As they paused to take a look, one of the monkeys came down from his ledge and poked his arm through the bars.

"Hello, Bennie," crooned Gary, shaking the little fellow's hand.

"You *name* these animals?" asked Adam, incredulous. "How can you allow yourself to get attached to them?"

Gary shot Adam a sheepish grin. "Well, Bennie is rather special. I can assure you that he will not be used in any terminal procedure. But that's not to get around, if you know what I mean."

Adam nodded. Then, with Gary leading the way, they stepped through another door into a kennel full of baying beagles. About twenty or so dogs, all barking at once, greeted them with merrily wagging tails. The runs were all amazingly spotless.

"You must do a lot of cleaning," Adam observed.

"Constantly," agreed Gary. "As you can see, they are a happy enough lot. But to them, they don't know there's any other life than that of a research beagle." He had to shout to be heard over the commotion. After patting a few heads, he motioned Adam into the next room. Gary closed the door behind them, blocking out the din from the kennel.

"This is our procedures area." A large stainless-steel surgical table stood in the far corner of the room. A gas anesthetic machine was positioned in front of the table with its green oxygen and blue nitrous oxide lines running to a central outlet coming from the wall. A massive overhead surgical light hung above the table.

"Over there is our surgical set-up, with halothane anesthesia and piped in nitrous oxide and oxygen." Gary nodded to a piece of equipment unfamiliar to Adam. "We have an electrocardiogram and a doppler device for measuring blood pressure. We hope to get an electro-encephalogram for measuring brain waves soon." He moved over to two smaller Formica-topped tables sitting next to a large counter. "And over here is our procedures and animal restraint area."

Various sized aquarium-type cages, Plexiglas boards, and snares were neatly arranged on the counter. There were several locked cabinets with glass doors, through which Adam could see hundreds of vials of drugs.

Gary gestured to a laboratory bench that took up the nearest wall. "This is our blood chemistry unit and coulter counter. We also hope to be getting a blood gas machine before too long."

The hematology units took up a good portion of the shelf,

which also held a microscope, assorted pipettes, stains, and a small centrifuge. Two high-backed lab stools sat side-by-side in front of the working area.

"I'm very impressed," Adam commented.

"We have two full-time veterinarians on staff, as well as four certified animal technicians."

"And what is your title?"

Gary laughed. "I'm the official animal maintenance officer. In short, that means I'm the cage cleaner, pooper-scooper, and general gopher."

"You seem to enjoy your job."

"Yes, I do." Gary became more serious. "You know, research takes a lot of flak because of animal control studies. But unfortunately, or fortunately, depending on your point of view, animal experimentation is a necessary step before FDA will approve human field trials of new products. You can well imagine where we'd be without the use of lab animals. It's my job to see that the animals are well-fed, clean, and treated as humanely as possible. And if I see something I don't feel is necessary or right, I have the authority to stop the procedure pending investigation." He paused. "Enough lecture. I need to finish this tour or Dr. Rothchild will be wondering what happened to you."

They backtracked through the kennel and through the primate ward, entering a small room containing mice, rats, rabbits, and guinea pigs. The pungent, ammonia smell of wet cage litter assaulted Adam's nostrils.

"Sorry. I haven't gotten to this room yet. Here we have the rest of the group."

Several shelves housed numerous cages filled with white mice. "These guys are great for research, especially cancer, because they are so prone to the disease. Over here," Gary stepped over to a cage containing an unusual-looking group of mice. "These are New Zealand black/white mice. This strain is noted for naturally occurring auto-immune disease. They have multiple dysfunctions, which we are studying in an attempt to understand immune-mediated disorders."

Adam peered at the little creatures. "How interesting!"

"Well, that about does it. I'm sure we'll be seeing a lot of each other, because as I said, Dr. Rothchild doesn't like to involve himself in this part of the research. He's brilliant, but he doesn't live in the real world most of the time."

"Sometimes maybe that isn't so bad," Adam commented, suddenly remembering his own real world. He was sorry he had been reminded of it. He'd had such an enjoyable day so far, despite his problems.

Gary raised his eyebrows. Then, as if deciding not to pursue the subject, he concluded with, "It's been a pleasure meeting you, Mr. Wallace."

"Oh, please, call me Adam. If we're going to be working together, we can't be so formal."

"All right, Adam. I'll convey you back to the doc."

They exited through a side door, which put them back into the food preparation area, where Dr. Rothchild stood waiting, apparently daydreaming.

"Ah! Here you are, then!" he boomed cheerfully. "Did Gary give you the grand tour?"

"Yes, sir. I'm quite impressed by everything so far."

"Splendid. But I've more to show you." He motioned for Adam to precede him through the door leading to the corridor. Once outside, he said, "You'll be spending a lot of time with Gary. Does that bother you?"

"I don't know yet," Adam answered truthfully.

"Ah, that's what I like," said the scientist. "An honest man." Then, lowering his voice, as if any number of ears strained to overhear in the empty hallway, "That's one thing I couldn't stand about Pescoe. Always a 'yes' man. I think we'll get along just fine, Adam."

They had been walking back to their starting point, the silence of the hallway contrasting sharply with the chaos of the animal area. Crossing to the opposite side of the corridor, Dr. Rothchild unlocked a door which read "data processing." Inside, sat a large IBM computer, two key punch stations, and a card sorter.

"We have two secretaries who handle all the paperwork. Thank goodness for that. I'm not a paper pusher."

Adam began to wonder just what the man actually did. He didn't care to know what went on in the physical workings of the plant, the animal control studies, or the paperwork. Apparently, he was one of the very few intellectuals who was brilliant in his one little niche, but hopeless everywhere else. Adam found himself wondering if he had a family, hobbies, or outside interests.

Beyond the computers were two desks with typewriters and computer terminals. In the room beyond was another quality control set-up, much smaller than the one Katrina had shown him. A spectrometer, which Adam recognized, and a gas chromatographer, which he didn't, took up the bulk of the room, the rest being given over to routine lab supplies and equipment.

"In here, our technicians double-check our work."

"Just what is it you're working on now, Doctor?"

"Ah!" Dr. Rothchild boomed again, a broad smile creasing his face. "I thought you'd never ask."

Adam had to grin at the man's enthusiasm. He obviously loved his work, even if he had little interest in everyone else's.

"I'm working on an anti-cancer drug. Chemotherapy. I tell you, Adam, it's the wave of the future." He draped his arm over Adam's shoulders and continued, his already loud voice rising with his enthusiasm. "We have a wide range of antibiotics to fight infections, and we've developed hormones for patients who, for whatever reason, have failed to produce their own, naturally. We even have medications to combat the inflammatory response, pain, depression—you name it. But what do we have to fight the dreaded disease that has rapidly become one of the leading causes of death in this country? Not much, I'm afraid." He paused, as if delivering a speech he had delivered hundreds of times before. He waved his arms as his voice became more animated. "It's a wide-open field. And just think. If we can discover a cure for cancer, imagine the millions of people we could help who previously had no hope."

"It's quite an exciting undertaking," Adam agreed, getting caught up in the idea. They reached the end of the hall, where Dr. Rothchild stopped in front of a door on which his name was printed in authoritative gold letters across the top. "Robert Rothchild, PhD, Head of Research and Development."

"My office," he explained, as though it wasn't obvious. "Please, come in and have a seat."

Adam entered a tastefully decorated room. Probably someone else's doing, he thought, as he doubted the scientist was even particularly aware of his surroundings. Dark oak paneling covered the walls over which numerous diplomas hung. As he stepped inside, Adam's feet sank into thick beige carpeting. Several shelves behind a beautiful mahogany desk held numerous volumes of scientific tomes. He noted the large picture window facing east, which would flood the office in morning sunlight. But the chocolate venetian blinds had been closed tightly, as if the doctor didn't want to be reminded of an outside world. The desk was incredibly messy, just as Adam would have suspected, with stacks of papers, books, and journals thrown helter-skelter.

"Have a seat," repeated the doctor, as he took his place behind the desk in a high-back leather swivel chair.

Adam removed some clutter from the solitary chair facing the desk and sat.

"Now, where was I?" grumbled the scientist, as though having interrupted his speech, he needed help finding his way back into it. "Ah yes, chemotherapy, the wave of the future."

The thought crossed Adam's mind that perhaps the man had done a paper on "Chemotherapy, the Wave of the Future," as he kept referring to it.

"You've definitely got my interest," Adam said. "Please, tell me everything. I will admit this is an area I'm not too familiar with."

"Not too many people are, Adam, my boy. That's what makes this work so exciting. It's all relatively new, even though the systemic anti-cancer effects of alkylating agents were first identified during government investigations into the sulfur-and nitrogen-containing war gases during World War Two. If you remember your pharmacology, you will recall that nitrogen mustards are direct vesicants, or in other words, they produce blistering of skin on contact. From these studies came attempts to improve the nitrogen-mustard compounds being used to treat lymphoma. In the late 1950's, this research resulted in the development of cyclophosphamide, one of our first orally available chemotherapeutic agents. It has been used to treat leukemias, Hodgkin's disease, lymphosarcoma, testicular sarcoma, and a number of other neoplasms, or cancer."

Adam nodded, trying to absorb as much as possible. "Yes, I have heard of cyclophosphamide, but it's not one of Fenner Pharmaceuticals products, is it?"

"No, it's not. In fact, Fenner has *no* anti-cancer drugs. None. That's why we've got to get with the program, or we're going to be left behind."

"Tell me, basically, how these drugs work, Dr. Rothchild. How do they know which cells are the cancerous ones?"

The doctor sat back in his chair, a self-satisfied look on his face. Contrary to what one might expect, he did not seem annoyed at Adam's lack of knowledge. He apparently loved playing the role of teacher.

"Well, you see, a cancerous cell is a normal cell gone awry. Stop me if I'm over-simplifying this."

Adam nodded.

"A single clonogenic malignant cell can multiply sufficiently to kill the host. To achieve a cure, it is necessary to destroy every single cell. In cancer diseases, unlike infections, the host immune system plays very little role in eradicating the disease, unless only a small number of malignant cells are present. The object of chemotherapy is to kill malignant cells, but in order to do so, the drugs must act at the most sensitive part of the cell cycle, which in most cases means cell division. The tumors that are most susceptible to these drugs are those with a high percentage of cells in the process of cell division. Unfortunately, there is very little, if any, selective toxicity for cancer cells as compared to normal cells."

"That accounts for the severe side effects," said Adam.

"Exactly. The normal tissues that proliferate rapidly are often affected during chemotherapy, such as the bone marrow, the intestinal epithelium, and the hair follicles. That's why we see the problems with nausea, hair loss, and the susceptibility to infections because of a decrease in white blood cells. What we desperately need is a selective drug. One that will recognize the normal from the abnormal, so as not to make the patient sicker than he already is. And that," he said, with a twinkle in his eye, "is what I am working on."

"How utterly amazing." Adam could now see why the man could not afford to waste time in the trivial matters of everyday life. He was trying to develop a cure for cancer. "And how close are you?"

"Oh, close. Very close. That is why Pescoe's blasted heart attack was very inconvenient right now."

Adam suppressed a smile. He imagined it had been inconvenient to Pescoe, as well. But Pescoe's bad fortune had been

Adam's big break. Imagine, being in on the research that could be such a major breakthrough. Not, he thought humbly, that he would really have much of a part to play, but he would be there, on the scene, while it was happening!

"I can't wait to get started."

"Good. I'm going to need you twenty-five hours a day for the next several weeks. Is that a problem?"

Adam hesitated. The doctor scrutinized him, his magnified blue eyes appearing owlish through his glasses.

Don't blow this. "No, sir. I'm at your beck and call, twenty-five hours a day."

"Splendid. In fact, we've got you a furnished apartment just a block from here. Although, you won't be seeing much of it."

Adam wondered if the scientist knew about his family. Better not to mention anything at this point.

"Well, are you ready to get started?"

"Yes, sir," Adam replied, ignoring the nagging hunger pains in his stomach.

CHAPTER FOURTEEN
CONNIE

onnie took her time driving back to Biloxi, as the condemning thoughts paraded through her mind. Why did she always say such awful things to people she loved? She would never forget the look on Charlotte's little face when she had blurted out in anger and frustration that Adam didn't love them anymore. How could she have said such a horrible thing to the child? She would have to try to explain she hadn't meant the awful words. Of course, Adam still loved them—well, the girls, anyway. But Charlotte would never believe her. Because of Connie's thoughtless words, the child was probably blaming herself. She knew only too well how children tended to take such burdens upon themselves.

She thought back to when her baby brother had died. She had been much older than Charlotte, but she had been intensely jealous. For twelve years, she had been the only child, the loved and pampered child, and then, all of a sudden, nobody had time for her anymore. Everyone was too wrapped up in the baby. A boy, yet. She remembered hating the baby and feeling guilty. She'd even allowed herself to wish for evil things to happen to the baby. Although she never consciously thought the word "die," she knew that was what she hoped for. And then she got her wish. But it hadn't been wonderful. Instead, she had felt solely responsible. She carried her crushing guilt, afraid that if her parents knew, they would stop loving her. Her parents said God had taken the baby away as a punishment for their sins, but Connie knew the truth. It was *her* sin, not theirs. And then, as time went on, it didn't matter anymore. Her parents stopped loving her anyway. They became strict and joyless, burying their grief in their bleak religion under the tutelage of Reverend Harmon, and constantly finding fault with her for wanting things to be the way they were before. For years, she carried the burden of blame, believing she was the cause of everything, just like Charlotte would now. Why did people so often repeat the mistakes of their parents? Especially when they tried so hard to be the opposite of their parents?

Her depression deepened as she attempted to banish the unwanted thoughts from her head. Going home had not worked—not that she'd had any expectation it would. But now what was she going to do? The desperateness of her situation forced her mind to face the fact there was only one solution.

She had to convince Adam to come back. She would call his district manager in the morning and get a message to her husband. Maybe he would come back for the children's sake. Of course! She began to relax a little. She had been foolish to panic and rush home to her parents. After Adam had a couple of days to think, he would realize he couldn't live without his children. And maybe, just maybe, she could make it up to both him and Charlotte for the things she had said and done.

It was late by the time she finally arrived home. The first thing she did was take the phone off the hook in case her parents called. She couldn't deal with another lecture tonight, and after dumping the children on them, her parents would hound her until she came back for them. Once this was all over, she would rescue the girls, and they would never have to see her parents again.

She fell into a troubled sleep, full of vivid nightmares in which her father turned into the devil and carried her down into hell for causing the death of her infant brother. Then Reverend Harmon's ominous voice seemed to come from out of nowhere, condemning her for her wickedness. Her whole life flashed before her as the preacher narrated page after page of her wicked days on earth. And her mother stood by, nodding in silent approval. Suddenly, her mother turned into a witch, riding off on her broomstick, cackling, "Charlotte's daddy doesn't love them anymore," while the sobbing child stood in the street.

Connie awoke in a cold sweat, her heart pounding in her throat. Groping for the lamp, she banished the night-time demons in the glaring light. But she was afraid to go back to sleep. On shaking legs, she made her way into the kitchen, where she searched for something to chase away her fears. Finding a half-bottle of scotch, she poured herself a generous shot and drank it straight, shuddering at the strong taste. But the warmth calmed her trembling body, and her anxieties began to fade into a numbing peace. She sat for a long time, forcing herself to take deep breaths before she felt strong enough to go back to bed.

She awoke in a daze. Then she remembered her dreams from the night before. Somehow, even the most frightful nightmares seemed silly in the light of day. She chided herself for being so easily terrified by a stupid dream. And drinking. She had never drank before to calm her nerves. What was wrong with her lately?

Thank goodness it was after nine o'clock. Connie raced to the phone, as though she might lose the opportunity, and replaced the receiver. After hearing the dial tone, she called Adam's district office.

"Fenner Pharmaceuticals, southeast district," answered a bored, slightly nasal female voice.

"This is Mrs. Adam Wallace," Connie blurted out. "I need to get a message to my husband as soon as possible."

"Hold please," the woman said, in the same bored tone.

Please don't put me on hold, Connie wanted to scream.

In a moment, the woman came back on the line. "I'm sorry, but Mr. Wallace is no longer employed with this office. If you'll please hold . . ."

Connie's blood turned to ice. With frozen fingers, she replaced the receiver. Adam didn't work for Fenner Pharmaceuticals anymore? That's why he had come home early Friday. Had he been fired? No, he was one of Fenner's best sales reps. They wouldn't have let him go. He must have quit his job. Why? Her mind churned. Because he had found something better. The vague memory of him shouting something about "news" when he'd walked through the door struggled to the surface of her brain. He had sounded excited, although at the time, she had been so caught off guard, it hadn't really registered. So, he was truly gone. There was no way to find him now. Apparently, that was the way he wanted it when he left, since he hadn't left a note. He'd finally had enough of her. Who could blame him? She was alone. Completely alone.

*   ●   *

When the district office secretary picked up the phone to report Adam's transfer to Atlanta, she found the line had been disconnected. "Oh, well." She shrugged and picked up her nail file to finish her interrupted manicure.

CHAPTER FIFTEEN
ADAM

———•●•———

Adam woke early on Monday morning, full of exciting expectations for the day ahead. Since he had been so tired the night before, he hadn't really taken the time to look around his new apartment. Now, after a refreshing night's sleep, he was anxious to explore a little, but first, he wanted to try calling Connie.

"Blast it!" he exploded, getting the busy signal again. That meant the phone had probably been off the hook all night. Why? Because she had company? He found himself getting angry at the thought of Connie's boyfriend spending the night and wondered if Charlotte had been in the apartment. His good mood quickly soured.

"Might as well make some coffee," he muttered, without stopping to wonder if there was any coffee in the apartment. He headed into the bright, cheery kitchen, painted in sunny yellow, with cream-colored tile. Ruffled, yellow flowered curtains hung at the window. Adam was delighted to see that someone had thoughtfully furnished everything from dishes to a coffee pot. And, thank goodness, a new can of coffee sat waiting for him on the kitchen table.

As the coffee perked, he explored the rest of the apartment in more detail. A small breakfast nook connected just off the kitchen, with a little round table for four. The living room had been furnished with a new sofa and matching armchair, a small coffee table, end table, floor lamps, and a small television set. Matching bookcases waited to be filled. There were two bedrooms, the larger one with the double bed that he had collapsed into last night, and a smaller one with twin beds. He felt a little tug in his heart, thinking about his daughters. Would they, one day, be sharing this room? For now, he didn't want to look at this room. Closing the door behind him, he made another attempt to call Connie.

Still busy. He slammed the receiver down, almost knocking the phone off the nightstand. If he could only talk to her. Surely, she had read his note. Maybe she would try to call him.

He took long, slow sips of his coffee, hoping the soothing steam and rich aroma would help him recover his earlier good spirits. His eyes drifted to the open breakfast nook window to a little playground area for the children in the apartment complex. Although still early, several children laughed and played on the swings, bounced up and down on the see-saws, and climbed on the monkey bars. How Charlotte would love it here. Their apartment in Biloxi didn't have a play area. Why did everything have to remind him of his daughters?

His heart gave an unexpected squeeze of longing for his family, and he couldn't stand another minute of watching the children play. He left for the plant. Once inside the now familiar lab, he began to feel better. Here, he wouldn't have time to think about his family.

As early as he was, Dr. Rothchild had beat him in.

"Adam, my boy! Aren't you the early bird! Why it's not even . . ." The scientist consulted his naked wrist. "Hhm, what time *is* it anyway?" He ran his hand through his disheveled hair.

"Seven-thirty, Doctor." Adam's eyes took in the fact the man wore the same clothes he'd had on yesterday, only they looked even more wrinkled.

"Aha!" cried the doctor, as if Adam had revealed a startling fact. "Have you had breakfast yet, boy?"

"No, sir. Only a cup of coffee."

"Well, then. Let me buy you breakfast while we wait for the others to come straggling in. They," he said, wrinkling his nose, "can't manage to get to work before eight o'clock."

So, the scientist *did* eat. Adam was amazed at just how much the man consumed. But he was fascinating. The whole time he ate, he talked nonstop about his research, past and present. In Dr. Rothchild's company, Adam found himself transported into another world. The man's knowledge seemed endless. Adam noticed, however, that not once during breakfast did Dr. Rothchild acknowledge the presence of anyone else in the cafeteria. It was truly unnerving the way the man could apparently close himself off from everything else. What a strange ability.

When they returned to the lab, they found it bustling with activity, people busily occupied everywhere. Dr. Rothchild introduced Adam all around and then put him to work.

The next few days passed in a blur of activity. Adam fell into the routine of having breakfast with the scientist every morning, during which time he had him all to himself. This early morning rendezvous with just the two of them became Adam's most treasured time. Here, his mind became so absorbed with Dr. Rothchild's fascinating stories of pharmaceutical breakthroughs and setbacks, he didn't even think about his family. During the day, he worked with different people in various areas of the lab, learning as much as possible about everything that went on. Lunch, if he ate at all, consisted of a hurried sandwich while he stood occupied at a workbench. Around five or six o'clock, most everyone else left for the day. Then he and Dr. Rothchild had the quiet lab to themselves. Adam worked side-by-side with his teacher, hoping that simply by being in Rothchild's presence, he could absorb some of the great man's vast knowledge. And he did. The speed with which he picked up the inner workings of the research lab staggered his imagination.

At night he went home, exhausted, but exhilarated. He would pick up some carry-out food and eat it mechanically while he poured over his old pharmacology books. Every night and every morning he tried to call Connie. She never answered. The mornings were the most difficult when he had to listen to the children playing outside his window.

Finally, after a few weeks, he placed his usual late-night call to Connie. But instead of an endlessly ringing phone, a recording interrupted. "The number you have dialed has been disconnected."

His heart froze at the unexpected message. Disconnected! A crushing pain paralyzed him as he realized Connie had probably moved out. How was he going to find her now? And his daughters? He fought the urge to panic. There had to be some way. She had probably gone to Stephen's. With mounting dread, he realized he didn't even know Stephen's last name. What was he going to do? Who would know where Connie was?

A thought occurred to him, and with shaking hands, he dialed his old landlady's number. He didn't care about the late hour.

"Yeah?" came a sleepy, annoyed voice. "What is it?"

"Mrs. Trapp!" he cried, his voice loud and urgent. "It's Adam Wallace."

"*Who?*" she snapped.

"Adam Wallace. I used to live in your building. Apartment fifteen," he said, thinly concealing his impatience.

"Oh, yeah. What do you want?" she grumbled. "Do you know what time it is?"

"Listen, I've been trying to reach my wife, Connie," he blurted out, without apologizing for waking her. "And just now I discovered the phone has been disconnected."

"Yeah, that little snip moved out without paying the last two weeks' rent."

Adam tried to suppress his irritation. "Well, do you know where she went? Did she leave any forwarding address?"

"The only thing she left was a gosh-awful mess for me to clean up. And if you see her, you tell her she owes me two weeks' rent plus a cleaning fee." The woman spat the words at him.

"Are you *sure* she didn't leave a forwarding address? Please, think. It's very important." His heart began hammering in a rising panic and he felt sweat break out on his forehead.

"Mister, with the stack o' bills that's piled up for her, I don't think she *wants* to be found. You know what I mean?"

He had to try something else. Mrs. Trapp was the only one he could think of who might know. Swallowing his pride, he said, "Please try to remember. She had a . . . a friend who used to visit her sometimes. His name is Stephen. Do you by any chance know his last name or where he lives?"

The woman snorted. "Honey, I don't stick my nose where it don't belong. If my tenants have friends, I don't ask questions, 'cause I don't wanna know."

"Do you know of anyone in the building who would know?" he asked, through clenched teeth.

"Look, Mister. I ain't no private eye. I don't know nothin'.

And I need to get my beauty sleep."

"Thanks anyway." His shoulders sagged in defeat. "Sorry to wake you."

—•●•—

The next day, Adam took an unprecedented lunch hour. He drove downtown to a tall office building, took the elevator to the sixth floor, and found suite number 609. He had no idea what to expect on the other side of the frosted glass door.

Stepping into the reception area, he told the schoolmarm-looking woman behind the desk, "I'm Adam Wallace. I'm here to see Mr. Peel."

The plain, tall woman removed her glasses from the bridge of her long nose, patted her tight, black bun at the nape of her neck and replied, "Yes, Mr. Wallace. Follow me, please."

She led him across the worn brown carpet and down a musty-smelling, narrow hallway, stopping at a door at the end of the corridor. She gave a sharp rap on the door, and without waiting for an invitation to enter, opened the door, ushering Adam in behind her.

"Mr. Wallace to see you, Mr. Peel," she said, and withdrew, closing the door behind her.

The middle-aged man behind the desk stood, extending his hand. "Mr. Wallace," he greeted pleasantly. "Please sit down." He indicated a chair in front of the desk.

Adam slipped his clammy hand into the other man's before perching on the edge of the chair. He tried not to fidget.

"Now, just what is it we can help you with?"

Adam took a deep breath, gripped the arms of the chair, and leaned forward. "I want my children back, Mr. Peel."

CHAPTER SIXTEEN
CHARLOTTE

C harlotte found the best way to cope with her grandparents was to keep out of their way as much as possible. Otherwise, they invariably found fault with her for one thing or another. On the first morning after her mother left, her grandmother handed her a basket and ordered her to gather the eggs from the henhouse.

"Yes, ma'am," Charlotte replied, taking the basket. She went out the sagging screen door leading from the kitchen to the back yard, careful not to let the door slam shut. Under other circumstances, gathering the eggs would have been an adventure, but this morning her spirits felt as though they were being trampled beneath her feet with each step she took. She ambled down the little cobblestone path that led to the chicken coop, contemplating what her life was going to be like from now on. Would her mommy ever come back for her? Would she ever see her daddy again? Even if he didn't love them anymore, she loved him. Maybe if she tried really hard to be good . . .

"Don't be takin' all day," scolded her grandmother from the kitchen window, startling her out of her daydreaming. "And don't forget to close the gate."

She turned to stare at her grandmother, and then took off like a scared rabbit down the path. A stubborn latch held the gate leading into the chicken coop. She struggled for a minute with the rusty hinges.

Her grandfather appeared behind her. "Here," he said, his voice gruff, as he wrenched the gate open for her. "If you'd eat, maybe you wouldn't be such a weakling."

He stood outside the fence watching her. Several large chickens stopped their scratching in the dirt to investigate the newcomer. Some of them pecked at her feet. She tried to move out of their way by dancing away from them, but they persisted.

"Gaw on. Don't let a bunch 'o stupid chickens scare you, for cryin' out loud."

Dodging the chickens, Charlotte ran into the henhouse, out of sight of her grandfather. Inside the darkened enclosure, she paused for a moment until her eyes adjusted to the dim light. A musty odor of old wood and hay permeated the building. She could make out three rough wooden tiers covered with straw. In the center of some of the nests, she spied abandoned brown eggs. She collected all the eggs she could see, thinking what fun this would be if her heart didn't hurt so much. But half-a-dozen possessive hens sat guarding their nests, refusing to budge. Charlotte wasn't about to argue with them over their territorial rights. If they were sitting on eggs, they could just keep them.

Satisfied she had enough eggs in her basket, Charlotte pushed her way back through the swinging wooden door to the outside pen, keeping an eye out for nosy chickens wanting to peck at her feet. She had almost reached the gate, when suddenly an irate leghorn rooster came bustling out from behind the henhouse. He strutted toward the intruder, his bright red comb erect in attack position. Charlotte struggled again with the rusty latch on the gate, only this time her grandfather was not around to open it for her. Setting down her basket, she tugged with both hands, terrified of the advancing rooster. Just as the gate flew open, he charged, knocking her to the dirt and dumping over the basket. Then the victorious rooster jumped on top of her, flapping his wings and crowing. She began to scream, fending off the attack with her hands.

Suddenly, she felt herself being pulled up and away. Her grandfather plopped her onto the hard ground outside the gate, and kicked at the belligerent rooster, who still danced his victory on top of the overturned basket. The rooster didn't try to bluff the old man. He took off squawking behind the henhouse.

"Just look at this!" yelled her grandfather.

Charlotte, still cowering in the grass, didn't know whether to be more frightened of the rooster or her grandfather. Almost afraid to look, she rose and edged toward the gate, taking care to stay outside it. Her heart sank as she spotted several eggs lying broken in the dirt.

Her grandfather snatched up the salvageable eggs, muttering under his breath. Then he disappeared into the henhouse.

"What in the . . ." He stormed back out, waving a handful of eggs at her. "And why did you leave these perfectly good eggs?"

Charlotte's lower lip began to tremble. "I . . . I picked up all the ones I saw," she whimpered. "The chickens wouldn't let me have the others."

"You were scared to move the setters off the nest?" he cried, as though he couldn't imagine such a thing.

"Y . . . yes, sir." Charlotte lowered her eyes in shame.

"Tarnation, child," he swore at her. "I never seen such a scaredy cat in all my born days." He yanked the gate open with a ferocious tug. Then, towering over her, he pointed his finger toward the end of her nose.

"I'm gonna tell you sump'thun, girl," he said, his voice softer, but more ominous. "Your grandma and me didn't ask to be burdened with your mama's mistakes. We got enough to do without havin' to look out for you. So if you're gonna stay here, you're gonna have to learn to pull your own weight. You hear me?"

"Yes, sir," she whispered.

"And if you can't stand up to a *chicken* . . ." He didn't finish his sentence. Instead, he stomped away, leaving her standing dejected and ashamed.

"What's takin' you so long?" called her grandmother, coming out onto the back step, wiping her hands on her apron. "What're you just standin' there for? Bring me them eggs."

Charlotte picked up the basket and carried it to her grandmother.

"Is this all?" The woman frowned as she assessed the basket.

"Yes, ma'am." Charlotte didn't feel up to explaining why.

"Hhmph." With that, the old woman turned and marched into the house. Then, seeing Charlotte still standing outside, she said, "Well come on in here, girl. I got me a mess of snap beans to put up. I could use a little help."

"Yes, ma'am."

———•●•———

Charlotte soon found that all the days seemed to be the same. She would be awakened early for a tasteless breakfast, usually oatmeal, then she would be sent to gather the eggs, which, over time, she learned to do without being afraid of the chickens—except for the bullying rooster. He was still capable of a few mean tricks, but she never let him make her drop the basket again. Then she would help her grandmother shell peas, snap beans, or husk corn all morning. After lunch, which usually consisted of home-grown vegetables with cornbread or biscuits, she was told to go take a nap. The escape came as a welcome relief, but she never slept. She didn't want to waste her valuable free time napping. Instead, she played quietly with her mother's old dolls, one ear cocked to listen for her grandparents.

Once, when she was deep in serious play, she looked up to see her grandmother standing in the doorway watching her. Frightened at being caught doing what she wasn't supposed to be doing, she quickly tried to replace the dolls on their shelf. But to her surprise, her grandmother said, gently, "It's all right, child. I take it you're not sleepy."

"No, ma'am."

Her grandmother came into the room, picked up a porcelain-faced doll, and sat on the edge of the bed. "This was Constance's favorite. She called her Roberta." Then the old woman actually laughed. "Can you imagine? I don't know where she got that name." Her eyes took on a glassy, far-away stare. "How she loved her dolls. When she was little, she always said she wanted lots of children, all girls."

Charlotte kept quiet. She knew her grandmother was in the midst of a rare revelation, and she didn't want to spoil the moment.

Her grandmother sighed. "Just like Joshua and me." She stopped and looked directly at Charlotte. "I'll bet you didn't know your grandpapa's Christian name, did you?"

Charlotte shook her head.

"Joshua. Joshua fought the Battle of Jericho. Do you know that story?"

Charlotte nodded.

"Joshua and me always wanted a big family. We wasn't blessed in that way, though. Probably because we hadn't lived a good enough Christian life." She fiddled with the doll, turning it over, smoothing the little dress, fluffing up the frizzy hair. "And because of our sins, God took our precious baby boy from us." Tears welled up in her eyes, and she swiped an index finger across her lower eyelids. She continued in a choked voice. "It was a bitter lesson to learn, but Reverend Harmon said it was God's way of telling us we had to change our ways. Sometimes . . ." Her voice broke. Then she went on, her voice so soft, Charlotte had to strain to hear her. "Sometimes, I think it would have been better had He taken Constance, instead."

"Is that why you're so angry with my mommy?" Charlotte asked. She was still a little afraid to speak, but she had to know. Was it because her mother lived and the baby died?

"I'm not angry with your mother, child. I'm burdened for her soul."

Charlotte didn't understand, but she didn't think she should push.

"She was such a beautiful child, such a good child." The older woman looked almost tenderly at Charlotte. "In fact, you look exactly like she did at your age. Maybe that's why . . ." She didn't finish the sentence. Then she frowned and her voice hardened. "But she departed from the ways of the Lord as she grew older. And that is why her life is filled with turmoil. Don't let that happen to you, child."

Charlotte nodded in agreement. She had no idea what her grandmother was talking about, but she wouldn't do whatever it was her mother had done, if she could help it.

"Well," the older woman said, rising from the bed, "you go ahead and play for a while longer. Then you'll need to get cleaned up for prayer meeting tonight." She left, closing the door behind her.

Charlotte was so dumbfounded by her grandmother's tender talk, she forgot to dread the prayer meeting. She had been in her grandparents' home ten days, and during that entire time, neither of them had opened their mouths for anything other than criticism or demands. This heart-to-heart talk was so unlike anything her grandmother had done so far. Charlotte could learn to like a grandmother like that. Unfortunately, those sweet moments were to be a rarity.

———•●•———

In the late afternoons, Charlotte usually helped her grandmother in the kitchen or cleaned the dreary house. Her grandmother gave her a feather duster with instructions to keep the dust off the furniture, an almost impossible job with the wind always blowing fresh dust in the open doors and windows. After dinner, she helped her grandmother with the dishes. Then they sat in the living room while her grandfather read from the Bible and her grandmother did darning or needlepoint. Bedtime came early, usually around eight o'clock.

On Sundays, she attended the dreaded church services and on Wednesday nights, prayer meetings. The strange rituals confused her and the giant Reverend Harmon terrified her. Once he had gotten right up in her face, with his blazing eyes and flaring nostrils, and the stench of his bad breath almost made her gag. He never smiled or laughed or teased her like Reverend Aaronson did. He never told her that Jesus loved her like her Sunday school teacher, Mrs. Russo did. There wasn't even a cheerfully decorated Sunday school class with pictures of Jesus and the little children, or Bible stories and crafts like they had at her other church.

The few people who attended the church were strange, too. They didn't bend down and hug her or talk with her, asking how she was doing or telling her how pretty she looked today. They were grim and somber like her grandparents, barely acknowledging her presence other than to turn around and scowl at her if she became too squirmy during the long services or whispered too loudly. They sat in stoic agreement, nodding as Reverend Harmon berated them without mercy from the front of the church, sometimes coming down the aisle to castigate one particular person or another. Her grandfather told her that's because the person had sinned. Her grandparents kept telling her that she had to "fear God," but Charlotte couldn't understand why she was supposed to be afraid of God when Reverend Aaronson and Mrs. Russo told her that God loved her.

She wondered, if perhaps that was why her daddy didn't love her anymore—because she wasn't a good enough child. Maybe her daddy abandoning them was God's way of punishing her for not being good. Her guilt overwhelmed her. What if her mommy didn't come back either? She remembered her last awful words to her. *I hate you!* Of course, she hadn't meant what she said, but what if her mother had been so hurt by those words that she decided to stop loving her, too?

Diana seemed to handle the adjustment to the new surroundings rather well. She rarely cried. Her grandmother attended to the baby's basic needs, but with little outward show of affection. She would change Diana's diaper or feed her, and then deposit the baby back into her playpen or bassinet.

Once, when Charlotte asked her why she didn't cuddle or rock Diana, like Mrs. McCarthy and her mother did, her grandmother had snapped, "Because I don't want to spoil her." From then on, Charlotte refrained from bringing up anything more concerning Diana's welfare. Since Diana didn't seem to mind, Charlotte decided it wasn't any concern of hers, either.

As the days went by, Charlotte began to lose track of time. She fell into a general routine, which although far from satisfying, kept her out of trouble as much as possible. Then, one day, as she sat at the kitchen table shelling lima beans, she heard a knock at the door. At first, she didn't pay much attention, for people were always stopping by from the church with the name of someone to pray for or other urgent business.

But then she heard her grandmother's flat, disapproving voice. "Oh, it's you. After all this time without a word, I was beginning to think you'd disappeared off the face of the earth, leaving us with your children to raise."

Charlotte edged to the kitchen doorway. It was *her*! She had come back. Unable to restrain herself, Charlotte raced into the living room, throwing her arms around her mother's waist. "Oh, Mommy, I'm sorry. I'm sorry."

Her mother's eyebrows shot up. When the older woman shrugged, her mother brushed the shaggy curls from Charlotte's forehead and asked, "What are you sorry about, Charlotte?"

"Because I said I hated you." With her face still buried in her mother's skirt, she said, "I didn't mean it, Mommy. I love you."

"I love you, too, honey. I know you didn't mean it." Her mother released her grasp and held her at arm's length. "She looks good, Mama."

"Of course she does," replied the older woman. "She's been in a Christian home." Then, her voice softening, "And if you don't mind my saying so, you look terrible."

"It's been a difficult few weeks for me, Mama. That's why I didn't call. I know I should have, and I apologize."

At her grandmother's observation, Charlotte studied her mother. She looked thin. Dark circles rimmed her eyes, and her cheeks appeared sunken and pale.

"Are you all right, Constance?" her grandmother asked, a little note of concern creeping into her voice.

"Yes, everything will be fine." She wiped a stray tear from her eye.

"You can stay here for a while, if you need to."

"Thank you, Mama. But it wouldn't work."

"Then you'd better get packed up and gone before your father gets home." The older woman's voice became brisk once again.

"Yes, I know." Her mother turned to Charlotte. "Go get your things together."

Charlotte shot a cautious look at her grandmother. When she didn't put forth an objection, Charlotte raced to her room to pack, her heart pounding in happy excitement.

With Charlotte working like a little whirlwind, afraid her mother or grandmother might change their minds, the car was packed and ready to go in no time. She climbed into the back seat, bouncing up and down with the anticipation of finally escaping from this place.

Her mother and grandmother lingered for a moment in the street. "I do appreciate everything you've done, Mama. And I do love you." Her mother reached over and gave her grandmother a hug.

The older woman's eyes widened as her hands came up to return the embrace.

"Well, we'd better be going," her mother said, after an awkward pause. "We've a long way to go. Thank you again, Mama."

"God be with you, Constance." The two women appraised

each other.

They hugged again and then her mother climbed into the car.

Her grandmother reached through the open window of the back seat and touched Charlotte's cheek. "Remember what I told you, child. Fear the Lord."

"Yes, ma'am."

And then, at last they were leaving. Charlotte turned around to watch her grandmother's figure grow smaller and smaller until at last she couldn't see her anymore. She burned with a million questions, but was suddenly too shy to ask any of them.

———•●•———

After several long minutes, Connie spoke. "You're awfully quiet, Charlotte. Are you all right?"

"Yes, ma'am."

Connie peeked in the rear-view mirror at her daughter who sat curled up in the back seat. She wondered what had happened to the child during the several weeks of her absence. But, with a stab of pain in her heart, she had a pretty good idea. Charlotte's spirit seemed to be broken.

"We're going to a new home, Charlotte," she said, feeling her way with the child.

"Okay."

Connie glanced at the apathetic child and sighed. It was going to take some time for Charlotte to come out of her little shell. "We're going to be living in Alabama. Do you know where that is?"

"No, ma'am."

The extreme politeness made Connie uneasy. "It's the state right next to Mississippi, where we lived before. We're going to be living in a city called Mobile."

———•●•———

Would her daddy be there? Her hopes were dashed with her mother's next statement.

"I've got a job there, Charlotte. Things are going to be just fine now."

But Charlotte wasn't fooled by her mother's forced cheerfulness. She had a most uncomfortable feeling that things were not going to be fine.

CHAPTER SEVENTEEN
ADAM

Adam waited in agony for the next two weeks to pass. Fortunately, his work kept him too busy to think most of the time. Otherwise, he would have gone crazy. Finally, the date arrived for his next appointment with Jonathon Peel.

Driving downtown, Adam's stomach churned. Mr. Peel had not given him any information over the phone. Was it good news or bad? Probably bad, since he insisted on meeting in person. Still, until Adam knew for sure what the man had to say, there was always the chance it might be good news.

With trembling hands, he opened the frosted glass door to office number 609, on which the words "Jonathon Peel, Private Investigations" were written in bold black letters. The same cool, efficient woman ushered him into the inner sanctum.

Mr. Peel held the telephone to his ear. He motioned for Adam to sit while he wrapped up his conversation. In an effort to distract himself, Adam studied his surroundings. When he had been here before, he had been too upset, too nervous to take much notice of anything but his own distress. Now, having to pass the time, he tried to relax and let his eyes wander around the sparsely furnished room containing Mr. Peel's desk, two uncomfortable wooden chairs for clients, and a cheap bookcase containing several books on criminology. Four framed documents hung behind Mr. Peel's head, but without his glasses, Adam couldn't read them. He had to admit he hadn't given much thought to the credentials or qualifications required of a private investigator. Now, his curiosity was aroused at just how a person got started in this line of work. Ex-cop maybe? He would have to ask later, when the more urgent affairs were settled.

Adam studied the man before him. Appearing to be in his mid-forties, Jonathon Peel exuded a kind, strong, self-assured manner which instilled Adam with a sense of confidence in his ability. He was soft-spoken, smiled enough, but not too much as to make one doubt his sincerity, and seemed to be genuinely compassionate. He had warm brown eyes, dark brown hair that was just beginning to gray at the temples, and a deep dimple in his left cheek. He wore a wedding band on his left hand. Adam wondered if he had children. If so, then he would be especially sensitive to Adam's problem.

Finally, the phone conversation ended. Jonathan Peel stood and shook Adam's hand, apologizing for the delay. Adam looked at him, his heart hammering in expectation, but hesitated to take the initiative, lest it bring him bad news. He realized this was irrational, of course, but felt he needed every advantage.

"Well, Adam—"

"Did you find them?" he blurted out.

Jonathon Peel pressed his lips together in a grimace of frustration and blew out a breath. "I'm afraid not yet."

"Oh." Adam's body sagged, along with his spirits.

"It's very strange," Jonathon continued. "I talked to the landlady—who is still, by the way, complaining about her lost rent and the mess Connie left behind—the other tenants in the building, and neighbors. Nobody seems to know where she's gone. I did, however, manage to locate this Stephen fellow. He's a doctor at St. Andrews Hospital. He is also very married. So we can cross that possibility off our list. I wonder if Connie was aware of that fact, or if perhaps he promised to get a divorce and marry her." He shrugged. "Anyway, it doesn't look like that's going to happen. Beverly Presswood Gates, his socialite wife, has lots of money, and it appears Stephen has become very accustomed to the manner in which she is keeping him. He refused to talk to me. Probably suspected his wife hired me." Jonathon gave a sad smile. "Connie was making inquiries around town about getting a job. I checked out several leads in that direction, but nobody I talked with was hiring or able to help her."

Adam shook his head. "Poor Connie." He sighed. "I wonder what happened between her and that creep. And why, if she was in trouble, didn't she at least call me? Even if she didn't want to come back to me, I would have given her alimony and child support. I don't understand."

Jonathon waited for a moment before speaking again. "Adam, can you give me any more ideas? Does Connie have any close friends or family she might have gone to or confided in?"

Adam shook his head again. "She really didn't have any close friends. She kept pretty much to herself. Maybe that was why Stephen . . ." His voice trailed off. He didn't want to voice the possibility that Stephen had filled a void in Connie's life that Adam couldn't.

"What about her family?"

Adam snorted. "No."

"She has parents still living in Mississippi, doesn't she?"

"Yes, but she never would have gone there. They haven't seen each other since they disowned her when we got married. She didn't want anything to do with them after that." Adam sighed again. "No, even if she were desperate, she wouldn't have gone there. I sincerely doubt they would have helped her, anyway."

"Well, I'll just have to keep looking for someone who knows something. I'll check with the moving companies, U-Haul, things like that. In the meantime, if you can think of anyone who she might have contacted, call me."

"I wish I could, but there's nobody I know of." Adam stood. "Thank you for your time, Jonathon."

"Cheer up. We'll find them. It's just going to be a little harder than we thought."

"I hope you're right." Adam turned and shuffled out the door, his shoulders slumped, his spirit defeated.

————— •●• —————

Jonathon watched him, hoping he could deliver on his promise. Usually missing persons weren't this difficult, but there was something about this case that bothered him. He couldn't put his finger on it, but it made him uneasy. He thought of his own daughters and sympathized with Adam. Sometimes this job really got to him.

"Oh well, back to Biloxi."

CHAPTER EIGHTEEN
CHARLOTTE

The hot afternoon sun awakened Charlotte, as she lay curled in the back seat. Even with all the windows down, the heat inside the small car had become stifling.

She sat up, feeling stiff all over from having fallen asleep in an awkward position. Rubbing her eyes, she asked "Are we there yet?"

Her mother glanced in the rearview mirror. "Almost. Look. You can see the bay."

Charlotte squinted through sleepy eyes at the expanse of blue water to the right of the highway. Sailboats, their sails flaccid, drifted along hoping to catch a bit of a breeze. Listless seagulls and pelicans sat on pylons, as though it were too much of an effort to fly. Here and there, she could see a motorboat pulling a water-skier. The car made a sharp turn toward the bay, and all at once, the smell of salt water blasted through the open windows along with the humid air.

"Isn't it pretty?" asked her mother. "Maybe we can go to the beach sometimes on weekends, like we used to. Remember? Before Diana was born?"

Charlotte didn't answer. She remembered playing in the ocean with her daddy, riding on his shoulders, running from the waves. But that was a long time ago. When he still loved her. It wouldn't be the same now. Her mother didn't usually like to get wet. Charlotte sat brooding for a minute before a little voice inside her head told her to be grateful her mother had come back.

"I like the beach, Mommy," she said, trying to sound cheerful.

They began to veer away from the picturesque bay toward the downtown area. The changes in the surroundings were subtle at first—the yards less cared for, the houses a bit shabbier—and then the scenery seemed to go from bad to worse. Charlotte began to feel uncomfortable and hoped they would pass through this area quickly. She was anxious to see her new home.

They proceeded a few more blocks before having to slow down for the heavy city traffic. The heat in the car became suffocating. An accident up ahead reduced their speed to a crawl.

"Our building is the gray one on the corner," her mother said in a falsely sunny voice.

Charlotte pushed her sweaty hair out of her eyes and craned her neck to see. A wave of repulsion enveloped her. Surely her mother wasn't serious. Charlotte's frantic eyes darted up and down the dirty street at the decaying buildings, stores with boarded-up windows, and tough- looking teenaged boys in tight, tattered denims loitering on the littered street corner, smoking and laughing. Their building sat right out on the street, unadorned by any grass, trees, or even flowers in a window box. Laundry hung from lines strung to the fire escapes, where a number of the tenants had pulled out kitchen chairs in an attempt to elude the heat.

They pulled into the parking lot next to the building. "Carry what you can, Charlotte. We'll come back for the rest."

As Charlotte got out, her mother locked the car doors behind her.

"Well, here we are," she said, a slight tremor to her voice. They went in through the creaky back door, which only partially closed behind them. As soon as they entered the dim, dirty hallway, the lingering odor of stale cooking and an overpowering, acrid stench of urine assaulted them. The walls were marked up with bad words and pictures which Charlotte didn't understand, but that she instinctively knew were nasty.

At the end of the hallway, they went up a flight of stairs covered with litter and debris and stopped in front of the first door on the right. Loud music spilled into the hallway from an apartment further down.

"This is it." Her mother struggled to open the door with Diana on one hip.

As Charlotte stepped into the little apartment, the first thing that caught her attention was the smell of fresh paint. Then she spied some of their familiar furniture, although it looked rather crowded and out of place.

"Well," said her mother, "what do you think? I've spent the last couple of weeks fixing it up so we could have a nice, new cozy home."

"Okay," Charlotte replied, without enthusiasm.

"Honey," her mother said, kneeling down, "I know this is not as nice as where we lived before. But with your father gone we're going to have to make do. Things are going to be a little bit harder for all of us."

Charlotte, who up to this point had said very little, blurted out, "Where is he? Where is my daddy?"

"I don't know." Her mother's shoulders sagged. "But I want you to know none of this is your fault." Connie tried to brush the curls out of her daughter's eyes, but Charlotte kept her eyes glued to the floor. "It's *my* fault. I did something very foolish and . . ." She stopped abruptly. Charlotte was tuning her out. "Anyway, it's just us now."

Charlotte didn't respond. She looked around at the familiar things her mother had moved from their other home. There were some things missing. "Where's the big cabinet?"

Her mother sighed. "I couldn't bring everything, Charlotte. This place is much smaller than our old apartment and there just wasn't room. But I tried to get everything clean and pretty. Come look at your room. I bought new curtains."

Charlotte shuffled behind her mother into the bedroom. The first thing she noticed was not the new curtains, however, but that there was only one bedroom. "Where are you gonna sleep, Mommy?"

"My bed is the couch. Remember our hideaway bed? I'll pull it out at night and tuck it away during the daytime."

Charlotte nodded. It was going to seem strange having her mother sleeping in the living room.

"Tomorrow, I have to start work. And you and Diana are going to a nice day care center where there will be lots of other children to play with. And in September, you'll be going to school. So there will be plenty of new things for you to do."

Charlotte nodded again. She was going to have to try awfully hard to like it here. If she didn't, she might get sent back to her grandparents' house. That thought alone kept her from voicing her opinion to her mother. As bad as this place was, it was better than living with her grandparents.

She had a hard time falling asleep that night. She could hear the television from the apartment next door through the thin wall. Dozens of worries weighed upon her five-and-a-half-year-old mind. But the worst one of all was what had she done to make her daddy stop loving her?

The next day her mother woke her early. "Hurry up and eat your cereal, Charlotte, while I get Diana dressed."

Charlotte gobbled down her breakfast, remembering how bad the oatmeal she had gotten used to tasted.

The day care center was only a few blocks from their home, occupying a large, faded brick building with a big front porch and a fenced-in playground in the back. The sign on the front of the building said "Children's Social Welfare Services," but Charlotte couldn't read it.

A plump middle-aged lady in a sleeveless blue cotton dress met them just inside the door, handed Diana off to another woman, and led Charlotte away, calling over her shoulder, "Remember, Mrs. Wallace, you must pick them up by six o'clock sharp."

The amount of loose flesh on the woman's upper arms that swayed when she walked intrigued Charlotte. Although the walk to the classroom wasn't very far, the woman's face was beet-red and her chest heaved with the exertion to breathe by the time she had shown Charlotte the way.

"This will be your classroom, Charlotte," she wheezed, as she led her into a room full of tiny tables and chairs occupied by preschoolers. "And this is your teacher, Miss Runge."

A tall, almost masculine-looking woman, Miss Runge initially appeared frightening. But she spoke kindly. "Thank you, Miss

Flaggerty. Will you please sit over there, Charlotte?" She pointed to a vacant seat.

Charlotte took a seat next to a freckle-faced red-headed girl. "What's your name?" asked the redhead.

"Charlotte," she answered, appraising the new child.

"Mine's Belinda. Are you unner-pribliged?"

Charlotte looked at her. "I don't know. What's unner . . ." She struggled with the new word.

"Unner-pribliged," Belinda repeated, with emphasis. "Everybody here is."

"Oh, I guess so, then," Charlotte agreed.

Belinda nodded, apparently satisfied.

The day passed pleasantly enough. They played on the playground, sang songs, had lunch, nap time—although Charlotte didn't go to sleep—then drew pictures, had milk and cookies, and story time. She didn't see Diana all day. The babies were in a different part of the building. But she had fun and made some new friends.

Her mother arrived at five-thirty to pick her up. "Well, how did you like your first day?" she asked, as they walked out to the car.

"Good," Charlotte answered. "Mommy, am I unner-pribliged?"

"What?"

"Unner-pribliged." She tried to say the word just right.

"Oh, honey," choked her mother. Then to Charlotte's astonishment, she began to cry.

CHAPTER NINETEEN
CONNIE

Thank goodness it was Friday. She had only been working at this lousy place for two weeks and already she dreaded each new day. One would think that someone with two years of college could get something better than a secretarial position in a plumbing supply warehouse. But Connie had to face reality. What marketable job skills did a psychology major drop-out have to offer the business world? A person certainly couldn't do anything in the psychology field without a degree, preferably a master's. At least she'd had the foresight to take basic typing and shorthand classes, although at the time, she had thought them a waste.

But her typing and shorthand skills were a bit rusty, which was probably why nobody had been eager to hire her. Thank goodness for Mrs. McCarthy who used her influence with her nephew, Jason, in Mobile, to give Connie a chance. Otherwise, she'd probably be on welfare.

Although Jason McCarthy loved his aunt dearly, she had really put him on the spot by foisting Connie on him. Connie had only been with him two weeks and already had fallen into the habit of coming in late and leaving early, and on top of that, she didn't get along with the other women in the office. And, as if those faults weren't bad enough, her secretarial skills left a lot to be desired. She was slow and, more often than not, made mistakes. If it weren't for Aunt Sarah . . . He rolled his eyes and sighed, as he stuffed the last of the paychecks into their respective envelopes.

———•●•———

At long last, the never-ending day was drawing to a close. Connie breathed a sigh of relief, anticipating a whole weekend away from Mr. McCarthy's continual harping and the other secretaries' snubbing. She would have slipped out a little early, but paychecks hadn't been distributed yet. Her impatience mounted as she watched the hands advancing on the ugly, industrial clock across the room. It was already after five. With each click of the minute hand, her stomach clenched in frustration.

Finally. The boss appeared with the coveted white envelopes, handing them to the two other secretaries first and then to her, before turning to retreat back into his office. With greedy fingers, she tore open the envelope, but her happy anticipation turned to annoyance.

"Excuse me, Mr. McCarthy," she called, running after him. "My paycheck is in error."

He stopped and turned to face her, his lips twisting in obvious irritation. "I beg to differ with you, Mrs. Wallace, but your paycheck is correct."

"But this is not the amount I asked for!" she insisted. Connie felt the heat rising in her face.

The other two secretaries stopped their preparations to leave and looked on with interest at the unfolding drama.

"May I remind you, Mrs. Wallace," he replied, in an icy tone, "I told you at the time you were hired that your pay would be contingent on your work performance. I made no promise to start you at your asking salary. You represented yourself as being in possession of certain qualifications which you obviously do not possess. Under the circumstances, you cannot expect to be compensated for work you cannot do. And need I remind you further that you are still in the probation period of your employment?"

"How is my family supposed to live on this?" Her voice broke.

"That, Mrs. Wallace, is your problem, not mine. Should your

work improve, then perhaps we can move you up to your asking salary. And it might not hurt to punch the time clock a little earlier in the morning and later in the evening, rather than the other way around."

Too upset to answer, her chest heaved with anger. Then, glancing at the other women, who were watching the interchange with widened eyes, she lowered her voice. Grasping at his sleeve, her words spilled out.

"Please, Mr. McCarthy. I really need the money. I know I'm a little rusty, but I just need some time. I used to be much faster." Stinging tears filled her eyes.

He looked down at her plucking at his sleeve, and a look of disdain spread over his face. Then he blew out a heavy sigh.

"If you like, Mrs. Wallace, you can take home some typing to do in the evenings. You can earn some extra money and practice your 'skills' at the same time."

"But—"

"That's my final offer. Take it or leave it."

She bit her lip, trying not to make a bigger fool of herself in front of everybody.

"All right," she whispered. She turned away, afraid the gathering tears were going to turn into an avalanche. *No. I will not cry.*

"And," continued Mr. McCarthy, in a voice loud enough to be heard by all, "if your work performance does not improve, I will have no alternative but to terminate your employment. Do I make myself clear, Mrs. Wallace?"

"Yes," she replied, her voice barely audible.

"Good. There are some handwritten papers on my desk that need to be typed. You may take them home and begin on them this weekend. Good day, Mrs. Wallace."

Her face burning with shame, she hurried into his office to collect the wretched papers. Then she fled past the other two secretaries, who sat with self-satisfied smirks on their faces. She didn't meet their eyes.

Once outside, she could no longer control the tears. Why couldn't anything go right for her? Maybe she *was* a failure at everything. Glancing at the time, she quickly brushed the tears aside. She would be late picking up the girls if she allowed herself to stand there weeping.

Her heart curled in on itself as her thoughts turned to her daughters. She was not doing so well in the motherhood department, either. Diana's incessant neediness rankled on her fragile nerves, which only ratcheted up Connie's maternal guilt over feeling so resentful toward the helpless infant. And Charlotte's quiet sullenness ever since she had come back from her grandparents gnawed at her. Connie knew Charlotte missed Adam. But that wasn't her fault. If Adam really wanted his daughters, like he said, he would not have gone away without a word. Why hadn't he tried to contact them? Connie could sure use child support. Maybe he really believed the awful lie she blurted out in anger about him not being the girls' father. She had made such a mess of things for everybody.

Connie had almost reached the day care center when she spied a liquor store on the corner. Why not? More than once in the past few months, she swore not to drink anymore, particularly after that embarrassing episode in the park. But she needed something to get her through the weekend. Especially after the setback at work.

"Mommy, you're late," chided Charlotte, when Connie finally showed up right before six.

"I'm sorry, I had to work late tonight." She avoided looking at her pouting daughter and Miss Flaggerty who waited with the few remaining children.

It was obvious, however, that Miss Flaggerty's sharp eyes and nose weren't fooled. "Are you all right to drive home, Mrs. Wallace?" she prodded.

"Of course, I'm all right," Connie snapped. She collected her daughters in a huff and stomped out to her car.

CHAPTER TWENTY
CHARLOTTE

As they drove home from day care, Diana began to fuss. Charlotte had been hoping for a day at the beach. After all, her mother promised to take her when they moved here and it had been two whole weeks with no trip to the beach. She knew that now was probably not the best time to bring the subject up, but she still felt somewhat miffed at having been picked up late from day care. If the truth be known, she had begun to worry about being abandoned again, and her growing fear made her cranky with her mother when she finally showed up.

"Mommy, can we go to the beach tomorrow?" she asked, in an accusing tone, which indicated there would be an argument if her mother did not say yes.

"No, I'm sorry, Charlotte," her mother replied, in a flat voice which didn't even hint at her being sorry. "I—"

"Why not?"

Her mother pursed her lips. "Don't interrupt me and I'll tell you." She turned around to glare at Charlotte, who sat with her little arms folded in defiance over her chest, bottom lip poked out, waiting for a fight.

"I have a stack of papers to type for Mr. McCarthy over the weekend. I'm going to have to spend a lot of time on them."

"But I don't see why—"

"I just told you why. Now don't argue with me anymore. I'm

not in the mood."

Charlotte wasn't in the mood, either. At least not in the mood to be sloughed off by some silly adult explanation that didn't make any sense.

"But you promised," she wailed.

Her mother yanked the car over to the curb and slammed on the brake, startling Diana, who momentarily stopped fussing. Charlotte pitched forward, her seat belt digging into her belly. Her mother twisted around in her seat, shaking her finger at her.

Uh oh. Charlotte knew she had gone too far this time.

"Don't you ever, *ever* talk back to me again. Do you understand?" Her dark blue eyes flashed with anger.

"Yes, ma'am," Charlotte said, dropping her eyes. She could still feel her mother's blazing glare on her, even though her own eyes were downcast.

"As if I don't have enough to worry about," she muttered, putting the car in gear and pulling out into traffic. "On top of everything else, I've got an ungrateful kid on my back."

Charlotte felt the prickle of cold fear creep up her spine. Why had she pushed her mother into this quarrel, knowing her mother wasn't acting like herself tonight? What if she made her mad enough to go away for good, like her daddy had done? Unwelcome guilt flooded over her. She had to try harder to be good.

After a dinner of canned soup, her mother told Charlotte to play in her room while she worked on her typing. Charlotte stayed out of her mother's way that evening while she listened to the clacking of the typewriter keys. For several interminable hours, the noise seemed to go on, broken up every so often by swearing and the sound of paper being ripped from the roller. Her mother didn't even come in to put her to bed.

Charlotte finally undressed herself and crawled under the covers, feeling forlorn and forgotten.

"Please, God," she prayed, "I'll be good. I don't haft'a go to the beach or anything. Just don't let my mommy go away." Then she drifted off to sleep, still listening to the typewriter.

In the middle of the night, Charlotte got up to get a drink. On her way to the kitchen, she crept into the living room, taking care to be quiet. Her mother had fallen asleep on the couch without pulling out the bed or changing into her nightgown. A large amber bottle and a juice glass sat on the end table beside the sofa, and the room smelled funny. Without getting her water, Charlotte tiptoed back to bed.

She woke early to Diana's crying. She waited a few minutes for her mother to come take care of the baby. When she didn't, Charlotte grew worried. Climbing out of bed, she padded into the living room to check on her mother. She was still lying in the same place.

Charlotte bent close to her ear. "Mommy," she whispered.

She didn't respond.

Frightened, Charlotte shook her hard and cried, "Mommy!"

Her mother bolted upright.

"What?" she shrieked, grabbing her forehead in her hands. "What is the matter with you?"

Charlotte shrank back. Her mother had never yelled at her like this before. "It's Diana," she answered in a trembling voice. "She's crying."

Her mother groaned. "All right. I'll take care of her." She squinted through puffy eyelids at Charlotte. "I'm not feeling very well, Charlotte. I want you to get dressed and pour yourself some cereal. Let me go back to sleep for a while. Don't make any noise."

Charlotte nodded and fled from the room, as her mother struggled to her feet. By now, Diana's insistent screams pierced the air.

"Oh, for the love of Pete, shut up," pleaded her mother as she staggered down the hall to attend to the demanding infant. She jerked Diana from her crib, causing the baby to wail even louder.

"Why me? I can't *do* this." She shook the screaming child. "*Shut up!*"

Charlotte cowered in the corner of her room, lest she, also, invoke the wrath of her mother. She knew babies shouldn't be handled roughly, but she was too scared to intercede on Diana's behalf. She threw on her clothes that still lay on the floor from last night and slipped out the door while her mother prepared a bottle in the kitchen.

Although still early, a heaviness hung in the air, promising another muggy, brutally hot day. The street was pretty much deserted at this hour. Charlotte sat on the front steps, which were already warm under the morning sun, and put her head in her hands to think. How was it, she wondered, that her life had changed so much in the last few weeks? She had been living for the day when her mother came back and took her away from her grandparents' house. Everything was supposed to be better after that. But it hadn't been. First, they had to leave their nice home and move into this horrible place. Then her mother was gone to work all day, and when she came home, she was always in a bad mood. At first, her mother tried to put on a false cheerfulness, but Charlotte had seen right through that. Now, her mother didn't even try. She was just unhappy and mean all the time. How had things gotten to this point? So out of control?

Her daddy. It was all *his* doing. The revelation hit her like a lightning bolt. Everything had been fine until he went away. Now her mother had to do everything by herself, and it was making her unhappy. And because she was unhappy, she was making Charlotte and Diana unhappy. Well, maybe not Diana. She was only a baby, after all. But Charlotte's life had never been so miserable. And it was all because of him.

She considered what she could have done to make him stop loving her and go away. She thought and thought, but could not come up with anything. Finally, another revelation hit her. It was not her fault. Her chin raised in defiance. She had not done anything wrong. It was *his* fault. He was the one responsible for their circumstances. A slow, burning hatred began to crowd out the old guilt feelings. If he didn't love her, then she wouldn't love him. It was as simple as that. Her guilt would be much easier to bear if she could just hate him. So she did.

"Well, looky here. What you doin' up so early, L'il Missy?"

The deep voice with its thick southern drawl broke Charlotte's meditation. She looked up into the face of the blackest man she had ever seen. At first, she was a little afraid, for she hadn't had much contact with colored people, especially really black ones. She knew there were a lot of colored people in this neighborhood, but thus far, she had not met any of them, except for some of the children in her day care.

"What'sa matter, L'il Missy? Cat got your tongue?" The man laughed, showing an expanse of very white teeth inside a very dark mouth. A gold tooth gleamed in the front. "Ole Luther ain't gonna bite ya."

The gold tooth caught her attention. Fascinated, she couldn't take her eyes off it.

"Oh," he drew out the "o" into two long syllables. "So, you like my tooth, huh?"

She nodded.

He smiled again, the corners of his lips stretching in a wide arc, giving her an opportunity to look at the tooth more closely. "Yep, Ole Luther's mighty proud'a his tooth. Real gold. What's your name, L'il Missy?"

"Charlotte," she replied, meeting his dark eyes for a moment before glancing away.

"Miss Charlotte," he repeated. "Mighty purty name. So, Miss Charlotte, what's you doin' out here all by yourself? Where's your mama?"

"She's sick. She told me to be quiet, so I came out here to think."

"Oh." Again, he drew out the "o."

"Did you get your thinkin' done?" His voice took on a serious tone.

"Mostly."

"I see. What's a purty l'il thing like you got to be thinkin' about so hard?"

She regarded him, wary. Should she trust this total stranger with her innermost worries? Then she shrugged. She might as well. He seemed nice enough, and he was the only grown-up who had ever asked her what she was thinking about. Nobody else cared.

"I was thinking about my daddy. He went away, you know."

"Oh, no, I didn't know." Frown lines appeared on the man's smooth face.

"He didn't love us anymore," she added, risking a peek at him to catch his reaction.

He didn't look shocked. He just looked sad. "I'm right sorry, L'il Missy. That's a tough 'un, all right." He reflected for a minute, then shared, "My pap went away, too."

Stunned by this confidence, Charlotte said, "He did?" Her curiosity got the better of her manners. "Why? Didn't he love you anymore, either?"

Luther sighed. "Well, L'il Missy, to tell you the truth, I don' rightly know why. Jus' happens sometimes, I reckon." He shrugged.

"But life goes on, as they say. What's your plans for this mornin', L'il Missy?"

"Plans?"

"Yeah. You got sumthin' to do?"

She shook her head.

"You wanna help Ole Luther?"

"Help you do what?"

"Well, I'll tell you. You see all those ole weeds in the back of the buildin'? Real eyesore, don'cha think?"

She nodded.

"I was thinkin' of gettin' rid of 'em and plantin' some flowers, so it would look purty."

"I like flowers," Charlotte said, her blonde curls bobbing in enthusiasm.

"Then Ole Luther could sure use some help. That is, if'n you ain't busy or nothin'."

"I'm not busy." A glimmer of excitement sparked at the thought of doing something fun with this nice man.

"Good. Come on, then."

Charlotte trotted happily along beside the big man to the rear of the building, where he had a couple of garden spades, a hoe, and a trash barrel. A cardboard box off to the side held an assortment of colorful perennials.

"Wow," she said, when she saw all the pretty flowers just waiting to be planted.

"Hold on, now, L'il Missy. We got lot'sa work to do, a'fore we can plant 'em. Here." He handed her a spade. "You set to work on that there patch of weeds." He pointed to one corner of the overgrown vegetation "An' I'll start here."

Charlotte launched whole-heartedly into the project, happy to be doing something useful. While she worked, she let down her guard, and she began to chatter nonstop to Luther, who listened with absorbed attention. He also shared pieces of his life with her. She found out that Luther was the maintenance man for the building and lived in an apartment on the first floor. He had two grown sons and four grandchildren, and his wife had died five years before. Charlotte was so involved in the conversation with her new friend that she failed to notice she wasn't making much headway in ridding the weeds from the patch of dirt.

"Charlotte?"

She looked up to see her mother looming over her, Diana on her hip. "I have been looking all over for you. Why didn't you tell me you were going outside?" Her face wore an impatient scowl.

"You told me to be quiet. So I came out here," Charlotte answered, disappointed her mother had turned up and ruined her pleasant morning with Luther.

"I don't know what I'm going to do with you. You had me worried sick!"

"She's all right, ma'am," interjected Luther. "She's been out here helpin' me."

Her mother turned her attention to the man kneeling in the dirt. "Surely, you realize, Mr. . . ."

"Luther, ma'am."

"Surely you realize, Mr. Luther—"

"Not Mr. Luther. Luther's my given name. Last name's Johnson, but I don' stand much on formalities. Just plain Luther'll do."

She let out an exasperated sigh. "It isn't safe for a small child to go wandering off by herself in this neighborhood."

"She wasn't wanderin', ma'am. She was just sittin' on the steps."

"Nevertheless—"

"But your mama's right, L'il Missy," Luther interrupted again, addressing Charlotte, "You should'a told her you were out here."

Charlotte was amazed at how smoothly Luther had handled the situation. Without arguing, he had averted her mother's anger and interceded on Charlotte's behalf. She had definitely found a friend.

"Is she in your way, Luther?" her mother asked, her voice losing its edge.

"Oh, no, ma'am! She's a big help."

She snorted. "I can see that." Then, addressing Charlotte, she said, "You come right back in when you're finished. And don't go out of the apartment again without telling me." She turned to leave, then looked back and added, "Thank you, Luther."

"My pleasure, ma'am."

Out of that day grew a special friendship for Charlotte. In the evenings or on weekends when her mother was busy with her extra typing, Charlotte sought out Luther, wherever he happened to be, and helped him with whatever he was doing. Sometimes she followed him into other apartments where he might have to replace a leaky faucet or check a faulty light switch. She trailed along behind him, carrying a tool or flashlight, and observed him with quiet seriousness while he went about his work. Afterward, he often invited her into his apartment for milk and cookies and a long chat, always telling her how much help she had been and how he couldn't have managed without her.

Other times, she followed him into the big, dark basement, where she was a little afraid to go by herself, and helped him empty the trash from the garbage chute or check on the various, mysterious meters. He was always busy, and therefore, she was always busy, as well. It never occurred to her that she might be in Luther's way, and since he never seemed to object to her hanging around, the subject never came up. Although her mother protested a little, at first, as time went on, it seemed as though she was relieved to have Charlotte out from underfoot. Eventually, her mother didn't seem to care about much of anything except her foul-smelling bottle, which she purchased every evening and opened earlier and earlier every night.

CHAPTER TWENTY-ONE
CONNIE

Although the end of the summer was quickly approaching, there was no relief from the heat. Today, Connie couldn't stand the thought of facing that airless office with its inefficient little circulating fans and pecking away for eight hours at that miserable typewriter, while her clammy fingers ached, and her sweat-soaked skirt clung to her legs. She would wait until nine o'clock and call one of the other secretaries to tell her she wasn't feeling well—which she wasn't. The magic bottles that erased the pain at night multiplied it ten-fold by morning. Still, she couldn't give up her nightcaps, as she had come to call them. They were the only thing she had to look forward to at the end of the day.

Mr. McCarthy had become even more intolerable, lately. Here she was, practically killing herself working on extra typing at home, and he still found plenty to complain about. She knew her skills had gotten a lot better, but the expected raise hadn't materialized. Then, just because she had made a few mistakes on customer orders, he had relieved her of her duties in dealing with the public.

This meant the other two brown-nosing secretaries had to spend more time on the telephone and talking to clients, which greatly increased Connie's typing load. How she hated those two. They had resented her from day one, probably because of her association with Mr. McCarthy's aunt and the fact she was young and pretty. They never missed an opportunity to enlighten the boss about any mistake Connie made or snipe at her about one thing or another. And they took full advantage in being relieved of the extra paperwork.

They would hand Connie a stack of invoices, saying in their haughty voices, "I didn't have time to type these up. I was on the phone all morning with Mr. So-and-so," or "Would you mind? I've had to spend the whole day straightening out Mrs. Who-sit's account."

Then they would smirk, in that self-satisfied way, to let Connie know she was clearly beneath them in position and didn't have a choice.

Well, to heck with them all today. She dialed the number. Fran, the lesser of the two evils, answered the phone.

"Hello, Fran, this is Connie," she whined, trying to sound as pathetic as possible. "I'm not feeling very well today."

She could actually hear Fran pursing her lips over the phone.

"Connie," Fran admonished, as if talking to a dim-witted child, "this is the fourth time this month. And you know we have to do the inventory by the end of the week."

"Well, I'm sorry," snapped Connie. "But I'm sick. What do you want me to do? Infect the whole office?"

"All right. I'll tell Mr. McCarthy. But he won't be pleased."

Connie almost retorted, "So what else is new? Mr. McCarthy is never pleased." But instead, she said, "Thanks, Fran, I'll try to come in tomorrow if I'm feeling better."

There. I've bought myself a whole day before having to go back.

But what was she going to do tomorrow, and the next day, and the next? She snatched up the newspaper lying on the end table to peruse the want ads. As if she didn't already know them by heart. Hadn't she read them over and over again from top to bottom every day since she'd started this job? She had even called about a few of the openings and interviewed for a couple. But there was nothing, outside of minimum-wage jobs, that she could do. At least she was making better than minimum wage where she was, although not much. And she couldn't afford to move again.

"Mommy, we're going to be late," announced Charlotte, hovering over her, as Connie lay sprawled out reading the paper.

"We're staying home today. I don't feel well."

"Again?" Charlotte's childish voice dripped with disapproval.

Connie glared at her precocious daughter. "Yes, again. That is, if it's all right with you."

Charlotte retreated to her room.

Honestly, why does that child insist on constantly aggravating me?

It was almost as if Charlotte deliberately thought up ways to annoy her, as if to punish her for the upheaval in her young life. And Diana. She was walking now and getting into everything. She had to be watched or confined every minute.

A wave of hopelessness washed over Connie. Was this what her life was going to be like from now on? There seemed to be no escape. An overwhelming sense of regret enveloped her. She never should have packed up and moved to a strange city on the promise of a job from a friend's nephew. She should have stayed in Biloxi and gone on welfare if she had to. At least there, she had some people she knew, people who might have helped her. Who did she have here? Nobody. If only she weren't saddled with these two children. No sooner had the thought formed in her head than a crushing remorse seized her heart. What kind of a mother thought that way about her children? She reflected on her own mother, and how she had promised herself in her younger, more idealistic days that she would never be like her. But lately, she had not been much of a mother, either. Poor Charlotte. Ever since they moved here, she'd had no time for the child. Things had to change.

"Charlotte," she called, rising from her bed of self-pity. "Find your bathing suit. We're going to the beach."

———•●•———

For one carefree afternoon, mother and daughter laughed and played under the hot sun, chasing the waves, walking the beach, eating a huge picnic lunch, and then flopping onto the blanket to rest, while Diana amused herself in her playpen. Later, they searched for shells and watched the funny little sandpipers scurrying up and down the beach on legs so fast that you couldn't even tell they *had* legs until they stood still. They fed the greedy, raucous seagulls and tried to catch the hermit crabs as they scampered sideways into their holes. Then, when the late afternoon breezes began to turn cooler, they packed up and headed home.

After dinner and a bath to remove the sticky salt, an exhausted Charlotte crawled into bed. Connie sat on the edge of the bed for a long time, as the child drifted off to sleep. Just before sleep overcame her, Charlotte mumbled, "I had fun today, Mommy. I love you."

"I love you, too," said Connie, bending down to kiss her brow.

That night, Connie didn't have a nightcap. She awoke refreshed and full of high spirits. Things were going to get better, she told herself. She made a big breakfast of sausage and eggs, and Charlotte sat at the table chattering away, just like she used to. Connie looked at her older daughter, her heart softening with affection. It took so little to make the child happy. She was going to have to try harder. These children were the only worthwhile things she had.

Walking into the office, Connie felt she could handle anything, today. The other two women looked up in surprise to see her there before nine o'clock.

"Feeling better?" Fran asked. She rolled her eyes toward the other secretary.

"Yes, thank you, much better. I apologize for any inconvenience I caused you yesterday," Connie replied, keeping her voice pleasant and ignoring the obvious barb.

"Oh, that's all right, dear," said Martha, the other secretary. "Fran and I are used to taking up your slack."

Connie gave her a sweet smile. Martha and Fran were not going to get to her today. She sat at her desk, removed the dustcover from her typewriter, and began to occupy herself with the enormous stack of paperwork left from the day before. Martha and Fran had saved her plenty.

Mr. McCarthy came in at nine, did a double take at Connie already hard at work, and proceeded to his office without a word.

With Fran and Martha occupied with inventory in the warehouse, the day passed in relative peace. Connie worked like a whirlwind to catch up with yesterday's typing as well as today's, as one or the other of the secretaries popped in every so often with a new batch of pages to be processed. Shortly before five, Connie finished the last of the work. She sat back in her chair, closed her eyes, and stretched. It felt good to have gotten everything done.

"Mrs. Wallace!" barked Mr. McCarthy, standing over her.

In the middle of her stretch, she hadn't noticed him approach her desk. She jumped, and, embarrassed, almost fell off her chair.

"You startled me," she said, with a little giggle. When she realized he was not amused, she added, "I've finished everything from yesterday and today," gesturing to the large stack of papers piled in the out box.

"I'd like to see you in my office, if you are finished with your yoga exercise," he said, his voice heavy with sarcasm.

She sighed and followed him into the office, where he motioned for her to close the door. "I was just stretching, sir," she said in her own defense. "I've been sitting there for hours without a break trying to get finished."

"Yes. Of course, if you hadn't been so sick yesterday, you wouldn't have had two days' worth of work to get done in one day." His cold eyes locked onto hers, causing her to look away.

"I'm sorry, sir, I . . ."

"I suppose your doctor ordered plenty of sunshine. You certainly have a healthy glow."

Her heart gave a sudden lurch against her ribs and her mouth went dry. She hadn't considered her mild sunburn. There was no excuse she could give. With trembling hands, she waited in expectation of what he would say next.

"Mrs. Wallace, let me be very frank. I have put up with a lot from you for my aunt's sake. Your secretarial skills, when you started here, were abominable, to say the least—"

"But I've gotten much better," she protested, daring to raise her eyes and meet his glare.

He held up his hand. "Please, do not interrupt me."

"I'm sorry, sir." She lowered her eyes again.

"Your work ethic has been sloppy. You have been consistently late getting to work and in the habit of leaving early, despite repeated warnings—"

"But I have two children in day care that I—"

His face twisted in anger, as she, once again, disrupted his tirade.

"Excuse me, sir, please, go on."

He let out a loud sigh. "In short, Mrs. Wallace, your

employment here has been more of a liability than an asset." Then raising his hand again, as though to ward off further protest, he continued, "But I was willing to overlook a lot in deference to your unfortunate circumstances. However, there is one thing that I cannot and will not abide in my office. And that is a liar."

He let the ugly word sink in. "I cannot stand being lied to, Mrs. Wallace. I'm afraid this is the final straw. As of right now, your employment here is terminated."

Connie's racing heart plummeted into her stomach. She could feel the color drain from her face and her muscles turn to rubber, making it difficult to remain standing. "But Mr. McCarthy—"

"There will be no further discussion. Please clear your things from your desk and vacate the premises." He turned his back on her, thus effectively cutting off any further communication.

With her whole body frozen in shock, she stood staring at his back, and tried not to panic. There was no point in arguing. Should she resort to begging? No. He was a stubborn man and his mind was made up.

She walked out of the office on legs that felt heavy and wooden, returned to her desk, and stared at it. Her brain had gone dull. She was supposed to do something . . . oh, yes. She was supposed to clean out her things. In a fog, she began to open drawers, having to concentrate with considerable effort on whether the items inside were hers or not. Out of the corner of her eye, she became aware of the other two women who had returned from the warehouse to collect their purses. They were exchanging glances and nodding to each other. They obviously knew what had transpired. How? Had they all discussed her dismissal yesterday? Finally, they walked over to her.

"I'm sorry, honey," gushed Fran. "If there's anything we can do—"

Something in the tone of the woman's voice roused Connie from apathy to acute, hot rage.

"Yes, there's something you can do, you back-stabbing old bat." She grabbed the mound of papers she had spent all day completing and hurled them to the floor, scattering them everywhere. "You can both drop dead." She stood glaring at them, her chest heaving.

The astonished women stepped back.

"I told you she was crazy," Martha cried, wasting no time in withdrawing to the other side of the room, Fran on her heels. They stood as far away as possible, until Connie finished stuffing her few personal items into her purse.

The commotion drew Mr. McCarthy from his office. His eyes widened at the sight of the mess Connie had made. "You get out before I call security!" he sputtered.

"And you can drop dead, too. All three of you!" she yelled, as she stomped out the door, slamming it behind her.

The impact of what had just happened and the dire circumstances she now faced did not sink in for several minutes. Fighting back tears, she knew she had to hurry to pick up the girls. It was almost six. But the familiar liquor store beckoned her with its long invisible arm. She didn't have time to stop, she told herself. But as she got closer, the more the long arm reached out and tugged at her with unrelenting, clawing fingers. She had to stop. It would just take a minute. She couldn't possibly get through this night without help.

A long line stretched in front of her to the cashier. She shifted from one foot to the other, her impatience mounting as she glanced at the clock above the clerk's head. The hands pointed to exactly six o'clock. The idiot ahead of her had to write a check, and getting clearance was taking forever. She ground her teeth in furious exasperation. She had to have a drink. Her nerves were shot. As she stood for what seemed like an eternity, another shelf caught her eye. Why not? She reached down and picked up a second bottle that said Jack Daniels. She'd never tried that.

It was almost six-thirty when she finally got to the day care center. Miss Flaggerty was not pleased. Charlotte and Diana were the only two children left, and they were not pleased, either. Diana's loud wails continued unabated, despite Miss Flaggerty's ineffectual bouncing of the child on her amply padded hip, and Charlotte's eyes brimmed with unshed tears.

"Mrs. Wallace," Miss Flaggerty admonished, her tone sharp. "You are half an hour late. If you had not shown up by seven o'clock, I would have had no choice but to take these children downtown to the county children's home for the night."

Connie didn't trust herself to answer. "Come on, Charlotte," she slurred, reaching for Diana.

"Mrs. Wallace, are you drunk?" cried Miss Flaggerty.

"Not yet," Connie snapped.

Mrs. Flaggerty's eyes narrowed. "I'm sorry, but I simply cannot allow you to—"

"You mind your own business, you old bat!" Connie yelled, yanking Charlotte along by the arm.

———•●•———

Miss Flaggerty stood in shock, her mouth hanging open. She struggled for a moment trying to decide whether to call the police and children's social services. But that would tie her up for possibly another hour or two, and after all, she did have tickets to the ballet tonight. And she was already running late. There was one thing for sure, however. That Wallace woman would have to make other childcare arrangements come tomorrow. And she still just might report her to the authorities.

———•●•———

Connie drove home, her hand unsteady on the steering wheel. Once in the apartment, she fixed a bottle for Diana and put her in her crib.

"Charlotte, make yourself a peanut-butter sandwich and then go play in your room," she said, forcing her thick words past her lips with considerable effort, ignoring the frightened look on her daughter's face.

Then, taking both her bottles, she curled up on the couch. This time, she didn't even bother with a glass. This time, the pain and the fear refused to be banished. But finally, the warm, peaceful feeling began to descend upon her, blocking out everything else, as she sank into welcome oblivion.

———•●•———

The coroner's report read "Cause of Death: Acute Alcohol Intoxication."

CHAPTER TWENTY-TWO
CHARLOTTE

Charlotte was mystified by the sudden change in her mother. Yesterday at the beach had been so much fun. Charlotte hadn't seen her mother that carefree for a long time. She had almost dared to hope maybe things had changed and they could be happy again. And then this morning, her mother had actually cooked breakfast, and they had laughed and talked. For once, her mother had not been tired or irritable. Charlotte had been both happy and scared at the same time. Happy for the wonderful change and scared it wouldn't last.

It didn't. Her mother picked them up from day care way past closing time. Everyone else had already gone. Miss Flaggerty did not even bother to conceal her annoyance at having to stay after hours with them. Charlotte had begun to panic again. What if this time her mother didn't come at all? Why did she always worry her mother wouldn't come back? She didn't know, but every time something happened to change her normal routine, her inner warning alarm sounded.

And then, when her mother had finally come to get them, Charlotte almost wished she hadn't. This was the worst she had ever seen her mother. Her mother had actually yelled at Miss Flaggerty. With a gnawing fear, Charlotte endured the ride home in silence. But even with the windows down, the overwhelming stench of liquor permeated the stale air in the car. She knew the liquor was what made her mother behave so oddly. Disappointment flooded her small body. She should have known better than to hope the good times would last.

At home, her mother told her to make herself a sandwich, but Charlotte was too miserable to eat. Her mother didn't even notice, as she headed for the living room with her bottle. Charlotte curled up in a tight little ball in the middle of her bed and cried herself to sleep.

Diana's crying woke her. Again, her mother did not come. These early morning rituals were becoming more and more frequent. Charlotte sighed and got out of bed. Again, she found her mother on the couch, still in the clothes she wore yesterday. Charlotte flinched at the dreadful odor that hung in the air around her mother. A strange, new bottle lay knocked over on the floor, and some of the contents had spilled onto the faded brown carpet. It smelled even worse than the others her mother always drank.

Charlotte poked her mother harder than she meant to. She was getting tired of this. Her mother should *act* like a mother. "Mommy, wake up."

There was no response. "Mommy!" she yelled. "Diana's crying." She shook her again. Still no response.

In disgust, Charlotte gave up and went into the kitchen to fix a bottle for the baby. She had seen it done enough times. It couldn't be that difficult. She wasn't supposed to touch the stove, but she didn't have any choice. Filling a pan with water, she set it on the burner and turned on the gas. The whooshing flame startled her as it rose up to lick the bottom of the pan, but in an instant, she dismissed it as she opened the refrigerator, grabbed a pre-filled bottle, and stuck it in the water.

While the bottle heated, she went back into the bedroom, scowling at her mother as she walked by, and tried to quiet the baby. Nothing worked.

"You're prob'ly wet," Charlotte informed Diana, in her most authoritative voice. "But I'm not s'posed to pick you up."

She waited for a few minutes, but the crying didn't stop. Oh well, if she got in trouble, so be it. If her mother would wake up and take care of Diana, then *she* wouldn't have to.

Charlotte lowered the railing on the crib and eased the heavy baby out onto the floor. "Yep, you're wet."

Should she try to change the diaper? She knew how it was done. She would probably get into trouble, though. But Diana was wet, and she wasn't going to stop crying until she was dry. Making up her mind, Charlotte removed the diaper pins and dropped the wet diaper into the diaper pail in the corner. Then, with clumsy fingers, she attempted to re-diaper the baby without sticking herself or Diana with the pins. It took a while, but she eventually got the job done, even if it didn't look as good as when Mommy did it.

Diana stopped crying and began to jabber.

"Oh, I forgot the powder. Oh, well . . ." Charlotte shrugged. "Now I've gotta get you back in your crib." She tried to lift the chubby baby, but couldn't hoist her high enough to get her over the lowered crib rail. After heaving and tugging, Charlotte gave up and left Diana on the floor. "You stay here," she ordered, as she left to get the bottle.

Her mother still lay slumped in the same position. As Charlotte trudged into the kitchen, her shoulders sagged under the burden of having to take care of Diana. She turned off the burner, making sure the flame went out, and checked the temperature of the milk, like she had seen her mother and grandmother do. She jerked her wrist away from the scalding liquid. Her frustration mounting, Charlotte poured half the milk down the drain and replaced it with cold milk.

Diana didn't seem to mind, as she reached for the bottle with eager, plump hands. But how was Charlotte going to get her back in the crib? She couldn't just leave her there.

Marching into the living room, she shouted, "Mommy! Wake up." She shook her as hard as she could. Then she noticed something strange. Her mother's skin felt so cold. Maybe she really was sick.

A sense of terror gripped her. Thinking fast, she raced out of the apartment downstairs to Luther's and beat frantically on his door. It took forever for him to answer. He still wore his pajamas.

"Goodness, L'il Missy, what's you doin' here so early?" Luther asked, rubbing the sleep from his eyes.

"You gotta come, Luther. My mommy's real sick. She won't wake up."

"Oh mercy," he cried, springing into action, as he pushed past her.

Charlotte ran after him. When she reached her apartment, Luther was bent over her mother, lifting her eyelids and running his hands down her neck. He turned when Charlotte came in, and his eyes were so big that the whites stood out shockingly against his dark face.

"Don't you come in here, chil'." His large body blocked Charlotte's view of her mother.

Luther's face scared her more than she had ever been frightened in her whole life. But she had to know. She eased across the room to stand next to him.

"What's wrong, Luther?" she asked, in a trembling voice.

He tried to usher her out of the room. "Now, Lil Missy, you just go back to my 'partment and wait. Ole Luther gotta call the po'lese."

The police? Why? Charlotte shrugged off his hand and clung to his leg.

"Why, Luther?" she begged, tears streaming down her face. "You gotta tell me what's wrong."

Luther squeezed his eyes closed, took a deep breath, and then knelt down, putting one big arm around her and drawing her close. "Your mama's *dead*, L'il Missy. She dead!"

— • ● • —

The policeman and the social worker found Charlotte and Diana in Luther's apartment. Diana contented herself with her blocks, oblivious to the tragedy that had just occurred, and Charlotte pretended to be absorbed watching her. She knew she should be scared, but nothing felt real. Still, what was going to happen to them now? Maybe they could live with Luther. That would be okay. Although the adults spoke in hushed tones, Charlotte's little radar ears tuned in to everything they were saying.

"You say the child found the woman?" asked the policeman, scribbling on a notepad.

"Yes, sir," answered Luther. "And she come and got me. I saw her mama was dead and called you right away and then brought them chil'un down here."

"The baby probably needs to be fed and changed," said the social worker, a pretty young brunette, as she started toward the children.

"No'm. L'il Miss Charlotte, she done had her changed and fed before she come got me."

"The little girl?" The woman stopped in her tracks, wide-eyed.

"Oh, Missy Charlotte, she's a smart 'un. She jus' like a grown-up."

"Can we get back to the mother?" asked the policeman. "Now then, Mr. . . ."

"Luther, sir, jus' call me Luther."

"All right then, Luther, do you have any idea what could have happened to the woman? Did you notice anybody else around her apartment?"

"No, sir, but maybe you can ask Missy Charlotte. She'd a known."

The policeman frowned. "I don't know if she'll be much—" he began.

"Well, it's worth a try," interrupted the social worker. She stepped over to the other side of the room, where Charlotte pretended she wasn't listening to the adults talking. Squatting down, she said, "Hello, Charlotte. My name is Carol."

Charlotte appraised the woman without speaking. The policeman followed the lady called Carol, but kept his distance.

"Charlotte, do you know what happened to your mother?" prodded Carol.

Charlotte nodded. "She died and went to heaven," she answered, matter-of-factly. Then, parroting a talk she'd had several months earlier with Mrs. McCarthy, she added, "When someone you love dies and goes to heaven, you're s'posed to be happy for them. But you're also sad 'cause you'll never ever see them again."

The social worker raised her eyebrows, but didn't respond.

"Isn't that right?"

"Why, . . . yes," stammered the woman. "Absolutely." She looked around at the policeman, who stood fidgeting. She turned back to Charlotte. "Charlotte, honey, do you know if there was anyone else in your apartment last night?"

"Nope, there wasn't anybody."

"Are you sure?" interjected the policeman.

"Reckon she done had a heart attack?" asked Luther. "She was mighty young to have a bad heart."

The policeman glared at him. Charlotte took an immediate

dislike to the man.

"No, we never had comp'ny," Charlotte volunteered, directing her answer to the social worker.

"Charlotte," asked Carol, taking her by the arms, "did your mother drink a lot? Do you understand what I mean?"

Carol's soft touch felt good against her bare skin. "Yes. Every night, almost." Charlotte bit her lip, wondering if she should have told the strange lady this information.

The woman exchanged glances with the policeman. "What do you think, Officer? It doesn't appear to be foul play."

"Thank you for your brilliant insight, but perhaps we should let the coroner decide that, Miss . . ."

"Sherman. And it's *Mrs*."

"Excuse me," he retorted. "Well, I don't think I'm going to learn anything else at this point. We'd better get the coroner over here to examine the body."

"Your sensitivity overwhelms me," Carol said to his retreating back. Then she returned her attention to Charlotte and lowered her voice. "Charlotte, where is your father?"

"He 'bandoned us," she answered with a shrug. "He didn't love us anymore."

Carol flinched. "And you don't have any idea where he is?"

Charlotte shook her head.

Carol glanced up at Luther.

"No'm, I don't. It was jus' Miz Wallace and the two young'uns. She never said nothin' 'bout Mr. Wallace."

"Charlotte, honey, do you have any relatives I can call? Any aunts or uncles?"

Charlotte shook her head again.

"How about grandparents?"

Charlotte hesitated. The thought of going back to her grandparents was unbearable. She knew it wasn't right to lie, but she couldn't let them send her and Diana back there.

"No," she whispered, avoiding Carol's eyes.

Carol sighed. "So you don't have anybody? Are you sure?"

Charlotte shook her head. "I guess now we'll haf'ta be 'dopted."

"What?" Carol's eyes widened.

Charlotte shrugged. "Well, Mrs. Grandma—she's not my real

grandma—said that if you don't have a real mommy and daddy to take care of you that you get 'dopted. And the people that 'dopt you love you even more 'cause they picked you out special."

Carol's mouth dropped open. "Uh, yes, sometimes."

Charlotte locked eyes with Carol, as the woman seemed to struggle for words.

"Charlotte," Carol began, then stopped. She took a deep breath and continued, "I'm going to take you and Diana to a nice place where you can be taken care of for a while."

Charlotte frowned. "Can't we stay here with Luther?" She glanced over at him, but he hung his head.

"No, honey, I'm sorry."

Tears filled Charlotte's eyes. Up until this point, she had held tightly onto her feelings. She had thought Luther was her friend, but now he didn't want her, either. "Just 'til we're 'dopted?"

Carol shook her head. "Don't worry, honey, everything will be all right." Then to Luther, "I'll get their clothes later."

Charlotte shot a pleading glance at Luther. Why did adults always say everything would be all right when it wasn't?

Luther knelt and pulled Charlotte into his big arms. She could see tears welling up in his dark eyes.

"Now, L'il Missy, Ole Luther's jus' too old to be takin' care of young 'uns, you see. But Miss Carol gonna take good care of you. You be a good girl and go with her, now." He crushed her tightly against his massive chest. "And don' be forgettin' your ole friend, Luther, now, you hear?"

"Yes, sir," she answered, her voice muffled against his chest. "I love you, Luther."

"I love you, too, chil'." Silent tears ran down the dark cheeks. Finally, Luther wiped his eyes on his sleeve and stood.

Carol picked up Diana, then stepped over and took Charlotte's hand. Charlotte allowed Carol to lead her out of Luther's apartment, into the hall, and finally out to Carol's car.

They rode downtown with Carol gabbing away, but Charlotte tuned her out. Again, Charlotte's heart squeezed with the sense of adult betrayal. Carol had acted so nice, but now she was taking them away to . . . where? Carol was just like all the others—full of false promises and forced cheerfulness. Charlotte kept her eyes averted out the window, but she wasn't actually focusing on anything. What was going to happen to them now? She wished she were a baby, like Diana, who was blissfully unaware of all the unhappiness that had plagued them the last few months, ever since their father had gone away. And now her mother had gone away, too.

They pulled up in front of a big brick building surrounded by a large fenced-in playground, filled with noisy children of different ages. Charlotte assessed the surroundings with an apathetic eye.

"Here we are," chirped Carol, opening the car door and lifting out the sleeping baby. "Let's go inside and I'll introduce you to Miss Millie. You'll love Miss Millie. She'll get you all settled."

"You mean we gotta stay here?" Suddenly the lack of other options became real. Charlotte wrestled with her lie about her grandparents. Should she tell Carol she did have family? She decided to wait and see.

"For a while, anyway, until other arrangements can be made." Charlotte didn't ask what other arrangements.

"You'll like it here," Carol chattered on, "there're lots of other children to play with." They were climbing the steep concrete steps leading to the front door.

Charlotte ignored her. Carol was still talking when they entered the large hallway and stopped in front of the first door on the right. Carol opened it and motioned for Charlotte to enter.

———•●•———

A harried-looking middle-aged woman with a flushed face looked up in surprise. "What's this?" she demanded.

"Where's Millicent?" countered Carol.

The woman threw up her hands and rolled her eyes. "Millicent had to go and break her ankle last night, of all things," she exclaimed, with a great deal of gesturing, as if to imply Millicent had deliberately broken her ankle to inconvenience *her*.

"She won't be back for another two or three days. And just tell me what I'm supposed to do? I've never had to manage on my own before. And here I was supposed to be leaving on vacation tomorrow. Then, on top of everything else, the plumbing backs up. We can't even flush the toilets, and do you think we can find a plumber on a Saturday?" Her voice rose in hysteria.

Carol broke in. "Well, I'm sorry about all that, but we've got a problem here. These two little girls need a place to stay. Their mother passed away last night and there don't appear to be any relatives we can contact."

The woman looked at the two children as if just noticing them for the first time. "I can't deal with two more," she cried. "I'm overfilled on my allowable capacity as it is. You'll have to take them somewhere else."

"What?" demanded Carol. She motioned for Charlotte to sit in a chair by the door and shoved the baby onto her lap. Crossing the short distance to the desk, she leaned over, practically touching her nose to the other woman's nose. "This is outrageous. You *know* there is nowhere else. This is the Mobile County Children's Home, for heaven's sake!"

The woman backed away and began to babble. "I *told* you! I'm not *supposed* to be in charge here. Millicent is the director." She waved her hands in a frantic display of helplessness. "I simply cannot take these children now. I have no space. My plumbing is backed up. We'll get cited for overcrowding and—"

Carol could see there was no headway to be made with this irrational woman. Even if there were, how could she leave the children in such chaos on their first day?

"All right," she conceded, making an effort to calm her voice. "Where do you suggest I take them?"

"Well, the nearest place with a county facility would be Montgomery," the woman said, then flinched, as if anticipating a blow.

"*Montgomery*?" cried Carol. "That's *hours* from here!"

"I'll call and tell them you're on your way," the woman volunteered, managing a feeble smile.

Carol fumed. But at this point, she had no choice. She was, however, going to report this woman for her extremely unprofessional conduct. "And what is your name?" she demanded.

The woman looked as if she were going to cry. "Clare Nelson. But, please, I'm doing the best I can."

"Of course you are," Carol replied, her tone dripping with acid. Turning, she caught a glimpse of Charlotte's stricken face. She reproached herself for allowing the child to witness this blatant display of bureaucratic ineptitude. But how was she to know the supposedly stable Mobile County Children's Home was in the midst of bedlam and in the hands of a woman who appeared to be on the verge of a breakdown? Everything always ran smoothly and efficiently under Millicent's strong hand. *This poor child.*

Putting on a smile, she said, "Well, Charlotte, it's looks like we're going to have to go for a bit of a ride."

"Yeah. She doesn't want us, either," grumbled Charlotte, who in the course of a few months had been rejected by her father, her grandparents, indirectly by her mother, Luther, and now the Mobile County Children's Home. As she allowed Carol to lead her away, she glared at the woman standing behind the desk wringing her hands.

CHAPTER TWENTY-THREE
ADAM

Adam sat in nervous expectation in Jonathon Peel's austere office, waiting, clasping his hands to keep them from shaking. Jonathon must have some terribly important news for him to have insisted he come downtown. His heart pounded so hard he could almost hear it.

"Sorry to have kept you waiting," greeted Mr. Peel, whose sudden appearance behind him caused Adam to jump.

"What did you find out?" cried Adam, dispensing with formalities.

Jonathon positioned himself behind his desk, a broad smile on his face. "I think I've found them, Adam."

"Where? Where are they?" Adam perched on the edge of his chair, barely able to contain his excitement.

"Do you know a woman named Sarah McCarthy?" asked Jonathon.

"No, no, I don't think so." Adam brushed the question aside with an air of impatience. "Who is she and what does she have to do with my wife and kids?"

"She used to babysit for the children. She lives a few blocks from your old apartment. Do you want to know how I found her?"

"No. Just tell me where they are."

A flash of disappointment crossed Jonathon's face. Then he sighed and continued. "Well, it seems Connie told her you left them, and she needed to find a job."

"She what?" cried Adam. "Why in the world would she say *that*?" He shook his head in disbelief. "She walked out on *me*. Told me she wanted a divorce."

Jonathon shrugged. "I don't know. That's what she told the old lady, anyway."

"I'm sorry. Please, please go on."

"Well, Connie was having a hard time finding employment and this Sarah McCarthy used some influence with her nephew in Mobile to hire her."

Adam jumped out of his chair. "They're in Mobile? Oh, thank God! Do you know where?"

Jonathon shook his head. "Not yet. I spoke to the nephew on the phone this morning at his home. He didn't have Connie's address at his house, but promised to look it up when he got to work."

Adam grinned and rubbed his hands in eager anticipation of a reunion with his family. He was hardly listening now, as the news of finally finding his family flooded him with euphoria. He paced with nervous energy.

"Adam, there is something else."

Adam stopped pacing and waited. Whatever else Jonathon had to say didn't matter. He had found them.

"Mr. McCarthy said he fired Connie a few days ago."

"Oh." Adam frowned, then shrugged. "Well, it really doesn't matter. I'll go to Mobile and take care of everything." With her latest setback, Connie might be more easily persuaded to come back to him. They would work things out.

"I thought you had already started classes," Jonathon reminded him.

Adam blew out a frustrated breath. "Yes, last week. But I'll take a few days off. I have to."

"Won't that be rather difficult right now? Why don't you let me go and talk to her? I'll leave first thing in the morning."

Adam shook his head. "No. I want to go with you. I need to talk to her myself. There're a lot of things to clear up."

"I really think it would be better if you stayed here. You'll have a tough time catching up with your classes. You don't want to ruin this opportunity."

"Do you think I could possibly concentrate on class?" snapped Adam. "Nothing matters but my family. I'm going with you."

"All right." Jonathon gave in. "I'll make the arrangements. We'll leave first thing in the morning."

Adam nearly danced out of the office. Back at the lab, the first thing he did was seek out Katrina. He found her busy in the animal control area, injecting rabbits.

"Kate!" he cried. "You've got to stop everything and come celebrate with me."

"Wh . . . what?" she looked at him as if he had gone crazy. "Adam, I am right in the middle of a crucial step here."

Adam bounced up and down like an excited child. "You *have* to." Grabbing her hands, he went on, his voice rising in urgency, "When was the last time you took a morning off? Come on, I need you."

She stared at him. "But I—"

Adam directed his attention to the lab technician who held a lop-eared creature. "Karl can finish up, can't you, Karl?"

"Honestly, Adam, this is really bad timing," Katrina scolded. She sighed. "Karl, can you get Sharon to restrain the rabbits for you? I'll show you what to do."

"Sure, Miss Graham."

"I'll be waiting for you downstairs in the cafeteria," Adam said, racing out of the room.

When she joined him, although her curiosity was piqued, Katrina's irritation still rang through the harshness of her tone.

"I absolutely have to be back in one hour," she informed him. "Otherwise, I can kiss the entire morning's work good-bye. That is, assuming Karl doesn't mess things up." Then, looking at his radiant face, she softened. "I'm sorry, Adam. What is it? What's your news that can't wait? Is it your re-entrance exams? I know how nervous you've been about taking them."

"Well, I had wanted to go somewhere a little more festive, but I guess this will have to do." He reached across the table and took both her hands. "Kate, I had to tell you first. You're my best friend."

She waited. "So, tell me."

"Jonathon found them! He found Connie and the girls."

The news came as a jolt, a sucker punch to her gut. Katrina remembered back to a few weeks before when he had first confided in her about his wife leaving him and taking his children. From that night of pain, a wonderful friendship had sprung up between them. She had grown to like Adam immensely, and felt that perhaps the feeling was reciprocated. Although there had been nothing more between them, she had tentatively hoped that maybe, someday . . . well, after all, Adam was so different from anyone she had ever met before. He was the only man she had ever truly felt comfortable with. But everything was about to change. If he worked things out with his wife, her role in his life would soon be diminished. She guessed she had never really considered that possibility. How foolish of her. He *was* still married, after all.

"Kate?" His voice sounded far away. "Did you hear what I said?"

She forced a smile. "That's wonderful, Adam," she said, her voice catching in her throat.

He didn't seem to notice her odd reaction.

"Have you talked to your wife?" she asked, pushing down an unreasonable tinge of jealousy.

"No, not yet. I'm flying to Mobile tomorrow. That's where they are, in Mobile."

"Oh." She had to force herself to pay attention. Guilt gnawed at her. She should be thrilled for Adam. But all she could think of was what she was about to lose.

Come on, Kate, Adam isn't in love with you, for heaven's sake. You're not losing him. And besides, her work was her love, her life. What would become of that dream if she fell in love like every other silly, romantic female? Her life was better off as it was.

Adam rattled on in his enthusiasm. She tried to concentrate, but it was difficult when so many emotions battled for her attention.

"Kate? Are you all right?" Adam paused, suddenly appearing to realize she was acting peculiarly.

"I'm fine, Adam." She smiled. "And I'm so happy for you. Really." She said the last to convince herself as much as him. She gave his hands a brief squeeze, then hopped up. "Come on. I'll buy you a coffee *and* a doughnut to celebrate. I wish it could be more, but we'll celebrate later, okay?" She doubted that later would ever come.

———•●•———

Downtown, Jonathon Peel's secretary announced a call from Jason McCarthy. Jonathon snatched up the receiver.

"Jason," Jonathon cried merrily into the phone, "I hope you don't mind my calling you Jason." Without waiting for a reply, he continued, "So do you have the address for me?"

"Yes, I do," Jason McCarthy replied, his voice flat. "But I've got some other news for you. It's going to come as a shock, I'm afraid."

"Oh?" A cold chill swept through Jonathon's body.

Jason sighed. "I just read it in the morning paper." Jonathon heard him take a deep breath. "Connie Wallace was found dead in her apartment three days ago."

"Oh no," Jonathon whispered.

———•●•———

Jonathon finally reached Adam at home around nine-thirty that evening.

"Jonathon, are we all set? What time are we leaving in the morning?"

"Adam, are you sitting down?" Jonathon asked, his voice grim.

"Am I what? What are you talking about?" Adam laughed.

"If not, please sit down. I have something to tell you."

CHAPTER TWENTY-FOUR
CHARLOTTE

———— • ● • ————

It was late by the time Carol Sherman, the social worker, drove Charlotte and Diana to the Montgomery County Children's Home. The office had already closed, and Carol had to contact the director, a man named Ray Ewing, at his home. Apparently, the inept Clare Nelson, temporary acting director of the Mobile County Children's Home, had also failed to notify Mr. Ewing of Carol's impending arrival with the two children. Carol was going to report that woman if it was the last thing she did.

By the time Ray Ewing finally materialized, Carol was angry and frustrated, and trying hard not to let her feelings show in front of Charlotte, who had already been through enough for one day.

Mr. Ewing appeared kind and competent. They met in his now quiet-for-the-evening office.

"Mrs. Sherman," he gushed, "what an ordeal you've had." He cast a broad smile at the two children and guided Charlotte to a chair. "What lovely little girls. Just have a seat here for a moment, young lady, and we'll get you taken care of. I know this has been a long day for you." He gently took Diana from Carol's arms and placed her on Charlotte's lap.

"It has been a rather trying day," Carol admitted. "I can't believe that stupid woman didn't bother to call you. And I also can't believe she sent us all this way. Surely, she could have made other arrangements for the children without all this hassle."

He put a conciliatory arm around her shoulder. "Well, I don't want you to worry anymore. Now that you're here, I will take care of everything. I have an excellent, temporary foster home where I can take the children for tonight, and we'll worry about the formalities in the morning after they've had a chance to rest."

Carol sighed. "That would be wonderful, Mr. Ewing. I can't tell you how grateful I am to find someone who knows what he's doing."

Ushering her toward the door, he said, "Now, I know you have a long drive home ahead of you, so why don't you just give me everything you have and I'll handle the rest?"

He was so sincere, so reassuring.

"Thank you, I appreciate it," said Carol, as she handed over the paperwork. She was so tired. She knelt by the chair in which Charlotte sat with Diana.

"Charlotte, I have to go now. This nice man, Mr. Ewing, is going to take care of you. You'll be all right."

Charlotte regarded her with an indifferent expression.

"Everything is going to be okay," Carol repeated. "All right?"

"Sure," Charlotte said, in a dull voice, without looking at Carol. "Bye."

Carol reached over and hugged the rigid little body. She knew Charlotte was somehow blaming her for leaving them here, but that was probably natural. She wondered if she would ever get used to this job.

"Goodbye, sweetheart. Take good care of Diana." She straightened up. "Thank you, again, Mr. Ewing," she said, as she turned to leave.

— • ● • —

Charlotte watched Carol disappear through the door. She was dumping them, too. Charlotte sat waiting and watching the new man. His whole manner suddenly changed. Where just a moment ago he had been nice and friendly, now he ignored them as he picked up the telephone.

Charlotte listened to the one-sided conversation. "Julia, I've got a couple of arrivals for you." A brief pause. "No, there's an older child, too, but that won't be a problem. I'll figure something out. I'll call William Gessel as soon as you pick them up." Another pause. Then his voice became brusque. "Well, I need you to come get them as soon as possible." Another pause. "Oh, all right then." He slammed down the receiver.

Looking up, he acknowledged the children for the first time since Carol had left. "I'm going to drive you out to your foster home for the night." His voice carried no emotion. "Grab your stuff." He reached for the baby and hefted her onto his hip.

Lugging her little overnight bag, Charlotte trailed him out to his car, although her stomach clenched in painful spasms. Quiet tears coursed down her cheeks, and she couldn't control the shaking which seized her whole body. Mr. Ewing didn't pay any attention. They rode in silence for several blocks, finally pulling up in front of a small, ranch-style house. A young woman opened the door. She had long, stringy, brown hair, and her brows were drawn in an ugly frown.

Without even glancing at the children, she launched into the man. "Ray, you *know* I don't take older kids!"

"It's just for a few days," he told her. "This is too good to pass up. Look at this baby."

Her eyes moved from the man's face to the gurgling child in his arms. "Yeah, I see what you mean." Then she frowned, "But are you sure there won't be any problem? With . . ." she nodded her head in Charlotte's direction. "You know?"

"No," Ray replied. "The mother's dead, father's whereabouts are unknown. He abandoned the family a few months ago. No other relatives." He stepped closer to the woman and handed her Diana. Caressing the woman's cheek with the back of his hand, he said, "I've got everything figured out, baby. Just sit tight for a few days. I guarantee we'll get enough for this one to make it worth the inconvenience."

"All right, but just a few days. If it's any longer, she'll have to go downtown."

"Trust me, baby," he said, as he went out the door.

Charlotte, in the meantime, had been standing on the porch, feeling totally left out of everything, but yet, somehow, in the middle of everything at the same time. The tears continued to flow.

"Well, come on in," the woman said, softening her tone a little.

"It looks like you're going to be staying with me for a few days. My name's Julia. What's yours?"

"Charlotte," she sniffled. She did not like this arrangement at all. Something was terribly wrong.

"Okay, Charlotte. Bring your bag and come with me. I'll show you to your room."

CHAPTER TWENTY-FIVE
CHARLES

It was a perfect Sunday afternoon for golf. With the promise of fall just around the corner, a subtle hint of a chill hung in the light breeze that gently relieved the harsh September sun. Charles DeVoux, who had recently achieved full tenure as a professor of English literature at Auburn University, and the Honorable Judge Theodore Bellamy, of the First District Court of Montgomery, had just finished nine holes and were heading to the club house to quench the thirsts they had worked up. They took seats at an outdoor table on the patio overlooking the green. A large, multi-colored umbrella shaded them from the glare of the sun, enabling them to enjoy the heavenly, soft breeze. After the waitress came and took their orders, Charles leaned back in his chair and sighed.

"What is it, Charles?" asked the judge.

"Hmm?" asked Charles, his mind elsewhere. He had been subconsciously studying a young couple at the next table. The woman held a small child on her lap. They had apparently been enjoying the club house while the man played a few holes, and he had just joined them for a snack. The toddler squealed in delight at the sight of his father, and the man, chuckling, reached for his son.

"I'm sorry, Ted," said Charles, turning his attention back to his friend. "What is it you were saying?"

"I was asking what's wrong with you today?" replied the judge, his tone conveying slight exasperation. "Your concentration is way off. Usually, I have to play like the devil to beat you, but today, you're just not yourself."

Charles forced a brittle laugh. "We won't talk about the game, if you don't mind." Then he became serious. "Actually, it's Andrea I'm worried about. After all the screening and interviewing and waiting for a baby, the adoption agency decided we are too old." He snorted. "Can you believe it? We *grew* old waiting for them to approve us, for crying out loud. As if forty-two is too old to adopt a baby, anyway."

"Oh, I am sorry," sympathized Ted. "I thought the adoption was a sure thing."

"So did we," replied Charles. "We found out yesterday we were turned down." His voice rose a little. "You know how well we could provide for a child. And Andrea. My word, the woman would spoil a kid rotten." He shook his head. "It doesn't seem right with all the unwanted children in the world. All we want to do is take one child into our home to love, and we're too old." He snorted again. "What a system."

The judge nodded in agreement. "So, Andrea's taking it pretty hard, is she?"

Charles sighed. "She's terribly depressed. I'm really concerned about her."

"Well, perhaps we should cut this short, and you should go home."

"No, she wanted me out of the house today. I think she feels she's dragging me down with her broken heart. But believe me, I feel bad enough for myself. I've always wanted kids. And I'd make a darned good father." His gaze drifted over to the next table.

They sat in silence for a moment as the waitress returned with their drinks. Ted took a long sip, then leaned across the table and said, in a soft voice, "Charles, maybe there's something I can do."

Charles perked up. Looking at his old friend, his curiosity aroused, he said, "But you don't deal in domestic law."

"No," replied the judge, "but I may know of someone who

might be able to help you."

"I'm all ears."

Ted took a furtive look around them. Keeping his voice just above a whisper, he said, "Sometimes arrangements can be made in situations like yours without having to go through the usual channels."

A flutter of hope rose in Charles' chest. But at the same time, he felt a warning of unease. "I don't want to look a gift horse in the mouth, Ted, but—"

The judge held up his hand. "Let me make some phone calls. Don't say anything to Andrea just yet."

Charles nodded. Whatever it took, it was worth it.

———•●•———

The Honorable Theodore Bellamy called Charles the next day and asked him to come to the law office of Gessel and Smythe at eight o'clock that evening. Although meeting with a lawyer at night seemed unusual, Charles did as he was told, arriving a little before eight to a dark, deserted outer office. A tendril of apprehension gripped him, and he almost turned around to leave, when suddenly an inner door opened. A tall man stood shadowed in a beam of light from the room behind.

"Ah," the man cried, coming forward in the nearly dark office. "You're early. Forgive me. I was just coming to turn on the lights for you." He stopped in front of Charles, extending his hand. "I'm William Gessel."

Charles took the hand in his own, slightly damp one. "I was referred to you by Judge—"

Gessel held up a hand. "Please, I'm familiar with your situation. Come into my office."

Charles followed him from the darkened waiting area into the well-lit office beyond. His nervous glance took in the expensively furnished room before he sank into the large leather chair where the lawyer directed him.

Gessel sat opposite him at a Louis XIV desk. He smiled in an apparent attempt to put Charles at ease, but Charles' first impression was the man had way too many teeth for his mouth and too much gel on his slicked-backed dark hair.

"I apologize for having to meet you so late," the lawyer began. "Busy, busy, busy, you know."

Charles managed a weak smile. "Will Judge Bellamy be joining us?" he asked.

The lawyer looked as though Charles had uttered a blasphemy. Then he quickly recovered his composure. Flashing Charles his toothy smile, he said, "No, he will not. And it would be better if we keep our business just between ourselves, if you understand what I mean?"

Despite the frigid air coming from the central air conditioning, Charles began to grow warm. What had Ted gotten him into? There was something not quite right about this meeting. He certainly didn't want to do anything that would get Ted or himself into trouble.

"Now then, Professor DeVoux. May I call you Charles? It would be so much more informal."

"Yes." Charles forced the answer from his dry throat. The man was making him uncomfortable. He reached up to loosen his tie, then realized he wasn't wearing one. He smiled, self-consciously. "A little hot in here."

William Gessel merely grinned again. Settling back in his chair, he laced his fingers together, palms outward. "Charles, from what I understand, you and your lovely wife have been trying unsuccessfully to adopt a baby."

How does he know Andrea is lovely?

"Yes," Charles answered, his tone wary, as he took a handkerchief from his front pocket and wiped sweat from his brow.

"My job," explained the lawyer, "is to, shall we say, facilitate the process. There are a number of wonderful, deserving couples, like yourselves, desperate to adopt, who simply get tangled up in all the bureaucratic red tape. I try to make the process a bit easier."

"And how do you do that?"

"By arranging for private adoptions, Charles. Say, for example, we have a young, unwed mother who wants to give up her baby for adoption. But she needs money to pay for medical care, living expenses, things like that. We arrange for the adoptive parents to cover her expenses. Everybody benefits."

Charles nodded. It sounded reasonable.

"And sometimes," Gessel went on, "we get babies who have

been abandoned or orphaned. It takes forever to get the customary paperwork cleared for them to be eligible for adoption. By then, they're no longer babies and they're much more difficult to place. Now why should a child have to suffer because of the ridiculous length of time required for the slow wheels of bureaucracy to turn?"

Warning bells sounded in Charles' head. "Do you mean, then, that these adoptions are not legal?"

Bill Gessel showed his teeth again.

The man should be a politician.

"Let's just say, Charles, that although they are legal, you could possibly run into a potential problem if some unknown relative showed up years later claiming the child. So we try to ensure that doesn't happen. But it takes money."

"No," said Charles, vehemently. "I don't like the sound of this. I want a legal, permanent adoption."

The lawyer allowed Charles' outburst to roll off him.

"Charles," he said, his voice soothing, "I'm afraid in your situation, this is your only option."

A wave of repulsion rose in Charles' gut. This man across from him was a snake-oil salesman, only he was peddling babies. No, he could not lower his standards to make a deal like this, no matter how badly he wanted a baby. He gripped the arms of the chair, intending to rise and walk out just as the lawyer tossed a photograph across the desk.

"Now here," Gessel offered, "is a beautiful little girl named Diana. Her mother died unexpectedly. The father abandoned the family several months earlier. There is no other known family."

Against his will, Charles' eyes were drawn to the picture. As much as he tried to resist, he couldn't help the longing that overcame him when he looked at the smiling, angelic face surrounded by a mass of blonde curls.

"I could arrange for you and your lovely wife to be the proud adoptive parents of this little bundle of joy as soon as a day or two." The lawyer waved his hand as if everything was a done deal.

Charles' hand seemed to move of its own volition as he reached for the photograph.

While he studied the picture, the lawyer's mellow voice continued, "The baby is almost a year old and in excellent health. If the normal channels of having to do an extensive, diligent search for living relatives is followed, she could get lost in the system for months or years. Then placing her in an adoptive home will be much harder. That would be a real pity, a waste, when *you* could give her a loving, comfortable home, and she could give you so much happiness in return. Imagine being able to go home tonight and tell your lovely wife she will have a precious little daughter in a day or two. You tell me, where's the harm in that? Who would be hurt?"

Charles had to admit the attorney had a point. Who would be hurt? It was a silly system anyway, denying him and Andrea the right to adopt. If it weren't for the stupid system, he wouldn't even be here considering a shaky adoption. His thoughts churned, but the seed had already been sowed and watered with his first glimpse of the picture.

"I want this baby." He heard the words come from his mouth before he even realized he had formed them in his head.

Mr. Gessel beamed. "I don't blame you, Charles. We both know that everyone stands to benefit from this. Especially the child." He gazed at the photograph Charles still held.

"What do I have to do?"

"Well, first of all, there is the adoption fee of fifty-thousand dollars. That will cover all the legal paperwork, immediate expenses of the child, and a generous donation to the county children's home, without whom this would not be possible."

Charles gulped. That would wipe out nearly their entire savings. A little voice in the back of his mind whispered there would be little cost to the paperwork and expenses, and probably no donation. Not anything amounting to fifty-thousand dollars, anyway. The money would be pocketed by this unscrupulous lawyer and his contact inside the agency. Uneasiness gripped him. But he was already in too deep. He wanted this adorable baby. And Andrea deserved some happiness. He stared at the little smiling face, imagining her in his home—his very own daughter.

Then a new fear wormed its way to the front of his brain. What if he got into trouble over this? What if someone came and took the baby away? But the lawyer was coming to that.

"What I would strongly suggest, Charles," Gessel went on, "is that you consider a move, a fresh start."

"Move?" Charles echoed. "But . . . ." He didn't have to ask why. People would ask questions about where the child had come from.

It would be hard to explain, especially if the adoption agency got wind of the news. It might cause trouble for Mr. Gessel and his contact, as well as Ted Bellamy. "I just received full tenure," he said, his voice betraying the pain over the loss of his life's accomplishment.

"Surely a professor of your ability will have no trouble getting another university position." The lawyer smiled again, and an image of a shark came to Charles' mind.

Charles nodded. What was he doing? He should get up and leave. Now! But the reality of having the baby was so close, actually within his grasp. He knew he would pay dearly for his compromises. Was it worth it? Blast that photo. If it weren't for the picture, he could have fought the urge to commit this highly unethical act.

"There is one other slight wrinkle," added the lawyer.

What more can there be? He had already agreed to something he would never have believed himself capable of.

"The natural father."

"What of him?" cried Charles. "He abandoned her." His indignation rose. "He has no rights anymore."

"Unfortunately, that is not always the case, Charles. As unfair as it may seem to decent men like you and me, the courts are usually quite lenient about upholding the rights of the biological parent, no matter what he or she has done. If he were to reappear—"

Charles had already come this far. He wasn't about to lose out now. "What can we do to prevent that from happening?"

"Well," said the lawyer, "I think we can make it rather difficult to trace the child through a little paper shuffling." He opened a drawer and pulled out a form. "For example, when we fill out the adoption papers, we *accidentally* leave the 'i' out of her name. So she becomes 'Dana.' The father isn't looking for a child named Dana, but if worst comes to worst, we can say it was a clerical error."

Charles suddenly felt very tired. "I don't want to know any more details. Just do what you have to do and let me know when everything's taken care of. In the meantime, I'll get ahold of some old contacts at some other universities."

"Very well. It's been a pleasure, Charles." Gessel stood and held out his hand.

Charles allowed the lawyer to take his limp hand. Then he turned to leave.

"Wait. You may take this for your wife." He held out the picture that had captured Charles' heart and forced him into buying a baby.

All the way home, Charles wrestled with the rights and wrongs of what he had just done. Whenever he tried to justify it, his conscience always interfered. But what was done was done. There was no turning back.

Andrea waited in anxious anticipation. With one look at her expectant face, he knew he had done the right thing. His face broke into a wide grin.

"We have a daughter, Andrea," he cried, waving the picture under her nose.

Andrea's mouth dropped open. Then she threw her arms around Charles' neck and began to cry. "I can't believe it," she sobbed against his chest. "I had given up hope."

"Her name is Dana," Charles told her. There was no reason to elaborate on anything more unless she asked. Still holding her, he said, "You know, dear, I was thinking. Maybe we should move somewhere new, make a completely fresh start for all of us."

Andrea raised her head and looked at her husband, her eyes probing his with unasked questions. "Whatever you say, Charles. As long as we're all together."

————•●•————

As soon as Charles left, William Gessel placed a phone call to Ray Ewing, director of the Montgomery County Children's Home.

"Good news, Ray," he said. "I've got a couple for the Wallace baby. You haven't processed her yet, have you?"

"No," came the reply. "I was waiting on you."

"Good. Nobody will ever know she was there."

"How much did you get, Bill?"

"Thirty-thousand."

"Not bad. Not bad at all."

"What are you going to do about the older sister? There could be a problem if she talks to the wrong person."

"I'll take care of it."

"Make sure you do. I don't need to remind you what would

happen to our lucrative sideline if we get caught."

"Like I said, Bill, I'll take care of it. You just get this baby out of here as soon as you can before anybody starts asking questions."

"It's as good as done, Ray."

CHAPTER TWENTY-SIX
ADAM

Adam was unnaturally quiet on the flight from Atlanta to Mobile. In fact, he had said very little at all after Jonathon had told him the news about Connie. Now, sitting next to him in the cramped airplane seat, Jonathon shifted his eyes ever so slightly to observe Adam. He sat with his head back, eyes closed, but Jonathon knew he wasn't sleeping. What was going through the man's head? Was he blaming Jonathon for not finding Connie sooner? Jonathon cursed the miserable timing. But for a few days, Connie might still be alive. He sighed. He hated this part of the job— when things didn't have a happy ending. Could he have prevented Connie's death? That question had been eating away at him ever since the phone call from Jason McCarthy. He still didn't know the cause of death. He would have to wait and talk to the police. At least it should be fairly easy to find the children and re-unite them with their father. They were probably either in the county children's home or with a foster family. How Adam was going to cope with a small child and a baby with no mother, Jonathon had no idea. But with Connie gone, Adam would have no choice. The main thing now was to wrap up as much as they could and get back home as soon as possible, so Adam could get on with his life.

As soon as they landed and deplaned, Jonathon told Adam "I'm going to pick up our rental car."

Adam nodded. "Then what?" he asked, the first time he had spoken since they'd boarded the plane.

"I think our first stop should be the police department. They'll have all the information we need. Then we can see about making arrangements for the children and cleaning out the apartment."

"And taking care of the body," Adam said, his voice flat, finishing the thoughts Jonathon hadn't spoken aloud.

"Yes," Jonathon admitted. He hadn't wanted to bring that subject up yet, but there was no avoiding it.

Adam started to say something else, but choked on his words. He waved Jonathon off to get the car.

— • ● • —

Adam rode to the police station in a daze, peering out the window without registering anything. Jonathon did not attempt conversation.

A burly desk sergeant greeted them as they entered the noisy precinct. Jonathon stated their business.

"I'm Jonathon Peel, a private investigator from Atlanta, and this is Adam Wallace, the husband of Connie Wallace. We're here to talk to whoever's in charge of that case."

The sergeant looked at Adam without interest. Then he flipped through some papers in front of him. "That would be Officer Jennings," he said. "Hold on, I'll get him for you."

As they waited, Adam became more and more uneasy. Up until now, he had existed in a state of frozen unreality. Now, he was about to be thrown face-to-face into stark reality. Suddenly, it hit him that Connie was truly dead. He hoped he could hold up. He jumped when another policeman approached.

"Gentlemen, I'm Officer Jennings." A large, thick-wasted man with close cropped hair and a ruddy complexion stood over them. He gave them only a cursory nod, not extending his hand, then beckoned them to follow him.

They passed through a large room filled with desks and police personnel, all appearing to be busy. The general chaotic atmosphere of phones ringing, people talking, filing cabinet drawers being opened and closed, and papers being shuffled, grated on Adam's fragile nerves. Officer Jennings led them to a small, stuffy room in the back, where he closed the door, shutting out the mass confusion.

Adam and Jonathon took seats on metal folding chairs at an old, scratched wooden table in the center of the room. The stench of stale cigarette smoke and sweat permeated the claustrophobic, confined space. A small, oscillating fan mounted on the wall made a futile attempt to stir the sluggish air.

The policeman stood, holding a thin file folder. "I must say I'm a little surprised to see you here, Mr. Wallace."

Adam's eyebrows rose in question. "Why?" He could feel the burning disapproval in the man's words and didn't know why.

"Well, from what little information we have on your estranged wife, you abandoned the family several months ago."

"What?" Adam jumped to his feet. His numbness dissolved into anger at the false accusation. He pointed a shaking finger at the officer. "I don't know where you got your information, Officer Jennings, but it's simply not true. Why would you have something like that in your report unless you knew for a fact it was true?" Heat rose in his face and he could feel sweat trickling down the back of his neck.

Jonathon hopped up and put a hand on Adam's shoulder, guiding him back into his chair.

"That's right, Officer. Mr. Wallace engaged my services several months ago to find his family. It was his wife who took his children and disappeared without a word. Mr. Wallace has been frantically trying to locate them."

The policeman narrowed his eyes and drew his brows together in a skeptical frown. "Why would she do that, Mr. Wallace? Did she have reason to be afraid of you?"

Adam jumped up again. "Of course not!" His voice rose with his increasing frustration. Then the image of the fight they'd had popped into his mind. How he had slapped her. But that was silly. That was certainly no reason for her to fear him. Was it? He sank back into his chair, his shoulders slumped.

"What Mr. Wallace is trying to tell you, Officer," Jonathon explained with infinite patience, "is we don't have any idea why Mrs. Wallace did what she did. But all that's really beside the point now. What we want to know is the cause of death, for which we have no details, and where we can find Mr. Wallace's daughters."

Jennings thumbed through the folder—it seemed to Adam— more as an irritation to prolong Adam's discomfort than for the sake of looking for information.

"Well, the cause of death is pretty straight forward. At least the coroner thinks so at this time, but we will have to wait for the final pathology reports."

"Well?" prodded Jonathon.

"She died of acute alcohol toxicity. Her blood alcohol level was 0.6%."

"What exactly does that mean?" asked Jonathon.

"It means, Mr. Peel, the woman had enough alcohol in her body to kill an elephant. A person goes into an alcoholic stupor or coma at about 0.4 to 0.5%. And with a woman her size and weight . . ." He broke off, shaking his head.

"You mean she died from drinking?" cried Adam. "I can't believe it. I *never* saw her drink. Never."

The policeman turned a cold eye on him. "It would seem you didn't know your wife very well, wouldn't it, Mr. Wallace?"

Adam had no reply. His brain reeled with this shocking discovery.

"Don't be so quick to blame Mr. Wallace for his wife's shortcomings," Jonathon retorted. "Mr. Wallace is a fine, decent, hardworking man who obviously loves his family very much to go to all this trouble and expense of trying to find them."

He started to elaborate further, but Adam held up a restraining hand. "Never mind, Jonathon, I'm not on trial." His defeat hung in his weary tone. He looked up at the judgmental officer. "If you'll just tell me where my children are, we'll be on our way. I will make arrangements for my wife's body at a later time."

Jennings hesitated. "I'm not sure I should release any information about the children until we've done a thorough investigation into the cause of your abandonment and your wife's obvious fear of you. I don't want to send children back into an unsafe environment."

Adam flew out of his seat before Jonathon could stop him. "Blast it, you fool! What do I have to do to get the truth through your thick head?" His hands involuntarily clenched into fists as he advanced on the officer.

Jennings backed up and tightened his own fists, his narrowed eyes daring Adam to make a move.

Jonathon rushed to pull Adam away. "Not like this, Adam.

Please. Let's just go."

Adam stood for a moment, tensed for a fight. Then his whole body sagged.

"Get him out of here," Jennings growled. "Before I throw him into jail for threatening an officer."

Jonathon pushed Adam through the police station. Once they were safely outside, he released his full fury.

"What is wrong with you?" he yelled in Adam's face. "What are you trying to do? Assure they'll never release your kids to you?"

Adam had calmed down a little. "I'm sorry. But that moron cop seemed determined to antagonize me. He didn't listen to a thing I said. He had his mind all made up."

"Well, if he didn't before, he certainly does now," Jonathon grumbled. "Do you want to have to go through a lengthy court battle to determine if you're stable enough to get your kids back?"

Adam shook his head. "I shouldn't have let him get to me like that," he said, his tone drained of all feeling. "I've been under such a strain for so long. I just lost my head."

Jonathon studied him for a moment. "Adam, I hate to even bring this up, but *is* it possible that Connie was trying to hide from you?"

"You too, Jonathon?" Adam shook his head and looked at the man he had considered his ally. "Look, I know I lost my temper just now, but to be as honest as I can, no, I do not know of any reason why she would do that."

"Then how do you explain her strange behavior? Nobody even knew where she was except for Mrs. McCarthy."

"I can't explain it, Jonathon. Maybe she didn't want to face me after her plans fell through with Stephen. Maybe she was hoping to start a new life. Maybe she was afraid I would make good my threat to divorce her and take the girls away from her. I don't know. I just don't know." His voice broke, as he ran his hand over his face.

"And now we will never know." Jonathon rubbed his hands together as if dispensing with that subject. "Well, what I suggest we do next is contact the county children's home and see if we can get the girls released before Jennings makes trouble for you."

"Let's go," said Adam, with a bit more enthusiasm. "I've waited a long time to see my daughters."

"You'll forgive me if I don't get up," greeted the middle-aged woman behind the desk. A pair of crutches lay on the floor beside her chair. "I'm Millie Longfield, the director of the children's home. What can I do for you gentlemen?"

Adam breathed a sigh of relief. On first impression, the woman appeared to be intelligent, compassionate, and competent. He wouldn't have to worry about controlling his temper with her like he had with the imbecile police officer.

"I'm Jonathon Peel, a private investigator, and this is Mr. Adam Wallace." Jonathon gestured to Adam. "We have just flown in from Atlanta. Mr. Wallace's estranged wife was found dead in her apartment a few days ago, and we believe his two daughters must have been brought here. His daughter, Charlotte, is almost six, and the baby, Diana, is eleven months old."

Millie Longfield clucked her tongue in sympathy. "Oh, I am terribly sorry about your wife, Mr. Wallace." She began to sift through some papers on her desk. "As you can see, however, I've had a little accident, and it's my first day back. But Miss Nelson didn't say anything to me about any new children. I'm sure she would have told me. Let me check through the records."

Her brow furrowed with intense concentration as she made a thorough search through her paperwork. Then, looking up, she said, "I am sorry, Mr. Wallace, but we haven't had any new admittances in two weeks."

"But that's impossible—" Adam began.

Jonathon interrupted. "Perhaps in your absence, Miss Longfield, your assistant did not keep the records as meticulously as you, yourself, would have. Could you maybe check with Miss Nelson?"

"Oh, I am sorry," she apologized again, "but Miss Nelson left on vacation this morning. She won't be back until the end of the month. But I can check with Mrs. Hall, the dormitory supervisor. She would know."

"Thank you, we would appreciate it," said Jonathon.

A rising panic began in Adam's gut as the woman cast him a

reassuring smile and picked up the phone.

"You'll have to forgive me," she said, placing her hand over the receiver, "ordinarily, I know everything about every single child who comes through these doors. But you wouldn't believe what I came back to after being gone just . . . oh hello? This is Millie. Let me speak to Norma Hall." She waited and smiled again. "Yes, Norma? Listen, Clare Nelson didn't take in any new children that I don't know about, did she? An almost six-year-old girl and an eleven-month-old girl? Hmm." A short pause. "Yes. Uh-huh." She frowned and rolled her eyes. "Yes, I know about that incident. Yes. Yes. I'll take care of that later. What about our foster homes?"

Adam waited in agony while the woman went on with her endless "uh-huhs" and "yesses." Finally, she put down the receiver.

"No, I'm sorry, Mr. Wallace, but they were not brought here. And none of our foster homes received them, either."

"But where else could they be?" Adam cried, his voice becoming shrill.

"Are there some relatives, perhaps, who might have taken the children?"

"No!" he yelled. The woman blinked at his outburst. His heart in his throat, he apologized. "Please, forgive me, Miss Longfield. I'm not myself. I didn't mean to shout at you."

"Miss Longfield," interjected Jonathon. "Is there any other facility around here where they could possibly be?"

"No," she said, shaking her head. "We are the official children's home for the southern part of the state."

To Adam's astonishment, he found tears rolling down his cheeks. To come so close and still be so far! Embarrassed, he hurried to wipe the tears away.

Millie handed him a tissue. "It's all right, Mr. Wallace. I realize what an ordeal this is for you. I suggest you check with the police who handled the report. Surely, if there were no relatives in the area, a social worker from the children's services was assigned to the children. You can talk to him or her. They could be staying with friends or neighbors while the social worker is trying to locate *you.*"

"Thank you, Miss Longfield," said Jonathon. "I will leave you my card in case you hear anything."

He took Adam's arm and led him outside. "Well, I doubt we'll get the social worker's name from the police, after this morning."

"Oh, please, Jonathon, do something. They've *got* to be here somewhere."

Jonathon thought for a moment. "What about their grandparents, Adam? Wouldn't they have been the logical people for social services to have contacted if they couldn't find you?"

Adam began to see a little ray of hope. "You may be right," he agreed, blowing his nose. "Quick, let's find a phone booth."

— • ● • —

Adam exited the phone booth, his face ashen. He shuffled to the car, where Jonathon waited, and got in slowly, like an old man.

Jonathon knew immediately that there was more wrong than just a lead that hadn't panned out. "What is it, Adam?"

"Her parents didn't even know she was dead," Adam whispered. "Oh dear Lord, it was awful having to tell them like that."

"Oh, no," groaned Jonathon.

"There's more."

Jonathon waited.

"Connie left the girls with them for a few weeks after she left me."

Jonathon inwardly kicked himself for not pursuing that possibility. But Adam had been so adamant they would not be there. He *knew* he should have gone with his instinct. He muttered a curse under his breath.

Adam leaned back and closed his eyes. "Yeah. Go ahead and say it. If I had listened to you and had you check with Connie's parents, I'd have had my children back months ago, and Connie might still be alive. I was so blasted *sure* of everything. Turns out, I didn't know anything. Not about Connie, anyway."

They sat contemplating their next move.

"I say we call the social services office and see if we can locate the case worker," said Jonathon.

"Good idea," agreed Adam, his tone listless.

This time, he waited while Jonathon placed the call. And this time, Jonathon was the one who came back to the car defeated.

"I'm afraid our Officer Jennings beat us to it," he said. "The office refuses to give out any information until they have an okay from the police department."

"Well, did they say if they were even contacted about the girls?"

"They won't say anything," replied Jonathon. He let out a long, deep sigh. "Let's grab a bite to eat and then head over to her apartment. Maybe one of the neighbors knows something." But even as he said it, he didn't sound very hopeful.

————— • ● • —————

As they neared the section of town where Connie's apartment was located, Adam grew more and more uneasy.

"Jonathon, are you sure about this address?"

"That's what I got from Jason McCarthy."

"But *look* at this area. It's worse than a slum."

"Be realistic, Adam," Jonathon told him, "Connie didn't have much money. Where did you expect her to live? In some waterfront villa?"

"No, but . . . I guess I never thought . . ." Adam's voice trailed off, as he imagined his wife and children in this terrible neighborhood. If only he could talk to Connie—ask her why.

"Here we are."

Adam looked at the building in horror. "Oh, my word, Jonathon."

With reluctance, he got out of the car. Even *he* felt vaguely uncomfortable in this rough neighborhood. Imagine what Connie and Charlotte had felt. As they entered the front door, the filth and offensive odors assaulted his senses. He fought a wave of nausea and made an effort to conceal his intense repugnance.

Jonathon, likewise, despite his tough outer facade of professionalism, appeared to be having difficulty hiding his abhorrence.

"Here's the super's number," Jonathon said, reading the mailboxes. "Let's go see if he knows anything, first."

After Jonathon had stated their business, Luther let them in, but he seemed guarded. Adam felt the undisguised distaste of the big man as he looked Adam over.

"Mr. Johnson, we're sorry to bother you, but—" began Jonathon.

"Luther," the man replied, his voice sullen. "Jus' call me Luther. Don' much stand on formalities." He folded his big arms over his chest.

"All right." Jonathon smiled. Luther listened to Jonathon, but kept his piercing dark eyes on Adam. Adam couldn't understand why he was being so hostile.

"Luther, were you around the day Mrs. Wallace died?"

"Yes, sir, I was. L'il Missy Charlotte come and got me that mornin'. Said her mama won' wake up." He glared at Adam.

"Oh, my Lord," Adam whispered, his voice trembling.

Luther went on, "An' I went up to her 'partment and found Miz Wallace dead. Then I called the po'lese. An' I brought them young'uns down here 'til the po'lese came."

Adam collapsed, sobbing, onto Luther's broken-down sofa, his noisy wailing echoing through the small apartment.

"Now, Luther," Jonathon went on, raising his voice to be heard over the din of Adam's weeping, "did a social worker come for the children?"

"Yes, sir, a woman came. And seein' as how L'il Missy told her they didn't have no family, the woman took them downtown." Luther gave special emphasis to the words "no family."

"Downtown. To the county children's home?"

"Yes, sir. I reckon."

"Well, Luther, Mr. Wallace and I were just there. And the children were not admitted to the home. Would you have any other ideas where they might have been taken?"

"No, sir. L'il Missy Charlotte, she wanna stay here with me. We got to be good friends." Again, he shot Adam a venomous look. "But the lady says no, she can't. So L'il Missy Charlotte says she go with the lady, but only until she gets 'dopted."

"But what about her father, Luther? Didn't anyone think about contacting him?"

Luther took a deep breath and settled his withering gaze on Adam. "Well, sir, L'il Missy Charlotte told me and the social worker her daddy 'bandoned her. Said he didn't love her no more."

"What?" cried Adam, jolted out of his hysterical sobbing, as if someone had slapped him.

Jonathon appeared ready to thwart another confrontation.

But Adam merely rose, as if he were a feeble old man. He held out his trembling hands, pleading with Luther to tell him it wasn't so.

"Charlotte told you that?" he croaked.

"Yes, sir, she did." Luther stood firm, bottom jaw thrust out.

Adam's body began to shake all over. "But it's not true," he whispered. He turned to Jonathon, as though needing to convince him, as well. "You know it's not true." His voice broke and he began to sob again.

Jonathon placed a hand on Adam's shoulder and pushed him down firmly again on the sofa.

"Luther," he said, "do you remember the name of the woman who took the girls away?"

Luther frowned. "Don' rightly remember if she said. I was in such a state, myself." He shook his head. "No, sir. I don' rightly remember." Then he brightened, "but the po'leseman would know!"

"Thanks, Luther," said Jonathon. "Perhaps you would be so kind as to let us into the apartment. Mr. Wallace will need to make arrangements for Mrs. Wallace's personal effects."

"Yes, sir, I can do that."

Adam trailed behind the other two men, wincing at the squalor all around him. They went up the dark, littered steps, and stopped at the door to Connie's apartment.

"Every time I clean the buildin' up, some low-life trashes it up again," Luther grumbled. "I do try, but . . ." He shrugged. "This here's it," he said, opening the door.

Adam stepped inside. All the familiar furnishings filled him with a sense of coming home again. He half expected to see Connie and Charlotte come running to greet him. He wandered aimlessly through the tiny apartment, occasionally picking up an item here or there. When he got to the bedroom, he found the bedclothes in disarray, as if the occupants had just woken up. The bars to the crib were down. He walked over and tenderly touched the little baby blanket wadded up at the foot of the crib. Diana always kicked off her blanket. Then he turned to the narrow twin bed, where Charlotte had slept. He picked up her pillow and inhaled deeply. He could still smell her childish scent clinging to the pillowcase. A beat-up rag doll lay on the floor.

Picking it up, he whispered, with a catch in his throat, "She left Betsy. How could they have taken her away without Betsy?" Silent tears began to make their way down his cheeks, once again.

Luther and Jonathon exchanged confused looks.

"It's her favorite doll," Adam explained. Tucking the doll under his arm, he snatched up the little blue blanket from Diana's bed. Then he walked out of the bedroom, hunting for something else. He found what he was looking for in the small living room, next to the sleeper sofa—the picture of Connie with Charlotte and Diana taken a few months after Diana was born. Identical faces, separated by twenty years smiled out at him from the photograph.

"That's all I want from this place," he uttered. "You can do what you want with the rest."

Luther nodded. "You might want this, too," he said, reaching into his pocket and pulling out a small gold pin in the shape of a heart. A single diamond was in the center.

"I took it for safe-keeping, so nobody'd steal it."

Adam grasped the pin with a shaking hand. He had forgotten about it. He had given it to Connie on their first anniversary. It had cost him a small fortune at the time.

"Thanks, Luther, I appreciate it."

Luther regarded Adam with sad eyes. "An' for what it's worth, sir, I don' believe you run off and left those girls. Someone's told L'il Missy a whoppin' lie."

Adam took the man's hand. "If only I could find her, now, Luther. God only knows what harm has already been done."

"Luther," said Jonathon. "What we really need is the name of that social worker. If by chance you can remember it, please call me." He handed him a card. "She's our only hope at finding those kids."

"I sure will, and good luck to you, sirs."

Adam's head spun with confusion. Who had told Charlotte he abandoned them and didn't love them anymore? Connie? Her grandparents? And why? How could anyone have told the child such a damaging lie? Until he got her back, she would believe he had actually walked out on her. What must she be going through now? Not yet six years old and all alone. He *had* to find her.

"Adam," Jonathon's voice cut through Adam's jumbled

thoughts. "I don't think there's anything more you can do here. I'm going to take you back to the airport and book you on a flight home."

"But—" Adam started to protest.

"Our only lead right now is that social worker. And at the moment, your presence here is more of a hindrance than a help. I may have to get a court order, but first I'm going to nose around and perhaps call in a few favors, and I need you out of the way. Especially if that policeman decides an investigation is in order."

"All right." Adam blew out a weary breath. Why had he been so reckless this morning? He had blown everything by losing his temper. "But you call me as soon as you know anything. I want to be here when you find them. Charlotte's probably frightened enough as it is."

"You'll know as soon as I know," Jonathon promised.

———•●•———

The surprise registered on Adam's face when he found Katrina waiting for him at the Atlanta airport.

"How did you know?"

"Jonathon called me," she told him. "He thought you could use a friend."

"But how did Jonathon—"

"I asked him to let me know. I hope you don't mind my interfering, but, well . . . ordinarily, I don't think he would have told me anything confidential, but under the circumstances . . ." Her words trailed off.

"You're a wonderful friend to care so much, Kate," Adam said, leaning over to kiss her cheek.

Katrina felt a twinge of guilt at Adam's obvious misunderstanding of her concern. She had asked Jonathon to let her know whether or not it looked like a reconciliation between Adam and his wife. She had not been prepared for what he told her, and that made her feel even worse.

"I can't tell you how sorry I am about everything," she said sincerely. "Would it help to talk about it?"

"No, I don't think so," replied Adam, who then began pouring out everything in his heart. When she pulled up in front of Adam's apartment, he asked, "Would you mind coming in for a while? I don't think I can stand being alone tonight."

"Of course," she answered, her tone sad and gentle.

They sat and talked, or mostly Adam talked, while she listened with a sympathetic ear. He showed her the picture of Connie and the girls.

"They're beautiful, Adam."

Tears sprang to his eyes, and she put her arms around him, letting him cry into her shoulder, as she rocked him like a heartbroken child.

She held him until he had exhausted all his tears. Then, before she knew what was happening, he was kissing her forehead, her cheeks, her chin, and finally her lips.

As much as she wanted him, she didn't want him this way.

Gently disengaging herself from his arms, she whispered, "This isn't the right time or place, Adam. Lie down and sleep. We'll figure everything out later." She kissed his wet cheek, brought him a blanket, and slipped quietly out the door.

CHAPTER TWENTY-SEVEN
CHARLOTTE

———•●•———

The next day passed uneventfully. Julia was not unkind to Charlotte, but neither was she overly friendly. She seemed to be uncomfortable around the child, so she didn't speak to her much. Charlotte watched out the window on Monday morning as the neighborhood children started out to school. She should be going to school, too.

Charlotte told her, "I'm s'posed to be in school, you know."

Julia looked at her, a blank expression on her face. "Oh, don't worry," she replied. "As soon as you get to your permanent residence, you'll be enrolled in school."

Charlotte didn't have any idea what a permanent residence was, but she didn't want to ask Julia any more questions. She didn't trust Julia to tell her the truth anyway.

On Tuesday, Ray showed up, obviously upset. He and Julia talked freely in front of Charlotte, who sprawled on the sofa watching cartoons, as if she were incapable of hearing them.

He ran his hand through his thinning hair, his eyes darting in all directions. "We've got trouble, Jules," he said, his voice high and tense. "There's been some nosing around about our sideline."

Julia's face went pale. "How did they find out?"

"I don't know," he went on, "but we've got to move fast. Gessel has a couple for the baby. I'm going to hang around long enough to close that deal, then I'm going to resign and leave town.

It's too dangerous for me to stay." He glanced at Charlotte, who shrank back against the cushions, trying to make herself invisible. "What I need you to do is take the kid and get out of the state."

"But, Ray," she protested. "Where are we going to go? What about you? Where will I find you?"

"It would be better for us not to be seen together for a while. Go to Florida. Make up some story and dump the kid somewhere. Then get lost. I want you to leave today."

"But couldn't we just take the baby and leave together?"

"No! We stand to make several thousand from this. I don't want to lose this chance."

"And how am I supposed to get my cut?" she snarled.

"I'll find you later, sweetheart. I promise."

"How?" she demanded. "You'll have the money and be long gone, and I'll have nothing."

His words came out loud and angry. "Fine. If you want to hang around and get caught, that's okay with me. I'll hold your share of the money until you get out of jail." Then his voice become menacing. "But so help me, if you mess things up for me, Julia . . ."

"You miserable creep," she spat at him. "I'll go. But don't you spend my share of the money. Because I'll find you. And when I do, I'll want my money."

Charlotte, after much protest over being separated from Diana, embarked on yet another long journey, this time ending up in the Escambia County Home for Children, in Pensacola, Florida. All she understood was that Diana was being adopted and she wasn't. She didn't know what Julia had told them at this new place. But for some reason, nobody believed anything *she* tried to tell them. At last, she gave up. After all, she really didn't know for sure what was going on. But she knew it wasn't right.

CHAPTER TWENTY-EIGHT
ADAM

———•●•———

Adam was not pleased to learn that Jonathon had returned to Atlanta. That could only mean one thing. He braced himself for the worst, as the receptionist showed him into the now quite-familiar office.

Jonathon sat behind the desk, a deadly serious expression on his face, as usually befits the bearer of bad news. He looked exhausted.

"Give it to me straight, Jonathon," Adam said, his heart weighing like a stone in his chest.

Jonathon Peel leaned back against his chair and let out a long, deep sigh. "Adam, I wish like the devil I didn't have to tell you this."

"Just tell me," Adam replied, now knowing with certainty the news was the worst possible.

"I don't know where they are. I'm at a dead end."

"So, what happened?" Adam demanded, a hint of accusation in his tone.

Jonathon pressed his lips together and swallowed hard, clearly dreading having to recount his last few days. He fixed his gaze on a point beyond Adam's shoulder.

"I finally got ahold of the social worker, a woman named Carol Sherman. Millicent Longfield, the director of the Mobile Children's Home called me. Mrs. Sherman lodged a formal complaint against the temporary director, a Miss Nelson, who was covering for Miss

Longfield when she broke her ankle."

"Is all this necessary?" Adam didn't think he could take any more. He just wanted the bottom line.

"Yes. I believe so," Jonathon told him. "It helps to understand the progression of events."

Adam grunted.

"Mrs. Sherman took the children to Miss Nelson who told her she didn't have room for the children. She sent them to Montgomery. Miss Nelson, by the way, suffered a nervous breakdown a few days ago, and was admitted to the county psychiatric hospital."

"As if I care," muttered Adam. The incompetent woman had cost him his children.

"Mrs. Sherman took the girls to Montgomery and turned them over to a Mr. Ray Ewing, the director of the Montgomery Children's Home. By the time they arrived, it was after hours. He told her he was taking them to a temporary foster home for the night. However, they were never admitted to the county home. Recently, there have been some investigations concerning Mr. Ewing's suspicious activities."

"What kind of activities?" cried Adam, in alarm.

"Embezzlement. Fraud." Jonathon hesitated. "Possibly black-market baby selling."

"*What*?" Adam felt the blood drain from his face. "You mean he *sold* my children?"

"I don't know anything for sure. Possibly Diana."

Adam jumped out of his chair, his hands clasped to his head. "Oh my Lord! Oh my Lord! Then where is Charlotte?" Horrible visions began to swarm through Adam's mind.

"Unfortunately, Mr. Ewing has disappeared. Mind you, there's no proof of anything, but there are a number of files missing, which looks suspicious."

"I can't believe this." Adam's knees became weak, and he sank back into the chair. Unable to control the shaking that had seized his body, he hugged his arms around himself. Despite his shivering, the room seemed unbearably warm and suffocating.

"There are criminal charges pending against Mr. Ewing. However, they have to locate him first."

"And what about my children?"

"If you want my honest opinion, Adam, I think Diana has been illegally adopted and Charlotte is either far away or . . . or dead." His voice trailed off in a whisper.

"Oh my Lord," moaned Adam, again. "How can they let criminals and lunatics run county homes for children?"

"I know it won't be any comfort to you, Adam, but believe me, this is quite a rare exception."

"That doesn't help my daughters, does it?"

Jonathon regarded the distraught client before him and allowed a moment of silence to pass before he spoke again. "Adam, you know I've done everything I can, don't you?"

Adam slowly nodded. "I know, Jonathon." He sighed. "So, this means you're giving up? I know I owe you a lot of money—"

"Adam," Jonathon stopped him. "Believe me, it's not the money. I simply don't know where to go from here. Those kids could be anywhere."

"You're telling me to give up," Adam said, his tone flat and defeated.

"Yes," Jonathon whispered, not meeting Adam's eyes.

"Will you tell me how I'm supposed to go through the rest of my life wondering where my little girls are and if they're okay?"

"I wish I could, Adam. I wish I could," Jonathon replied. His sad gaze locked on Adam's eyes and lingered there.

"The worst part is if Charlotte is still alive, she's thinking I did this to her. She'll grow up hating me. If I could only tell her how much I love her."

There seemed to be nothing left to say. Jonathon promised to pursue any new leads, which they both knew were unlikely to come. Then Adam left. If he were going to survive, he was going to have to try to put the girls out of his mind and get on with his life, such as it was. If only he knew how to deal with the big hole in his heart.

PART 2
DIVERGENT PATHWAYS
1966

CHAPTER TWENTY-NINE
DANA

———•●•———

Dana showed her first sign of musical ability at the age of three. It came about in a rather unexpected way, much to the surprise and delight of her doting mother. Andrea, who believed in exposing her young daughter to as much culture as possible in her early years, had just received yet another classical record album from her record-of-the-month club. Up until this point, Dana had not paid much attention to the constant concertos and sonatas which echoed throughout the house. But today was different. Among the selections on this particular album was *The William Tell Overture*. Dana, who loved watching *The Lone Ranger* with her father, perked up her ears when she heard the familiar theme song.

She listened for a moment, and then announced, "Mommy, that's *The Lone Ranger* song."

Why, yes, it is, darling," said her thrilled mother.

"But they're playing it wrong."

Andrea's brows knitted in confusion. "What do you mean, darling? How are they playing it wrong?"

Dana's chest heaved as she struggled to explain. They're playing it *wrong*," she insisted, lifting her stubborn little chin, her childish voice filled with increasing frustration.

Andrea knelt in front of her daughter. "I'm sorry, darling, but I don't understand what's wrong."

Dana pursed her lips and stomped her foot. "It's *wrong*!" Then she marched to the baby grand piano in the corner of the living room, hoisted herself onto the piano bench, and pecked out the melody to *The Lone Ranger* theme song with two fingers. "*This* is how it's supposed to sound."

Andrea strained to hear the difference. Then suddenly, it dawned on her. Dana was playing the tune in a different *key* than what was on the recording.

"Darling," she cried, in amazement, "do you mean the song is in a different key on the television?"

Dana shrugged. "It's not the same. It's wrong."

But how would she know that? Andrea could hardly contain her excitement until Charles came home.

———•●•———

When at last he appeared, Andrea rushed to meet him at the door. "Charles, wait until you hear what Dana did today."

Charles laughed. Every day it was something else new and extraordinary. Everything Dana did was exceptional to his wife. Nobody would dare tell her that Dana was a normal, healthy three-year-old. To Andrea, Dana was the smartest, most talented, prettiest—and every other superlative adjective one could think of—child in the world.

"Now, Charles, don't you make fun of me. I'm serious. I've always told you Dana's special. Just you listen to *this*."

She called Dana into the room. "Darling, tell Daddy what you told me this afternoon."

Dana frowned.

"About *The Lone Ranger* theme song," prompted Andrea.

"Oh." The child smiled. "Mommy bought a record with *The Lone Ranger* song. But they played it wrong."

"I don't understand," said Charles, looking to his wife to clarify the significance of this observation.

"Neither did I," said Andrea. "But just listen." She turned to Dana. "Darling, go play the song for Daddy, like it's supposed to sound."

"Okay." Dana boosted herself once again onto the piano bench

190

and proceeded to pick out the tune without missing a note.

"Wow, that's good," said Charles, his tone placating. "That's very good, sweetheart."

Andrea gave an exasperated sigh at her husband's condescending attitude. "That's not what I'm trying to show you. Now you listen to *this*." While Dana was finishing her mini-concert, Andrea put her record on, so Charles could compare the two versions.

Charles, as Andrea had done earlier, failed to see the difference.

"See, Daddy?" said the child. "They're playing it wrong."

He shot a helpless look at his wife.

"The record version is in a different *key* than the television version," Andrea explained, with barely concealed patience.

Having a tin ear, Charles didn't fully grasp the significance of this observation, but it sounded important.

Andrea went on. "I think Dana's got natural musical ability. She's only three years old and she can distinguish one key from another, without even hearing them at the same time. Plus, she can pick out a melody on the piano by ear."

While Charles struggled to ascertain whether this ability was truly something special or just another of Andrea's exaggerations, Dana, clearly enjoying all the attention, launched into another piece.

"Here's the first song, the one on the new record," she announced.

Andrea's mouth dropped open. "Charles! That's from the new record album she heard today. It's Shubert's *Ave Maria.* She only heard it once."

This time, Charles was stunned, as the tiny child pounded out the melody to the complicated piece. She stopped abruptly. "I forgot the rest."

"Charles, we've got to find her a teacher. The best."

"I'll do some checking at the university tomorrow."

— • ● • —

The next day, Professor Charles DeVoux, Associate Professor of English at Union University in Schenectady, New York, made some inquiries into locating a music teacher worthy of his daughter's exceptional talent. Because seldom a day went by in which Charles' colleagues were not treated to a detailed account of Dana's "latest," many of his colleagues often rolled their eyes and made snide comments behind his back. Although Charles usually attributed most of the exaggerating of Dana's outstanding achievements to his wife, his colleagues would have disagreed with him. And most of them failed to be as impressed by the child's remarkable accomplishments as her doting parents were. So no one seemed overly eager to hear Charles regale those who had not managed to escape with the newest accomplishment of his precocious daughter.

However, he did end up with a few names of piano teachers, including the woman who was regarded as the number one in the state. Her name was Esther Winstein, and she came highly recommended by several people who knew what they were talking about. Esther Winstein required auditions and refused to take on a child who did not show obvious ability. Charles called her that afternoon.

—— • ● • ——

"Professor DeVoux," came her chilly response, "I don't accept children under the age of six."

"But Miss Winstein," Charles replied, "if you would only—"

"My time is quite valuable, Professor. It is completely out of the question to even consider the absurd possibility of taking on a student at the age of three."

"Please, Miss Winstein. I've heard you are the best."

"I *am* the best, Professor," she answered in a haughty tone. "And that is why I simply don't have the time to waste on—"

"Look, Miss Winstein. I'll pay you whatever you ask if you'll just listen to her. Then if you still feel the same way, I won't bother you anymore."

"It's your money, Professor," she said, her voice conveying her opinion he was throwing the money away. "My fee is twenty-five dollars for an evaluation. Have her at my studio tomorrow at four o'clock."

"Thank you, Miss Winstein. You won't be sorry."

———•●•———

The next day, the nervous parents dressed Dana in her finest red taffeta and patent leather Mary Jane shoes and presented her to the formidable Miss Esther Winstein.

A large-boned, imposing figure in her late sixties, Esther Winstein had seen and heard it all. Impressing her was next to impossible. Most of her pupils were terrified of her not only due to her intimidating physical appearance, but because she was also uncompromisingly demanding. Many a student developed an upset stomach or a severe headache before his or her weekly lesson with Miss Winstein. But in this way, she weeded out those who had what it took from those who didn't. In her opinion, if a student didn't have the ability or the dedication, he was wasting her time and his parents' money.

Although Charles and Andrea were visibly anxious—forcing smiles, wringing their hands, and perching on the edges of their chairs, holding their breath—Dana took the old crone in stride. In all her young life, nobody had ever been anything but enamored with her, so she wasn't particularly worried now.

"All right, young lady," boomed the teacher, in her deep, almost masculine voice, "show me what you can do." Then she sat back with her arms folded across her chest, lips flattened, and eyes narrowed—her dismissive posture showing her intent to burst the bubble of this spoiled brat and her overly indulgent parents.

Displaying no outward signs of fear whatsoever, Dana pushed the large piano bench a little closer to the console and hopped up. Andrea sat forward, clearly dying to coax her young daughter. But one look from the dragon-lady made her hold her tongue.

Even the doting mother was shocked by Dana's performance. Out of the blue, the child had added harmony to her selected tune with her left hand. Although her technique was still quite primitive, Dana played perfectly, not missing a note.

Then she stopped, announcing to the skeptical teacher, "That's how they play *The Lone Ranger* song on TV. This is how it is on the record."

Even Esther Winstein didn't get it at first, but when Dana began to play the music in the new key, her jaw flew open. Charles and Andrea, their eyes darting back and forth between their darling daughter and Miss Winstein, could tell the old bird was stunned.

Dana finished her little recital and turned to face her audience, a look of smug satisfaction on her cherubic face. She didn't really see what all the fuss was about, but it was making her the center of attention more than anything else she had ever done, and she was enjoying it.

Charles and Andrea dared not break the silence. But the unflappable Miss Winstein was truly unnerved.

Finally, she spoke in a hoarse whisper, "Who has been instructing this child?"

Dana's parents exchanged glances. "Why, nobody," said Charles.

"This is incredible. I have been teaching music for forty years, and never in my life have I seen such natural ability in a child. Let alone a child this age."

Charles and Andrea beamed with pride. Dana stayed in position, obviously hoping for a chance to show off a little more.

"Then again," the teacher mused, "Mozart started at the age of three." She pointed a long bony finger at the parents. "Do you *know* what you have here?"

"Of course, we do," Andrea said. "We've always known Dana was special."

"No. No, you don't. I'm talking another Mozart here." The old dragon-lady stood and paced, as her voice rose. "It's going to take a firm hand and lots of discipline to keep her on the path. I can handle that. But *you* . . ." She whirled around, causing Charles and Andrea to jump. "Don't you ruin this child's future."

"What are you talking about?" demanded Charles. "We want what's best for our daughter. Why would we ruin anything for her?"

"I'm not talking about what's best for your daughter, Professor DeVoux. I'm talking about what's best for the music world. You can't treat this extraordinary talent as some whim or passing fancy to be squeezed in around a schedule of dance classes, girl scouts, boyfriends . . ." She waved her hands, running out of examples. "She must dedicate her life solely to music. Do you understand? And nothing must interfere with that."

Andrea spoke up. "She's that good, then?"

Miss Winstein clasped both hands to her head. Through clenched teeth, she answered, "My dear woman, that is what I have been trying to get across to you."

Chastised, Andrea sat back and closed her mouth.

"Well, where do you suggest we go from here?" asked Charles.

The old woman put her bony index finger to her puckered lips and frowned, deep in thought. Then, relaxing her wrinkled face, she withdrew her finger and reflected aloud, "I think twice a week lessons at the beginning. Half-hour sessions. And she should practice for two hours at home every day."

"Two hours," cried Andrea. "But she's only three years old."

Miss Winstein's little bird eyes bored into Andrea's. Andrea lowered her eyes. She began to feel extremely uncomfortable and wondered if they had made a mistake subjecting their darling Dana to this obviously mentally disturbed lady.

"My dear woman," Esther Winstein explained, as if to an exceptionally stupid child, "I'm afraid you fail to grasp the significance of your daughter's ability. I do hope you will not cause her more harm than good in her endeavor to become a great pianist."

"But suppose Dana doesn't want to become a great pianist?" Charles asked.

"She has no choice," Esther Winstein stated. "Her calling has already been determined."

Andrea cast an apprehensive glance at Charles.

"We'll think about it, Miss Winstein," said Charles, standing and reaching into his pocket for his wallet. "Come along, Dana."

"Don't let this child's talent be wasted," implored the old woman. "Please, let me teach her, mold her." She closed her eyes.

"Yes, well, as I said, we'll think about it. Thank you for your time," Charles reiterated in a no-nonsense tone. He deposited twenty-five dollars on the piano. Then, prodding his puzzled daughter and worried wife along, they rushed from the studio.

"What do you think, Charles?" asked Andrea, once they were outside.

"That woman disturbs me," he admitted. "I felt quite uneasy with her." He paused. "Although, she was sure Dana has exceptional ability."

"But we can't decide our daughter's future for her," Andrea protested. "And we certainly can't allow that . . . that *woman* to take total control over her life. Dana's only three years old."

Charles patted her hand. "Let's not worry about it now, dear. I'm sure that what is meant to be will be."

But when Dana continued to display more and more interest in the piano, becoming increasingly more adept at working out melodies strictly by ear, her parents decided she needed some formal training. They didn't take her back to Esther Winstein, however. Instead, they found Mrs. Kennedy, a housewife in their neighborhood, who gave piano lessons to school children at her home in the afternoons.

CHAPTER THIRTY
KATRINA

Dr. Katrina Graham, now PhD, sat in her office simultaneously wrestling with two unrelated problems. The first problem dealt with the chemical reactions occurring within the body when progesterone, the pregnancy hormone, is given orally. Theoretically, if she could just find a way to make the hormone effective when administered by mouth, she could trick the female body into believing it was already pregnant. This would trigger a negative feedback reaction to the pituitary gland in the brain, thus suppressing the release of follicle-stimulating hormone and luteinizing hormone, which would, in turn, suppress ovulation. Thus, a perfect method of birth control. A synthetic progesterone was the answer—one that retained its hormonal-like activity when given orally, as natural progesterone did not survive the digestive enzymes long enough to enter the bloodstream. She would also have to work out the potentially harmful side effects of progesterone, such as chronic stimulation of the endometrial tissues of the uterus and stimulation of the mammary glands, which could possibly lead to an increased risk of uterine or breast cancer. Toying with her chemical structures on paper, she drew in radical groups here and there. Then, with a sigh, she put down her pencil. She couldn't focus on her first problem. Her second problem took up too much of her concentration.

Adam Wallace. How was she ever going to break through the

invisible barrier he had built around himself three years ago? It seemed as though he had erected an impenetrable outer shell in order to keep anyone from getting too close to his heart and hurting him again. She could understand his reluctance to let his guard down—up to a point. After all, he had been through a terrible ordeal. But after all this time, shouldn't he be willing to let go a little, live a little . . . love a little? God knew she loved him. She loved him so much she ached. Oh, they were still best friends—crying on each other's shoulders, working side-by-side, encouraging each other, being there for each other, and sometimes dancing around the possibility of a more intimate relationship. But he had never once said he loved her.

She had to laugh at herself. Imagine. Her, Dr. Katrina Graham, PhD, at twenty-six, with several medical breakthroughs to her credit, who ate, slept, and breathed her work . . . imagine her mooning over some man like a love-sick teenager. It was absurd. Nevertheless, even as her head told her how ridiculous it was, her heart replied she was still a woman in love.

But there was another reason why today, after three years in limbo with Adam, her problem had become so acute. Fenner Pharmaceuticals wanted to transfer her to Los Angeles. Should she just go and forget Adam? It might be easier if she could make a clean break and start over, with total and complete dedication to her work. On the other hand, she had grown quite comfortable having Adam around, even if it wasn't the relationship she wished for. Should she swallow her pride and just out-and-out ask Adam how he felt about her? Should she ask him to go with her to L.A.? She knew how he worshipped Dr. Rothchild. Which of them would he choose, given the choice? Perhaps the answer to that question made her reluctant to delve further.

Katrina shook her head. She never thought she would be in this position. She had never wanted anything but her work, her career. There had never been even the tiniest suggestion in the back of her mind that she would ever find a man who understood her, identified with her. That she should be no different in this regard than all the other members of her sex annoyed her. She had believed herself above all that romantic nonsense.

"Confound it," she muttered. "I can't concentrate."

Temporarily abandoning her efforts, she stood and stretched.

Then she became aware of a great deal of commotion across the hall. Curious, she wandered into the hallway and looked inside the open door to Dr. Rothchild's lab.

Inside, several people stood, all talking at once. One of the technicians popped open a bottle of champagne, which gushed forth, splashing those in the immediate proximity. Quickly, they jumped back, laughing, as the man with the bottle began to pour the bubbly into waiting glasses.

A tendril of irritation squeezed Katrina's gut. Why hadn't she been invited to the party?

"What's the celebration for?" she asked, allowing a petulant tone to creep into her voice.

"Kate," said Adam, leaving the happy circle and coming over to put his arm around her. "We're celebrating Robomycin's approval by the FDA. We just got the news."

"Oh," she replied, still pouting.

"Now don't be hurt, Kate. You were so absorbed with your work. But I was just coming over to tell you, when I saw you in the doorway."

"Oh. All right, then," she said. "Pour me some champagne." She broke through the little crowd surrounding Dr. Rothchild. "Congratulations, Robert. It's wonderful news."

"Ah, Katrina!" boomed the scientist, bestowing a look of gratitude upon her. He looked desperately like a man needing rescuing from his circle of admirers. Clearly uncomfortable in the social atmosphere, he nevertheless had to suffer through the celebration after all the work and waiting for Robomycin's approval. Everyone had worked hard on the drug.

Adam pushed his way to Katrina, handed her the champagne, and put his arm around her again.

"This will completely change oncology protocol," Rothchild said, excitement ringing in his voice. "The studies showed a better response to the drug than even *we* expected. Now we have a fighting chance against cancer!"

His fervor became contagious. Everyone talked at once about the amazing breakthrough. This was *big*—one of the most important discoveries to come out of Fenner labs in years.

"Dr. Rothchild," came a voice from the doorway. "Sydney Lane, Channel Six News. Can you please tell us more about your new wonder drug?"

The well-known reporter shoved his way through the crowd and stuck his microphone under the chin of the surprised scientist. A cameraman, loaded with equipment followed on his heels.

Dr. Rothchild recovered his composure, clearly in his element—explaining the intricate workings and practical applications of his research. Katrina grinned, knowing what poor Sydney Lane was in for.

"Well, Mr. Lane," said the instant celebrity, squinting myopically into the rolling camera, "Robomycin is actually one of the anthracycline antibiotics obtained from a Streptomyces sub-group. Robomycin has several biochemical properties which appear to be relevant to its cytotoxic properties . . ."

As he warmed up, Katrina caught a glimpse of the reporter's face. She knew most of this footage would wind up on the cutting room floor.

" . . . and it appears to be active during all phases of the cell cycle, although maximal effects are observed during the S phase of the cell cycle—"

"Uh, excuse me, Dr. Rothchild," interrupted the reporter, "could you tell us what this means in terms of a medical breakthrough? In English?"

Everyone laughed but Dr. Rothchild, who looked rather startled. Clearing his throat, he said, "It means, in simple English, young man, that we at Fenner Pharmaceuticals have developed a drug that from all early indications may be palliative or possibly, in some cases, curative in certain types of cancer."

"Wow! That's incredible. Please, continue, Dr. Rothchild."

"In English?" asked the scientist, tartly.

"Yes, please," replied Sydney, a spot of red appearing in his cheeks.

"Very well then. For the last three years, Robomycin has undergone rigorous testing in numerous controlled cancer studies. Significant improvement and sometimes apparent cures have been seen with its use, although I would caution you that it is still too early to speculate on long-range effects. However, it has showed considerable promise in the treatment of acute lymphocytic leukemia, certain other leukemias, Hodgkin's and non-Hodgkin's lymphomas, osteogenic sarcomas, breast cancer, ovarian carcinoma, gastric carcinoma, and oat cell carcinoma of the lung.”

“And what side effects have you seen with Robomycin?” asked Sydney Lane. The cameraman moved to the side to get a different angle of the scientist.

“Relatively few. That is the beauty of this drug. There have been some problems with slight decreases in the hemoglobin concentration, as well as the usual leukopenia and thrombocytopenia. These usually resolve in a few days. Some hair loss with chronic use. But not too much in the way of gastrointestinal symptoms. The test subjects have reported very little discomfort during their treatment regimes.”

“Thank you, sir.” The reporter turned to face the camera. “I’m Sydney Lane, Channel Six News. We have just heard from Dr. Robert Rothchild, head of Fenner Pharmaceuticals, the developer of Robomycin, the new miracle drug for curing cancer. Dr. Rothchild, the world thanks you for such a major medical breakthrough.” He signaled to the cameraman to stop the film.

“But young man, I didn’t say Robomycin would cure cancer,” objected Dr. Rothchild. “I *said*—”

“Thank you for your time, Dr. Rothchild,” Sydney interrupted, looking at his watch. “Gotta run.”

The group stood looking after them as the newsmen fled the scene.

“Blasted press,” grumbled the scientist. “Don’t listen to a thing you say and then twist your words all around.”

“Well, look at it this way, Robert,” said Katrina. “Robomycin *is* the best drug we have to fight cancer at this point in time. And there’ll be dozens of new drugs on its heels. It’s only a matter of time until we do have a cure for cancer.”

After the interruption by the news team, the little party began to break up, and people drifted back to their work.

“Well, congratulations again, Robert,” said Katrina, turning to go back to her office.

“Thank you, Katrina. And congratulations to you, too, by the way.”

Adam looked at her, his eyebrows raised in question. “Oh? What for? You’ve already saved the rabbit population from the pregnant women of America.” He chuckled.

His teasing sarcasm failed to amuse Katrina. But before she

could open her mouth to say anything, Robert intervened. "Why on her promotion. Didn't you hear? Katrina's going to head up the new lab on the west coast."

Adam's face fell. "Oh. You didn't tell me, Kate," he said, stinging accusation punctuating his words.

"I only just found out myself," she replied, annoyed at Robert for spilling the beans before she'd had a chance to break the news to Adam.

"Well, congratulations," Adam uttered briskly. "I've got some work to finish up." He left Katrina and Rothchild staring at each other.

"What's the matter with him?" asked Robert.

"Oh, Robert. You really are an ostrich with your head buried in the sand." She turned and headed for the door.

"What did I do?" cried Rothchild at her retreating, stiffened back.

If Katrina had thought she couldn't concentrate before, she knew the rest of the afternoon was now hopeless. She decided to do something she never did—go home early.

———— • ● • ————

After a long soak in a hot bathtub, she felt less on edge. She still hadn't come to any sort of conclusion as to what to do about Adam, but maybe Rothchild's premature announcement was actually a blessing in disguise. Perhaps it would put the burden on Adam to make the first move.

At eight o'clock, her doorbell rang. Looking through the peephole, her heart did a little leap when she saw Adam standing on her porch.

She made herself wait until she counted to ten, then she opened the door.

"Hello, Adam," she greeted, her voice deliberately cool.

He didn't attempt to come in. Instead, he stood shuffling his feet on the doorstep, his eyes darting everywhere but her face. "I just came by to apologize, Kate. I tried to stop by your office, but you were already gone."

"Oh? Apologize for what?" she asked, as if she didn't know.

She didn't invite him in.

Adam still didn't meet her eyes. "For being such a jerk this afternoon. You know. When Rothchild mentioned your promotion."

Katrina kept quiet, waiting for him to go on.

"It took me by surprise, Kate. I just . . . look, do you mind if I come in?"

She stepped aside, arms folded across her chest, chin jutted forward.

"I guess I was hurt that you didn't tell me first," explained Adam. "It seemed like everyone knew but me."

"Everyone? Dr. Rothchild is hardly everyone, Adam. And he is the one who recommended me for the position, after all."

"I know. I was being childish. And I said I was sorry." He looked into her unyielding face. "Why are you being so unforgiving, Kate? Can't you just accept my apology and let's be friends again?"

She forced out a brittle laugh. "Is that what we are, Adam?" She threw up her hands in an "I give up" attitude and turned her back to him.

"Well, of course we're friends. I don't know what I would have done without you these last three years. And I'm going to miss you. Terribly."

She nodded. So now she had her answer. She would not humiliate herself by throwing herself at him. A huge lump lodged in her throat.

"What in the world is the matter with you, Kate? This surely can't be just over my insensitivity this afternoon? Tell me what's wrong."

Angered to find tears welling up in her eyes, she snapped, "Confound it, Adam Wallace. If you don't know, then I'm not going to tell you." With that, she turned and ran from the room, leaving Adam alone in the foyer.

After a minute, he followed her into her bedroom, where she lay weeping into her pillow. He eased himself down on the side of the bed and lightly stroked her back.

"Please go away," she sobbed, her words muffled by the pillow.

Instead, he gently took her in his arms. Almost against her will, she wrapped her arms around him, clinging with a sense of desperation. As her tears subsided, he began placing tentative kisses on her wet face. She responded with an eagerness that explicitly implied what she wanted. But then, just as quickly as the feelings had overtaken her, she pushed him away and searched his wounded eyes.

Poor Adam, he really doesn't have a clue. I'm such a foolish woman.

"Kate, please tell me what's wrong."

Should she tell him? Why not? What difference could it make now, anyway?

"All right, Adam," she replied, looking into his crestfallen, little-boy face. She snatched a tissue from her nightstand and attempted to repair the damage to her face. After a long moment, she took a halting breath and, not bearing to look at him, lowered her eyes.

"It's not your fault. You see, like an idiot, I happened to fall in love with you." She heard him catch his breath. "And since you obviously don't feel the same way about me . . ." She let the words trail off.

"But Kate!" he cried. "I love you, too."

"*What?*" she gasped, her wide eyes meeting his.

"I love you, too. I have for a long time. But I didn't want to interfere with your career. I know how important it is to you. Plus," he said, lowering his eyes, "You deserve better than me. I'm damaged goods."

She stared at him. "What on earth do you mean?"

He sighed. "My past."

Her mouth dropped open. "Adam, none of that is your fault. Don't you see that?"

He shook his head. "I never wanted to put you in the same position as Connie. To have you grow to resent me for holding you back."

"Oh, Adam," she groaned. "That will never happen to us. We're entirely different people. Yes, I want my career, but that doesn't mean I don't want you, too. I love you, Adam." She took a hesitant breath. Her heart pounded so loudly she was sure he could hear it. Then, without thinking further, she blurted out, "Marry me, Adam, and come to L.A. with me!"

CHAPTER THIRTY-ONE
CHARLOTTE

———•●•———

In the three years Charlotte had been at the Escambia County Children's Home in Pensacola, she had learned a few things. First of all, don't make friends. With the high turnover in the number of children coming and going, there were few who stayed for any length of time. Most of the children were just there temporarily while families were going through domestic problems or dealing with a drug or alcohol addiction. Some were runaways who were eventually returned to their parents. Some were the victims of child abuse who needed a safe shelter while other relatives were located. A few were there while a single parent was sick, when there were no other relatives to care for them. But there were very few who were orphans in the true sense of the word. It seemed everyone had some family. Hardly anyone had the actual misfortune of having two deceased parents and nowhere else to go.

Of course, if Charlotte were honest with herself, she wasn't actually an orphan, either. She had grandparents. Thankfully, however, nobody knew about them. And her father hadn't died. He had abandoned them. But he might as well be dead for all the good he was doing her.

When she had first come to the home, she had tried to make friends. But as she watched them leave, one by one, she had finally given up on building any lasting relationships. It was better not to become fond of someone, only to be sad when they were taken away. Thus, most of the children found her to be rather aloof, mistaking her forced indifference for snobbishness. She didn't worry too much about her lack of popularity. If a particular child didn't like her, chances were that child wouldn't be around long, anyway.

At first, she had grieved over her loss of Diana. Strangely enough, she seemed rather resigned to the death of her mother, but somehow, she had always pictured she and Diana would be together. She wondered why the people who had adopted Diana hadn't wanted her. In the beginning, she thought someone else would adopt her. But as the weeks turned into months, and then finally into years, she realized that adoption apparently wasn't all that simple.

Although rather lonely, after a while, even that didn't bother her so much. She learned to be happy being alone, and often spent her spare time drawing pictures or writing stories.

School, however, proved more difficult. There, she had to endure being in a class with normal children, who had mothers and fathers, and who regarded her as something of an oddity. Children, being what they were, could be quite cruel to someone who was different, and Charlotte was no exception. At first, she had been hurt when she was shunned or made fun of by the other kids. Since few of the others wanted to be social outcasts either, there weren't many willing to risk ridicule by being friends with her. Occasionally, she was lucky enough to have one of the other children from the home in her class. Then they could stick together. But it was usually only temporary, so Charlotte didn't count on always having another outsider to pal around with.

Sometimes, she simply refused to go out for recess. It was bad enough in the classroom, where she was under the protection of the teacher, but when forced to fend for herself on the playground, the teasing often became unbearable. Since she was well-behaved and quiet, the teachers usually gave in to her requests to stay inside, and she would sit silently at her desk drawing her pictures or writing her stories. Sometimes, a sympathetic teacher would attempt to engage her in conversation. Although always polite, Charlotte was no more outgoing than she absolutely had to be. It was better not to become too dependent on the friendship of an adult, either. In the end, while they were nicer than children, they deserted you, too.

Two other factors accounted for her lack of popularity in

school—her keen intelligence and her beauty. Learning came easy to Charlotte, who just naturally absorbed new facts, whereas other children often had to struggle. She usually completed her assignments in half the time it took the others; thus, the teachers, in order to keep her occupied, often let her do special tasks or go to the library. This favoritism became an intense source of jealousy among her peers. Then, on top of being an orphan and a teacher's pet, she had beautiful, curly blonde hair and unusual, deep blue, almost violet eyes. To the other little girls who were cursed with straight hair and endured the discomfort of their mothers' curling irons or home perms, Charlotte's blonde curls constituted a sore point. And while her looks were enough to attract the attention of even the most confirmed "anti-girl" young boys, her brain was enough to turn them off again.

It was a far cry from her happy, earlier years, when she had been such a sociable little chatterbox with lots of friends. But for Charlotte, her dependence on only herself became her survival.

CHAPTER THIRTY-TWO
ADAM

When out of the blue, Katrina announced she was in love with him, it had completely caught Adam off guard. He had never dreamed a woman like Katrina could be romantically interested in him. She had always been so adamant about her goal to climb the ladder of success. He always thought, or so he told himself anyway, that Katrina was only being nice to him because she felt sorry for him. Besides, she was nice to everybody. It was true they had become good friends, but how could a woman like that, with her vivacious beauty and extraordinary intelligence, possibly be in love with a common man like him?

He had to admit he was in love with her, too, although he had never actually allowed himself to acknowledge it. After all, where could it lead? She was so far above him—a PhD, making three or four times as much money as he made, developing new pharmaceuticals as easily as some women might knit a scarf. And with a senior vice-president of the company for a father, no less.

And what was he by comparison? An aging pharmacy student, struggling to finish his master's degree, while working as an errand boy. No, it would have been too preposterous to even think she might reciprocate his feelings. Of course, part of what attracted him to her was his awe of her—the uncanny ability she had to do everything well and still be human enough to relate to the less-gifted individuals who worked under her. Unlike Rothchild, who lived within his own narrow confines of the lab, Katrina was interested in everything and everyone around her.

But what could she possibly see in him? He wasn't being overly humble. He truly didn't see anything out of the ordinary about himself that would attract Katrina. Surely, if she wanted, she could have had her pick of dozens of men. But she had never displayed the slightest interest in other men, and she had certainly never talked to him about a relationship with anyone else. He had always thought she lived for her work alone. Hadn't she told him her goal in life was to become another Robert Rothchild, only greater?

He tried to recall what they had talked about when they had spent so many quiet evenings together. The lab, obviously, and their research, and in the beginning, a lot about Adam's family and his anguish over losing them. But had they ever really talked about *her*? He couldn't remember. Perhaps that was why Katrina apparently had the impression he should have known her better than he did. Was he being obtuse? He didn't think so, but then perhaps he was also a little afraid of falling in love again. Maybe his misunderstanding was deliberate, unintentional as he tried to tell himself it was. He had come close to telling her he loved her on several occasions, but always stopped himself, not wanting to appear a fool. Now this amazing woman was his fiancé, and he had to periodically reassure himself it wasn't a dream.

———•●•———

It was to be a large wedding. Katrina wanted a lavish affair with all the trimmings. Although Adam would have preferred a quick, quiet ceremony, he went along with what his excited bride-to-be wanted. After all, it was her first and, hopefully, only wedding. He supposed all women harbored a secret desire for their own big day in the spotlight, so he resigned himself to grin and bear it. Watching her fuss over all the last-minute preparations, he couldn't help but be amused at the bundle of nerves his cool and competent little PhD had become.

He had cause for nervousness himself, however, when it came time to meet his future in-laws. From all he had heard, Trenton

Graham, in particular, was an intimidating, formidable man.

"Will you relax?" Katrina fussed at him as they drove out to her parents' home. "They'll love you."

Adam sweated, feeling like a teenager who had been caught in the backseat of a car.

They pulled up in front of an impressive colonial-style home.

"Come on," she said, as the reluctant Adam tried to stall the inevitable moment for as long as possible by taking his time getting out of the car.

Katrina took hold of his arm and propelled him up the sidewalk, stopping in front of an ornate front door with beveled glass. Before they had a chance to knock, the door opened, and an attractive woman in her mid-fifties, with stylishly frosted hair swept up in a French twist at the nape of her neck, stood beaming in the foyer.

"Katrina," she cried, hugging her daughter. Then she extended a gracious hand. "And you must be Adam."

Just as Adam grasped the offered hand, she reached up, pulling him into a hug, as well. Then, holding him at arm's length, scrutinizing him, she said, "Well, he's certainly a handsome one. I can see why you are smitten."

"Oh, Mother." A blush spread across Katrina's face.

"Come in, please," her mother said, her voice cheerful and welcoming. "Trenton is dying to meet you."

Adam could see where Katrina got her vitality. Although the woman must be twice Katrina's age, she bounced from the foyer into the elegantly furnished living room like an excited child. Following her at a distance, Adam got his first look at the imposing Trenton Graham, senior vice-president of Fenner Pharmaceuticals. He stood by the marble fireplace, a cocktail glass in one hand and an unlit cigar in the other.

"Trenton, darling," gushed Mrs. Graham, "this is Adam."

Although not a physically intimidating person, being somewhat on the short, stocky side, Trenton Graham's sharp, hawk-like eyes could melt a glacier. Fixing Adam with a cold glare, he stuck his cigar in his mouth and offered his free hand to Adam.

"Nice to meet you, sir," Adam stammered, pumping the man's pudgy hand with his own clammy one.

"Yes, well," growled the older man, his words somewhat

inarticulate as he chewed on his cigar.

"Katrina, I have a million details to go over with you," said her mother. "We'll leave the men to get acquainted while I get my list. Come into the kitchen."

Throwing Adam a helpless glance, Katrina left him to face her father. Adam stood with his hands in the way, trying to figure out what to do with them.

"Drink?" muttered the older man.

"Please," croaked Adam. It would give his hands something to do.

This is ridiculous. You're thirty-four years old, for crying out loud.

Without asking Adam what he wanted, Trenton Graham poured a generous martini from a blender on the bar and handed it to Adam. Then, grunting as he lowered himself onto the taupe leather sofa, he motioned for Adam to join him.

Adam accepted the glass and sank into the soft cushion, leaving a large gap between himself and his future father-in-law, and took a sip of his drink to wet his dry throat. He didn't particularly care for martinis, but he kept his mouth shut. A trickle of sweat worked its way in an agonizing, slow path down his back. He attempted to stem its progress by sitting back and digging his upper torso into the plush cushion behind him.

They sat in an uncomfortable silence for several minutes, during which Adam tried to appear interested in looking around at everything in the expensively furnished room except Trenton. His blank mind worked feverishly to come up with a scrap of scintillating conversation. He wondered why Trenton didn't light the cigar, but decided against pursuing that topic. Cigar smoke would only make his stomach queasier.

"So, Alan," barked Trenton, abruptly breaking the uneasy silence, "you know Katrina's our only child." He stated the remark as a fact rather than a question.

"Yes, sir," Adam replied, his voice hoarse around the dryness in his throat. He swallowed and took another tentative sip of his unappetizing drink. He didn't bother correcting what he suspected was a deliberate mistake of his name.

"And you know what she's accomplished in her life. She's no ordinary woman."

"Oh, no, sir." Adam could feel the sweat now beading up on his brow and he stifled the urge to wipe it off. His shirt collar suddenly seemed overly tight and strangling.

The older man turned and fixed Adam with a scowl. Removing the cigar from his mouth, he said, "I don't mind telling you, young man, that I'm not pleased about this marriage."

Heat rose up Adam's neck into his face. His heart began to pound, and his gut clenched. He felt the fingers of his free hand digging into the edge of the sofa, and forced them to stop, wiping his damp palm on his pants.

They'll love you. Katrina had promised. Right now, he wasn't feeling the love. He didn't know whether he was expected to respond to Trenton's statement or keep quiet. He opted for the later.

"Of course, her mother's thrilled," grumbled the older man. "Says it's unnatural for a woman to be so involved in her career. Thinks every woman should get married and have kids." He stopped and stared Adam in the eye.

Adam scooted forward, forcing his eyes to meet Trenton's, and cleared his throat. "I can assure you, sir, Katrina's career will have top priority. I won't do anything to hinder her."

Trenton Graham snorted. "You say that now, Alan, but what's to happen if a baby comes along? Babies do have a way of changing one's plans, in case you don't realize it."

Oh, don't I.

"It's 'Adam,' sir."

The older man gave no indication he'd heard. "I can't understand how such a brilliant girl like Katrina managed to get herself in this situation in the first place," he grumbled under his breath, but loud enough for Adam to hear.

"Mr. Graham," said Adam, "I understand your feelings. But I love Katrina and she loves me. We'll work things out if or when a baby comes."

"Hmph." The older man snorted again. "A brilliant career and a PhD down the drain in exchange for dirty diapers. She could have gotten her M.R.S. degree a lot easier." Again, he muttered as though to himself, but loud enough for Adam could hear.

"That's not going to happen, I promise you."

His future father-in-law wrinkled his nose and waved his hand, effectively ending the conversation. Adam reached up and swiped his finger under the strangling collar of his shirt.

The older man sat, apparently lost in his own thoughts, while Adam fervently wished Katrina and her mother would finish their business and come to his rescue.

Then, out of the blue, Trenton Graham spoke softly, "Just take good care of her. Because if you don't, you'll have *me* to answer to." He sounded almost pitiful and Adam almost felt sorry for him.

To Adam's relief, at that moment, the women reappeared.

"Oh, good. You're getting along," said Katrina.

Adam shot her a look of disbelief.

"Dinner's almost ready," announced her mother, "let's all get to the table."

— • ● • —

Adam remembered very little about the actual wedding ceremony. He recalled standing at the altar in front of the packed church with the minister and Dr. Rothchild, who was his best man, hoping he wouldn't faint. Then, as the organist began playing the Bridal Chorus and he got his first glimpse of Katrina coming down the aisle on the arm of her scowling father, his fears dissipated. To say that Katrina was a radiant bride was an understatement. Of course, all brides were radiant, but Katrina . . . well, she gave a whole new meaning to the word. Even through the filmy veil he could see her sparkling green eyes and her sunny smile. And to think he had almost let her get away.

The rest of the ceremony passed in a blur as they exchanged their vows and the soloist sang, and then the minister gave the benediction and pronounced them husband and wife.

At the reception, Katrina danced the obligatory first dance with her father, who then handed her over to Adam, admonishing him, "Remember what I told you, Adam."

Adam smiled.

As they danced, the love for his new bride swelled in his heart to the point he was afraid it would burst. Surely his feeble heart couldn't contain this much love.

"Adam, I'm so happy," she declared, tears shimmering in her eyes as she looked up into his face.

For the first time in his life, Adam knew true love. This marriage would work. God had given him another chance. This time things would be different. He wouldn't make any of the same mistakes. He would make Katrina happy. Anything she wanted.

—•●•—

With the wedding and the move and the stress of starting a new job, Katrina didn't pay much attention to her body's changes. However, within a few weeks, Katrina confirmed what she suspected, using the pregnancy test she had developed. She was pregnant.

Adam was euphoric at first. He had another chance to be a father. This child would want for nothing. But then a piercing grief assailed him as visions of his daughters filled his mind. Although the pain of his loss always stayed with him, it had dulled a bit through the years. Now, the pain became agonizing.

"Please, God," he prayed, "let this baby be a boy."

Then he began to worry about Katrina. Was he going to be responsible for destroying another woman's dreams?

Please, God, I can't bear that.

How was this baby going to affect her? Would she have to give up her life's work? And what would this baby do to his own career? Although Adam was hardly in Katrina's league, he had come a long way in three years. Was all that going to end?

CHAPTER THIRTY-THREE
CHARLOTTE

In the spring, a new student enrolled in Charlotte's third-grade class. Her most notable attribute was her obvious limp. She was a small, plain child, with mousy brown hair braided into two short pigtails, and large, puppy-dog brown eyes that made her look as if she were constantly begging for something.

On the playground at recess, Charlotte observed the new child from a distance. Charlotte had been slighted too many times to take the initiative anymore. The newcomer stood on the periphery of a group of children, watching as the others played jump rope or tag. Nobody asked her to join them. After a while, she wandered away and sat by herself in the corner of the fenced area. Then she glanced in Charlotte's direction.

Charlotte tried to look away, but it was too late. The little girl struggled to her feet and limped over to where Charlotte stood.

"Hi," she greeted. "What's your name?"

"Charlotte Wallace." Charlotte's tone invited no further conversation. It wouldn't do any good to be friendly with this girl. She'd just find out Charlotte was an orphan and shun her like everyone else. Maybe Charlotte should save her the trouble. "I'm an orphan."

The child stared at her with interest. "Oh. How awful. Did your mother and father die?"

Well, that had been a mistake. She had only succeeded in

arousing the girl's curiosity. Now she was going to have to play "twenty questions."

"Yeah." Charlotte turned away, not wanting to explain any more.

"How did they die?" the child persisted.

"What's wrong with your leg?" asked Charlotte, whirling around, turning the tables on the child's rude questions.

The girl looked taken aback. Then she shrugged. "I was born like this. One leg's shorter than the other. I have to wear a special shoe."

Charlotte's eyes were drawn to the girl's feet. She noticed that one shoe was thicker than the other. Now *she* became curious. "Does it hurt?"

"No. But I can't run very fast." She gazed with obvious longing over to where the others were playing.

It dawned on Charlotte that she might have a soulmate. "Do people make fun of you?" she asked, already knowing the answer.

"Sometimes," admitted the girl. "My mother says not to let it bother me, but . . ." She shrugged again. "Sometimes I'd just like to be like everybody else."

"Yeah," Charlotte agreed. "What's your name?"

"Amy Klein." She remained quiet for a minute. "Why are you standing here by yourself?"

"Because the others don't want to play with me. I told you. I'm an orphan."

Amy's brow wrinkled in a frown. "But that's terrible. You can't help it if your parents are dead. Why should it matter to them?"

"Why should it matter because of your leg?"

"I guess we're both different," said Amy. "But I'll be your friend if you want."

Against her will, Charlotte felt a spark of hope. But before she allowed herself to be drawn into another friendship that would be ripped away, she made sure Amy was going to be around for a while. Amy assured Charlotte she would. Her father had bought a marina, the fulfillment of a life's dream for him, and the family expected to settle in the area permanently. Also, her mother's parents lived nearby. Amy confided she had been lonely, as she was not only handicapped, but an only child. Charlotte felt her own loneliness responding to Amy's. At last Charlotte had a friend. A friend who needed her, too. A friend who wouldn't be moving away just when they had grown close.

One day, Amy invited Charlotte to come home with her after school. Charlotte's heart gave a skip of excitement. Then her face fell.

"I don't know if I'll be allowed."

"Well, you won't know unless you ask," insisted Amy. "Here's what we'll do. My mother always picks me up after school because . . ." She paused. "Because I can't walk very far. We'll ask her to drive you to the orphanage so you can get permission."

Charlotte laughed, her brain conjuring up images from *Oliver Twist*. "They don't call it an orphanage." Then she became a little anxious. "What will your mother say? About me, I mean?"

"Oh, she can't wait to meet you," Amy said. "I talk about you all the time at home."

"Really?" Charlotte didn't think she was important enough for anyone to talk about, but she was flattered, nevertheless. "Well, okay, then."

It was agreed. The two little girls looked forward to a normal after-school friendship with such happy anticipation that they found it difficult to get through the rest of the day.

Three o'clock finally arrived, and Amy hurried Charlotte out to the curb as fast as her deformed leg would go. Her mother had just pulled up.

Amy opened the car door and breathlessly cried, "Mommy, this is Charlotte, the one I was telling you about. The *orphan*."

Charlotte hung back a little. At the word "orphan," she winced.

"Amy," scolded her mother. "Don't be rude." Then, leaning across the seat, Mrs. Klein said, "I'm sorry, Charlotte. Amy gets a little carried away sometimes. She didn't mean to hurt your feelings. Anyway," she said, her face breaking into a soft smile, "I'm very happy to meet you. I'm Mary Klein."

Mrs. Klein, a delicate, gentle-looking woman, had the same light brown hair and eyes of her daughter, but she was much prettier. She had a sweet, natural smile that formed little creases around the corners of her mouth and eyes.

"Mommy, will you take us over to the orphanage . . . I mean to the children's home so Charlotte can ask permission to come over to our house and play? Please?"

"Would you like to come over, dear?" Mary Klein's eyes searched Charlotte's in a way that seemed almost pleading.

Puzzled at first, Charlotte realized that perhaps Amy didn't have many friends.

Charlotte nodded. "Yes, ma'am, if it's okay."

"Of course, it's all right," said Mary. "We'd love to have you. Hop in, girls."

Charlotte still felt a bit shy, but Amy's enthusiasm soon rubbed off. By the time they had obtained the necessary permission and driven to Amy's house, Charlotte was giggling and chattering, completely at ease with Amy and her mother.

The Kleins lived in a recently renovated old house. The outside wood had been repainted an elegant cream with brown trim. A broad, wooden porch wrapped around the front of the house, and two swings hung from the porch roof. Inside, the floorboards creaked when walked on, but the beautiful, original hardwood floors had been polished to a brilliant shine. The heavenly aroma of freshly baked cookies drifted into the foyer from somewhere near the back of the house.

"I made oatmeal cookies," said Amy's mother.

"Later. Come on, Charlotte, I want to show you my room." Amy grabbed Charlotte's hand and dragged her away from the enticing cookies.

Charlotte followed Amy up a narrow staircase opposite the front door to a large room at the back of the house. Charlotte's eyes took in the delightful bedroom with a slanted ceiling, under which the children could stand, but adults could not. Amy's high, canopied bed occupied the opposite wall. Charlotte had never seen a bed so magnificent outside of storybooks. A frilly, starched white dust ruffle covered the entire foot and sides of the bed, and a thick, padded white comforter lay in perfect geometric configuration over the top. Several pleated, lacy pillows in various pastel colors rested atop the bed, with dolls and stuffed animals nestled among them.

Every toy and game imaginable crowded the rest of the room. A large dollhouse took up most of the third wall, and a child-sized table and chairs sat against the fourth. Two floor-to-ceiling windows in the shorter wall overlooked a huge backyard with a small vegetable garden. A beautiful apple tree in full blossom shaded a small doghouse.

"Oh," cried Charlotte, trying to take everything in. "You have a dog, too?"

"Yes. Her name is Sissy."

"Wow," murmured Charlotte, her voice conveying the small pang of envy in her heart. "I've always wanted a dog. Can we go play with her?"

"Sure." They went back downstairs and out to the backyard where they were greeted by a non-descript animal of questionable breeding. About the size of a small beagle, with wiry, tan hair and long, floppy ears, Sissy surely ranked among the world's happiest dogs, even if she would not win any canine beauty contests. She barked, wagging her tail in furious glee, and dropped a red rubber ball at Charlotte's feet, obviously hoping for a game of fetch.

Glad to oblige, Charlotte picked up the ball and hurled it to the far corner of the yard. She and Amy laughed as they watched the tireless beast return the ball again and again. Then finally, when Sissy's tongue hung out in exhaustion and the children grew tired of the game, Amy's mother called them in for milk and cookies.

Sitting in Mary's kitchen, nibbling on homemade oatmeal cookies, Charlotte thought this was the happiest she had ever been. At least, the happiest she had been in a long time. She felt a little jealous of Amy, who was surrounded by so much, and didn't even seem to realize what all she had. But then a twinge of guilt overcame her, and Charlotte thought about the fact that Amy would always be crippled. She would never be able to run and play like the other kids.

After their snack, Amy took Charlotte back upstairs, where they played with the dollhouse until it was time for Charlotte to leave. The time had passed much too quickly.

Reluctantly, Charlotte rose from the floor.

"I wish you didn't have to leave," Amy said, putting Charlotte's own thoughts into words.

"Yeah, me, too." Charlotte thought of the lonely weekend stretching ahead of her.

"But maybe you can come back tomorrow," Amy said, brightening. "Then we could spend the whole day together. You could stay for lunch. And maybe some time you could spend the night." Her excitement grew as she formed plans.

Charlotte couldn't imagine anything better. Her eyes lit up. "Do you think I could?"

"Sure. My mom and dad will say yes. Would you be allowed?" Charlotte frowned. She didn't know. But she sure hoped so.

As it turned out, getting permission to spend time with the Kleins was fairly easy, as long as Amy's parents were willing to drive Charlotte back and forth to the home. And they were happy to do so, for Amy's sake. Both Mary and her husband, Neal, doted on Amy, and had suffered along with her over her loneliness. Charlotte had been an answer to their prayers. Different and lonely herself, Charlotte filled a need in Amy's life, just as their family filled a need in hers.

Charlotte ended up spending a lot of time at Amy's house, sometimes even spending the night in the big, overstuffed bed, where they would lie for hours talking and giggling until Mary or Neal would come in and gently tell them to go to sleep.

As the weather grew warmer, Mary often took them to the beach. Surprisingly, although slow on land, Amy was an excellent swimmer. Charlotte, who had never learned to swim, stayed in the shallow water, afraid to venture out too far.

"Why didn't you ever learn to swim?" asked Amy, with her usual blunt questioning that Charlotte had grown accustomed to.

Charlotte answered before she thought. "My daddy was going to teach me. But the summer he was supposed to teach me, he abandoned us."

They all stared at her.

"But I thought you said he was dead," Amy said, confusion on her face.

Charlotte immediately realized her slip-up.

"Well," she replied, "he's dead now." *Or at least he should be.*

CHAPTER THIRTY-FOUR
DANA

———•●•———

Dana's first piano recital was held at the Oakridge Elementary School on a Saturday afternoon in April. A small gathering of proud, expectant parents sat fidgeting in the first few rows of the school auditorium waiting for the moment when their little darling took the stage and showed up all the other lesser-talented kids. Mrs. Kennedy kept her dozen pupils safely tucked away backstage where she tried, without much success, to keep the noise level down.

The budding musicians ranged in age from about seven to fourteen, except for little Dana, who, at the age of four-and-a-half, was clearly the class pet. Most of the older children showed protectiveness toward the fragile, doll-like little girl, who resembled a storybook princess in her full, white muslin dress with its wide, bright blue sash. They obviously assumed this awful ordeal of having to perform in public must be twice as traumatic for a tiny child Dana's age.

Dana, however, was not the least bit nervous. On the contrary. Not only was she "somebody" in this elite group of older children, but she was actually going to be allowed to play in front of grown-ups. She couldn't wait for her turn.

The first performer, a red-headed boy of about eight, was to play a simplified arrangement of Bach's *Minuet in G*. He took his time as he shuffled to the center of the stage and bowed. Then, seating himself at the piano, he adjusted the bench up and back, up and back, until unable to stall any longer, he finally placed his trembling hands on the keyboard. His technique left a lot to be desired—taking extreme liberties with the strict tempo as he pounded out the loud, monotonous notes—but it was par for what one expected to hear in a piano recital of grade-school children. When he finished, he jumped up, a look of overwhelming relief on his face, took a quick bow, his hair falling into his face, and hurried backstage as the audience clapped its polite applause.

The boy sank into his chair, wearing a huge smile, as the others kidded and complimented him.

Dana studied him and the others. Then, climbing down from her chair, she marched over to him and announced, "You made ten mistakes, Kevin. I counted."

The boy's mouth dropped open. "Oh, yeah?" he shot back. "Well, let's see how great *you* do, Little Miss Know-it-All!"

Unruffled, Dana went back to her chair, where a couple of the older girls attempted to stifle their giggles.

The next girl onstage played Beethoven's *Fur Elise.* Although her phrasing showed lack of artistic judgement, she was somewhat better than Kevin.

When she finished and escaped backstage, Dana said, "The middle's supposed to be soft, Debbie. Why'd you play it so loud?"

The astonished pre-teen stared at the miniature critic. "So who asked *you*, anyway?" she snarled. She moved as far away from Dana as possible.

By the time Dana's turn came at the end of the recital, she had managed to alienate most everyone in the class. She didn't know why everybody was so hostile. She had just told the truth. But it didn't bother her. If they wanted to act that way, so what?

The other students watched and waited for Dana to fall flat on her little angelic face as she strode with confidence across the stage to the enormous grand piano. There were whispers in the audience of how "cute" and "adorable" she was, as she stood, unsmiling, by the bench and announced, "My name is Dana DeVoux and I'm going to play *The Swan* by Camille Saint-Saens."

Chuckles filtered through the small crowd as the endearing little child struggled to climb onto the high bench.

"Isn't she precious?" gushed one old lady, a bit too loud.

But the platitudes stopped abruptly the moment those tiny hands hit the keyboard. The placating smirks and whispers gave way to looks of disbelief as the audience listened to the soft, legato running chord in the left hand and the sweet melody in the right build to a crescendo with the first run. Dana's tiny body swayed with the rhythm, lost in the beauty of the music, seemingly unaware of the dozens of eyes focused upon her. After building up to a mezzo-forte climax, she made an abrupt decrescendo, her notes becoming increasingly softer to the end, and with a slight ritard, ended her final notes so faintly the audience had to strain to hear.

At first, after she finished, a complete silence filled the auditorium, as most of the audience sat too stunned to react. Then a thunder of applause rang out, with several people jumping to their feet and clapping. Nobody had ever heard anything like this before at one of Mrs. Kennedy's piano recitals.

Afterward, at the small cookies and punch reception held in the school cafeteria, everyone buzzed about the tiny protégé. The other children, many of whom realized that even their own parents regarded their performances as second-rate compared to Dana's, stood in an unhappy group off to the side, making snide comments.

Andrea and Charles beamed with pride, surrounded by a constant mass of people, all talking about the greatness of their daughter. Mrs. Kennedy looked rather bewildered, as though she were somehow responsible for the child's exceptional performance but wasn't quite sure exactly how.

"Why can't you do that with my Kevin?" complained one mother. "If you can get *that* child to play so well, why can't you do more for him?"

"Well, you see," stammered Mrs. Kennedy, who was fortunately interrupted by someone else before having to think of a diplomatic way to tell the poor woman her son had no musical talent.

Dana sat alone, munching a handful of cookies, watching her parents accept their due compliments, while the other students glared at her. She had learned an important lesson today. It was lonely at the top.

CHAPTER THIRTY-FIVE
CHARLOTTE

A s June and summer vacation approached, Charlotte worried about how her friendship with Amy would fare. She needn't have been concerned, however, for Amy was making all kinds of plans for the two of them. It didn't look as though Charlotte was going to be spending much time brooding all by herself at the home.

On the first weekend after school let out for the summer, Amy invited Charlotte to spend the day with them at her grandparents' house just across town. Charlotte wondered what the grandparents were like. Were they like Mrs. McCarthy, her "adopted" grandmother who babysat her, or were they like her real grandparents? An involuntary shudder ran down her spine at the thought of them. She would have to be careful not to accidentally mention them. Until recently, it had not been difficult, for nobody had gotten close enough to her to be taken into her confidence. But now she had a dangerous tendency to forget herself in her happy chattering with her completely open friend, Amy, and Amy's warm mother, Mary, who always seemed as interested in Charlotte as she did her own daughter.

Early Saturday morning, the Kleins swung by the home to pick up Charlotte. Although she had become quite comfortable with Neal and Mary, Charlotte was not particularly looking forward to meeting a new set of strangers. Amy, as usual, did not notice Charlotte's discomfort, as she rambled on excitedly about how much fun they were going to have. It seemed that Grandma Bess, as Amy called her, was the world's greatest cook and would no doubt have all kinds of culinary delights waiting for them. And Grandpa Tony, who had made her massive wooden dollhouse, was the best grandfather who ever lived. Although there were other grandchildren, Amy informed Charlotte, Amy was, by far, the favorite.

"Amy," fussed her mother, in an ineffectual scolding.

"Well, you know it's true," Amy shot back.

"Nevertheless, it's not polite to talk about such things. Besides, your grandparents love all their grandchildren equally."

Amy's smug look spoke otherwise. Charlotte wondered if perhaps Amy's grandparents went a little overboard in spoiling her to make up for her handicap.

They pulled up in front of an attractive white stucco house with bright blue window boxes full of colorful flowers. Charlotte saw a swing set and a small plastic wading pool in the backyard. Not waiting for her parents, Amy rushed Charlotte up the steps to the porch and into the house, banging the screen door in her haste.

"Grandma Bess? Grandpa Tony?" she called out. "We're here."

Amy's grandmother emerged from the kitchen, wiping her hands on her apron.

"Amy," she greeted, as the child ran to her, throwing her small arms around the woman's ample waist. "How's Grandma's little lamb?"

Just then, an older man appeared, a broad smile spreading across his wrinkled face. "Come give your Grandpa Tony a hug," he ordered.

Amy tore herself away from her grandmother and ran in the other direction, throwing herself at her grandfather. He swept her off the floor and swung her around, as she squealed with delight. By that time, Mary and Neal had come in the house, exchanging hugs and kisses with the older couple. Charlotte stood feeling out of place, waiting for someone to notice her.

Finally, Mary turned to her with a sweet smile. "We've brought someone we want you to meet," she said. "This is Amy's friend, Charlotte. And Charlotte, dear, these are my parents, Elizabeth and Anthony Jordan. Amy calls them 'Grandma Bess' and

'Grandpa Tony.'"

Grandma Bess looked like the product of her own good cooking, short and plump, with a ruddy complexion and short gray hair. Grandpa Tony stood taller, but also appeared quite well-fed, with a paunch overlapping his belt buckle. A few scraggly white hairs stuck straight up from his almost bald scalp.

"We're happy to have you, Charlotte," said Grandma Bess. "If you girls go out into the kitchen, I've got a surprise for you."

"Yay!" cried Amy, clutching Charlotte's hand and dragging her along. "Gingerbread men."

"Now, Amy, you've just had breakfast," said Mary.

Ignoring her mother, Amy grabbed a handful of the goodies and ordered Charlotte to "come outside and play."

———— • ● • ————

Mary and her mother sat at the kitchen table watching the children at play.

"I'm so happy Amy found Charlotte," mused Mary. "They seem to get along so well together."

Her mother frowned. "Awfully pretty child."

"Yes, she is." Mary sighed. "She's a nice little girl, too. Such a shame, being an orphan."

"Almost *too* pretty, if you ask me," continued her mother, a touch of disapproval in her tone.

"Why, Mother," said Mary, "why is that a bad thing?"

Her mother shrugged. "Bound to be trouble later."

"What do you mean?" asked Mary, bewildered by her mother's attitude.

Her mother pursed her lips. Mary could sense an inner struggle with her mother as to whether to speak her mind or keep quiet.

Finally, she replied, "I just don't want to see Amy get hurt, that's all."

"I don't understand what you're talking about."

Her mother gave a long, exasperated sigh. "Do I have to spell it out for you, Mary? Very well, then. How long do you think this friendship will last? That child will use Amy for all she can get, and then suddenly, one day, she's not going to want to be saddled with a handicapped playmate anymore. Then she'll break Amy's heart."

"Oh, Mother, I hardly think so."

"I wouldn't be so sure."

"Charlotte has her own problems," said Mary. "I think she needs Amy just as much as Amy needs her." She paused, debating whether to go on. Then, in a defiant voice, she said, "And I'll tell you something else. Neal and I have been thinking of adopting her."

The blood drained from her mother's face. "Oh, Mary," she whispered. "You can't be serious."

"Yes, we are," declared Mary, immediately sorry she had mentioned anything to her mother. She and Neal had only casually discussed the possibility. There had been no definite plans. But now her mother had forced her hand.

"You're making a big mistake," her mother warned. "There'll be trouble with that one. I promise you."

———•◉•———

During the course of the summer, they visited Amy's grandparents several times. Charlotte could never quite put her finger on why, but she could detect an obvious coolness toward her on the part of the older couple, especially the grandmother. But Amy never seemed to notice.

———•◉•———

One of the adventures Charlotte loved best was when Neal took the girls down to his marina. They would play for hours in the cuddy cabins of the display models or watch the mechanics working on the strange-looking outboard motors. Sometimes, they were allowed to go out for a test drive with one of the mechanics. Invariably, the young workers showed off for the girls, going too fast while they bounced across the rough waves, the girls giggling with delight. Other times, they lounged on the docks, watching boats coming in and going out. There was always activity going on somewhere.

When Neal wasn't busy, he instructed the girls in marine terminology and pointed out various differences in boats. Sailing was his passion, and soon, Charlotte and Amy were well versed in the art of distinguishing cutters from sloops, yawls from ketches, and the numerous rigs of the schooners. They would argue over whether a particular vessel was a gaff-headed yawl or a jib-headed yawl, and usually, the boat would be long gone before they agreed to consult someone in authority to settle the matter.

One day, as they were engaged in one such heated discussion, Neal called to them. "Come see what I've got."

Curious, the girls hopped up from the dock and hurried to where Neal stood grinning, next to a new catamaran.

"What is it?" asked Amy.

"It's a catamaran, silly," answered her father, his eyes shining.

"I know that, Daddy," she said, exasperation in her tone. "Why did you want to see us?"

"It's not just a catamaran. It's *our* catamaran."

Amy's eyes widened. "Ours? Can we take it out?" she cried, her voice rising in hopeful excitement.

Neal laughed. "That's why I called you. Run get your life vests. We're going to try her out."

"Wow!" they both cried at the same time, racing off as fast as Amy's legs would go.

When they returned, Neal attempted to give them a mini lecture on the proper procedure for hoisting the sails and the difference between the apparent and the true wind. But his words fell on little ears too impatient to listen, so he laughed and shoved the vessel off the beach, as the two excited children climbed aboard the platform connecting the two hulls.

Neal expertly took the tiller and began putting the craft through her paces. Still trying to combine the thrill with a learning experience, he yelled over the noise of the wind beating in the sails, "Amy, which side of the boat are you sitting on?"

"The starboard, Daddy," she answered, rolling her eyes.

"And you, Charlotte?"

"The port." She leaned back, enjoying the stiff breeze and the sound of the waves as the catamaran skimmed over the tops.

"Very good," said Neal. "Now, which way is the wind blowing?"

The girls exchanged looks, each trying to see if the other knew the answer. Then, both satisfied that neither knew, they waited for

Neal to tell them.

"It's coming from the starboard rail," he explained. "That means we are on the starboard tack."

He continued, going through several maneuvers demonstrating the points of sailing, showing them how to tack, jibe, run, and beat. The day couldn't have been better for sailing. There was enough wind to keep the catamaran moving swiftly and easily, but the bay was relatively calm, allowing them to glide smoothly across the water. Neal explained they were lucky to get this unusual combination of good wind and calm water. And although the hot sun beat down from the cloudless blue sky, the soft breezes made the scorching heat more bearable.

Charlotte closed her eyes, gulping deep breaths of the clean, salt air. This was the next best thing to heaven, she thought, wishing she could save this moment forever.

"Ready about," called Neal, alerting her to duck as he swung the boom over. Now he turned back, heading directly into the wind.

"Oh, Daddy, do we have to go in already?" complained Amy.

"I'm afraid so," said Neal. "I'm supposed to be working this afternoon. Not taking you two joyriding."

Amy smacked him playfully. "When are you going to teach Charlotte and me how to sail?"

"Soon. Maybe next time."

With practiced skill, Neal moved the vessel against the wind, taking the wind on one tack at a forty-five-degree angle, letting the wind pass quickly across the bow before the direct pressure stopped the boat, then taking the wind on the other tack, repeating the procedure over and over until they beached at the marina.

As he hauled the boat up on the beach, Amy reminded him, "Next time, you're going to teach Charlotte and me."

He ruffled her hair. "We'll see. We've also got to teach Charlotte to swim if we're going to make a sailor out of her."

Charlotte's spirits soared. This wonderful man was going to teach her to swim and to sail. Just as if she were his own daughter. With sudden longing, she wished fervently that she were.

CHAPTER THIRTY-SIX
KATRINA

Katrina took her pregnancy in the same easy stride that she took everything else. She still insisted on working excessive hours, although her research on a birth control pill caused many a raised eyebrow and suppressed chuckle among her co-workers, especially as her girth expanded. Adam fussed at her constantly about her overdoing it, but his wife laughed away his concerns, as she assured him she was fine.

Working under Katrina hadn't been as difficult as he had imagined. He was already familiar with a lot of her research, and they had always worked well together in Dr. Rothchild's lab. Still, he sometimes had vague, uneasy feelings, imagining what their co-workers must be saying about him, tagging along on her coattails.

One afternoon, Adam wandered into the break room, where he found his wife in a rare moment of taking a breather from her work. He refreshed her coffee, grabbed a cup for himself, and sat opposite her, relieved to see they were alone. Taking a deep breath, he revisited the conversation they had started that morning over breakfast, but didn't have time to finish. He had difficulty admitting that while he enjoyed his job, he still harbored a degree of insecurity.

"Don't be paranoid, Adam," Katrina scolded him, gently. "Nobody thinks less of you because you work in your wife's lab. Nobody is talking about you." She took a sip of her coffee.

"Not in front of you, perhaps," he said, "but I'm sure people have plenty to say privately about the bum you married." He fiddled with stirring sugar into his cup.

She laughed at him. "Oh, Adam, you know that's not true. You just got your master's degree, for heaven sakes."

"I should get a PhD like you," he grumbled.

Her sharp green eyes locked onto his. "Why? Because you really want to? Or because you feel you have to compete with me?"

"Both, I guess," he answered honestly.

"I'll never understand men," said Katrina, shaking her head. "Why is it they can never accept a wife who's more educated or making more money than they are, yet the converse is perfectly acceptable? Are all men so insecure?"

"Male ego I guess," said Adam, a sheepish grin on his face.

Katrina rolled her eyes. "Well, far be it from me to hold you back. If that's what you want, Adam, go ahead and get your PhD. I can tell you from experience, however, it won't be easy."

He rose from his chair, pulled her to her feet, and hugged her, his arms stretching to reach around her expanding waistline.

"Kate, everything for you is easy. You're the most remarkable woman I've ever known. I just want you to be proud of me."

"I already am. But if my assurance isn't enough, you'll just have to prove it to yourself."

———•●•———

Much to her annoyance, Katrina's advancing pregnancy forced her to slow down a little. She was furiously trying to tie up loose ends before the blessed event, but the swelling in her ankles and the aching in her back made it difficult for her to work for any length of time without having to rest. Then, much to her dismay, she went into labor almost three weeks early.

The timing couldn't have been worse. She had a scheduled meeting with the board of directors that afternoon. As she hefted her bulk from her seat to outline some figures on the overhead projector, to her utter horror, her water broke in front of the whole board. Most of them froze, not knowing what to do. Fortunately, one of the men had the good sense to summon a secretary, a matronly woman, who assessed the situation, called an ambulance, and cleared the room.

Feeling like a bloated whale, Katrina half sat, half lay back in one of the thickly padded leather armchairs of the boardroom, her skirt soaked, wishing desperately Adam were there. The kind secretary sat with her, patting her hand and assuring her everything was going to be all right. She told Katrina she had given birth to three children, so she should know what she was talking about.

"Is there somewhere I can reach your husband, Dr. Graham?" she asked.

"No," panted Katrina. "He went to Stanford this morning to meet with his PhD advisor."

She had never been so frightened or felt so alone in her life. How she wished she could get in touch with Adam. Hating herself for being such a coward, she asked, "Would you mind riding to the hospital with me, Dorothy? I don't want to be alone."

The secretary hesitated for a minute. Then she smiled. "Of course, dear. But there's nothing to worry about. You're going to be just fine."

Katrina squeezed her hand. "Thank you. I know it's silly, but I'm so scared." She attempted a brave little laugh. "This is a definite first experience for me."

Then she gasped as a searing pain shot through her swollen abdomen. "Oh, dear God, I don't know how I'm going to get through this."

———•●•———

Adam Scott Wallace Junior came into the world breech, after an agonizing eighteen hours of hard labor on the part of his mother. The exhausted obstetrician had just alerted the operating room to prepare for a Caesarian section, when his assistant, a fourth-year resident, finally dislodged the infant's stubborn, anteriorly bent legs from Katrina's narrow birth canal. The baby came forth complaining with a mighty wail from his lusty lungs. Katrina, weak and fatigued, lay back on her sweat-soaked pillow, and drifted off into a drug-induced sleep.

Adam Scott Wallace Senior, meanwhile, had endured a miserable night in the hospital's waiting room lounge, where the hospital staff had banished him as soon as he arrived, several hours after his wife. If only he hadn't gone up to Stanford yesterday, he chided himself. He *knew* he should have stayed nearby, with Katrina's due date so close. But she had insisted, promising him she was nowhere near going into labor yet.

She had even laughed, saying, "I've still got too much to do." He shouldn't have listened to her. Then, as the hours went by with no results, he had become terrified, begging to be allowed to see Katrina.

"I'm sorry, Mr. Wallace," the head obstetrical nurse told him firmly, "but there are some complications with the delivery. It would be better for you to stay out of the way."

The waiting became agony. If anything happened to Katrina . . . But he couldn't allow himself to think about that possibility. With feelings of guilt, he thought about Connie giving birth to their daughters. Connie, in contrast to everything else in her short life, had had no problems, breezing effortlessly through the deliveries. And now Katrina, for whom everything had always been easy, was exactly the opposite. He tried to banish the memories. Not only did he not want to compare the two women, he didn't want to be reminded of his daughters. Not today.

Finally, as he watched the first sliver of light break through the graying sky outside, Katrina's doctor appeared. As he walked into the waiting room, pulling off his sweat-soaked surgery cap and running a hand over his unshaven, weary-looking face, Adam jumped up and ran to him. "How is she, Doctor?"

"She's all right, Adam," said the obstetrician, sinking into a chair. "You have a son. He's a little premature, but from all initial evaluations, he appears to be healthy."

With an immense feeling of relief, Adam finally acknowledged his own fatigue. "Oh, thank God." He sighed. "Can I see my wife?"

"For a minute. She's been through a tough time. She's pretty well drained."

Adam followed the doctor to Katrina's room where he got his first shocked look at his wife. Her thick, auburn hair lay limp and matted against her pillow, and her normally warm, rosy face appeared deathly pale.

He saw her struggle to force her dull, glazed eyes open for just a second before closing them again. Adam sank into the chair next to the bed, reached for her hand, and held it tightly.

"Oh, Kate," he whispered, his voice choked with raw emotion, "I love you."

He could see her chest rising and falling with her even breathing. She moved her lips, but her voice was so weak, he had to lean over to hear what she was saying.

"It was so awful," she whispered.

A stab of pain pricked his heart. He was responsible for the ordeal she'd been through. "I'm so sorry, sweetheart. If I could have taken the pain on myself to spare you, I would have." He rubbed her limp hand on his cheek.

She opened her eyes. "But we have a son." Her lips turned up in a thin smile.

"I know. I'm so happy, darling."

"Have you seen him?" Her words slurred from the pain medication, as her eyelids closed again.

"Not yet."

"He's beautiful." Then she lost the battle with drowsiness, falling asleep almost as she said the last two words.

Adam smiled. The baby was probably red and wrinkled and looked just like all the other newborn babies in the nursery. But he was *theirs*. Adam reached down to untangle the sheet and pull it up over her, when something caught his eye. A stain of bright red was seeping into the sheet underneath her flaccid legs.

"Nurse!" he croaked, his frightened voice barely above a harsh whisper. Then, in rising panic, he bellowed, "Nurse!"

"What is it?" demanded the Florence Nightingale who stomped into the room at his noisy summons. "We *do* have call buttons, you know."

Then, her eyes following Adam's finger pointing at the steadily increasing flow of blood, she shoved him out of the way. Pushing the intercom button, she called in a trembling voice, "Dr. Hutchinson to room 311, *stat!*"

The next few moments passed in a blur. As the room began to fill with people, Adam found himself pushed to the back.

"What's wrong?" he tried to yell above the confusion, but his words were lost in the general chaos. The next thing he knew, a gurney had been wheeled, in and Katrina was being rushed from the room.

"Wait!" Adam cried, running after them, clutching at Dr. Hutchinson's sleeve. "Somebody tell me what's going on."

"She's hemorrhaging," snapped the doctor, jerking his arm free. "We have to do an emergency hysterectomy. Now."

CHAPTER THIRTY-SEVEN
CHARLOTTE

T he summer passed too quickly. Amy and Charlotte managed to finagle as much time as possible at the marina, begging and teasing Neal until he agreed to let them spend more and more time with him. On the weekends, Neal and Mary took them out on the catamaran, with Neal slipping in seamanship lessons. Under his guiding hand, Amy and Charlotte took turns at the tiller, as they proudly displayed to Mary how adept they had become at sailing.

Usually, every couple of weeks or so, they spent an afternoon at Amy's grandparents' house. Charlotte often caught Grandma Bess pursing her lips whenever she looked Charlotte's way, and then, as if suddenly aware of what she was doing, Grandma Bess would fake a tight smile. But Charlotte was not fooled. She sensed the woman's disapproval.

As the new school year approached, Mary took Amy and Charlotte shopping, buying both of them new clothes, shoes, and school supplies.

Overwhelmed by the amount of money Mary spent on her, Charlotte said, "They'll give us all this stuff at the home."

"I know that, dear," said Mary, "but I want you to have some nice new clothes."

Charlotte spirits soared with gratitude. Although the home provided clothes, they were rarely new. The children usually received somebody's hand-me-downs or second-hand clothes collected by charitable organizations. The clothes might or might not fit right, and most certainly would be out of style. Still, she had to be thankful for what she got, so Charlotte never got her hopes up at the prospect of having any nice clothing. But Mary made her feel so special, buying things for Charlotte just as if she were her own daughter. How Charlotte wished she were.

The Saturday before school started, the Kleins planned a picnic on the beach. Charlotte, waiting as usual for Amy's parents to pick her up at the home, was surprised to see Amy's parents drive up alone.

"Is Amy sick?" she asked, her voice filled with worry, as she opened the back car door. She sure hoped not. Amy was awfully delicate, however, and although she tried valiantly to keep up with Charlotte, she often tired easily.

"No, Amy's fine," Mary said. "She's visiting with our neighbor."

Charlotte frowned. Why would Amy be somewhere else instead of with her parents?

"We wanted to talk to you alone," added Neal.

Charlotte looked from one to the other, her stomach fluttering with a twinge of concern. She didn't know what the Kleins were about to say, but whatever it was, it must be important. A fleeting, troubling thought crossed her mind. Were they going to tell her they were moving away? Or she wasn't welcome to spend so much time with Amy anymore? But Mary's sweet face softened with a gentle smile.

"Come up in front with us," she invited, stepping out, so Charlotte could sit between them.

Charlotte closed the back door and climbed in between the two adults. All at once, she felt safe and important. Sitting this close to Amy's parents, she breathed in the comforting, spicy scent of Neal's aftershave and Mary's flowery shampoo, and her earlier apprehension faded.

As soon as they all settled into the car and Neal pulled away from the curb, Mary reached over and took Charlotte's hand. "Charlotte, do you like spending time with us?"

"Yes," Charlotte replied, wondering why they were asking. Didn't they know how much she loved being with them? A hot breeze moved through the open car windows, blowing her curls into her face. She reached her hand to brush the hair from her eyes as Neal spoke up.

"And you really like Amy a lot, don't you?"

"Yes. She's my best friend." In truth, Amy was her only friend. Charlotte turned to look at Neal's profile, her hand still holding her hair away from her eyes.

"Does it bother you that Amy's different?" asked Mary, with a small tremor in her voice.

Charlotte twisted the other way to address Mary.

"No." She bit her lip and thought for a moment. "I'm different, too. I think that's why we get along so good."

Neal glanced her way before returning his eyes to the road. "What if you weren't different?"

Charlotte squinted her eyes. "What do you mean?"

He cleared his throat. "Well, what if . . . say, you weren't an orphan? Would you still want to be friends with Amy?"

"Sure." This was a mighty strange conversation.

They slowed down, then stopped at a red light next to a rumbling motorcycle, interrupting their talk for the moment.

When the light turned green and the motorcycle sped off leaving a trail of gray smoke and acrid fumes, Neal continued. "Even if the other children were nicer to you? Wouldn't you rather have lots of friends instead of just Amy? Especially if the others were making fun of Amy?"

Charlotte didn't know where this line of questioning had come from, but she suspected Grandma Bess was somehow behind it. Anger rose in her chest.

"Amy is my best friend," she told them, her words coming out more forcefully than she intended. "And I don't *want* any friends who wouldn't also be Amy's friends."

Neal and Mary exchanged glances. Neal nodded.

"Charlotte," Mary said, squeezing Charlotte's hand, "what would you think if Neal and I told you that we have grown to love you very much? Amy adores you and you seem to love her, too. Neal and I have talked it over and we think we could all be happy together. If you would be willing, Neal and I would like to adopt you."

Charlotte's eyes widened in surprise. Never had she imagined her dream would come true. With a rush of pure joy, she threw herself into Mary's arms.

"I take that as a 'yes'?" Neal glanced at her and laughed.

"Yes! Yes!" cried Charlotte, feeling she was going burst with happiness.

"We'll still have to be approved by an adoption board. It's going to take several months," Neal explained.

"Oh." Her initial excitement began to deflate.

"But," he went on, "we have already begun the process. Until we are officially approved, you will be allowed to live with us as our foster child. It's only a formality of completing the necessary waiting period and paperwork."

"That's right," Mary said. "Everything will be the same. The adoption just makes things legal, that's all." She gave Charlotte a hug.

"I'll be real good. You won't be sorry."

The adults laughed.

—•●•—

Amy waited for them at her neighbor's house, bouncing up and down with excitement. She sure hoped Charlotte had said "yes." As soon as she heard the car pull up, she hobbled outside as fast as she could go. One look at Charlotte's face was all she needed. The two little girls grabbed each other and jumped up and down.

"We're going to be sisters!" they cried happily.

CHAPTER THIRTY-EIGHT
ADAM

After an hour in surgery and four units of blood, Katrina was transferred to the intensive care unit. Adam, having been plunged back into the depths of paralyzing fear, after such a brief reprieve, reached his breaking point. After ascertaining that Katrina was out of danger, he unleashed all his pent-up emotions on Dr. Hutchinson.

"What happened?" he shouted at the hapless physician, when he finally emerged from the ICU. Adam's eyes took in the appearance of the haggard doctor who looked on the verge of physical collapse, and Adam felt a momentary twinge of sympathy—but not enough to stem his own anger.

Dr. Hutchinson closed his eyes, took a ragged breath through his nose, and blew it out slowly through his compressed lips before answering. Then, running a hand over his face, he answered, his voice quiet and controlled.

"She had a post-partum hemorrhage from the placental site. We had to do an emergency hysterectomy."

"Why didn't you know that sooner?" demanded Adam. "Confound it, if I hadn't been there, she could have bled to death."

The doctor knew Adam was right. Katrina should have been

monitored more closely. After a prolonged labor like hers, the potential for an atonic uterus increased. And hemorrhage from the placental site associated with an atonic uterus was always a risk. He would find out who was responsible for not doing their job. But ultimately, it all came down to him. No matter how good of a doctor you were, you were still responsible for seeing your orders were carried out—and taking the blame when they weren't.

"Adam," he said, his tone conveying all the weariness that shone on his face, "these things happen. Fortunately, they happen rarely, but there are always potential complications even with the simplest delivery. And although we do our best, we are, after all, only human."

"That's not much of an answer," grumbled Adam.

"It's the only one I have," admitted the doctor. "Now I suggest we try to work together for Katrina's sake. Her recovery is all that really matters now, don't you agree?"

Adam gave a grudging nod. But at least Katrina would be all right.

———•●•———

Katrina's stay in the hospital stretched into ten days. But as she grew physically stronger, her mental state declined. Never in her life had she had a setback such as this. Not only did she hurt everywhere, but her research had been interrupted at a very inconvenient time. And now the doctor wanted her to wait even longer before going back to work. Then, as if that weren't enough, she wasn't even able to take care of her baby, having to rely on her mother and a hired nurse. On top of everything else, she would never be able to have another child. Although, at this point, she felt she would never want to go through this ordeal again, who was to say how she would feel a few years from now?

———•●•———

Adam had been accepted for the PhD program at Stanford, but remembering his earlier mistake in being away from his wife and new babies so much, he decided to turn down the opportunity. He also decided not to tell Katrina.

He scrutinized the baby—whom they called "Scott" to avoid confusion over junior and senior—looking for any physical resemblance to the girls. Fortunately, there didn't seem to be much similarity, at least from what he could tell at such an early age. But then, Charlotte and Diana resembled Connie, so he didn't really expect Scott to favor his half-sisters. That was one relief. He didn't want to be reminded of his daughters every time he looked into the face of his son.

Perhaps it was because he was home so much more with Scott than he had been with his infant girls, or perhaps it was just the difference in the nature of the babies, but Adam became aware that Scott seemed to be a difficult baby. He cried constantly and he didn't sleep well. Adam and his worried mother-in-law took the baby to the pediatrician, who found nothing wrong.

— • ● • —

One morning, in particular, Scott was extremely fussy, and nothing Katrina's mother did could quiet him.

"Let me have him," said Katrina, who reclined in the living room.

"Now, Katrina, the doctor said you're not supposed to be lifting the baby yet. You've just had surgery, sweetheart. You're not that strong."

"Oh, hogwash," snapped Katrina. "I'm just sitting here, for crying out loud. I'm not lifting him."

Katrina's mother sighed. She knew Katrina wasn't strong enough yet, but on the other hand, the baby's persistent screaming was starting to wear on her. She was too old, she told herself, to deal with a newborn fulltime.

"Just give him to me, Mother," repeated Katrina, the irritation palpable in her tone.

Reluctantly, the older woman laid the infant in her daughter's lap, hovering over them for a moment until Katrina's glare drove her from the room. She escaped to the kitchen, where she sat at the table, her hands over her aching head.

A few minutes later, Adam came home for lunch and found

her there.

"Mom?" he asked. "What's wrong?"

"Oh, Adam." She sighed and looked up. "Everything. I can't seem to do anything right."

"Why? What do you mean?" He pulled out a chair and sat beside her.

She shook her head. "I don't know. I've never seen such a fussy baby. I'm exhausted with trying to comfort him. And Katrina." She rolled her eyes. "I've never seen *her* like this either. Every time I open my mouth, she bites my head off. She insists on pushing her limits, and every time I try to do anything for her . . ." Her voice trailed off.

Adam rose, leaned down, and put his arm around her shoulders. "You're just tired, Mom. We all are. These last couple of weeks have been a strain on everybody."

She rested her head against Adam's hand for a moment. Then suddenly, she sat up straight. "Listen."

"What? I don't hear anything."

"Exactly." She jumped up and headed into the living room, Adam right behind her. There, they found Katrina rocking the infant, humming softly to him. And he was quiet.

Seeing the astonished looks on their faces, Katrina said, "What are you staring at?"

"Scott quieted down so quickly," said her mother.

"Of course," replied Katrina. "All he needed was his mother."

———•●•———

There seemed to be a special bond between the two of them, even more than the usual mother-infant tie. Katrina was the only one who could consistently quiet the baby, and she derived a great deal of satisfaction from this ability. As the days turned into weeks, Katrina became more herself again, with one major exception. Motherhood had changed everything. Fiercely protective of Scott, she didn't want him out of her sight. Almost as if there were some secret code between them, Scott, likewise, wailed inconsolably when separated from his mother.

When Scott turned three months old, Adam approached his

wife, who sat on the sofa after nursing Scott and laying him down.

"Kate, honey, don't you think it's time to consider going back to work?"

She glared at him, but didn't answer.

He coaxed a little harder. "Sweetheart, you only wanted to take a month's leave of absence. It's already been three."

"Well, things didn't exactly turn out like we expected, remember?" Her tone became defensive. "In case you don't, I almost died."

"I know, sweetheart, but it's been three months. You're fine now."

"Well, thank you for your diagnosis, Dr. Wallace," she bit out. "You obviously are unaware of what my body has been through. How dare you tell me I'm fine! What do you know?"

"What about your work, Kate? Weren't you beside yourself because you had to leave in the middle of your research?"

"It'll be there when I get back," she replied, dismissing the subject with a wave of her hand. "I'm not well enough yet."

"Kate," he said, more firmly, "your health is not the issue here, and you know it. Scott is the issue."

Her eyes filled with tears. "That's not true."

"You're going to have to leave him sooner or later and go back to work." He sat beside her on the sofa and took her trembling hands in his.

"I don't want to leave him," she whispered, as the tears spilled over her lower lids and trickled down her cheeks. "Other women stay home with their babies. Why can't I?"

Adam took her in his arms. "Oh, sweetheart. If that's what you truly want, then fine. But I don't think you'll be happy for long. And I don't think it's good for Scott to be so dependent on his mother."

"But he's only three months old," she sobbed. "He needs his mother."

Adam sighed. "All right, Kate. Whatever you want." He held her for a long time, until Scott's insistent wail summoned her.

CHAPTER THIRTY-NINE
CHARLOTTE

Charlotte easily settled into a happy routine with the Kleins. Mary gave her the guest room down the hall—over mild protests from Amy who wanted them both to share her room—and with Mary's help, they redecorated it in shades of blue. The girls assisted in the painting, and although they got more paint on themselves than on the walls, Charlotte had never been so happy.

School was better, too. Now, instead of having to fend for themselves, the girls each had an ally. They found the other children were not as quick to harass two of them as they had been when the girls were alone. A few children were actually friendly, at least toward Charlotte, perhaps because she no longer wore funny clothes and was not considered an orphan anymore. Amy's situation, however, remained mostly unchanged with her physical impairment. Still, Charlotte's intense loyalty and protectiveness toward Amy kept the other children from excluding her. Remembering Mary and Neal's concern on that wonderful day when they had offered to adopt her, she finally realized why they had asked her those strange questions. They had wanted to protect Amy. They had to be sure Charlotte wouldn't abandon Amy, too. But they didn't need to worry. Knowing firsthand how it felt to be abandoned by someone she loved, she would always be loyal to Amy and would never consider her a burden. Their special friendship and soon-to-be sisterhood would always come first.

With the pressure off at school, Charlotte excelled scholastically, even more than before. And because Charlotte did well, Amy, in turn, worked hard to keep up with her. The competition was good for Amy, who up until this point, had only done what she had to do in order to get by. Her parents, thrilled with the improvement in her grades, proudly pointed out to the doubtful grandparents just one more of the many advantages to adopting Charlotte.

"Sure, everything's peaches and cream *now*," said Grandma Bess, one day when they were visiting for the afternoon, "but wait until the adoption goes through. Then she won't be so anxious to gain your favor."

"I honestly don't know why you're so worried," Mary replied. "These last few months of having Charlotte in our home have been a blessing for all of us. We love her already as if she were our own."

"Well, that's just fine," snapped her mother. "It looks like everybody's forgetting Amy. Just shoving her out of the way because this waif of questionable heritage has wormed her way into your hearts and home. I'm warning you, she's just using you and as soon as she gets what she wants from you, she'll be nothing but trouble and heartache."

Charlotte, unfortunately, had picked that moment to come into the house.

Mary stared over her mother's shoulder at Charlotte's wounded face. It was obvious she had overheard them.

"Charlotte . . ." She started toward her, but Charlotte pulled away.

Her lower lip trembling, Charlotte said, "I don't know why you don't like me, Grandma Bess. I've never done anything to hurt any of you. And I never will."

The older woman looked as if she had been slapped. "I'm *not* your grandmother, young lady! And don't you forget it."

It was Charlotte's turn to look as if she had been stricken. She turned and bolted out the door.

"Mother!" gasped Mary. She ran from the room, following

Charlotte.

———•●•———

Charlotte sat on the porch steps, sobbing. Mary slid down next to her, rubbing her back until Charlotte's sobs gave way to faltering hiccups.

Charlotte turned her tear-stained face to Mary. "Why? Everything is so perfect. Why does she have to spoil it all?" She knew she shouldn't speak disrespectfully of Mary's mother, but after all, Grandma Bess had started it.

Mary hugged her. "With some people, it takes time. Be patient. Grandma Bess will grow to love you just like we do. In the meantime, you're going to legally become our little girl in two months. And nothing is going to spoil that."

Charlotte hugged her back. How wonderful it was to have someone like Mary to love her. Grandma Bess or no Grandma Bess, nothing was going to ruin her relationship with the Kleins. In two months, she would become their daughter. And then she would never have to be alone again.

———•●•———

"But Amy, it's still awfully cold to take out the catamaran," said Neal.

"Please, Daddy? It's April," Amy begged. "And tomorrow we're adopting Charlotte. We need to do something special to celebrate."

"It's not cold," Charlotte chimed in. "It's seventy-five degrees outside."

"The water will be cold," insisted Neal. He looked at all the females of the house staring at him with longing eyes and acknowledged defeat. "Oh, all right. But I don't want to hear anyone complaining about how cold the water is."

"Yea!" cried the two girls, at once, running off to get into their bathing suits.

Mary smiled. "They're so excited, Neal. Tomorrow is a big day for them."

"And for us," he said, smiling back.

"If only Mom and Dad would come around." Her voice took on a wisp of sadness. "I'm afraid things there will always be strained."

"They'll get used to Charlotte. Give them time."

Their conversation was cut short by the return of the children. "Come *on*," said Amy, "you're not even in your bathing suits, yet."

"All right, all right," said Neal, in mock protest. "How am I ever going to live with *three* nagging females in the house?"

The warm sun shone brightly from the clear blue sky and a subtle breeze blew in from the bay as they all crouched on the hot sand to ready the sails. Neal unfurled and inspected the sails that had been stored away for the winter, making sure there were no tears. The impatient girls assured him the sails were fine. Not allowing their enthusiasm to deter him from his thorough inspection, however, he methodically checked the spars and rigging, explaining what he was doing and why. He'd had the foresight to mark the buckles on the standing rigging with tape to indicate where their position had been last year when the mast was properly tuned. That saved some time.

Finally, they were ready to hoist the sails. Neal showed them how to stretch the canvas along the boom, mast, and gaff, and tighten them by means of the boltrope, which was sewn into the edge of the canvas.

"Daddy, hurry up," cried Amy, as he handed the ropes to Mary to pass around the brass grommets.

"Always hoist the aftermost sail first." Neal instructed in his patient voice, ignoring his eager daughter's outbursts. "And when lowering the sails, begin with the headsails and proceed toward the stern, lowering the aftermost sail last."

"We know," groaned Amy. "The whole day's going to be over before we even get started."

"Have patience, Amy. It's important to do things properly."

"I'm afraid patience is not one of Amy's virtues," Mary said.

The whole procedure took a while, since it was the first time this season they had taken the boat out. But at last, they were ready.

"Okay," said Neal, "we're all set. Into your life jackets, girls."

Charlotte donned hers, but Amy, as usual, protested.

"Aw, Daddy, it's too uncomfortable. We can swim good. We

don't need life jackets."

"Amy," scolded Mary, "why can't you do as you're asked? Like Charlotte. You know it's dangerous not to wear a life vest."

Amy scowled at Charlotte. "*I'm* a good swimmer, anyway." Her pointed little chin lifted in defiance. "And I don't want to wear a life jacket." She crossed her arms across her chest.

Mary sighed and rolled her eyes at Neal. Charlotte glanced between the adults and her friend and bit her lip.

Neal pursed his lips. Amy could be difficult when she wanted her own way. If Amy were forced to wear the life jacket, they would all suffer the consequences of Amy's sulking for the rest of the day. It had been so nice, thus far. Besides, Amy was right. The life vests were cumbersome, and she was an excellent swimmer.

"Oh, all right," he said. "But be careful."

Amy flashed Charlotte a victorious smile and they raced down to the edge of the water. Just as Neal had predicted, it was cold. For a few seconds, Amy seemed to wrestle with the idea of complaining about the water temperature, then obviously thought better of it.

Neal frowned. "We've really got to do something about Amy's stubbornness. It's beginning to get out of hand."

"She's hopelessly spoiled," Mary agreed. "Maybe having Charlotte around as an example will help."

Neal laughed. "I just hope Amy's bad habits don't rub off on *her*."

———•●•———

The choppiness of the bay made sailing a little rough, but having come this far, they were all determined to make the best of it. The wind, meanwhile, had picked up, carrying them away from shore at a rapid pace. Even the warmth of the bright sun didn't stave off the chill of the water as it sloshed over the side of the catamaran. Still, the crisp, clear day and the excitement of having the boat out for the first time that spring more than compensated for the minor discomforts of the rolling waves and cold sea.

After they had been out for about an hour, Neal said, "I should have checked the weather report before we came."

"Why?" asked Mary. "The sky looks perfectly clear."

"I don't like the way the wind is increasing. And I don't like the way that cloud looks over there." He nodded to an innocent-appearing white cloud.

They all turned toward the cloud in question. "It's just a cumulus cloud, Daddy," Amy said.

Charlotte began to grow uneasy. Although it looked like a cumulus cloud, it had begun to take on a more vertical position, with a spiraling column that seemed to reach higher and higher.

"I think we may be in for a storm," said Neal. "See the shape of that cloud? It looks like there's a thermal updraft developing in the center of it."

Sure enough, even as he finished speaking, they saw a flash of lightening and heard its accompanying clap of thunder. The rapidly increasing wind beat the already lurching waves into a creamy white froth.

Suddenly, the appearance of the sky changed, deepening to an ominous grayish blue, darkening toward the horizon.

"Neal, do you think we can make it back?" shouted Mary, as the wind shifted, almost drowning out her words with its intense force.

"We'll have to try," he yelled back. "There's nowhere around here to pull in for protection. And we don't want to sit out the storm here. We'll have to try and outrun it."

Deftly, he maneuvered the boat around as the first blast of the storm hit them, drenching them with a blinding spray. The angry waves bounced them with ruthless force, as Neal struggled to gain control of the wind-beaten sail.

With the blackening veil of the storm descending over them faster than they could outrun it, Neal shook his head. "It's no use. We're going to have to sit it out. Mary, help me get the mainsail down."

The wind blew harder now. After admonishing the girls to hold on tight, Mary gingerly made her way to Neal's side.

Charlotte glanced at Amy's frightened face and wished Amy had donned her life vest. But it was too dangerous to attempt to retrieve it now.

The flapping canvas seemed to take on a life of its own, as it flailed under the assault of the fierce wind. It took the full strength of both Mary and Neal to pull it down. Another streak of lightening lit up the darkened sky, causing Mary to flinch.

"I hope we don't get hit," she yelled above the shrieking gale, casting a nervous peek at the naked aluminum mast.

"If we can just hang on, the storm will be over in a few minutes," said Neal. He shot a quick look at the girls. Charlotte clung to Amy, who had abandoned all pretense of bravery. "We'll be all right," he yelled to them. "Just hold on."

Turning to Mary, he said, "We need to unstep the mast, if we can. But first we have to get the other sail down."

She nodded, moving slowly over the precariously pitching leeward hull. Just as she had nearly reached her destination, she lost her footing and fell backward against the tiller, causing the heavy boom to swing out of control. It caught Charlotte and Amy unaware, striking them both full in the chests. In a split second, they toppled overboard into the churning waves.

Charlotte, still clinging to Amy, felt her grasp broken as they hit the icy water. She bobbed like a cork, momentarily relieved she hadn't gone under. Then, remembering Amy wasn't wearing a life jacket, she began to scream.

Frantically, she twisted her body to scan the immediate area for her friend. The cumbersome life vest made it difficult for her to maneuver. She could see nothing but the endless stretch of lashing white foam. Why hadn't Amy reemerged? Had she hit something or gotten caught on something? Where were Neal and Mary?

Raising her head as high as she could, she saw that Neal had rushed to help Mary and hadn't seen what happened. She screamed louder, but her cries were deadened by the wailing of the storm. Desperately, she fought her way against the waves to the side of the catamaran. As she clawed to get a grip on something solid, she felt Neal's strong arms heaving her out of the water.

"Where's Amy?" he shouted, his voice rising in panic. He didn't wait for an answer as he dove into the water.

"Amy! Amy!" shrieked Mary, searching the chaotic mass of dark water with its rising white caps. She dove in after her husband, leaving Charlotte, who clung with all her strength to the furled mainsail, completely alone on the boat.

Too frightened to look over the side, Charlotte buried her head in the wet canvas and prayed. It had been a long time since she had felt the need to call upon a higher power, but now she prayed for all she was worth.

Suddenly, a tremendous force shook the heaving vessel—a force so alien and deafening that, at first, Charlotte didn't know what had happened. The impact slammed her body several feet forward into the cockpit, and the noise made her ears ring. Then looking around, she saw that lightening had hit the metal mast, knocking it loose from where Mary had been trying to unstep it. It now dangled grotesquely at an angle, its tip dipping into the water, electrifying the area surrounding the catamaran. Terrified, Charlotte pulled her knees against her chest as her eyes were drawn to the smoking metal sizzling in the tumult of the angry sea. A charged circumference of water encircled the sailboat.

Still reeling from the impact of the jolt, the significance of what had just taken place didn't fully occur to her until a few moments later. Then, with the slowly dawning realization that Neal, Mary, and Amy had all been in the water when the electrifying current had shot through the water, she opened her mouth and screamed.

— • ● • —

A Coast Guard cutter found her several hours later. She had long since screamed herself hoarse and now sat motionless in a catatonic state. Although it was pretty obvious what had happened from the look of the charred, distorted mast, her rescuers' attempts to question her were futile.

"She's in shock," said one of the officers, who wrapped her in a warm blanket and gave her a cup of hot tea. She sipped the tea, but her unfocused, unblinking eyes attested to the fact her mind had shut itself off.

"She looks all right physically," said the other officer, "but we need to get her to the hospital for evaluation. She's bound to be hypothermic, if nothing else."

It didn't take long for the authorities to find out who owned the catamaran. What they didn't know, however, was the identity of the little girl who had been found aboard. With swift competence, they notified the Jordans, informing them that their daughter and son-in-law were presumed dead, but a little girl had been rescued.

Charlotte sat frozen, only dimly aware of the noisy confusion heralding the grieving Jordans' arrival at the hospital.

"Where is she?" shrieked Grandma Bess. "Where's Amy?"

Charlotte heard three sets of insistent footsteps hurrying toward her cubicle. The curtain was yanked aside, and the shocked grandparents got their first look at the sole survivor of the afternoon's tragedy.

Grandma Bess let out a high-pitched, hysterical scream.

Charlotte stared at the woman, her mind numb. Grandpa Tony threw himself at the doctor, who was trying without success to remove them from the scene.

"It's not our Amy," he cried in a shrill voice, clutching at the doctor's sleeve as if by pleading hard enough, the doctor could change Charlotte into Amy. "It's that *orphan* child," he spat, before breaking down into racking sobs.

"Please," said the doctor, "come, let me take you somewhere private."

As he led them away, Charlotte heard Grandma Bess wail, "Why couldn't it have been Amy who was saved? Nobody would have cared if *that* child had been lost. Oh, dear God, why Amy?"

Charlotte would always remember those words.

CHAPTER FORTY
KATRINA

D r. Graham," said Milton Rasner, the executive director of the Los Angeles-based Fenner Pharmaceutical Company, "I think it is only fair to warn you that the board is getting a little impatient with your extended leave of absence."

They sat in Rasner's exquisitely furnished, corner executive office. The well-fed, perfectly coiffed and manicured administrator leaned back in his expensive leather swivel-chair, placed his fingertips together, and appeared to be contemplating his buffed nails. He had probably not seen the inside of a working laboratory in twenty years.

Katrina shifted in her chair. She had quite naturally assumed she was indispensable, and the board would have no choice but to agree to her terms. From the chilly reception from Milton Rasner, however, she began to fear her assumption might not necessarily be true. Still, she would not be bullied.

"Perhaps you are unaware, Mr. Rasner," she replied, with more confidence than she felt, "there were numerous post-partum medical complications which necessitated my having to be gone from work longer than originally expected."

Mr. Rasner's slightly bored expression told her he wasn't interested in her "female" problems. "And perhaps you are unaware, Dr. Graham," he said, in an acid voice, "that Quiven Pharmaceutical is very close to perfecting a birth control pill."

An involuntary gasp escaped her lips. She hadn't known that fact. But for the past six months, she had not known much of anything except her son's needs and wants.

"And," he continued, still contemplating his nails, "if they succeed in getting FDA approval before we do . . . well, I suppose I don't have to tell you what that will mean."

No, he didn't have to tell her. It would mean several years of hard work down the drain, as well as a tremendous loss of potential profits for the company. She felt a band of constriction in her chest.

"So, Dr. Graham, this is Fenner's position. And it is backed up by the board. If you don't return to your job in the next two weeks, your employment here may be in jeopardy."

Katrina burned with indignation. How dare this pompous figurehead treat her like an errant schoolgirl?

She sat up straight and addressed him in a firm tone. "Frankly, Mr. Rasner, I resent your threat. I have worked my butt off" . . . She noticed his raised eyebrows at the word "butt" and took secret pleasure in the fact it had shocked him. "For ten years, I have devoted my life to this company and have produced more marketable products than anyone else in the country, with the possible exception of Robert Rothchild." Her momentum built as she continued. "If the board cannot bear with me in a time of personal need, then I shall tender my resignation immediately. I'm sure I will have no problem finding another position in a competitor's company. Maybe even Quiven."

With the end of her monologue, she stood and glowered at him, poised for a quick exit.

———•●•———

Bother, he thought. He hated these modern women who couldn't be intimidated. If Fenner Pharmaceutical lost Katrina Graham to the competition, his head would roll. Now he would have to eat crow, placate her—whatever it took to wheedle her back. He attempted to plaster a smile on his jowly face.

He stood, extending his hand to her in a peace offering. "Now then, Katrina," he said, his voice solicitous and smooth, "we both know that's not in either one of our best interests."

"Then back off, Milt," she snarled at him, as she stomped out of the room, slamming the door behind her.

* ● *

"Dr. Graham," said one of her co-workers, spying her in the hall. "When are you coming back to work?"

"When I'm darned good and ready," she snapped.

She seethed with rage all the way home and then sat brooding for the rest of the day. But one thing Rasner had said she couldn't get out of her mind. Quiven was close to marketing a birth control pill. Confound it, that was *her* project. She had been working on it for years. If she lost this opportunity . . .

It wasn't as though Dr. Rothchild hadn't warned her about this possibility. She knew other companies were working on the same thing. But she had thought she could beat them to it. And she would have if she hadn't taken off the last six months. She could have had everything wrapped up in four weeks, tops. Maybe she still could. As the idea took root in her mind, she began to feel the old rush of excitement again. Perhaps it wasn't too late. If she could just—

Scott's cries broke into her thoughts. Still pre-occupied with her ideas for finishing her research, she forced herself to his crib. One look at the baby, however, with his thatch of dark brown hair and grayish-blue eyes which looked so much like his father's, and her heart melted.

"Oh, Scotty," she cooed, picking up the crying infant, "what am I going to do?"

The baby, as if on cue, stopped crying as soon as his mother lifted him from the crib.

"I can't bear the thought of leaving you all day," she said, holding him so she could look into his face. "And yet, I've got to go back to work. If Quiven markets their pill before I do, I'll . . ."

The infant watched her with a puzzled look, as if he were trying to understand what she was saying.

She laughed. "Well, never mind. But I won't be happy. That's *my* project, Scotty." She held him close, cradling his fuzzy head. "Oh, Scotty, I never thought it would be this hard."

She sat with him in the rocker, wearily rocking back and forth, letting her spoken thoughts bounce off her son.

"We'll have to find you someone very special to look after you during the day, someone you'll like—but not *too* much. I don't want you to forget who your mother is. And then, when I get home at night, we'll play and read stories and sing songs and have such a good time."

Unbidden tears stung her eyes. With a catch in her voice, she continued, "I love you so much, Scotty. I wish you could have a normal mother who stayed home with you and baked cookies and all the things that other mothers do." Hot tears began to course down her cheeks. "But I'm not like other mothers. I'll make it up to you, baby. I promise. You'll have everything you want."

1971

CHAPTER FORTY-ONE
CHARLOTTE

When Charlotte was first sent back to the Pensacola Children's Home, she remained in a state of shock. She neither spoke to anyone nor responded when anyone spoke to her. She appeared to be locked deep inside herself, and nobody could find the key. At mealtime, someone would lead her to the table. Once there, she managed to eat on her own, but seemed totally unaware of what she ate. At bedtime, she undressed herself and got into bed, but whenever one of the matrons checked on her, they would find her lying with her eyes wide open, staring blankly into the darkness. Obviously in no condition to be sent to school, she remained isolated for several weeks while everyone waited for her to "snap out of it."

If the other children had thought Charlotte strange before, her behavior now displayed a whole new definition of strange. Her unresponsiveness earned her the nickname, "The Zombie," but, unlike before, Charlotte appeared completely unaware of the taunts and teases from the others.

The adult supervisors tried everything they could think of to reach her. Finally, in desperation, they sought help from a child psychologist. Dr. Marion Jaffe sipped coffee in the office of Evelyn Young, the administrator of the children's home, as Evelyn filled her in on Charlotte's background. After learning about the multiple tragedies that had befallen the little girl, the psychologist clucked her tongue in sympathy.

"I don't wonder she's disassociated herself from everything around her," Dr. Jaffe said, setting her cup on the table beside her chair. "I don't know if I would want to be part of a world that had treated me so unjustly, either."

"Isn't there something you can do?" begged Evelyn, as she clenched and unclenched her hands with nervous energy. "It's heartbreaking to see her like this day after day."

"I'll talk to her," Dr. Jaffe said, "but I think you had better consider the possibility she may not get better."

Evelyn gasped. "You mean we may have to put her in an asylum? Never in my twenty-five years of working with children's social services have I had to commit a child for insanity."

"It's possible. But, as you said before, you thought she'd improve with time. Perhaps she still might." Dr. Jaffe bit her lip and met Evelyn's worried eyes. "Anyway, I would not be authorized to make that decision. I would have to turn her case over to a child psychiatrist."

"Oh dear." Evelyn's lower lip quivered. "Please do what you can."

Despite her extensive experience in working with troubled children, Dr. Jaffe was unprepared for the child who was brought to the small conference room next to Evelyn's office. She shut the door, closing out the noise of happier children, and studied Charlotte as she was led to a chair. She could see that Charlotte had once been a pretty child, but the traumas the little girl had endured had taken their toll. Dark shadows colored the skin underneath her striking violet-blue eyes, and her cheeks appeared sunken and hollow. The paleness of her porcelain complexion made her look on the brink of death. The crop of sunny curls on her head had been neglected, hanging in a long, tangled mass.

Charlotte's vacant eyes appeared to register nothing. She didn't blink. She didn't turn her head or look around. She just stared straight ahead.

"My name's Marion," the doctor said. "What's yours?"

Charlotte gave no answer.

"Miss Young thought it might be a good idea if we talked. Would you like to do that?"

No answer.

"Charlotte," she continued, "Sometimes, things happen in our lives that are so painful our minds simply cannot deal with them. So in order to protect ourselves, we shut ourselves away from the world. And that's understandable. But sometimes, we go too far. And then it's not just the painful parts we don't acknowledge, it's everything. Is that what you're doing, Charlotte?"

No answer.

Dr. Jaffe sighed. Of course, she hadn't expected much from this first session, but she had hoped.

"Charlotte," she said gently, "you don't have to think about anything unpleasant. But surely you've had some happy times. Why don't you tell me about some of them?"

No answer.

Perhaps Charlotte needed a more authoritative tactic. "It's time to come back to the world, Charlotte," Dr. Jaffe said, in a no-nonsense tone. "Do you want to stay this way forever?"

No answer.

"Charlotte, you are trying to isolate yourself from further hurt by turning off all your feelings. But that approach doesn't work. Why don't we start with some good feelings? May I give you a hug?"

The psychologist rose slowly from her seat and cautiously approached the rigid little body. Charlotte didn't move. The doctor knelt in front of the child and placed her arms around her, pulling the child's body toward her. Charlotte's stiff arms remained at her sides, and although she did not resist, she also did not respond. It seemed as though she didn't even feel the woman touching her. Marion released the embrace and sat back on her heels, searching the child's face for any sign of a reaction. Nothing.

"Well," she said, a little disheartened, "I think that's enough for one day. I'll see you tomorrow. All right?"

As she expected, Charlotte didn't reply.

The sessions continued much in the same fashion for two weeks. Dr. Jaffe, frustrated at seeing no visible change in the child, consulted Miss Young.

"I think it might be time to call in a psychiatrist. Maybe some anti-depressant medication would help."

"Oh dear," said Evelyn. "Aren't those drugs habit forming?"

"Not necessarily. In some cases they work quite well." Dr.

Jaffe paused, rubbing her forehead. "I really don't know what else to try. Do you have any other ideas?"

"Such as?"

"Well," mused the therapist, narrowing her eyes in concentration. "Is there anything else you can tell me about Charlotte to help me break through to her. For instance, what was she like before she met Amy Klein?"

"Hmm." Miss Young frowned. "That was a long time ago and there have been so many children in and out." She took a deep breath and closed her eyes, obviously struggling to force a hidden memory from the recesses in her brain.

"Wait. A picture just popped into my mind of Charlotte sitting at the picnic table on the playground with her sketch book in her hand." Evelyn's voice rose with excitement. "She was always a little withdrawn, always drawing pictures or writing stories. She pretty much kept to herself before she met Amy. She didn't seem to make friends easily. But I seldom saw her without pencil and paper."

Dr. Jaffe chewed her thumbnail, then removed her hand from her mouth. "So, she is an introverted child." She pondered a moment. "This does make things tougher. But I have an idea."

"What?"

"Let me try it out first."

The next session started out like all the others. After some initial one-sided small talk, Dr. Jaffe said, "Charlotte, I hear you are quite an artist. And a writer as well."

No answer.

"I was wondering, Charlotte. Do you think you could draw me a picture for our next session?"

Silence.

But the next day, Charlotte came in carrying a tattered piece of paper.

"What's this?" cried the therapist, her voice raised in excitement. Had she finally found a way to reach the child?

Charlotte did not offer her the paper.

"May I?" Dr. Jaffe put out a tentative hand. Although no expression crossed Charlotte's wooden face, she gave up the content of her hand without resistance.

Dr. Jaffe unfolded the sheet of paper which revealed a drawing.

"Did you draw this, Charlotte?"

No answer.

She examined the picture. It showed the face of a man, but it had been grotesquely distorted into an angry, ugly image. Dr. Jaffe found the illustration disturbing.

"Charlotte, who is this?"

Nobody could have been more shocked than the unsuspecting therapist when the child broke her vow of silence and answered in a voice dripping with hatred, "My daddy."

It was the breakthrough she needed. Although Charlotte still refused to converse freely with Dr. Jaffe, the doctor was finally able to delve into the child's mind through stories and pictures. After the divulgence of the identity of the face in the drawing, Charlotte had clammed up, refusing to answer any more questions. So Dr. Jaffe asked her to write a story about her daddy for the next session.

Charlotte wrote only a few words. "My daddy didn't love us anymore. He abandoned us. Then all the bad things happened."

Dr. Jaffe tried to ferret out what bad things, but Charlotte stubbornly refused to talk. She was, however, more alert. Her eyes followed the therapist and the other people in the home, although they remained blank and unreadable. She still made no effort to communicate, although she occasionally answered a question with a grunt. Still, it was progress.

———•●•———

Over the course of the next several weeks, Marion Jaffe gradually pieced together the story of Charlotte's life and how she felt about it. The child's history was even worse than what Miss Young had been able to tell her. Then Charlotte told her the horrible words Bess Jordan had said in the emergency room—no one would care if *Charlotte* had died in the accident.

"That's not true," Dr. Jaffe said. "There are a great many people who would care if you had died."

"Yeah, who?"

"Me, for one."

Charlotte shrugged.

Dr. Jaffe caught her skeptical look. "Look, Charlotte, I know you feel you're all alone in the world—"

"I am. And I like it that way." Charlotte lifted her chin.

"—but there are other people who care about you and want to help you.

Charlotte remained quiet.

"I know you've been deeply hurt and you feel you can't depend on people, but you can't be afraid to reach out to people, to let them into your life."

Charlotte merely regarded her with a cynical eye.

Charlotte appreciated what Dr. Jaffee was trying to do, but how could Dr. Jaffe possibly know how badly Charlotte had been burned? Every time she had dared to love, she had lost. But she gave the therapist the answers she wanted so she would leave her alone.

Little by little, Charlotte began rejoin her world. She only gave as much of herself as she had to, however, preferring to remain detached. She still shunned friendships—from both children and adults—and still kept to herself, but at least she was now capable of responding to her environment. Since she had missed so much school, she had to work extra hard to catch up. Although not terribly difficult for her, the schoolwork gave her an added layer of insulation against anyone getting close to her. It became her excuse to remain isolated.

After a while, people just naturally left her alone, which suited her fine. And after an even longer time, nobody even bothered to talk about how strange she was. For the most part, people simply ignored her. Dr. Jaffe still insisted on a once-a-week session. Charlotte learned to say the things the therapist wanted to hear, and this kept them both happy.

Over time, her writing became therapeutic, and as a result, it became better. She could put into written words the thoughts and feelings she couldn't talk about. Her insightful and sensitive writing amazed her teachers, and with their help, by the time she was twelve, Charlotte had become a published author of short stories in a national women's magazine.

CHAPTER FORTY-TWO
ANDREA

D ana, sweetheart, you've been practicing for hours," said Andrea. "Don't you want to take a break and go outside and play?"

The soon-to-be eight-year-old sitting at the baby grand piano cast Andrea a scornful look. "Mo-*ther*," she replied in a contemptuous voice, "I *have* to get this right."

Dana had been having a bit of difficulty with Chopin's *Polonaise Militaire*, mainly because her small hands couldn't span the octaves, so she had to improvise.

"But sweetheart, it's such a pretty day outside. Besides, you don't have a recital coming up. There's no need to push yourself."

Dana let out a loud sigh and rolled her eyes. "I *want* to get this right. *Okay?*"

Andrea gave up. She didn't know why she even bothered. Except for the few minutes out of the day when Dana rushed through her homework to get it over with, the only thing that occupied her spare time was the piano. She never watched television, never played with her toys, and she had no friends. And anyone who interrupted her incurred the wrath of her nasty temper.

Andrea left the room, thinking if she heard Chopin's *Polonaise Militaire* one more time, she would go crazy. Why couldn't they have adopted a normal child? Then she immediately felt guilty. They were blessed to have such a gifted daughter. Perhaps in another environment, Dana's precious talent would be stifled.

No, it was meant for her to be with us, where her abilities can be nurtured without any outside interference from people who might not understand.

But Andrea worried. It couldn't be healthy for an eight-year-old not to have any friends or play any childish games.

Although Andrea attributed Dana's moodiness to artistic temperament, she never was quite sure whether Dana truly possessed artistic temperament or just plain bad manners that she and Charles had failed to correct. She fretted constantly that they were somehow to blame for Dana's peculiarities. There was no question that they spoiled Dana. But other spoiled children were not so moody. Brats, yes, but one couldn't really call Dana a brat. In fact, Dana had never seemed to be a child at all. She had never talked like a child or played like a child. Since the age of three, she had always acted like a miniature adult, with perfect pronunciation and grammar, and a single-minded focus—her music.

One day, Mrs. Kennedy asked the DeVouxs to stop by for a discussion.

"Oh dear," said Andrea, as she and Charles walked the short distance to the piano teacher's house. "I wonder what Dana's done now."

Charles laughed. "What makes you think she's done anything?"

"She's always insulting someone or hurting somebody's feelings." She added quickly, "She doesn't do it deliberately, of course. She just says what's on her mind without considering how it might affect other people."

"I'm afraid our daughter marches to her own drummer," said Charles. "And from what I understand, a lot of truly talented people do."

"I'm worried about her, Charles. It's not normal for a little girl to be so isolated by her own choice. She should be playing house, having slumber parties, playing dress-up . . . all the things other little girls do."

"I think we're going to have to get used to the fact that Dana is no ordinary little girl. I imagine all parents of great protégés have felt the same way." He slipped his arm around her. "Anyway, what's so bad about being different? We really don't want her to be like everyone else, do we?"

Andrea sighed. "I don't know. I guess I just don't understand her. Maybe I'm trying to impose my concept of happiness on her when that's not what Dana wants at all."

"Well, here we are." They stopped in front of the rambling Kennedy home. "Let's see what Mrs. Kennedy has to say." They walked up the cracked cement steps and knocked on the door.

The door was opened by one of the numerous Kennedy children, who turned and loudly announced their arrival.

"Joey, ask them to come in," called Mrs. Kennedy, emerging from the kitchen, wiping her hands on her apron. She brushed a wayward strand of hair from her flushed face, leaving a dab of flour on her forehead. "I'll swear, kids have no manners these days. It's not because I don't try. Please, come in."

The DeVouxs made their way through the cluttered living room to the den where Mrs. Kennedy gave her piano lessons.

"And turn down that television." She closed the door, muffling the noise. "Honestly. Sometimes I think I'm going to go out of my mind." Then, as if realizing she had been the one to summon the couple, she continued, a little more calmly. "I'm sorry. It's been one of those days. Please, sit down."

Andrea sat wringing her sweating hands in apprehension, afraid of what Mrs. Kennedy had to say. Had Dana been such a problem that Mrs. Kennedy was going to ask them to withdraw her from the class? No, that was ridiculous. This woman lived in constant chaos. An outspoken eight-year-old wouldn't unravel her. So why did she want to talk with them?

Their anxiety must have shown on their faces, for the frazzled lady before them suddenly smiled.

"I'm sure you're wondering why I've asked you here."

They nodded in unison.

"Has Dana done something wrong?" asked Andrea, her voice hesitant, dreading the answer.

"Oh, no," cried Mrs. Kennedy, her smile broadening. "Quite the contrary. I've never had such pleasure working with a student. Dana has truly been an answer to prayer. You wouldn't believe what I've had to work with." Then she laughed. "Of course, you would. You've been to the recitals."

Andrea's lips drew upward in a weak smile, and she wished

Mrs. Kennedy would get to the point.

"No, Dana is not the problem. I am. You see, I don't feel I can continue as Dana's teacher."

"But why?" asked Andrea, her distress mounting. She just knew Mrs. Kennedy was trying to make up an excuse to get Dana out of her class.

"Because her talent as a student has surpassed my ability as a teacher. I've taught Dana everything I know. There's nothing more I can do for her."

Charles and Andrea exchanged surprised looks. "Are you saying we need to find her another teacher?" asked Charles.

Mrs. Kennedy nodded. "Believe me, Professor DeVoux, it will be difficult for me to lose Dana. She has been such a joy. But I'm also fully aware of my own limitations. I'm simply not qualified to go on teaching her. I would only hold her back. And she deserves better."

The parents sat in stunned silence for a minute, pondering what the teacher had told them. Finally, Charles spoke. "She's that good, then?"

"Oh yes. Dana is destined for great things."

"Well then, do you have any suggestions as to who we should find to continue Dana's lessons?" he asked.

"There is only one person I can think of offhand who would be capable of handling Dana's talent, but I'm not sure she's still teaching. She must be at least seventy."

"Esther Winstein," said Charles and Andrea at the same time.

"Oh, you know of her, then?"

Andrea sighed. "Yes. We know of her."

— • ● • —

So the dragon-lady got her claws into Dana after all. With reluctance, putting their daughter's needs ahead of their own misgivings, the DeVouxs contacted Esther Winstein. They only hoped they hadn't insulted her five years earlier to the point where she would refuse to help them now. Esther, however, was only too glad to come out of retirement in order to take over Dana's instruction.

As she put it, "We shall have to work very hard. We have five years' worth of damage to undo. I only hope it is not too late."

CHAPTER FORTY-THREE
CHARLOTTE

Today was Diana's eighth birthday. Usually, Charlotte tried not to think about Diana, but the date brought back the memories. She wondered what Diana looked like now, what her life was like. Was she happy? With a twinge of sorrow, Charlotte fervently hoped her baby sister's life was better than her own. She pushed down the question that periodically arose as to why the family who had adopted Diana hadn't wanted her, too. That thought inevitably took her down the path of her almost-adoption into the Klein family and how everyone she had ever dared to love had been snatched away from her.

Charlotte had recently turned thirteen. Unlike most young girls at that awkward age, Charlotte was completely self-assured and as content with her life as possible. She found the fuss over teenaged boys and the constant fretting over one's appearance frivolous. Happily for her, the teenaged boys who knew Charlotte knew enough to leave her alone. And although strikingly pretty, she gave little thought to her appearance. Occasionally, a newcomer, dazzled by her unusual violet-blue eyes, blonde curls, and exquisite china doll complexion, would attempt to become familiar. If someone didn't warn the unsuspecting fellow, Charlotte wasted no time in letting him know she wasn't interested. In her opinion, teenaged boys were even sillier than teenaged girls, and she wanted no part of either.

As she sat in her usual spot, on the picnic table overlooking the playground, Charlotte found her mood to be even more melancholy than usual. She couldn't seem to shake the painful memories from her mind, but perhaps if she put her feelings in writing, it would help. She picked up her inevitable pencil and began to scribble down her thoughts. Totally absorbed in her writing, she failed to notice the tall boy hovering over her until he moved, blocking her light. Charlotte looked up, annoyed. A new boy. That figured. The others knew better than to interrupt her.

"Hi," he said, a broad grin on his face. "I've been standing here for five minutes. Whatever you're writing sure must be important."

Charlotte glared at him. "It is and I don't like being disturbed when I'm writing. So if you'll please go away . . ." She turned her attention back to her notebook.

"Oh. Sorry. I was just going to introduce myself. I'm new here."

Charlotte's body went rigid. "I don't really care," she muttered. She lifted her head and attempted to fix him with one of her icy stares. Without meaning to, she appraised him. He was older, possibly fifteen or sixteen, with dark blond hair and warm brown eyes. She supposed other girls her age would find him handsome.

To her amazement, he laughed. "I was warned about you."

"You should have listened," she replied, her voice cold. "Now will you go away?" Her unblinking eyes challenged him.

"But I thought I was just being chased away by jealous admirers," he continued, ignoring her request. "And I wasn't going to give up without a fight."

"You're crazy," she snapped. "What must I do to get rid of you?"

"Stop fighting it, Charlotte. There's nothing you can do. Because I'm going to marry you some day."

Her mouth dropped open. "Who *are* you?"

"Jeff Bower," he said, bowing, in a ridiculous display of pageantry. "And I'm in love with you."

She made a noise of disgust, got up, and fled.

CHAPTER FORTY-FOUR
ADAM

W hy didn't you tell me you had been accepted into Stanford's PhD program?" demanded an angry Katrina, as Adam walked in the door after work.

"What?" asked Adam, temporarily confused. Then he remembered. "Oh. That was four years ago, Kate. Why are you bringing it up now?"

"Because I just found out about it," she replied testily. "How could you pass up an opportunity like that?"

Adam shrugged. "It didn't seem so important at the time."

"Not important. Are you crazy?"

Adam could see his wife winding up for a good rant when he held up a restraining hand.

"It was when Scott was born, Kate. If you remember, there were more pressing matters."

"Oh." The fight immediately went out of her. "It was my fault."

"No, sweetheart, no." Adam rushed to assure her, pulling her into his arms. "I just didn't want to make the same mistake twice— you know, being so far away from my family when they needed me."

"But what about you? And your needs?"

"I'm happy."

"Oh, Adam," she said, laying her head on his shoulder, "I

know that isn't completely true. You've never been totally comfortable working under me."

"Sure I am. I have job security. You wouldn't dare fire me."

She lifted her head and fixed him with a stony glare. "Adam, this isn't funny. Why don't you see about re-applying?"

He shook his head. "Kate, I'm almost forty. I don't think I have the stamina to go through all that now. And besides, Stanford is too far away. Let's just forget about it, okay?"

"What about U.C.L.A.?" she persisted.

"They didn't have a program for me when I checked before."

"They might now. Why don't we look into it? Then you could commute."

"Oh, Kate, I don't know . . ." But he knew his brief moment of indecision would be the catalyst she needed.

"Well, I do. I'm going to make some phone calls."

Within a week, an interview was set up. Feeling a hundred years old, a nervous Adam presented the doctoral thesis idea he had put aside four years ago. It was accepted with enthusiasm. He requested an extended leave of absence from Fenner starting in September.

———— • ● • ————

"Scotty, don't bother Daddy," said his mother, as he roared through the house one Saturday morning.

"Why?" he asked, his challenging response to everything.

"Because Daddy is very busy today."

"But it's Saturday."

Both Adam and Katrina had agreed after Scott's birth that they were going to devote weekends to their family. No more living at the lab on Saturdays and Sundays. At first, their decision had met with some disapproval from those who were used to the husband-and-wife team being available twenty-four hours a day, seven days a week. But gradually, when it became apparent their decision was firm, nobody bothered them after Friday afternoon for a work-related problem. It had always been something young Scott could count on. Even when his parents often didn't come home from work until he was already in bed, he always knew the weekends were for him. And now they were changing the rules.

"Daddy is going back to school," his mother told him. "And he is going to need some time to himself on the weekends. We are going to have to be patient and understanding."

"Why is he going to school? He's a grown-up."

She laughed. "Because Daddy wants to be even smarter. It's important to him."

It didn't make sense. Grown-ups didn't go to school. And how could you be smarter than you already were? But he knew that his father was no longer available to do things with him, and that wasn't fair.

"It won't be forever, sweetheart, and in the meantime, you and I are just going to have to find things to do by ourselves. It'll be fun. Just the two of us."

Scott pouted. It wasn't going to be the same.

* * *

"Daddy, can I go with you today? Please?" begged Scott. It was a rainy Sunday afternoon, and he was bored.

"I'm sorry, Scotty, not this time."

"But why? I never get to go to work with you anymore."

"Because I'm going to be busy today and I can't keep an eye on you. Maybe some other time."

"But you won't have to keep an eye on me. I'll be good."

"No, Scotty, not today."

The child's face fell. Adam suddenly felt guilty. Since he had started his PhD work, he had hardly had time to eat and sleep, let alone spend time with his son. He had never dreamed the program would be so time-consuming. How in the world had Katrina managed to complete her PhD and still live a relatively normal life? Well, she had been younger, for one thing. She'd had more energy. And she was smarter than he was. She hadn't had to work as hard. Everything came easily to her. But was getting his PhD really worth it? Was his own self-gratification worth the price in terms of his relationship with his son? Was history repeating itself? Katrina continually assured him Scott was fine. But was Adam slowly losing him? He had already lost his daughters. Scott was all he had.

Adam smiled. "All right, pal, just this once. Get your jacket."

"All right! I'll be right back."

"Where are you going?" called Katrina, as Scott raced past the den where she sat reading a journal.

"I'm going with Daddy," he replied, his voice full of excitement.

Katrina stood, the journal dropping to the floor. "Oh no, you're not."

"But Daddy said—"

"I don't care. Your father is very busy and doesn't need you bothering him. Besides, I've got something I want you to help me with today."

"What?" Scott's tone became suspicious.

"I bought a new jigsaw puzzle yesterday. I was hoping you could help me with it."

"I'd rather go with Daddy." He stuck his lower lip out.

"Hey, pal, what's taking so long?" asked Adam, poking his head into the den.

"Mommy says I can't go," said Scott, his lower lip quivering and his eyes filling with tears.

Adam looked at his wife.

"Now, Adam, you know you can't get any work done if you're having to ride herd on Scott."

"One day won't matter."

She put her hands on her hips. "I thought you told me you were behind. Adam, this isn't a game. It's your only chance to get your PhD. Scott will be all right here with me. We're going to work a jigsaw puzzle."

Adam sighed. Katrina was right, as usual, but he sometimes wished she weren't so stubborn about everything. If she said Scott couldn't go, then it would take nothing short of a major confrontation to get her to change her mind. And he didn't want to argue in front of the boy.

He forced his face into what he knew was a pathetic excuse for a smile and said, much too cheerfully, "Tell you what, pal. What do you say I bring home some ice-cream tonight? How would that be?"

"Fine," muttered the child, turning away from him.

— • ● • —

He had been bought off again. Why, Scott wondered, didn't his father ever stand up to his mother? Why didn't his father just tell her he was taking Scott to work, despite what she said? Because his father really didn't want to take him in the first place, that's why. If his father really cared, he would have fought her.

"Good." His father tousled Scott's hair. "See you later. And I want to see that puzzle all put together when I get back. Okay?"

"Sure," said Scott, his voice glum.

CHAPTER FORTY-FIVE
JEFF

Charlotte's initial rebuff failed to discourage Jeff. It might take a while, but he was positive he would win her friendship, and hopefully more. In the meantime, he would look upon her as a challenge.

Jeff thrived on challenges. Nothing in his short life had ever come easily to him. He'd had to work hard for everything he got. But far from wearing him down, his adversities had made him stronger. And his solid faith in Jesus, along with his perpetual optimism and cheerfulness, had helped him succeed.

At sixteen, Jeff Bower was more grown up than many adults twice his age. And also, unlike many adults, he knew exactly what he wanted. He had his life all planned out and, God willing, nothing was going to stop him. Not even Charlotte.

Deserted by his father as a baby, Jeff lived with his mother, a frail woman debilitated by multiple sclerosis, until the age of seven. Although physically limited in many ways, his mother had the faith and courage of a warrior saint. She instilled her strong faith in her small son, making sure he went to church, even when she was too sick to take him, and constantly talking to him about Jesus when he climbed up in her bed during those times when she was too fatigued to get up. She showed him through her own life that hardship and difficult circumstances were just part of life, and everything could be borne in the strength of Jesus.

Finally, unable to care for her son any longer, his mother sent him to her sister's house until her health improved. Jeff's aunt, although a strong Christian woman, herself, was already overwhelmed with six children and an alcoholic husband who had trouble holding a job. She cared for Jeff the best she could, but ultimately her impoverished household simply could not support another child. With a heavy heart, she turned him over to the county children's services, where he was blessed to be placed in a wonderful foster home with the Whitfields, a sweet Christian couple.

In their late forties, the Whitfields had three other foster children, all of whom were in various stages of being adopted into the Whitfield home. The Whitfields also would have adopted Jeff, the energetic little blond boy with the big brown eyes—except for one thing. His mother refused to give up custody. Although she had been ill for years, she clung to the hope that one day she would be strong enough to raise her child again. His mother constantly assured Jeff, during her few brief visits, that he would soon be coming home. But all he had to do was look at her thin, pale body, and her sunken eyes surrounded by dark circles, and he knew the truth. So Jeff remained without permanent roots for most of his childhood.

Mr. Whitfield, a contractor, taught Jeff the basics of carpentry, plumbing, electrical wiring, drywall, painting, laying flooring, and roofing. Many evenings and weekends, Jeff accompanied his foster father, soaking up knowledge and gaining valuable hands-on experience.

Mrs. Whitfield also served as a guardian-ad-litem for children in the foster care system. Jeff soon came to realize she was one of the few people who actually fought for the best interests of the children in the system. He also came to understand that many of the children she advocated for were not nearly as fortunate as he was.

She would tell him passionately, "Jesus loves the little children, Jeff. We must never forget that."

Because of her tireless crusade in speaking out for the "least of these," he made up his mind that when he grew up, he would advocate for children who had no voice.

While with the Whitfields, Jeff learned even more about the love of Jesus, both through the Whitfields' words and actions. At the age of eleven, he accepted Jesus as his Lord and Savior, and committed to live his life for Him.

When he turned thirteen, his mother finally succumbed to the disease she had battled off and on for many years. The last two years of her life, she was too ill to visit him at all. But even as she lay on her deathbed, with Jeff standing beside her, clutching her skeletal hand, she insisted that when she got well, she would come back for him.

"It's okay, Mom," he said gently. "I'll be all right. You go be with Jesus now."

Shortly after his mother died, Mr. Whitfield got transferred across the country. Because there was not time to initiate and formalize a legal adoption, they were not allowed to take Jeff with them. They said goodbye through buckets of tears. Jeff managed to keep a stiff upper lip, assuring them that God had a different plan for his life. But even though his head believed, his heart was crushed.

"What now, God?" he asked through his tears.

He ended up in a series of different foster homes until the age of sixteen, when it became too difficult to place an older teenager. Contrary to what one might expect of a child raised under those difficult conditions, Jeff maintained his sunny outlook. He learned to be flexible, making the best of each situation, and never wasted time wishing for things that couldn't be. He believed God's hand was on his life—leading him, teaching him, molding him for something special— and considered each setback an opportunity for growth. He thrived on hard work and challenges, perceiving them as steppingstones on his life's journey. Jeff had ambition and a goal. He wanted to go to law school someday. It didn't worry him that he was a penniless orphan. Jeff knew if he worked hard enough, with God's help, he would eventually get what he wanted.

And now, he wanted Charlotte. He tried to analyze why he felt so drawn to her. It wasn't just because of her incredible beauty. It wasn't even because he felt sorry for her. After all, everyone at the children's home had a sad story. Nor was it that he perceived her as a lost soul in need of Jesus, which she surely was. But there was something about her, some undefinable quality. He had the distinct feeling God was leading him to her, and deep within this withdrawn and untouchable creature resided an abundance of overflowing love.

The person lucky enough to find the key that unlocked that dormant reservoir of love would be richly blessed. His instincts were rarely wrong.

Charlotte, however, proved to be even more of a challenge than expected. He had heard the talk and the warnings about her. But that only made him all the more determined.

His first approach had gone much the way he had expected, although, on reflection, his impetuous declaration of his love for her might have been a bit much. He had meant to lighten her mood, but his actions had only driven her away. The next day he tried again. He scrutinized her as she sat with her ever-present notebook or sketch pad, totally absorbed in her work. She interacted with nobody. Every so often, she looked up, her eyes focused on her subject, and then bent down again to record something on her pad.

He eased over next to her. "Are you drawing a picture of me?" he asked, his voice teasing.

She glanced up, her eyes flashing with annoyance. "Hardly."

"Why not? Don't you think I'd make a good subject?"

She blew out an exasperated breath. "Look, whatever your name is—"

"Jeff."

"*Jeff*," she sneered, "I just want to be left alone, okay? I told you that yesterday. I don't feel like playing your stupid games." She bent her head to indicate the conversation was over.

"It's not a game, Charley," he said, refusing to be put off. "I told *you* that yesterday." He heard himself blurt out, "I'm in love with you."

"That's ridiculous," she huffed, making no comment on the nickname he had bestowed upon her. "You don't even know me. And if you don't stop bothering me, I'm going to report you to Miss Young."

"For what? Being in love with you?"

"For annoying me," she hissed, her eyes blazing in anger. "I mean it."

"All right, I'll go away," he said, his voice still cheerful, "but I'll be back."

"Don't bother," she muttered.

For the next several days, Jeff made various attempts to break down Charlotte's barriers. She either coldly rebuffed him or walked away from him. After a while, she began to scan the play area to be sure Jeff wasn't around before settling down with her pads and pencils. Finally, she took to staying in her room. This irritated her because she liked being outdoors. She could think better. But Jeff's persistence was driving her crazy.

Her resistance was driving Jeff crazy, too. He had tried all his charm, his wit, his intelligence, and even prayer, but nothing worked. He even tried jealousy once or twice, for it was no problem getting the other girls to pay attention to him. But he didn't want the other girls. He talked to everyone, trying to gain more insight into what made Charlotte tick. Nobody really knew much, and everybody said the same thing. She was strange. Leave her alone.

Finally, the answer came to him. What was the receptacle for all of Charlotte's thoughts, dreams, sorrows? Her inevitable notebook. He had to find a way to read it. But how? She always carried it with her wherever she went. Perhaps at mealtime? He watched, surreptitiously, astonished to see she even scribbled in it while eating. At night? She had to sleep sometime. But what if he got caught? Still, there were always risks in every important venture. Charlotte was worth it.

He lay awake one night, waiting until the house settled down for the night. Then, when all was quiet, he slipped out of bed, his bare feet hitting the cold tile. But he dared not put on his shoes. Slowly, so as not to wake his roommates, he tiptoed to the door. As he opened it, the hinges protested with a loud creak. Jeff stood for a moment, holding his breath. No one stirred and he let out a sigh of relief. Still, he was safe as long as he stayed on this floor. After all, he could simply say he was going to the bathroom. It would only be after he descended the flight of stairs to the girls' dormitory area that he dared not be caught. Being found on the floor of the opposite sex was strictly forbidden in the children's home and carried stiff punishment. He crept to the stairway, stopping every few feet to listen.

Now came the point of no return. His heart beat like a fist against his ribs, and he feared the whole building would wake from the imagined noise of his thudding heart. His feet were freezing, but the rest of his body dripped with sweat. Taking a deep breath, he forced his foot onto the first step. No big deal. After that first step, getting the rest of the way down the flight of stairs seemed relatively easy. At the bottom, he paused again, listening.

Then it dawned on him he didn't even know which room Charlotte was in. Chiding himself, he focused his eyes down the dimly lit hallway. This floor was identical to the one above, with three bedrooms on each side of the corridor and the dorm supervisor's room at the end. Calculating that the girls' living quarters were arranged like the boys, he figured the older girls would be at the opposite end from the supervisor. But that still left two rooms on either side from which to choose. He padded quickly to the end of the hall and stood trying to make up his mind which room to check first.

Hurry up. Don't just stand there, his brain admonished him, spurring him into action to open the door on the left, the one closest to him. Relieved the door opened quietly, he paused a moment to let his eyes adjust to the sudden change from the dim hallway to the utter darkness of the room. He searched the four beds for the tell-tale blonde curls, but didn't see her.

Carefully, he backed out, easing the door closed behind him. He tiptoed across the hall, again, ever so gently opening the door. A shaft of moonlight from the open window across the room cast a warm, golden glow over the two beds on the south wall. And there she was. A halo of light illuminated her pale face, peacefully relaxed by sleep. The effect made her appear like an angel. Jeff could have stayed transfixed forever by that beautiful sight, but he knew he had important business to finish. He crept to the side of her bed.

Resisting the urge to reach out and touch her, he tried to think. Where would she keep that notebook? He crouched and peeked under the bed. Nothing but her shoes. Then, straightening up, he spied her closet. The door squeaked when he opened it, and he stood still, holding his breath, his blood thrumming in his ears. One of the girls mumbled in her sleep and rolled over. Only after he heard the sound of the girl's even breathing did he dare let out his own breath. He frantically searched Charlotte's clothes, ran his hand over the top shelf, and checked the floor. No notebook.

Where then? His pulse raced and his sweaty hands shook with apprehension. He couldn't risk staying here much longer. As he tried to think, his eyes were drawn back to the bed, to the odd way in which the sheet stuck out. His eyes registered why the sheet looked so strange before his brain did. She *slept* with her notebook. He ran his hand across his forehead, as his gut clenched with dread. How in the world was he going to get it now?

At that very moment, almost as if by divine intervention, Charlotte moved her arm and released her grip, allowing the notebook to slide to the floor. With cat-like reflexes, he reached forward and snatched it, just before it hit the floor. By then, his legs were shaking so badly he had to wait until he felt strong enough to move. But as he stood, willing his rubbery legs to advance, a gust of wind from the open window blew through the room, causing the door he had left ajar to slam shut. The startled girls awoke in alarm. Before they could register what had caused the noise, Jeff turned and ran, not stopping until he reached his own room.

He lay in his bed, eyes tightly closed, listening to the commotion from the floor below. The noise had awakened the dorm supervisor and most of the other girls. A brief search was made for the intruder that a couple of the girls swore they had seen, but after a while, it was decided that one of them must have left the door open after returning from the bathroom.

As the house once again settled down for a quiet night, Jeff crawled from his bed. Praying nobody would have to use the restroom, he crept down the hall to the one place where he could have light. There, he sank down on the chilly tile to unravel the mysteries of Charlotte.

Just before dawn, he finished. Bleary-eyed, his fuzzy brain urged him to hurry and return the notebook before people started waking up. But his leaden feet refused to move. Weighed down by the sorrow and bitterness that consumed the lovely Charlotte, he just wanted to sit and weep for her. Or take her in his arms and promise to protect her from all further heartache.

He rose from the cold, hard floor where he had been sitting for hours, totally unaware of the discomfort, his stiff body now protesting. His head warned him that the danger of getting caught returning the notebook equaled the danger of when he took it, but for some reason, he didn't care. He felt drained and numb.

He wandered back down the hall to the stairway, and without even attempting to muffle his footsteps, proceeded back to Charlotte's room. He laid the notebook on the floor next to her bed, resisted the urge to bend down and kiss her, and left.

CHAPTER FORTY-SIX
CHARLOTTE

For the next several days, Charlotte noticed an obvious distance in Jeff. She didn't know whether to be relieved or worried about what he would do next. He didn't approach her while she sat absorbed in her writing, although occasionally, if she looked up, she would catch him staring at her with a sad tenderness in his eyes. Once, she caught herself actually staring at him. Then a thought occurred to her. She reached for her pencil and sketchbook.

She had almost finished, when they happened to look up at the same time. Embarrassed at having been caught, she allowed a thin smile to tug at the corners of her lips. He smiled back. But he made no attempt to come over.

After dinner, she walked past his table.

"Here," she said, handing him the drawing she had made of him.

His jaw dropped, but he didn't say a word. She hurried away.

The next day, he wandered over to the picnic table where she sat drawing.

"You're a good artist," he said, with no hint of the tease he had been earlier.

She nodded. "I like to draw. It's not difficult."

"It is if you haven't got any talent, like me. I can't draw a straight line." He sat next to her, leaving a wide space.

"I'm a good writer, too," she said, casting a sideways glance at him.

"I know."

She met his eyes with an unblinking stare.

"I mean, I've heard." He corrected himself, his face turning red.

She bit her lip, debating whether or not to speak her mind. Then she blurted out, "You did *read* my notebook after you took it, didn't you?"

His eyes widened and the color drained from his face. "H…how did you know?"

She shrugged. "I was awake when you brought it back. Then I realized what had caused the noise earlier. You."

He blew a noisy breath out through his lips. "Why didn't you say anything?"

She shrugged again. "Why bother? What good would it do?"

"Aren't you angry with me?"

"I don't know," she replied honestly. "I guess I'm surprised that anyone would be interested in reading it."

He turned to her, searching her eyes. "Charlotte, for what's it's worth, I'm sorry. It was a terrible invasion of your privacy, and I had no right to do it."

"Then why did you?" There was no anger in her voice, only curiosity.

He sighed and looked away for a moment. Then, turning back to her, he said, "Because I was desperate to know more about you. And you wouldn't let me get close to you."

"But why? Why on earth do you want to know about *me*?"

"Because, Charlotte, as I told you before, I love you. You just wouldn't believe me."

She frowned. "That's the silliest thing I ever heard." She turned her back on him.

"You may think I'm being silly, but I'm not. It was love at first sight, Charley. I knew from the first time I saw you that we were going to be together. Don't you believe in love at first sight?" He reached a tentative hand to her shoulder.

Her body tensed.

"No, I don't," she replied, her tone becoming cold. "That's just in fairy tales and movies."

He withdrew his hand. "Sometimes in real life, too."

They sat not speaking for a moment, as the noise from the other children on the playground crept into her consciousness. Thankfully, no one paid them any attention.

"Anyway," she said, turning back to face him, "I'm never going to fall in love."

"Why not?"

She gave a little snort. "Because bad things always happen to the people I love. I'm like a jinx or something."

"Oh, Charley—"

"Why do you keep calling me 'Charley'?"

"Well, I don't know," he admitted. "Affection, I guess. Like a nickname. If it annoys you, I won't call you that anymore."

She scowled. "Oh, what does it matter? Anyway, as I was trying to tell you, I don't want your love or whatever it is you think you feel for me. And I'm not going to love you back, so you're just wasting your time."

"So, you want to be alone all your life, is that it?"

"Yes. I do just fine by myself."

"You don't even want a friend? How about if I just be your friend?" He raised his eyebrows and grinned, giving him the comical look of a hopeful puppy.

She resisted his charm and pursed her lips. "I don't need any friends."

"Oh, come on, Charlotte. Everybody needs friends. Even you. And you can't keep shutting everybody out who wants to be your friend just because you're afraid of getting hurt again. That's not living."

"I'm perfectly happy with—"

"Oh sure. You're real happy." His voice rose, causing a few of the other children to stop and look. "That's why you sit around brooding all the time. Well let me tell you something, Charlotte. You're not the only person who's ever had problems. You're not the only person who's ever been hurt. You're not the only person whose mother died." His words rushed out, becoming more heated. "And you're not the only person whose father has ever walked out on them. So why don't you stop feeling sorry for yourself and get on with your life?"

With that, he stood and stomped into the building, leaving an astonished Charlotte staring after him.

"Who does he think he is?" she asked angrily, to no one in particular. "My shrink?" But even as she burned with indignation, she could not escape the truth of what he had said. And then there was the other truth. He cared about her. He really cared.

CHAPTER FORTY-SEVEN
SCOTT

I'm sorry, sweetheart, but I have to work this weekend," Katrina explained.

"But you promised we'd go to the zoo," Scott said, jutting out his lower lip and crossing his arms over his thin chest.

"I know," his mother said, her voice full of regret, "and I wish we could, sweetheart, really, I do. But I've got some research that has to be completed before Monday."

He continued to pout.

"Scott, you're old enough to understand that sometimes we can't always get our own way. And you're also old enough to understand that Mommy's and Daddy's work is important." She started for the door.

"I'm impor-nan't, too," he yelled.

Katrina stopped in her tracks. Was Scott deliberately trying to make her feel bad? As if she didn't carry enough guilt around with her. Did other working mothers have these terrible conflicts? She turned to him and knelt down, taking him in her arms.

"Oh Scotty, of course you're important. You're the most important thing in my life. You know that, don't you?"

"Yes," came the child's muffled, unconvincing reply.

She held him away from her and studied his face. His eyes were downcast.

"After this project is over, I'll be able to spend more time with you. Please, Scotty, be patient. Your father and I love you very much, even if we can't always be with you."

He squirmed out of her grasp and ran to his room. She debated for a moment whether she should go after him. She was already late. *No,* she told herself, *he'll be all right. He needs to learn to be a little less selfish, anyway.* Picking up her briefcase, she went out the door.

———•●•———

Scott heard the door close. So she was gone again. First his father and now his mother. They were always at work. They always had something more important to do. How many times had he heard those empty promises, "When this is over?"

Anger bubbled up in his chest. He picked up his stuffed teddy bear and threw it against the wall. Then he tore up his bed, hurling the pillows across the room and yanking off all the covers and sheets, leaving them in a wad on the floor. He felt a little better. As he sat contemplating what to vent his rage on next, Lucy, the housekeeper, walked by his room.

"Why Scott! What on earth are you doing?" She stepped into the room, hands on her hips.

"None of your business!" he shouted at her. "And get out of my room."

The housekeeper glared at him and waved her finger. "That's it, young man. This time I'm telling your parents."

"Go ahead!" he yelled. "If they ever come home, you can tell them."

Lucy stomped out of the room, and Scott slammed the door after her.

———•●•———

"Scott!" bellowed his father. "Come here this instant." Adam stood in his study, holding his precious data sheets. Stray crayon marks appeared here and there from where Scott had been drawing at Adam's desk.

Scott appeared in the doorway, his chin tilted in defiance.

"What's the meaning of this?" yelled Adam. "You *know*

you're not supposed to be in this room. And you *know* you're not allowed to touch my work." He waved the ruined sheets of paper in front of Scott.

Scott didn't reply. He challenged his father's angry glare with wide, unblinking eyes.

"What has gotten into you? It seems like you have been going out of your way to get into trouble lately. I'd like to know why."

"I don' know."

"You did this on purpose, didn't you?"

Scott shrugged.

"Didn't you?"

"I just wanted to draw at your desk," Scott mumbled.

"Why?"

"I don' know." In truth, sitting at his father's desk made Scott feel a little closer to his father, but he didn't say this.

Adam gritted his teeth. "Well, you know what this means, don't you? It means no baseball game tomorrow because now I have to re-do all my notes. Maybe that will make you think twice before pulling something like this again."

Scott turned and walked away. He had no doubt there would not have been a baseball game tomorrow, anyway. His father would have found something else more important to do.

— • ● • —

"Honestly," Adam said to his wife. "I don't know what is wrong with Scott these days. He used to be such a good little boy, but lately it seems like he's got the devil in him."

Katrina set aside the journal she had been reading and sighed. "I know. It's because we're both working so much right now. He's resentful. I think he's being deliberately troublesome because he feels it's the only way to get our attention."

"That's ridiculous," said Adam. "With Charlotte . . ."

They both looked at each other. Adam shook his head. Recently, he had been comparing the two more and more. Why couldn't he seem to stop?

"It's okay." Katrina put her hand on his shoulder.

"I don't know why I keep doing that. Charlotte's been gone

nine years now . . ." His voice trailed off.

Katrina laid her head against his chest. "Maybe it's because Scott is about the same age now that Charlotte was when you lost her. Or maybe it's because her birthday is next week."

"Why do you always have all the answers, Kate?" he asked, laying his head against hers.

"I don't. I don't know what to do for Scotty. Neither one of us can afford to take time off right now. And I don't think punishing him is the answer. Maybe the best thing to do is just ignore it and hope he'll grow out of it."

"And what if it gets worse?"

Katrina shook her head. "I don't know, Adam."

The next day, she bought Scott a shiny new bicycle.

1973 – 1974

CHAPTER FORTY-EIGHT
CHARLES

C harles and Andrea had just returned from their weekly dinner out, which they did to pass the time while waiting to pick up Dana from her weekly piano lesson.

"Dinner took a little longer than usual," Charles said, looking at his watch.

"It won't matter. Dana and Esther are always so absorbed in their music, they never notice the time." As they pulled up in front of Esther Winstein's simple ranch house, Andrea said, "I'll go in and get her."

But before she could open the car door, they were surprised to see Dana running out to meet them.

Dana yanked open the car door and crawled over Andrea to sit in the middle of the front seat.

"Guess what?" she said, her voice full of excitement. "Miss Winstein is taking me to Europe!"

"What?" cried her parents in unison.

"What do you mean she's taking you to Europe?" demanded Andrea. "She didn't discuss this with us."

Charles took a deep breath through his nose, his nostrils flaring with irritation. Esther Winstein never discussed *anything* with them. She always made it clear that she considered Dana's parents more of a hindrance than a help to the child.

"That's it, Charles," Andrea huffed. "This time she's gone too far.”

Charles frowned over his daughter's head, admonishing Andrea not to say any more in front of Dana.

“Sweetheart,” he said, forcing his voice to remain calm, “what exactly did Miss Winstein say?”

Dana squirmed in delight, as she relayed her conversation with her teacher. “She said that this summer she wants to take me with her to Europe so I can go to all the music festivals and see all the important music places. She's going to introduce me to famous conductors and concert pianists. We'll be gone the whole summer.” Her pale face flushed with happy anticipation.

“That's out of the question,” said Andrea, until her husband's warning look quieted her.

Dana, as usual, ignored her mother's protests. “We'll go to Austria and Germany and England and . . .”

Charles and Andrea held their tongues as Dana chattered on about her plans. The drive home seemed endless.

Finally, after getting their wound-up daughter settled down for the night, they slipped into their own bedroom to talk.

Andrea began her tirade the moment the door closed. “How dare that woman make plans like that without so much as consulting us?” She paced the length of the room, flapping her hands in agitation. “Maybe we made a mistake letting her teach Dana. She's filled her head with all sorts of wild ideas and turned her against us.”

“Now, Andrea, calm down. Actually, it's not such a bad idea.”

“What?” She stopped pacing and stared at him. “Surely you're not serious.”

“Let me finish.” He held up his hand. “I'm not saying I approve of the way the old crone just sprung it on the child without asking us first. But think of what a wonderful opportunity this would be for Dana.”

“We take her to the symphony,” Andrea argued. “At least two or three times a year we go to Manhattan—”

“But that's not enough. She does need the exposure to the greatest music from all over the world.”

“Well,” said Andrea, thrusting out her chin, “I'm still not about to turn that woman loose with my ten-year-old daughter for an entire summer.”

“I agree. But what if we go with her?”

Andrea looked taken aback. "Us?"

"Yes, us. I've always wanted to go to Europe. And it's about time I take some of my vacation."

"Oh, Charles! That's a wonderful idea. But I'm still going to give that woman a piece of my mind."

Charles placed a restraining hand on her shoulder. "Let me talk to her. You know how flustered you get around Esther."

Andrea compressed her lips, but finally nodded.

— • ● • —

The next day, Charles went to see Esther Winstein. Although in her early seventies, she was an imposing, intimidating woman. It struck Charles as ironic that Esther Winstein could make him, a highly respected man in his profession and, himself often the source of intimidation to recalcitrant students, so uneasy. And Esther, astute to every detail, always seemed to take full advantage of his apprehension.

"Professor DeVoux," she barked, in her deep voice, a frown creasing the thin strip of skin between her narrow-set eyes, "just what is it you wish to see me about?" She had, again, put herself at an advantage by asking him to sit, while she towered over him, her arms crossed over her flat chest. Her sharp, dark eyes pierced his.

"Well, Miss Winstein." Charles stopped and cleared his throat. His heart pounded erratically. *Why are you being so timid? Are you afraid she's going to swoop down and attack you?* To his disgust, he found his words coming out in a thin voice. "My wife and I are a little displeased at the way in which you took it upon yourself to make elaborate travel plans for our daughter without discussing it first with us."

From her contemptuous look, Charles had the impression she regarded him as something distasteful in which she might have accidently stepped.

"The plans don't concern you," she said, waving her hand, dismissing his objection.

Charles' jaw dropped. In the past couple of years, he had witnessed the woman's unmitigated gall on numerous occasions, but this total disregard of his concern went too far. He suddenly found his backbone.

"I beg your pardon?" he demanded. "Need I remind you, Miss Winstein, that Dana is only ten years old?"

Esther tossed her head. "Dana is a pianist, Professor DeVoux. Her age has nothing to do with anything."

Not about to let her keep the upper hand, he replied in a firm tone, "That may well be, Miss Winstein, but she is still a child. And I am still her father. In the future, I would appreciate it if you would consult my wife and me before promising Dana things you may not be able to deliver."

Her shoulders drooped, and to his relief, Charles saw that Esther knew she had overstepped her bounds. But he also knew she would not give in easily.

She uncrossed her arms and held up her hands. "But how could you possibly object to what I have offered to do for Dana? I would think you'd be grateful."

"I *am* grateful, Miss Winstein, but your method leaves much to be desired. I wish you could learn to think of Andrea and me as being on your side, rather than fighting us. After all, we are all interested in what's best for Dana, aren't we?"

Esther sighed and finally took a seat opposite Charles. "Yes, of course, although I don't think either you or your wife is fully aware of Dana's capabilities. You seem to want to make her into your own concept of 'normal,' which she can never be."

Charles nodded. "I will confess that sometimes Dana's exceptional talent has been difficult for us to understand. But we are trying. Having a gifted child takes a bit of adjustment."

Esther looked thoughtful. "There's something I've always wondered about, Professor."

"What?"

"Where does Dana get her talent? Neither you or your wife is musically inclined. Were her grandparents, by chance?"

Heat flushed his cheeks. He had often worried when this question might come up. He and Andrea had discussed at length about the right time to tell Dana she was adopted. But the time never seemed right.

"No," he mumbled, dropping his eyes. "Freak of nature, I guess."

"I suppose." They sat in silence for a moment. "Well," she

said, finally, "I guess I do tend to get carried away with Dana at times. Sometimes. . ." She paused as her eyes misted over. "I see myself in the child, being able to re-live my own life, re-capturing my own lost opportunities." Her voice took on a faraway quality, as the old woman reminisced.

"You know, I once had a promising future, just like she does now. But then the war came and . . . well, my parents were not very supportive of my ambitions, anyway, and I had to go to work to help the family. I was young and eager to travel, to perform. But in those days, young, unmarried women did not have the freedom they do now. And when the war came, travel was severely restricted, so . . ." Her voice trailed off.

After a moment, she seemed to return to the present.

"Anyway," she said, looking Charles in the eye, "I don't want the same thing to happen to Dana. She needs your encouragement, not your objections. Because I won't always be around to look after her interests."

This was the first time Charles had ever seen anything vulnerable in the hard old woman. He felt a touch of sympathy and understanding. And for the first time, they seemed to be working together.

"Andrea and I talked it over last night—your offer to take Dana to Europe. We both feel it is an excellent opportunity for her and we truly appreciate your generosity."

Esther waited.

"But I hope you don't mind if Andrea and I tag along. Perhaps it will broaden our musical horizons as well as our daughter's. And maybe it will help us to help her."

Esther didn't smile, but she came as close to it as she could, with the corners of her mouth turning up, slightly. "I think that is an excellent idea, Professor."

CHAPTER FORTY-NINE
CHARLOTTE

—— • ● • ——

I'll be eighteen next month, Charley," said Jeff. In June, after I graduate from high school, I can't stay here any longer."

"I know," Charlotte said, her voice tinged with sadness. They were sitting in their favorite spot, the picnic table overlooking the playground, on a beautiful spring day. The clear blue sky and warm, gentle breeze promised an end to a cold winter. Most of the children were light-hearted and carefree, laughing and playing happily, as they tasted the first sweetness of spring. But for the young couple on the picnic table, the perfect day only served as a reminder that June rapidly approached.

"I'm going to wait for you," he told her.

Charlotte's usual practicality asserted itself. "In three years, you'll have forgotten all about me." She stared, unseeing at the younger children at play.

"No, I won't. Charley, look at me." He reached over and gently forced her chin toward him. When she finally met his eyes, he repeated, "I won't forget about you. Who's been your best friend for the past two years?"

"That will change once you're not living here anymore. But

it's all right, Jeff, really. I understand." She breathed out a nervous laugh. "I'm not the basket case I used to be, if that's what you're worried about."

That much, at least, was true. In the two years since she had met Jeff, Charlotte had gradually released some of her pent-up anger and let her perpetual guard down, just a little. The barriers were still in place, but a bit less rigid. At least she didn't demand to be left alone all the time. Close relationships, except with Jeff, were still difficult for her, but she was making an effort to be friendlier to people.

After Charlotte discovered that Jeff's father had also deserted him, she came to realize she was not so alone. She began to see that carrying around so much hate for her father was counterproductive, especially when she didn't even matter to him. Did her father waste time thinking about her? She doubted it. *Then why*, she asked herself, *should I waste time hating him?* It was better to let go, as Jeff told her, and get on with her life.

As time went by, she found herself dwelling less and less on the injustices life had dealt her. Her style of writing began changing to reflect her more positive attitude. And little by little, she became happier. And little by little, Jeff began to share Jesus with her.

He broached the subject again as they basked in the glorious spring day. All around them, new life budded—from the azalea bushes, exploding in an array of magnificent colors, to the dogwood trees competing in display with their glorious blooms. It seemed easier to talk about God while surrounded by the beauty of His creation.

"I liked going to church with my daddy when I was little," Charlotte said, "but after living with my grandparents . . . I don't know. I felt like God was always angry with me. It seemed that way, too, like He was always punishing me for not being good enough."

"Well, the part about not being good enough is true," he told her.

She looked at him, questioning. "How can you say that? You think I'm a bad person? It's not like I've ever murdered anyone or done anything really bad like a lot of other people."

"God doesn't compare our goodness with other people's goodness. He compares us to Jesus. Jesus is the standard. And none of us can live up to His standard." Jeff paused, allowing Charlotte to absorb his words before continuing. "The Bible says, 'all have sinned and fallen short of the glory of God. And the wages of sin is death.' Not only physical death, but spiritual death, or in other words, eternal separation from God."

"If nobody's good enough, then what's the point in trying?" she replied, her shoulders slumped in defeat.

"Because the Bible also tells us that 'while we were still sinners, Christ died for us.' Jesus took the punishment we deserved for our sins upon Himself when He died on the cross, so that we might be right with God. You see, God loved the world so much that He sent His only Son, Jesus, to save us from our sins. God truly is a God of love."

Charlotte snorted. "That doesn't sound like the God my grandparents worship."

Jeff nodded. "Sometimes, people get caught up in trying to live by rules. They get so busy doing things for God or not doing things they believe God won't like, they lose sight of the love and the grace and the mercy of God. They get so wrapped up in the laws and regulations they think are required by their religion that they lose the joy of the Lord."

She sighed. "My grandparents sure didn't have any joy in the Lord. They kept telling me to fear the Lord."

"Well, we certainly need to do that, too, but fearing the Lord doesn't mean being afraid of God. It means recognizing God for Who and What He is—Creator of the universe. He created all there is. He created you and me. He is King over everything. It means He's boss and we're not." He gazed into her eyes with an intensity reflecting his eagerness to make her understand.

She remained silent, mulling over what he said

"You see, Charley, we do good things for God out of gratitude for what He has done for us—not because it will get us to heaven. The only thing that will get us to heaven is accepting the salvation God has offered us through Jesus, not by living with a lot of rules."

Charlotte chewed on her lip. "So God really wasn't punishing me by causing all those bad things to happen?"

"No, Charley. God is love. Sometimes we suffer because of bad choices others make. God gives us the freedom to make choices, even if those choices sometimes hurt others. But the Bible tells us that He can take any bad situation and make it for good."

"How is anything that's happened in my life good?" she demanded, her voice rising.

Jeff took her hand and caressed it with his thumb. "I don't know, Charley. I don't have the big picture. Only God does. But I do know He has a plan for your life."

"A plan?"

"Yes." He grinned." One that includes me."

She withdrew her hand and slapped him playfully on the arm.

He grew serious. "My feelings for you are not going to change. You think I'm going to run out on you like everyone else?"

She didn't answer.

"Well, I'm not. I know you have trouble believing that, but it's true. The only reason I even brought up the subject of my leaving the home was to reassure you. And I'll prove it to you when the time comes."

Her relationship with Jeff, thus far, had remained chaste, partially due to the fact that teenage romances at the home were frowned upon, and partly because Jeff wanted it that way. He was not unaware of the fact that he was three years older than Charlotte, and although she was mature for her age, she was still little more than a child—a deeply wounded child. He didn't want to do anything to cause her to question his true intentions. He could wait until she was ready. She was worth waiting for.

As they talked about the future, he became more and more excited. "I've got everything lined up, Charley. I'll be working for Chandler Construction during the day, and I'll be going to the University of West Florida at night. It'll be hard work, but there's good money to be made in construction."

His enthusiasm for his future did not rub off on her. For his sake, she was glad he failed to notice her lack of response. She wanted to be happy for him, but her heart felt as though it were being crushed.

"And I should be able to save some money for law school, if I'm careful. Maybe I can even get a scholarship."

"Sounds like you're going to be too busy for me," she said, starting to feel sorry for herself.

He put his arm around her and pulled her close. "No, I won't, Charley. I don't care how busy I am, I'll have time for you. After all, I'm doing this for us."

"What do you mean?" She drew away.

He gave her an exasperated look. "Haven't you heard a word I've said?"

She didn't answer.

"I'm not doing it all for myself, you know. I want to make something of myself so that when we get married, I'll be able to support you. I don't want us to have to struggle for every penny like my mother and my aunt did."

For the first time since they had begun this conversation, Charlotte allowed herself a little spark of hope. Then she quickly doused it. Everyone important to her had made false promises and nobody had ever kept them. She wasn't going to be hurt again. Jeff had told her that God had a plan for them, but she couldn't quite let herself believe it. But she could see it was important to Jeff that she believe him.

Lest she say anything to give her true thoughts away, she just smiled. He hugged her tightly again. This time, she did not pull away. Sitting there with Jeff at that moment, she felt safe and loved. She could feel the beating of his heart against her own, reassuring her he was here. Fervently, she wished she could keep this moment forever and that June would never come.

— • ● • —

June came much too quickly. Charlotte dutifully attended Jeff's graduation and made a pretense of being brave. But as she watched him walk forward to receive his diploma, she felt tears well up in her eyes. Quickly, she turned away, afraid he would look up and see.

Drat, I wasn't going to cry.

It took a great deal of effort to get her tears under control. By the time the ceremony ended, her chest felt constricted with grief, and it took every shred of strength she could summon to hide her feelings. She had to appear happy for Jeff's sake. After all, it was his big night.

He sought her out of the large crowd. "There you are!" he cried cheerfully, waving his diploma. "Well, what do you think? I made it! I didn't even trip going up the steps to the podium." He wrapped his arms around her, crushing her against his chest.

For a moment, she felt like she would burst into tears. She mustn't now. It would spoil Jeff's graduation. Taking a deep breath, she pushed herself away and smiled up into his face. "I'm so proud of you, Jeff."

"Hey Jeff!" called a group of other graduates. "You coming, or what?" Several members of the graduating class waited to leave for the after-graduation party. The happy group laughed and teased one another, oblivious to Charlotte's broken heart.

"Yeah, just a minute."

"Hurry up. We don't want to miss all the fun."

He sighed deeply, turning back to look into Charlotte's face. She wore a pasted-on smile, but her lower lip trembled. He pulled her to him again.

"Oh, Charley. I wish you could go with me tonight," he breathed into her hair.

She did, too, but unfortunately, she had to go straight back to the home after the ceremony.

"It's okay. You go and have fun," she said, in a wavering voice.

"It won't be nearly as much fun without you." He continued to hold her.

"I . . . better go. I'll miss the bus back." She put up a hand and brushed away a tear.

"I love you, Charley. I'll be back next weekend to see you."

So now it begins. Already his new life can't include me. Next weekend, he'll have something more important to do. The tears started to roll down her cheeks, as she fought to hold them back.

Jeff reached down and tilted her chin up toward him. Then, for the first time, he kissed her, gently at first, and then more urgently. She didn't know how it was possible to feel so wonderful and so miserable at the same time. She could taste the salt of her own tears intermingled with the sweetness of Jeff's lips.

Then, abruptly, he pulled away. "I love you, Charley," he repeated. "I'll be back for you." He blew her a kiss as he ran to catch up with his friends.

"I love you, too," she called after him, shocking herself.

CHAPTER FIFTY
DANA

As the trip to Europe grew closer, Esther Winstein coached Dana every evening on the various music festivals they would be attending. Dana could barely contain her excitement, as a whole new world of music opened up to her. With her limited experience, she'd had no idea how much more there was to learn. In her eager anticipation of the upcoming adventure, she even displayed less of her frequent artistic moods, which probably would not have been tolerated in an "ordinary" child.

Charles and Andrea grew excited, too. Andrea purchased guidebooks for the various cities they were to visit and spent hours perusing the numerous pages for the "must see" tourist attractions. She scribbled vast amounts of notes which lay here and there all over the house, although, much to her frustration, Dana showed no interest. When Andrea would rave about a cathedral in Vienna, Dana would counter with how thrilling the Salzburg Festival was going to be. Charles, meanwhile, kept out of the discussions as much as possible, for it was obvious there was no way they were going to drag Dana away from her music long enough to see much else of Europe. Dana did allow her mother to take her shopping for a suitable wardrobe, but that was as close as they came to seeing eye-to-eye about their trip.

Although school was not yet out, they left late in May so Dana could begin her tour with the Glyndebourne Festival in Sussex, England. And, as Esther Winstein stated, "Dana will get a much better education on this trip than she will cooped up in that stuffy classroom." For once, Charles and Andrea agreed, for Dana's grades were well above average. Besides, they were as anxious to leave as Dana was.

During the several hours flight across the Atlantic, Dana peppered Esther with dozens of questions. Charles and Andrea, sitting behind the teacher and their child prodigy, listened with immense pride, if not understanding.

"Tell me again about the Glynebourne Festival," Dana begged.

Esther did not need to consult her lists, for she knew each and every festival, soloist, orchestra, conductor, and opera by heart. She also knew Dana already knew everything about the festivals, for she had gone over all the details in depth. However, she loved talking about them as much as Dana loved hearing about them, so she obliged. For Esther, it was the concert tour that had never been.

"The Glyndebourne Festival is held on the grounds of the estate of a man named John Christie, who was a wealthy manufacturer of pipe organs. It is considered one of England's major cultural events of the year," Esther explained, while Dana sat wide-eyed, taking in everything, although she had heard it all before. "Mozart's operas are usually performed, although others are represented, as well. We're very fortunate this year. *The Marriage of Figaro* is going to be presented."

"Oh, you never told us that," Andrea said, leaning forward in her seat. "I love opera."

Charles rolled his eyes.

Dana bounced in her seat as best she could with the constricting seat belt. Esther had made sure to expose Dana to all the music she would likely be hearing on her tour, and Dana had listened to *The Marriage of Figaro* several times.

"*The Marriage of Figaro* is one of my favorites. Remember when you told Mother and Father that I was like Mozart?" prodded Dana. "When you first heard me play, when I was three years old?"

"Charles, she can't possibly remember that," whispered Andrea.

Esther chuckled. "Yes, my humble one, you are a child genius, just like he was. Only you will be greater."

———•●•———

Dana squirmed with delight. She never tired of hearing how wonderful she was. "But Mozart wrote a whole symphony when he was two years younger than I am now." Dana pretended to fret. "And he wrote two operas when he was only twelve."

"Yes, but you, my dear, are a performer, not a composer. Although, as your musical education expands, you shall study composition and, no doubt, will do quite well. But for you, it is more important to develop your natural ability at performance, for this is where your strengths lie." She patted Dana's hand. "Let others write the music. You have the power to make the music live. And for this, you will be remembered."

Dana fell solemn.

Esther squeezed the delicate little hand. "You've plenty of time, my dear. Don't try to beat the time clock of another. I promise your day will come."

Satisfied, Dana leaned back and closed her eyes, dreamily visualizing the future in which she would play for important people in exotic places and be appreciated.

———•●•———

The Marriage of Figaro, performed in the small theatre on the John Christie Estate grounds, was even more enchanting than Dana could have imagined. Crowds of people overflowed from the little structure, but somehow, Esther managed to get them excellent seats near the front. Afterward, Esther took them backstage and introduced them to the conductor and several of the main performers. Andrea stood in awe at being in the presence of such prominent people, but not Dana, who took the meeting in her stride.

Before they left, the conductor took Dana's small hand and said, "I shall look forward to hearing you when you are a famous pianist, as Miss Winstein says you shall be. If she says so, I've no doubt that it will be."

Dana, filled with pride for her teacher who was so well thought of all over the world by important people, replied, "I shall try to live up to her expectations."

The conductor looked taken aback. "Such humility," he declared. "I hope that in the next few years you will consider returning to our festival as a guest soloist rather than a spectator."

"When my playing is perfectly polished, I will be honored to come back."

The adults exchanged startled looks at the poise and maturity of the ten-year-old.

Then the conductor took Esther's hand. "It's been a delight seeing you again. I do hope you can stay a few more days." He brought his lips to her wrinkled hand, his eyes lingering on her face a moment too long.

Andrea watched the interchange. "Yes," she piped up in her timid voice, "we would very much like to stay and see some of the country."

Esther's eyes narrowed. "No, I'm afraid it's impossible. We're off to London tomorrow."

"But . . ." Andrea began to object. They had only just arrived and hadn't had a chance to see anything.

"We're on a very tight schedule," Esther stated emphatically.

"Oh, I am so disappointed," said the conductor, still holding Esther's hand. "I would love to show you around myself."

"Oh, that would be lovely," said Andrea, a sense of longing in her tone.

Esther shot her a piercing look. "As I said," she repeated, "we're off to London tomorrow. But thank you for the invitation."

As they exited the theatre, Andrea demanded, "Why must we leave for London tomorrow, Esther? We've only just arrived and we're all tired from traveling."

"Because I'm presenting Dana to the guest pianist with the London Symphony Orchestra tomorrow night," Esther told her.

"The Russian pianist, Nadia Karushnikoff."

All three of them stared at her, too stunned to speak.

"I had wanted to save it for a surprise," she added, the corners of her mouth turning downward.

—•●•—

London in late May was delightful. Bright, cheerful sunlight filled the normally dismal, gray sky, gently warming the damp, cool air. All around, the promise of life renewing itself showed in the gentle pastels of spring. They stayed in a hotel overlooking the Thames River and the Houses of Parliament. Although they were all tired, Andrea's lists of things to see precluded them from resting.

Esther begged off, but Andrea insisted on taking Charles and Dana on a sightseeing boat trip on the river, and then on to St. Paul's Cathedral. She was trying to decide which museum she wished to see next, when Dana reminded her of the time.

"Oh, dear," Andrea said, "how could it have gotten so late? I did so much want for Dana to see the National Gallery and the Tate Gallery."

Charles smiled. "We don't have to see everything in one afternoon."

"That's right, Mother," said Dana. "Besides, I don't care all that much about museums."

Andrea bristled. "Well, young lady, be that as it may, you are going to see everything you can. This is a wonderful opportunity for you, and I want you to experience some other culture in life besides music."

"But, Mother, how can you expect me to get excited about some old paintings when I'm going to meet Nadia Karushnikoff tonight?"

Andrea threw up her hands. "Oh, honestly. I give up."

Charles laughed and tucked her arm through his. "Patience, my dear, patience. We will see to it that Dana suffers through every museum and art gallery in London, if that's what you want. But let her have tonight."

For perhaps the first time in her life, Dana was nervous. She said very little during the ride to the Royal Albert Hall, where the concert was to be given. She watched, spellbound as the most famous concert pianist in the world, Nadia Karushnikoff, strode confidently across the stage to a thunderous applause. Close to six feet tall, with jet black hair swept up into a French twist adorned with a large, glittering clip, Nadia's very presence demanded esteem. She wore a simple, but elegant black dress with a flowing skirt and a tight bodice that softened her rather angular features. She stood by the piano, bowed slightly without smiling, and then gracefully slid onto the bench.

Dana felt her mouth go dry. *I'll never be like that,* she thought, suddenly miserable. She reflected on her petite build and delicate coloring. How could she ever present a commanding appearance?

Her inner musings were broken, however, the moment the pianist's fingers hit the keyboard with Rachmaninoff's *Prelude Opus 32, Number 12 in G-sharp minor.* Then nothing mattered as Dana became totally lost in the emotions of the music. As the notes built and died, Dana's imagination conjured a beautiful, frozen Russian wonderland, like something out of a Dr. Zhivago movie. Although a short selection, when the last few notes tinkled away like tiny snowflakes gently falling against a frosty windowpane, the audience sat hushed. Then, after a long pause, they let loose with a roaring applause. The remainder of the concert consisted of mostly Rachmaninoff concertos. Dana found herself wishing the orchestra sitting behind this extraordinary woman would be quiet so Dana would not miss a note from her magic fingers.

The concert ended much too quickly. To her surprise, Dana found three hours had flown by. As they waited for the crowd to thin out before going backstage, Dana felt Esther's sharp eyes on her, picking up on her increasing anxiety.

"What is this?" she demanded. "Surely you're not nervous?"

"No," Dana lied. Then seeing it was no use hiding anything from Esther, she admitted, "Well, maybe a little."

"Ha! You've nothing to be afraid of. In ten years, you'll have replaced Miss Karushnikoff as number one."

For once, Dana wasn't so sure. They made their way backstage while Dana's discomfort intensified. What was the *matter* with her, anyway?

Nadia stood in the center of a large group of admirers, easy to pick out in the crowd with her imposing height and presence. They waited patiently until the last of the group departed and Nadia's eyes fell on them. Holding her head high, she floated over to where they stood.

"Ah, Miss Winstein," she said, in a deep, thickly accented voice. "I would know you anywhere. What a pleasure to meet you at last." She extended a stiff hand.

Esther took it with her own firm hand. "I've waited for this moment a long time. Your father would have been proud of your performance."

"You knew her father?" blurted out Andrea.

Nadia turned her piercing dark eyes on Andrea. "Oh, but yes. They studied together at the conservatory. My father, the late Boris Prokochev spoke of Miss Winstein quite fondly." She came close to a half smile. "In fact, he always said that if Esther Winstein had completed her tour, he would not have been considered the greatest pianist of his day."

Color flooded into Esther's face.

Dana's eyes widened at seeing Esther actually blushing. She wondered what other secrets her music teacher held.

"How very kind he was," said Esther, "although I would heartily disagree. Your father was unquestionably the greatest. And now you. What a pity he didn't live to see your talent surpass even his own."

The pianist's eyes glazed over with unshed tears. Then she quickly composed herself. "Ah," she said, "but that is ancient history." She turned her attention to Dana. "And this must be the child prodigy you spoke of. You shall play for me, yes?"

Andrea's hand reached out to touch Dana's tiny shoulder.

Dana began to tremble. "To be honest, I'm a little nervous, Miss Karushnikoff."

"Ah. But that is good," said Nadia. She raised her exquisitely arched brows. "Let me tell you something, my young friend. Nervous is good, for it gets the adrenaline pumping. It keeps you from becoming too complacent about your performance."

Dana stared at her, open-mouthed. "But . . . but surely, *you* don't get nervous anymore?"

Nadia nodded. "Every time. Before every performance. God help me the day that I do not."

"But *why?*" cried Dana, her amazement overcoming her own

fears. "You're the best in the whole world."

Nadia bent down, bringing her eyes level with Dana's. "Because, my dear child, when you are no longer nervous about your performance, then the heart has gone out of your music."

Those words would remain engraved in Dana's mind for the rest of her life.

"Now, come. Play for me. I promise I will not bite you."

Dana grinned. "All right."

Her parents exchanged looks filled with pride.

— • ● • —

Next, it was off to France for the Prades Festival, with Andrea pouting that they had not had enough time to see everything in London.

"But, Mrs. DeVoux," Esther explained, in a barely concealed tone of exasperation, "if we stay in London any longer, we'll miss the festival."

"Well, I fail to see why we can't skip just *one* festival," Andrea replied.

They all looked at her as if she had lost her mind. She returned their stares for a moment, then backed down. "Oh, never mind me." She forced a small laugh. "I know this trip is for Dana. Besides, there's a lot in France I want to see."

— • ● • —

This time, however, while Dana and Esther delighted in the works of Bach, Shubert, and Brahams, Andrea made her own arrangements for a side-trip to Paris, with her uncomplaining husband. There, they delighted in the Eiffel Tower, the Notre Dame Cathedral, the Arc de Triomphe, and the Louvre, without having to worry about the concert schedule. One afternoon, while Charles rested at the hotel, and she had shopped until she was exhausted, Andrea sank into a chair in one of Paris' delightful open-air cafes and reflected upon her strange existence.

The warm sun bathed her in peace as she sat watching the busy world go by. Would she really want to trade her life for a more normal one? After only a moment of pondering, she realized that even with the difficulties that came from being the mother of an exceptional child, she wouldn't have it any other way. In a few years' time, Dana was going to be world famous, and *she* was going to be the mother of a world-famous pianist. What would all their lives have been like had Dana not come into their world? She compressed her lips. In a word—dull. She and Charles would still be in sleepy little Auburn, Alabama, he with his comfortable tenure, and she . . . she had to laugh. She would still be filling her days with busy work, charity work—all the things that wives of successful men were supposed to do. And feeling empty, aching for a child.

And what would have become of Dana? Suppose she had ended up in an orphanage or with parents who were unable to devote their own lives to her special needs? Would another great genius have been lost to the world forever? Andrea shuddered to think of the possibilities. No, without the right parents to nurture and support her talent, Dana could not have achieved her remarkable success, regardless of how gifted she was. Andrea felt a warm glow of satisfaction in the knowledge of just how important she and Charles were in shaping Dana's future. Their role in their daughter's destiny was just as important as if they had endowed her with her musical genes.

Andrea frowned. They should have told Dana she was adopted by now. But the time never seemed right. Dana was always so moody, so wrapped up in her own world. How would such a revelation affect her? Perhaps it would be better never to tell her. After all, how would she ever find out?

Andrea glanced at the time. Heavens! Had she really been sitting here this long? Charles was probably getting worried. She rose and made her way back to the hotel.

"I'm sorry to be so late," she called out, as she entered the room. "I lost track of time. I was thinking, Charles," she continued, without waiting for him to answer, "perhaps tomorrow we could go on to Versailles. I would love to see Louis the Fourteenth's Palace."

"Oh, I'm sorry, dear," replied her husband, "but Esther just called. She wants us to leave for Germany tomorrow."

Andrea's face fell. "Of course." She sighed. "The Bayreuth Festival?"

He nodded, crossed the small length of carpet separating them, and took her in his arms. "We'll come back some day, just the two of us. I promise."

"Oh, it's really not important. I was just thinking this afternoon how incredibly fortunate we are to have Dana. And what's a small amount of inconvenience when we are so blessed with her?"

Charles smiled. "You're so right, my dear."

———•●•———

It was on to Bayreuth, Germany, with Dana talking non-stop about the Prades Festival.

"Well, tell us about the Bayreuth Festival," said Charles. "I swear I can't keep them all straight. What's this one about?"

"Why, Daddy," cried Dana, as if horrified by the thought that he didn't know. "Bayreuth is the shrine of Wagnerian opera."

Charles tried not to wince. Not more opera. How much more could he take? "Oh. That's nice, dear," he said, his tone saying otherwise.

"The festival was first held when Wagner was still alive. His very first performance was the complete *Ring of the Nibelung*."

"Oh, I see," said Charles. He had never heard of *Ring of the Nibelung*. He glanced at his wife, who was having difficulty controlling her amusement.

***

Sight-seeing in Germany was drastically reduced in order to take in the Bayreuth Festival, and then on to Bonn for Beethoven Week, and finally, to Ansbach for Bach Week. Andrea did manage to find a few hours, however, in which to subject her uninterested daughter in the Cathedral of Cologne and the attractive towns of Nuremberg and Rothenburg, built in the Middle Ages.

"It's incredible, Dana," she said. "These buildings have been beautifully restored. They look just like they did five-hundred years ago."

"How do you know that, Mother?" asked a bored Dana.

"Well, because. My guidebook says so."

Dana let out a dramatic sigh.

"But darling, don't these streets look like something out of a fairy tale?"

"If you say so, Mother."

"I wish we could be here for Oktoberfest. Wouldn't that be fun?"

Dana's mouth dropped open. "Surely you're not serious?"

"Well, why not? They have *music*, don't they?" A touch of sarcasm crept into Andrea's voice.

Dana snorted. "Mother, I would hardly call 'oom-pah bands' music. Besides, who wants to be in the middle of a crowd of barbarians drinking beer and eating bratwursts and dancing in the streets?"

Andrea flattened her lips. "Honestly, I don't know when you became such a snob, Dana. It's a most unattractive trait."

Dana rolled her eyes. "Are you finished looking at these gothic cathedrals, Mother?"

"Yes, I suppose so," said Andrea, her shoulders sagging.

Andrea suppressed her disappointment at not being able to get to Munich, with its world-famous art collections and historic treasures, and the Black Forest at Stuttgart. Berlin, of course, was out of the question, for it was way too far. But Salzburg waited.

CHAPTER FIFTY-ONE
JEFF

The first few days after graduation kept Jeff too busy to think much about Charlotte. With the help of one of the social workers, he found a small, furnished efficiency apartment close to Chandler Construction, where he was to start work three days later. During those three days, he cleaned up his new home, bought necessities, and paid his utility deposits with the dwindling amount of money he had left.

Realizing he was truly on his own now, considered an adult, and totally responsible for himself could have been a little frightening, had he let himself dwell on his circumstances. But Jeff handled the transition like every other new challenge in his life— cheerfully and optimistically, and praising God. His apartment, while not lavish, served his needs, and after a thorough cleaning, actually looked quite cozy. It had a combination living room/bedroom, with a hide-a-bed sofa, a tiny kitchenette, and an even smaller bathroom. The one window overlooked the parking lot, but he didn't expect to be spending much time looking out the window. With the last of his money, he bought a few frozen dinners, and hoped to be able to save enough to have a telephone installed and buy a small second-hand television by the end of the month.

The day before he started work, he went to the University of West Florida and applied for a student loan. For just a moment, he stood on the warm concrete steps of the administration building watching the carefree students sauntering along with their armloads of books, and wished he was fortunate enough to be able to go to college full time.

But I'll make it eventually.

Then he went on his way, not allowing the unattainable to depress him.

The construction job also kept him busy. With good weather on their side, the crews often put in overtime, working until it grew dark. Sometimes, Jeff would get to work by six in the morning and not get home until eight or nine o'clock at night. Although hot, back-breaking labor, he was young and strong, and liked being outdoors. After the first week, his skin turned a deep bronze, and the sun bleached his dark blond hair, giving him the appearance of a beach bum. He ached in places he didn't even know he had muscles, but his body became firm and strong.

The first weekend, the foreman offered him double-time if he would work Saturday. He fleetingly thought of Charlotte. But she would understand. That kind of money was just too good to pass up. Besides, he'd see her at church on Sunday. On Saturday, however, they still hadn't finished, and as they were working on a deadline, a handful of men volunteered to work Sunday. After a brief hesitation, Jeff decided to join them. He could make almost as much in two days as he had made all week.

On Sunday night, he dragged himself home, bone tired. How he wished he could afford a telephone so he could at least call Charlotte and let her know why he hadn't gone to see her. He hated waiting another whole week. But every dollar he made put him that much closer to his ultimate goals. Without undressing, he collapsed into bed.

The next weekend brought rain. It was probably for the best, Jeff told himself, so he wouldn't be tempted to put in overtime again. Early Saturday morning, he cleaned his small apartment, made a dash through the drizzle to the corner deli to pick up lunch supplies, and then caught the bus to the other side of town. The rain subsided as he stepped off the bus a block away from the home.

Although anxious to see Charlotte, he took his time as he ambled up the street, taking in his surroundings with new eyes. The dreary, overcast sky added to his melancholy mood. He didn't know why he felt so strange, as if he didn't belong here anymore. Then, like a jolt, it hit him. He *didn't* belong here anymore. The old saying, "you can't go home again," was true. He stood across the street from the familiar faded brick building which had been his home for a little over two years. After only two weeks away, it seemed as if it were a lifetime ago that he was a part of that world. However, he knew one thing for sure—no matter how much else had changed for him in the short span of two weeks, his feelings for Charlotte were stronger than ever.

At the thought of her, his heart began to beat faster, and he couldn't bear to waste any more time. He raced across the street and up the cracked concrete steps. He paused for a moment after entering the building, the uneasy feeling that he was an intruder settling in his gut. He tried to shake off the feeling as he wondered where Charlotte was. She wouldn't be outside on the wet playground, so that meant she was probably either in her room or in the recreation room. He decided to look in the recreation room first, and then, if she wasn't there, he would ask someone to check her room.

He strolled with purpose through the nearly empty corridor, his wet sneakers squeaking loudly on the tile floor. He passed the dining room, where lingering odors from breakfast hung in the humid air. His stomach rumbled in protest, reminding him he had skipped breakfast. Ignoring his stomach, he paused at the entrance to the recreation room and searched the group of noisy, restless children who were forced to be cooped up inside. But he didn't see Charlotte. He backed out of the room, without watching where he was going, and collided with the home's director, Miss Young.

"Why, Jeff," she cried, after regaining her balance and her composure. "How nice to see you. How are you?"

"I'm fine, Miss Young," he replied, his tone polite, but distracted.

She placed a firm hand on his arm, leading him back down the hall.

"And how is the new job? And the new apartment?" She chattered on, craning her neck to look up into his face. "It looks as if you've been out in the sun quite a bit."

"Pardon? Oh, yes. Yes, ma'am."

Finally, after it became apparent that Jeff wasn't listening to her small talk, she stopped, let go of his arm, and asked point blank, "What are you doing here, Jeff? Is there a problem we can help you with?"

"Oh, no. No, ma'am. I came to see Charlotte."

Miss Young's face clouded over. "Oh, I see." She looked around the hallway. "If you would, Jeff, please, I'd like you to step into my office for a few minutes. I need to talk with you privately."

Eager to see Charlotte, he hesitated. But how could he refuse? Finally, he said, "Well, all right."

They moved inside and she closed the door, shutting out the din from the recreation room. "Please, Jeff, sit down."

His eyes cut to the chair. Then clearing his throat, he said, "If you don't mind, ma'am, I am in kind of a hurry."

She flattened her lips and turned sideways to him, staring out the window. "Jeff," she said, then paused, as a breath of air escaped through her lips. "I don't know quite how to say this, except to just say it."

"Ma'am?"

Letting out a sigh, she turned around and faced him again. "You see, Jeff, you are now considered an adult in the eyes of the law."

"Yes, ma'am."

"But Charlotte is still a minor."

A knot began to form in the pit of his stomach.

"Ordinarily, as you know, the home discourages boy-girl relationships under its roof. Surely you can appreciate the problems that would undoubtedly arise in such close living quarters if such relationships were not dissuaded." She met his eyes.

Jeff swallowed around the tightness constricting his throat and looked away, fearing her next words.

"But frankly, I allowed your friendship with Charlotte to continue while you were here because it seemed to be good for her. As you know, she has had a lot of problems."

He forced his eyes back to hers, waiting, holding his breath.

"However, as you are now legally an adult and Charlotte is still a minor, I simply cannot allow your relationship to continue. I have a responsibility toward the children in my charge."

His heart plummeted. "But, Miss Young, you know me. You know I would never do anything to hurt Charlotte."

She regarded him with sad eyes. "Yes, Jeff, I do know that. But I cannot allow a precedent to be set. I would lose my job if I allowed our teenaged girls to carry on relationships with adult men. You do understand, don't you? It has nothing to do with you, personally."

At a loss to respond, Jeff grasped for anything he could think of to change her mind. It had never occurred to him that he would not be allowed to visit Charlotte. She wouldn't be eighteen for three whole years. How were they supposed to be apart for three years?

Finally, fighting to hold his emotions in check, he asked, "Could I just see her for a few minutes? Just to explain why I can't come see her anymore?"

She hesitated. "Oh, all right. I really shouldn't let you, you know. It is against the rules." Then her face softened. "But I'm not totally unsympathetic to your dilemma."

"Thank you, Miss Young."

"But only for a few minutes. Then you're going to have to leave. And I'm sorry to say you will not be permitted to visit with her anymore after this."

CHAPTER FIFTY-TWO
DANA

S alzburg, the fourth largest city in Austria, and the birthplace of Mozart, famous for its music festivals, would require more time than all the other cities they had visited so far, for the Salzburg Festival began the last week of July and continued through August. Featured in the festival were the Vienna Philharmonic Orchestra, the Vienna State Opera, and many other famous conductors and soloists. Interspersed among the various classical themes and operas were a number of contemporary works, as Salzburg was also the original city for the Festival of the International Society for Contemporary Music. At this particular festival, only twentieth century music was performed. Many of these pieces, Dana had not heard.

Here, Dana was introduced to Hugo von Reichmonn, one of the guest conductors, and perhaps the first person during the entire trip not to be immediately taken with the budding prodigy or Esther Winstein.

"I am quite busy, Miss Winstein," he told her, after she pushed her way into his private sanctum. "I don't have time for . . ." He waved his arm, attempting to find the right insult. "For piano recitals by little American urchins." His nose wrinkled in disdain. "Or conferences with old-maid piano teachers."

Dana's chest heaved with anger.

"Now see here, Herr von Reichmonn," Esther lashed out at

him, "I was a close friend of your late mentor and teacher, Herr Frederick Baum." The conductor's eyes widened just a hair. "In fact, he spoke to me often about you, when you were first under his guidance. He did not exaggerate your ability, but either he exaggerated your character, or you have learned your appalling manners along the way." She drew herself up to her full height and locked eyes with him. "I brought Dana to you as a favor to him. She will be famous one day, with or without your having given her an audience, but I thought I would do you the courtesy of having the opportunity to hear a young prodigy. However, we are quite busy ourselves, so we shall be on our way." She turned to escort Dana from the room.

His features softened a little. He turned to Dana with a critical eye. "She certainly doesn't *look* like an artist."

Dana returned his rude appraisal with a cold stare.

"Very well, then. Show me how wonderful you are." He crossed his arms over his chest and thrust out his chin.

Esther motioned for Dana to take her place at the piano. Instead, she said, "No, Herr von Reichmonn. But I'll tell you something. You'll live to regret this day." With that, she turned on her heel and walked out, Esther's laughter following her.

Vienna awaited, with its world-famous opera house. This time, it was Charles who initiated side trips to the Belvedere Palace, the Hofburg, and the Kunsthistorisches Museum. The closest he came to music was visiting the statue of "The Waltz King," Johann Strauss, in the city park. Even Andrea couldn't drag him to a performance by the Vienna Boys' Choir.

"But Charles," she said, "this isn't opera."

"I don't care. All those high voices will remind me of opera."

"Very well." She left him to his own amusement, as she accompanied Esther and Dana. She later discovered he had attended a soccer game.

There was no question of his attending the Bregenz Festival, which also featured opera.

The hectic pace continued on to Italy for the Florence Festival and the Festival of Two Worlds in Spoleto. While Esther and Dana delighted in the operas, ballets, chamber music concerts, dramas, and solo recitals, Charles and Andrea visited the massive Cathedral of Florence, the Uffizi and the Pitti Galleries, and the Medici Palace.

"Look, Dana," her mother exclaimed, showing her the numerous polaroid snapshots, "here is the statue of *David* by Michelangelo. It's eighteen feet high."

"Mother, it's positively obscene," she declared, after examining the life-like male anatomy.

"Oh, for heaven sakes. It's *art*! It's Michelangelo. Well, look, here is the statue of *Perseus* by Cellini."

Repulsed by the figure in bronze standing atop a nude, decapitated female figure, Dana wrinkled her nose. "How disgusting." She put down the photographs. "Let me tell you what we did today." She didn't wait for her mother to comment. "We heard Monteverdi's *Orfeo*. Can you imagine? It was one of the very first operas."

"Did you?"

"And tomorrow we're going to hear a harpsicord concert featuring the sonatas of Domenico Scarlatti. Wouldn't you like to come, Mother?"

"Well . . ." She hesitated. "Your father did want to see the Palazzo della Signoria."

"Oh, Mother, another old building. Daddy will like this concert. It's not opera."

"All right. I'll love it, I'm sure. But only if you promise to come with us to the Bargello Museum the day after tomorrow. You really must see *The Madonna and Child* ceramics."

"But, Mother, the day after tomorrow, we leave for Greece."

The effects of the fast-paced travel were beginning to take their toll on all of them, as they flew to yet another country. Esther, who up until this point had persevered with the boundless energy of a woman half her age, was unnaturally quiet as Dana chattered away about all the previous things they had seen and heard.

"I had no idea there were so many different forms of music," she said, for perhaps the hundredth time. "It's all so exciting."

Esther smiled and nodded.

"And you know so many famous people," Dana continued. "You haven't told me how you met all of them. Please, tell me everything."

"Some other time, maybe."

"But, Esther, you're as famous as most of them. I had no idea. I know you must have a lot of stories to tell."

"I'm not famous, my dear," Esther replied, her tone taking on a sadness, "although in my time, I . . ." Her voice trailed off. "I'm awfully tired just now. Let's talk of this later."

Disappointed, Dana let the subject drop. She glanced back to her parents, sitting in the airplane seats behind them, as Esther dozed off. As usual, her father napped and her mother had her nose buried in a tourist book. She looked up before Dana could look away.

"Dana," she said, "you absolutely *have* to see some of the history of Greece." Dana rolled her eyes. "As soon as we get to Athens, I'm going to arrange for tickets for a performance at the theater of Epidaurus."

Against her will, Dana's interest sparked.

"Here," said her mother, handing over her guidebook. "See? It's an ancient, outdoor theater, where they perform Greek tragedies. You'll enjoy it."

"Well," Dana replied, "if it doesn't interfere with the Athens' Festival. But really, Mother, please don't drag me to all those crumbling ruins."

"Of course not," replied her mother tartly. "Whoever heard of wasting their time in Greece visiting the Parthenon? And I suppose the Acropolis and the Acropolis Museum are out of the question."

Dana hated it when her mother became sarcastic. Why couldn't she understand that Dana simply wasn't interested in old ruins and museums and cathedrals? Dana had but one love—music.

——— • ● • ———

Andrea didn't push for Dana to join her and Charles in their sight-seeing, although Dana did agree to accompany them to the theater of Epidaurus to see Euripedes' *Medea*. Esther declined the invitation, saying she was too tired.

"I'm a bit worried about Esther," Charles remarked, as they set off for their evening.

"She's probably exhausted, like the rest of us," said Andrea, "and at her age, it isn't good for her."

"Maybe we can persuade her to slow down. We've about come to the end of our festival tour."

"Oh, no," said Dana. "We still have the Holland Music Festival and the Edinburgh Festival."

"But we'll have to backtrack," said Charles.

"We were never told anything about going to Holland and Scotland," added Andrea.

"We have to go west, anyway, in order to get home," said Dana, with obvious forethought. "We won't be backtracking."

"But what about school? I don't think it's a good idea for you to miss the beginning of the school year."

Dana wrinkled her nose. "I can catch up, you know I can. But when will I ever get the chance to hear the Holland Music Festival and the Edinburgh Festival again?" She parroted Esther.

"More opera, I suppose?" asked Charles, sighing deeply.

"Some, but there'll also be orchestral and chamber music, recitals, and choral works."

"Tell me," groaned her father, "have we left *any* festivals out?"

"Oh, yes," cried Dana. "The Lucerne and Zurich Festivals, the Israel Festival, the Sibelius Festival in Finland . . ."

"Never mind. I suppose I had to ask," muttered Charles.

——— • ● • ———

By the time they got to Amsterdam, they were all dragging. Nevertheless, Andrea made a valiant effort to expose them to boat trips on the canals and visits to every museum and art gallery she could.

"After all," she told them, "The Netherlands have produced some of the world's greatest painters, and we owe it to ourselves to see the art of Rembrandt and van Gogh."

While she and Charles trudged through Amsterdam's Rijksmuseum and the Stedelijk Museum of modern art, Dana, who begged off, and Esther devoted their time to the various operas, chorales, and concert music of the world-famous Amsterdam Concertgebouw Orchestra.

To her disappoint, Andrea had missed the Tulip Festival, which was held in the spring. But she still managed to persuade Charles and Dana to accompany her to the Keukenhof Garden in Lisse, where every type flower in every color imaginable greeted them.

And, of course, what would be a visit to Holland without seeing the windmills? Charles and Dana humored her in this, for they were both too tired to argue.

———•●•———

Finally, they came to Edinburgh, home of the Edinburgh International Festival of Music and Drama. Even Dana showed signs of weariness.

Here, Esther introduced her to Max Frasier, an American pianist, who played predominantly jazz. For him, Dana played the first movement from Beethoven's *Moonlight Sonata*.

"Of course, it is excellent," he mused, his head tilted and his eyes thoughtful, "but how about something more modern? *Rhapsody in Blue*, perhaps?"

"I'm afraid I don't know much modern music," Dana admitted, suddenly feeling very limited in her range.

"What?" He turned accusing eyes on Esther.

"Dana's studies have dealt primarily with the classics, Mr. Frasier."

"But this is a grave injustice!" He tossed his long, somewhat unkempt brown hair back in a dramatic gesture. Waving a bony hand, he continued in his tirade, "How can you expect the child, good as she may be, to become a complete musician if she's stuck in the classics?"

"She had—"

"Miss Winstein, I am appalled. Appalled! You, of all people, should realize what limitations you have placed upon your student."

"But she has shown no interest in anything but the classics."

"And who is *she* at her young age to know what's best for her?" He bent down, bringing his face level with Dana's. "You listen to me, young child. It is well and fine to be accomplished in one type of music. But you will never be a true musician until you have the versatility to appreciate and perform *all* types of music, whether it is to your liking or not. Do you understand?"

"Yes, sir," she said, feeling a bit ignorant for not having realized this fact before.

"You mark my words," he continued, so close that she could feel his hot breath, "when you go to Juilliard . . ." He paused when he saw the confused look on her face. "Well, *of course* you are going to attend Juilliard." He shot a look at Esther.

"We hadn't discussed it," she said. "It is a little far down the road."

"It's never too early to plan for one's future," he exclaimed, straightening up and waving his hands with another theatrical display. "Anyway, when you go to Juilliard, you will have to be versatile, so you had better get started now." He turned to his piano. "Here. Take this with you and learn it."

He handed her sheet music to Gershwin's *Rhapsody in Blue*.

Dana's eyes widened. "Thank you, Mr. Frasier."

"Don't mention it. Oh, and one other thing. It wouldn't hurt you to learn another instrument."

"Thank you for the advice," Dana repeated.

When they had gone, Esther said, "My dear, when we get back home, I think it's time to find you another teacher."

"But I want you!" cried Dana, in dismay. "You're the best!"

"Not anymore, I'm afraid," replied the old woman.

Andrea was almost too tired to insist on seeing the Edinburgh Castle, but she managed.

— • ● • —

When the exhausted group finally arrived home, Dana announced, "Next year, Esther's taking me to all the American Music Festivals!"

Her parents groaned and collapsed on their bed.

CHAPTER FIFTY-THREE
CHARLOTTE

———•●•———

Charlotte fidgeted in her seat at the public library, her secret meeting place with Jeff. Nobody ever questioned her about going to the library, so it seemed a safe place. And, she thought in defiance, *nobody* was going to tell her she couldn't see Jeff. She didn't care about any silly legal description of minor and adult. After all the time they had spent together at the home, it didn't make sense that simply because Jeff was a few months older they weren't allowed to be friends anymore. The fact was Jeff had come back for her, and she would be darned if something as ridiculous as their ages was going to keep them apart.

The first weekend after his graduation, when Jeff hadn't shown up as promised, she feared her doubt about his commitment to her had come true. He had a new life that didn't include her. But then, the second weekend, much to her relief, he had come. Her heart skipped a beat when Miss Young called Charlotte to her office, and she saw Jeff standing there. Miss Young then stepped out of the office, giving them a moment of privacy. With a choking voice, Jeff tried to explain to her what Miss Young said.

"No," Charlotte replied, her voice firm in refusing to accept the situation. "That's unfair. They can't keep us apart."

"Yes, they can, Charley," he replied. "They can get in a lot of trouble. And besides, Miss Young made it clear I'm not welcome here anymore."

Not to be put off, she shrugged. "So, we'll find a place to meet."

His eyes widened at her suggestion. "Charley! We can't. What if we get caught?"

"So what? If we get caught, all they can do is tell us to stop seeing each other. We really don't have anything to lose, do we?"

His brows furrowed in thought. "Okay," he finally agreed. "Where do you think we should meet?"

"It can't be at school. There're too many people who might see us." She chewed on her lip for a minute. "Wait. I know. The public library." Her voice filled with excitement, as her plan unfolded. "I go there all the time, and hardly anyone else from the home does. It's perfect."

He nodded. "All right. The library. Tomorrow after church."

———•●•———

There he came! After taking a furtive glance around to be sure nobody was watching, she wiped her sweaty palms on her slacks and beckoned him over to where she hid behind a stack of reference books.

He crossed the space between them in a few short strides and hugged her. "Oh, I've missed you," he whispered into her hair.

"I've missed you, too." She allowed herself a moment to snuggle against his firm chest.

He disengaged their embrace and said, "Come on. Let's get out of here."

"Where are we going?"

"You'll see. I've got lots to show you."

They glanced around again, and after ascertaining the coast was clear, made a hasty exit. Once outside, Jeff laughed. "We did it, Charley. And you know what? The bus stop's right around the corner." He took her hand, and they ran all the way, their feet pounding in happy unison along the hot pavement.

Only after they boarded the bus did they stop to catch their breath. He held her hand and gazed with longing into her eyes. Suddenly, a strange shyness inserted itself into Charlotte's outer bravado. Being with Jeff under the constant supervision of the home was one thing—being completely alone with him out in the real world was another. She didn't feel quite as courageous as she had the day before when she had boldly suggested her plan. A mix of emotions swirled through her head. Although doing something she was not supposed to be doing filled her with rebellious excitement, it also scared her a little. She loved Jeff, but in the short two weeks they had been apart, she had to admit he had become an adult. Her status as a child unable to follow him into his world frustrated her. But then, was she really ready to step in his world?

As though reading her thoughts, Jeff gave her hand a reassuring squeeze and smiled. She forced a timid smile back. They spoke very little as the bus drove to the other side of the city. Although Charlotte had lived here for almost ten years, she had actually seen very little of the area. She had vague memories of places she had gone with Amy's family, but she tried not to think about them too often. They brought back too much pain. So, free at last, she watched with interest all the new and unfamiliar sights that rushed by the window.

"We're here, Charley," Jeff said, interrupting her private reverie.

"Where?" She half stood and craned her neck to see, as the bus stopped with a whoosh of its air brakes, throwing her off balance. Jeff caught her and grinned. The entrance to the college campus stood just outside the window.

Jeff rose and pulled her after him. As they alit from the bus, Charlotte got a better look at the huge brick buildings set back from broad walkways and neat lawns.

"This is where I'll be starting night school in September. Isn't it wonderful?" Jeff's voice filled with excitement.

"It's so big." She looked around at the sprawling campus. "How will you ever find your way around?"

Jeff chuckled. "This is a very small campus, Charley. When I go to law school, I hope to go to a big university. One where it takes two hours to walk from one end to the other."

She tilted her head and looked up at him. "Why would you want to go somewhere like that?"

"Because the biggest universities are usually the best. Then when I get my degree, I'll have a better chance of hiring on with a good law firm."

He took her hand, and they moseyed along the hot walkway as Jeff pointed out various buildings. Small groups of students sat clustered in the grassy areas, absorbed in their books, talking with other students, or just lying back on the sweet-smelling summer grass, basking in the warm sunshine. Charlotte watched Jeff's demeanor change as he savored the moment. She knew he wanted her to feel the magic of the campus the same way that he did. His gaze became wistful.

"What's the matter, Jeff?"

"Hmm?" Then, with a sheepish grin, he looked down at her and said, "Oh, just a little wishful thinking, I guess. Some of these kids have no idea how lucky they are to be fulltime students."

"But don't you like your job?" Charlotte had always pictured the ultimate freedom in being out of school and working so she could finally be independent and away from the home.

Jeff motioned for her to sit with him on the wide, shaded steps leading into the student union. She plopped down onto the warm concrete.

"It's okay, but it's not what I want to do for the rest of my life."

"But you said you were making a lot of money."

"It's all right for now. But, Charley," he said, turning to face her, "don't you see? There's so much more to life than just working and making money. You've got to be able to do the things God has laid on your heart, and for me, that's becoming a lawyer so I can help people. I just have to get through all the required education." He sighed. "And since I can't afford to go to college full time, it's going to take longer."

She pondered his words. She had never considered school from his point of view. "So," she said, thinking aloud, "you would be happy if you could go to college full time."

Jeff nodded. "But it takes a lot more money than what I have." He hopped up, attempting to pull her up, too, "Come on. You've not seen the whole campus."

She pulled back from him, her brows knitted in contemplation. He stood towering over her on the steps, as she sat.

"How much money?"

"What?" His eyes narrowed in confusion.

She looked him in the eye. "How much money would you need?"

He laughed. "What difference does it make, Charley? It's a pipe dream. I'll get my degree eventually. It's all in God's timing. Come on."

"Would five-hundred dollars be enough?"

"What?" he cried, his mouth dropping open.

"I *said*," she dragged out the word, "would five-hundred dollars be enough?"

For a long moment, he just stared at her. Then finally, he answered. "Yes, Charley, it would certainly help. I suppose you just happen to have that much in your pocket."

"No, in my bank account." She returned the stare.

"What are you talking about? Where would you get that kind of money?"

"I've been publishing short stories for magazines since I was twelve. I get a few dollars here and there." She shrugged. "And I haven't spent any of it."

Jeff's eyebrows shot up. "A few dollars? Charley, that's a small fortune. I had no idea. You never told me."

She shrugged again.

"But why haven't you spent any of it, Charley?"

"On what?"

He threw up his hands. "I don't know. Some decent clothes maybe, instead of these hand-me-downs." He gestured to her attire.

His words stung. Charlotte looked down at her clothes and, for the first time in her life, she felt ashamed of her appearance. Anger bubbled to the surface at Jeff pointing out her shabby clothing.

"Well, it's not like kids from the home have much opportunity to shop," she snapped. "Anyway, I didn't spend any of it. If you want it, it's yours." She bit out the last few words, her chest heaving with indignation.

Tears sprung to Jeff's eyes. He sank back down on the steps next to her and took her rigid little body in his arms.

"Oh, Charley," he whispered. "I love you so much." He felt her relax just a little. "But I can't take your money." She started to interrupt, but he didn't let her. "I wouldn't feel right, Charley. I need to make it on my own. I know you offered the money to me out of love and it's the most beautiful and unselfish thing anyone has ever done for me."

"But—"

"Come on," he said, hopping up. "We don't want to waste the whole day sitting here. I'll buy you a milkshake at the student union and then I'll show you my apartment."

She gulped, and a strange fluttering sensation settled in her stomach. But not wanting to spoil their precious little time together, she nodded.

After their milkshake, they walked the several blocks to Jeff's apartment. "Maybe I can get a used car in the next couple of months," he said, "so I won't have to walk your legs off all over town."

She smiled. It didn't matter. She was content and with the person she loved, and free, if only for a few hours. As they walked along, she drank in the everyday sights and sounds, magnified into the extraordinary by her own happiness. The singing of cheerful birds, the brightness and warmth of the sun, the rush of the traffic—everything seemed wonderful today. All of her senses seemed to be heightened by her own awareness. She could only attribute it to being in love. Periodically, she gazed up at Jeff, as if somehow amazed that he was actually there, and afraid that if she blinked her eyes, he would be gone.

All too quickly, the magic walk ended.

"Here we are," he announced, his voice full of pride, standing before an attractive apartment building.

Her heart began to pound. What would happen now?

He led her inside and up the stairs, his eagerness palpable. "It's the last one of the right, with an excellent view of the parking lot." He inserted the key in the door and opened it, displaying his living area. "I even cleaned it up, just for you."

Charlotte stood in the doorway and surveyed the neat little room. "It's very nice." Her voice sounded tight and strange to her ears.

"Well, come on in." He laughed, as she stood fixed to the floor. "How about a Coke or something? Are you thirsty after that long walk?"

"Sure." Why did she feel so uncomfortable? She loved Jeff. She trusted Jeff. But her inner voice told her she shouldn't be here alone with him in his apartment.

She was still standing in the same place when Jeff came back from the tiny kitchen bearing two Cokes. He handed her one, closed the door, and headed to the couch, where he sat back and took a long swig from the bottle.

He wiped his mouth with the back of his hand and patted the spot next to him. "Come sit down, Charley."

She took a deep breath and crossed the small expanse of floor between the door and sofa on rubbery legs, lowering herself to the cushion, her body stiff, her gaze straight ahead.

"Oh, Charley," he murmured, putting his arm around her and drawing her to him. "Alone at last." His lips brushed her forehead. "You don't know how long I've waited, how long I've dreamed of this." He leaned in and touched his lips to hers, then pressed a little harder.

She tensed and pulled back, wincing at the perplexed look on his face.

"Charley," he said gently, "you're not afraid of me, are you?"

"No." She averted her eyes.

He removed his arm. "Charley, look at me."

She rolled her eyes up to meet his. She hated this feeling. How could she love Jeff so much and be so scared right now? It wasn't as if she were totally ignorant. She had read enough books to know how wonderful the physical love between a man and woman was supposed to be. So why the sensation of panic?

"Charley, I love you. I'd never hurt you. You know that, don't you?" His soft brown eyes searched hers.

She nodded and gulped, unable to speak.

He pulled her to him, hugging her tightly. Buried against his chest, her muffled words came out. "I'm sorry, Jeff."

He stroked her yellow curls. "No, *I'm* sorry, Charley. We shouldn't even be here alone like this. I know better. It's just that I'm so happy to be with you and anxious for you to experience everything new with me and . . . and sometimes guys get carried away in ways they shouldn't, which is why we shouldn't be here alone."

She relaxed and looked up at his face. "Oh, Jeff, it's just that I hear the other girls at school talking and . . ."

He held her at arm's length. "I love you, Charley. And I will always respect you and protect you." He stood, pulling her up with him. "All right, then. What do you say we get out of here and go check out the park down the street?"

Charlotte's heart soared as she understood how much Jeff truly loved her. How would she bear a week-long separation?

CHAPTER FIFTY-FOUR
KATRINA

Scott had been in kindergarten only two months when Katrina received a summons to appear at the school for a parent/teacher conference. The timing couldn't have been more inconvenient. In the process of breaking in a new assistant, her work had fallen behind. The thought crossed her mind to ask Adam to go in her place, or at least attend with her, but his PhD project was not going well. Everything was taking much longer than expected, and his nerves were constantly on edge these days. For quite a while now, she regretted her role in encouraging him to get the degree. It seemed as though the pursuit of his PhD was making him miserable, but he had too much time invested to quit at this point. And now, on top of everything else, Scott had to act up at school.

Feeling overwhelmed, Katrina left work early for the dreaded conference. With her mind still focused on her research, she sank onto the uncomfortable child-sized chair opposite Scott's teacher.

One would think, she thought in irritation, *they could at least provide the adults with something more suitable to sit on for these conferences.*

She felt ridiculous squatting eight inches from the floor while the thin, bird-like teacher perched above her.

"I apologize for the chair, Mrs. Wallace," said the teacher, although she did nothing to offer a more comfortable option.

"It's *Doctor* Graham. And if you don't mind, I'm rather in a hurry. I've still got a lot of important work to finish today."

The teacher flattened her lips. With her bifocals threatening to slide down the length of her sharp, pointed nose, and her sparse, graying hair drawn tightly into a bun, she reminded Katrina of a bird of prey.

"Doctor Graham," said the teacher, exaggerating Katrina's title in a tone just short of derision, "I realize you are a busy woman. However, it is your son whom I am concerned about. Therefore, I would hope you could spare a few moments for his sake."

"Well, of course," snapped Katrina. "I do care about my son, Miss Vernot. That's why I'm here. What's the problem?"

The teacher spoke through clenched teeth. "Well, Mrs. . . . Dr. Graham, Scott appears to have problems adjusting to the academic and social environment of the classroom."

Katrina's impatience grew. "So, what does that mean? 'Academic and social environment'?" She waved her hands as she echoed the teacher's words. "Cut the scholastic mumbo-jumbo, Miss Vernot, and just tell me what he's done." The little chair was becoming increasingly unbearable, and she felt at a ridiculous disadvantage in this position.

Miss Vernot took a deep breath through her nose, and Katrina could mentally calculate the woman counting to ten, as she no doubt did when provoked by one of her little pupils.

Then the teacher replied in an overly calm voice, "Scott is disruptive. He's uncooperative. He's defiant. He does not interact well with the other children. He picks fights. And he's a bully."

Katrina sat dumbfounded.

"Surely, you've noticed problems at home?"

"No," replied Katrina, shifting her weight. "He's a good little boy."

Miss Vernot raised her eyebrows. "Doctor Graham, just how much time do you spend observing your son's behavior at home?"

Katrina flew off the tiny chair, toppling it and almost falling in the process. "What are you implying?" she demanded. "That I'm not a fit mother? That I don't spend enough time with my child?"

"Certainly not, Dr. Graham, but—"

"Let me tell you something. If Scott has problems, it's because of *you*, Miss Vernot. Scott was fine until he was put into your class."

Katrina stormed out of the room, her angry footsteps resounding on the tile floor.

How dare she say those things! She fumed as she exited the building and marched to her car. She yanked open the door and fumbled for her keys. But as the engine turned over, Katrina began to recall little incidents that she had tried to ignore, hoping they would go away. She'd had a conversation with Adam not too long ago in which they discussed Scott's unruly behavior. Lucy had also complained about Scott's insolence and disrespect.

"I suppose it's all *my* fault," Katrina grumbled. "It's always the mother's fault."

Why is it, she wondered, her heart still pounding with indignation, *a woman can't have a career and still be considered a good mother? Men don't have these issues. Men can have it all—a home, a family, and a career. But if there are problems with the children, the blame always falls on the mother.*

A slow sensation of shame for the way she had attacked the poor teacher crept into her angry thoughts. She knew Miss Vernot was right. Katrina just hadn't wanted to admit that fact. But hadn't she already made supreme sacrifices in her career for her child? She was only now beginning to get back to where she should be professionally.

Confound it. She had an important job as the only female head of a pharmaceutical research facility. Plus, she had lost years of research on the birth control pill to Quiven Pharmaceuticals, who had beaten her to marketing. The board had not been pleased about that. And now? Now what was she supposed to do? Obviously, she couldn't be a good mother and a good scientist at the same time. She was going to have to choose.

It isn't fair, she thought, growing bitter again.

Then her mind flashed back to right after Scott was born—when she hadn't even *wanted* to go back to work. When had her priorities changed? Now it seemed she resented the time she had to give up from her career for her son. Guilt flooded over her.

No, that's not really true. I don't resent my son. I love Scott. It's the constant pressure at work. I can't just put in my eight hours a day and then come home and leave the lab behind. It's always there with me. And my child is suffering because of it.

Scott, the only child she would ever have, had become a lonely little boy who needed his mother, and he was crying out for help in the only way he knew how. He should be the most important thing in her life. What job in the world was more important than being Scott's mother?

She took a deep breath. "Oh, dear Lord …"

How long had it been since she had really talked to God? It seemed that relationship had suffered lately, too. Her feelings of guilt threatened to engulf her. Her faith had always been so important to her, but in the busyness of life since her marriage, the move to LA, the new job, and Scott's birth, she had to admit she had allowed her relationship with God to be placed on the back burner. Oh, they still went to church when there wasn't some crisis or another at work, but they hadn't really gotten plugged in to the body of believers like they had in Atlanta. How had things slipped so far out of control? She tried to pray for guidance, but she sensed no answer from above.

Then and there, she made up her mind. She drove back to the plant, her face set in determination.

After parking in her usual spot, she squared her shoulders, marched into the office of Milton Rasner, and announced to the astonished executive, "Milt, I'm resigning immediately. My son needs me."

CHAPTER FIFTY-FIVE
ADAM

The telephone was ringing as Adam walked in the door. He had just come from donating blood at the local Red Cross center, a habit he had gotten into after Katrina's emergency surgery requiring several pints of blood following Scott's birth. Usually, the procedure didn't bother him, but for some reason, today, he felt especially drained, and his head throbbed. Perhaps he was coming down with something.

The insistent ringing of the telephone told him nobody was home. He rushed to grab the receiver and, somewhat breathless, answered, "Hello?"

"Trenton Graham here," growled the angry voice on the other end. "What's this nonsense about my daughter quitting her job?"

Adam stared at the receiver, his brows drawn into a frown of confusion. "I don't know what you're talking about," he told his father-in-law. Maybe the old geezer had finally flipped his lid. "She's at work right now."

"Then why," demanded Katrina's father, his voice becoming more heated, "did I just receive an hysterical phone call from Milton Rasner telling me Katrina had resigned in order to 'be a mother'?" He spat the last three words with disdain.

Adam rubbed his throbbing forehead and sank onto the sofa. This news couldn't be true.

"Where is Katrina, anyway?" barked Trenton Graham. "I want

to speak to her."

"I don't know. I just walked in the door. This is all news to me. You've caught me completely off guard."

"Don't you and your wife ever talk to each other?" snarled the older man.

"Look," said Adam, growing irritated, "I don't know any more about this than you do. When Katrina gets home, I will have her call you."

"You do that."

Adam winced at the sound of the phone slamming down on the other end.

He sat holding the phone for a long time before replacing the receiver. The pounding in his head intensified after the disturbing call. He had been so tired lately. But he had been working so hard. That must be the reason. He couldn't remember ever feeling so weak from having donated blood before. It must just be fatigue.

His eyes wandered to his briefcase that he had dropped on the floor in his haste to answer the phone, and with a weary mind, he mused on the hopelessness of ever completing his PhD. It seemed like every time he made a little progress, he had two setbacks. And the added burden of the required teaching load on top of everything else was becoming overwhelming. He hardly ever saw his son anymore, a familiar pattern he had vowed would not be repeated with *this* child. This was not the way he had planned his second chance at fatherhood. So why was he killing himself over this degree?

You know why. Because you can't bear the thought of constantly feeling inferior to Katrina.

How he envied his wife, sometimes. From all outward appearances, everything came easily for her. So then, what was her father talking about? Surely, she hadn't actually quit her job. Her career was important, not only to her, but to the entire company. She must have had a run-in with Milton Rasner again. Adam grimaced. Fenner Pharmaceutical should have gotten rid of that unproductive old windbag years ago. He had no concept of how to adequately do his job.

Shaking his head, as if that might help the insufferable headache, Adam headed to the kitchen in search of aspirin, growing frustrated as he rummaged through the cabinets and drawers. Drat!

He couldn't ever find anything in his own house.

Of course, that's because you're so seldom at home.

Where the heck was Lucy? Was this her day off? He had just managed to locate the elusive medicine bottle when he heard the front door slam.

"Adam? Are you home?" called Katrina.

"In here," he answered, swallowing the tablets with a gulp of water from the sink. He heard her clacking heels on the parquet floor, the sound magnifying in his throbbing brain. Scott followed behind.

"You're home early," said his wife.

"Daddy!" interrupted Scott. "Guess what. Mommy and me went shopping and—"

"Mommy and *I*," corrected Katrina.

Scott, obviously impatient to tell his news, threw her a dirty look. "And she bought me a 'rector set! Can you help me put it together?"

Adam pinched the bridge of his nose and willed the aspirin to kick in. Right now, he could hardly think straight. "Maybe after dinner, son." He sunk into a kitchen chair and closed his eyes.

"But I want to *now*!" Scott screwed his face up into an ugly scowl.

"Your father said after dinner," Katrina repeated, in her calm, patient voice. "Now do you remember what we talked about earlier?"

"Yeah." The pouting child walked away, his shoulders slumped.

"Good," Katrina called after him. "Besides, I want you to get cleaned up for dinner."

She grabbed three potatoes from a bowl on the counter, and started pulling out pots and pans, talking over her shoulder to Adam as she worked. "How come you're home so early?" she asked, as she attacked a potato with a paring knife.

"I gave blood today. Kate—"

"Oh, that's right. Well, how did your day go?"

"Fine. Listen, Kate—"

"Did you start on the animal controls yet?"

"No," he answered, his voice rising. "I need to—"

"Well, when are you going to start?"

"Confound it, Kate!" he exploded. "Put down that knife and listen to me!"

She jumped at his outburst and turned, searching his eyes. Then she laid down her knife and plopped into the chair across the table from him. "What is it, Adam?"

He rubbed his forehead. "I got a call from your father just a little while ago."

Her eyes flickered with annoyance. "So. Milt 'the Rat' Rasner has already been on the phone to Daddy. And?" she asked, her tone becoming icy.

"He said you quit your job," Adam answered, adding a little laugh as if he knew it was ridiculous, but was afraid it might be true.

"I did," she replied, matter-of-factly. She didn't elaborate. "I really don't want to have this conversation now." She started to get up.

Adam stared at her. "For Pete's sake, Kate! Weren't you even going to discuss this with me?"

"Of course, I was," she answered briskly. "But now is not the best time. I've got to get dinner started and—"

"Well, where's Lucy?"

"I let her go."

"What?"

She huffed out a loud sigh and settled back into her chair again. "I let her go," she repeated. "I really didn't want to have this discussion now, but it looks like I'm going to have to whether I want to or not." Her lips flattened and she glared at her husband.

"I would appreciate being enlightened here, Kate," Adam grumbled. "What's going on? Why did you quit your job?"

Katrina took a deep breath. "Because of Scott. I—"

"Scott?"

She held up her hand. "Adam, we are both going through our lives with blinders on. We're so wrapped up in our careers that our relationship with our son is seriously deteriorating. And until today, I refused to admit it to myself. But I had a conference with Scott's teacher today and—"

"What conference? You didn't tell me anything about a conference."

"Because you're always so busy!" she snapped. Then she lowered her voice. "And *I'm* always so busy. Scott is growing up without parents, Adam. And it's already having adverse effects on him. His teacher said he is having a lot of problems at school. He's only six years old. If we don't correct these problems now, imagine what he's going to be like in ten years."

"But, Kate, you can't just quit your job. A lot of people depend on you." A knot began to form in his stomach as he tried to assimilate the ramifications of her actions through the blinding headache.

Katrina shook her head. "Nobody is indispensable. Except maybe a mother. Scott needs his mother."

"Well, maybe you can cut back your hours a little, you know, like you did when you first went back to work."

She shook her head. "You know that won't work. First, it's this little thing, then it's that little thing, and before you know it, you're back to putting in eighty-hour weeks again."

Although a direct assault on his pride, he had to bring up the next point. "Katrina, we can't make it financially on my teaching assistant's salary."

"Of course we can. You'll have your degree soon, and until then, we have some savings."

What was the use? Katrina was the most stubborn woman he had ever known. Besides, his head hurt too badly to continue arguing. And now his neck was beginning to ache, too.

"All right, Kate," he said, rising from his chair with considerable effort. "I'm going to go lie down for a while before dinner."

Her sharp eyes locked on his. "Are you okay, Adam?"

"Yes. Just a little tired." He started across the kitchen floor, which suddenly looked endless to his swimming vision. He grabbed his head with both hands to steady his dizziness. Then everything went black. The last thing his mind registered was the sound of Katrina screaming.

CHAPTER FIFTY-SIX
JEFF

As time went by, Charlotte became more and more comfortable being alone with Jeff, and they both looked forward to the weekends when they could be together. Jeff, for his part, was careful to respect boundaries.

In September, Jeff started night school. Although the construction work had slowed down a little, there were still days when he raced the clock to get home from work, shower, and make it in time for his first class. Then, when his classes let out at nine or ten o'clock, he went home and studied until midnight or one, grabbed a few hours' sleep, and woke up by five-thirty or six the next morning. He kept up the pace for several weeks before the exhaustion caught up with him.

One night, in his English class, during the professor's discourse on Chaucer, he closed his eyes for just a moment. The next thing he knew, he felt a gentle nudge. Startled, he sat up and looked around.

The nudger turned out to be a pretty brunette, with long straight hair and twinkling blue eyes.

"I'm sorry to wake you," she whispered. "I let you sleep as long as possible, but you were starting to snore."

Jeff ran a hand over his head. His brain felt fuzzy. He cast an anxious look at the professor, but the man still droned on, apparently oblivious to the exchange in the back of the room.

"How long was I asleep?" he asked.

"About a half-hour," replied the girl, laughing quietly.

"A half-hour?" he cried, in a hoarse whisper. A few people turned to glare at him. He lowered his voice. "Why didn't you wake me up when you saw me fall asleep?" He began to flip through his notes in a panic. "How much have I missed?"

"Relax. You can borrow my notes. You looked like you needed the nap."

He sighed. "Yeah, I guess I did. Thanks."

After class, as Jeff gathered his books, the pretty brunette tucked her arm through his and flashed him a dazzling smile.

"Look, why don't we go over to the student union for a cup of coffee? You can copy my notes there. Besides, you look like you need a cup of coffee."

Jeff hesitated. "Well, I really should be getting home. Perhaps I could just borrow your notes and return them tomorrow?"

"Oh, come on. I'll buy." She tugged at his arm.

Too tired to fight her persistence, he reluctantly agreed. It seemed the only polite thing to do since she was lending him her notes.

As they walked along, she said, "My name's Lisa Williams. What's yours?"

"Jeff. Jeff Bower."

"Well, Jeff, it's nice to meet you. I've seen you in class, but you always rush away so quickly afterwards, we've never had a chance to talk."

He studied her face for a moment. He didn't remember seeing her in class, but then he seldom noticed the other students. He hadn't wanted to form any friendships that might put demands on his already limited time.

"Yeah, well, I have to get up early for work."

"Oh?" she said, with a spark of interest. "Where do you work?"

"Chandler Construction."

"Oh. So that's why you have such a great tan. And such . . ." She paused and raised her eyes to his face, batting her lids flirtatiously, "such a strong-looking body."

Starting to become uncomfortable, he avoided her eyes and remained silent.

She still clung to his arm. "I'm going to be a model, but the only way I can get my parents to pay for my modeling school is by promising to get a college degree." She sniffed. "Big deal. Like I'm really going to need a college degree when I'm a super model making the big bucks. How about you? What do you want to be?"

He didn't want to have this conversation, but he couldn't be rude. "I'm going to be a lawyer."

"A lawyer? Wow! I think that's great. You must be really smart. So how come your parents make you work? Don't they want you to be a lawyer?"

"My parents are dead," he said bluntly, wishing he could get away from this girl.

"Oh, I'm sorry." Her face showed the appropriate degree of sympathy before her tone brightened. "Here we are." She propelled him up the steps to the student union.

They got their coffee and found a table. He reached for her notes, but she refused to be quiet so he could concentrate.

"So where do you live? You live alone?"

"Yes."

"Wow! That's neat. I wish I could get my own place. My parents are always on me about something. It's a real drag around my house. Maybe I could see your apartment sometime."

He didn't comment as he scribbled the notes as fast as he could.

"So, do you think you might want to hang out with me sometime?"

"Uh, I don't really have much free time."

"Oh. I guess you don't have a lot of extra money, either. We could just go to your place."

Again, he didn't answer, as he finished transcribing the notes, thinking it would be a miracle if he could read them. "Well, that does it. I really need to be getting home."

"But you haven't even touched your coffee."

"Oh." He took a quick swig of the bitter coffee and stood to go. "Listen, thanks for the use of the notes. See you around."

"Wait," she cried. "How are you getting home?"

He stopped. He didn't want to be rude, but he really wanted to get away from her. "There's a bus that leaves every half hour."

She consulted her watch. "You just missed it. Come on, I'll

drive you."

"Oh, no, I couldn't put you to that trouble. I'll just walk. It's not that far."

She stood and latched on to his arm again. "Don't be silly. I don't mind."

Unable to resist, Jeff allowed her to lead him to the parking lot. She talked non-stop all the way.

"This is it," she said, pausing in front of a red Mustang convertible. Tossing her books into the back, she hopped in the driver's seat. "Get in."

There wasn't much else he could do, so he did.

"Where to?" She put her head back and shook out her long, silky hair in a sensuous manner.

Jeff gave her directions and she took off, flooring the gas pedal, her hair flying in the night wind. He caught a faint whiff of her fruity shampoo as her hair blew freely.

"Don't you just love the freedom of the road?" she yelled, over the noise of the engine.

"Yeah." He kept his voice noncommittal, and tried to suppress the unwelcome feelings that were creeping into his consciousness as he sat next to this pretty, free-spirited girl on this warm, breezy ride through the city. She turned to him and smiled again, that spellbinding smile. He didn't want to encourage her, and he knew it would take very little encouragement. But she was so pretty and so . . . available. And the night was so balmy and beautiful and liberating after his wearying schedule. He leaned back and closed his eyes, trying to think of other things.

"Here we are," she said suddenly, pulling up in front of his building and turning off the engine.

He opened his eyes and started to gather up his books. "Thanks. I do appreciate everything, really."

"Jeff." She put her hand on his arm.

His body stiffened.

"I'm really attracted to you," she murmured. "Do you find me attractive?" She moved closer to him.

"Yeah, sure I do, but I… I have a girlfriend."

Her eyes narrowed slightly. Clearly, she thought he was making an excuse. "We don't have to be involved," she whispered, scooting even closer and running her hand down the front of his shirt. The door handle dug into his back as he moved away. She began lightly kissing his ear.

Against his will, he relaxed a little. It felt so good. He closed his eyes again and breathed in the clean scent of her. After a moment, he felt her lips seeking his, gently at first, and then, at his reluctant response, she pressed her body into his and kissed him harder. Her hand expertly undid the buttons on his shirt and found its way next to his skin. As if in a dream, his left arm seemed to move by itself, wrapping around her shoulders and pulling her closer, while he buried his right hand in her long, lovely hair.

Prickles of heat and desire warmed his body as the kiss intensified. Then she broke away and whispered, "Why don't we go up to your apartment?"

With a sense of unreality, he opened the car door, pulling her after him. She clung to him, kissing and caressing, as they slowly made their way up the steps. He felt a raging conflict between his head and his body. He knew this encounter would bring nothing but trouble, yet he was powerless to stop.

They had just ascended the flight of steps leading from the downstairs hallway, when he saw her. Huddling with her back against his door, her knees pulled up to her tear-stained face, sat Charlotte.

"Jeff?" she croaked, in a thin voice.

Jeff's blood ran cold, as he thrust Lisa away from him. "Charley!" he cried, rushing to kneel by her side. "What are you doing here?"

"I ran away from the home." She dropped her head and began to sob.

CHAPTER FIFTY-SEVEN
KATRINA

———•●•———

It took hours before the doctors could tell her anything. Unfortunately, Katrina couldn't tell them much either, for Adam had not complained of feeling ill. And she had been so preoccupied worrying about breaking the news to him about quitting her job, she hadn't been particularly attuned to anything different about him. She had noticed, now that she thought about it, that he kept rubbing his head.

I should have asked him if he had a headache.

Katrina contacted Lucy to come back and take care of Scott while she took up vigil at the hospital. Adam remained in a coma the whole night while the doctors ran test after test. Finally, at mid-morning, a nurse summoned Katrina to Dr. Phister's office.

Her legs jiggled with nervous energy and her eyes darted over the numerous diplomas hanging on the wall, while she sat and waited for the verdict. It had to be bad news. They never called people to a doctor's private office unless it was bad. Probably because they didn't want a public scene of hysteria.

At last, Dr. Phister appeared, looking like he hadn't slept, either. Dark circles ringed his bloodshot, puffy eyes, and he sported a day's worth of stubble on his face.

"What's wrong with Adam?" Katrina burst out, the minute he stepped into the office.

Dr. Phister collapsed into his chair, rubbed his eyes with his index fingers, then shuffled through the stack of papers on his desk.

The agony of not knowing anything became unbearable.

"Well?" she prodded, her voice rising.

"Katrina, we still don't know for sure," the physician replied, "but from the tests so far, it looks like he has a viral meningoencephalitis."

Katrina felt the blood drain from her face. "Oh, dear Lord," she whispered.

"The cerebrospinal tap showed a number of abnormalities. There was increased pressure, extremely high protein, and a high white blood count, predominantly lymphocytes. We've started viral isolation, but it will be a while before we know for sure what we're dealing with. We're also checking serum titers for the more common viruses, but as you know, we really need paired samples at about three weeks apart to get a definitive diagnosis. However, a high titer in a single sample can give us a reasonable degree of suspicion."

Hot tears coursed down Katrina's cheeks as her stunned brain tried to grasp what Dr. Phister was saying. His words seemed to bounce off her skull without penetrating it.

"It would help to know what kind of virus we're dealing with," he went on. "Katrina, has Adam had any recent vaccinations?"

She shook her head.

"Has Scott been sick with the usual childhood diseases? Measles? Mumps? Chickenpox?"

She shook her head again.

"Do you live near the water? Have you experienced an increase in mosquitoes?"

"Wait!" she cried. "Adam's research. He's been working on an anti-viral drug. He's bound to have cultures. Could he have accidentally gotten infected from one of his lab specimens?"

The doctor sat forward, the weariness in his voice giving way to hope. "Do you know what virus he's been studying?"

She frowned, trying hard to think. "No," she said, finally, "but you'll have the cultures within the hour."

After bullying her way into the U.C.L.A. research facility and threatening the lab supervisor with numerous unnamed unpleasantries if he didn't release the cultures to her, Katrina managed to produce the organisms most likely responsible for Adam's deathly predicament.

"He was working with the arboviral groups," Katrina told Dr. Phister.

"Do you know which ones in particular?"

"The A group, whatever that means." Katrina wasn't sure she wanted to know.

Dr. Phister stroked his chin, his brows furrowed in concentration. "Well, if I remember correctly, there are three important disease-producing agents in that group. They vary somewhat in severity and mortality rates."

Katrina gulped. How she wished he hadn't said "mortality." But she had to face facts. Adam was seriously ill. He could die.

"Which has the best prognosis?" she forced herself to ask.

"They're all serious, but the Western Equine Encephalitis virus carries the best prognosis."

"Equine?" cried Katrina, her eyes widening in horror. "You mean Adam's got some *horse* virus?"

Dr. Phister shook his head and attempted a chuckle, which fell flat. "No, Kate. You see, in the early 1900's, there was a widespread disease of horses affecting the central nervous system. It wasn't until around 1930 that a virus was isolated from a symptomatic horse—hence the name equine encephalitis. Actually, the equine encephalitis viruses are infectious for a large number of animals, including man."

"I've never heard of these viruses. Tell me everything you know about them."

The doctor paused, closed his eyes, and appeared to draw from his memory. "We don't see cases too often. The viruses are spread by mosquitoes. The main reservoirs appear to be birds and reptiles."

"Then it isn't contagious?" asked Katrina, suddenly worried about Scott.

"No. Man is essentially a dead-end host."

Katrina froze.

"I'm sorry, Kate, poor choice of words. A 'dead-end host' simply means that the infection in man is incidental, or accidental, if you will. The virus does not multiply sufficiently in man to infect mosquitoes. Thus, the life cycle is interrupted. Usually, virus is not even demonstrable in the blood of infected humans."

"Blood! Oh my gosh. Adam gave blood yesterday."

Dr. Phister frowned. "Okay, I'll have to notify the blood

bank."

The strain of the last twenty-four hours coupled with no sleep finally caught up with Katrina, as she slumped in her chair.

"So, what do we do now?" she asked, in a small voice. "How do we treat this virus?" She thought she already knew the answer, but she had to hear it from the doctor.

Dr. Phister massaged the back of his neck. "I'm afraid there is no specific treatment, Katrina. We will just have to give Adam supportive care and hope for the best." He added under his breath, "And pray it isn't the Venezuelan strain."

———•●•———

Katrina sat next to the bed, holding Adam's lifeless hand in hers.

Oh, Adam, how could you have been so careless as to let yourself get infected with your own tissue cultures? Weren't you taking precautions? You know *how dangerous it is to work with viable microbials.*

But, she thought, if he had been successful in finding a drug to treat these viruses, he wouldn't be lying here helpless now. Her eyes traveled over the endless plastic tubes and wires inserted in Adam's body. Two intravenous lines carried fluids into him, his urinary catheter carried fluids out of him, and worst, and most frightening of all, the hideous endotracheal tube taped to the side of his mouth, attached to the alien-appearing respirator with its constant "whooshing" noise pumping air into his lungs. His heart rhythm beeped across a green-screened monitor in a mesmerizing pattern, while his blood pressure registered prominently on the lower left side of the screen. This couldn't be her Adam. Her Adam was strong and healthy. He had been trying to find a way to help other people who suffered from untreatable viral infections. It wasn't fair.

"Oh, Adam," she said, her voice catching. "I'm so scared. Please don't die. Please get well. I need you so." She wondered if Adam had been this frightened when she had almost died after Scott's birth. She squeezed his hand.

Rain pattered against the window. Katrina gazed through bleary eyes at the gray, gloomy sky outside and realized she felt gray and gloomy on the inside. Droplets spattered the window and ran vertically, coalescing into formless globs of condensation. The steady beat of the rain combined with the cyclical "whooshing" of the respirator lulled Katrina until, without realizing it, she fell asleep.

She awoke to a darkened room. For one brief moment, she wondered where she was. Then the reality descended upon her. Rubbing her grainy eyes, she remembered having a strange dream about Adam being critically ill and wishing she could wake up so the dream would go away. But it hadn't gone away. She glanced over at Adam, who lay exactly like he had lain for over twenty-four hours. If only someone could tell her when to expect some improvement. She rose from her chair, stretched her stiff back, and wandered to the window. The rain still came down, bleak and dreary.

"Mrs. Wallace?" came a voice from the doorway. Katrina turned. A young nurse stood framed in the dim light from the hallway, holding a tray of medications. "Why don't you go home and try to get some rest? It's almost midnight."

The idea of a hot shower and a soft bed seemed heavenly, but she couldn't leave Adam. "I . . . I can't." She turned back to Adam.

The nurse set her tray on the bedside table and came over to put her arm around Katrina. "Really, Mrs. Wallace, there's nothing you can do. You need your sleep."

Katrina shrugged off the unasked-for touch. "I'm fine," she snapped. "And it's *Doctor Graham.*"

The nurse retreated without another word. Katrina went back to her chair, flopped down with exhaustion, and began to smooth the hair from Adam's forehead.

"You're forty-one, Adam Wallace, and you still have a head full of dark hair. Not a gray hair in sight and no receding hair line . . ." Her voice trailed off. "Now why, would you please tell me, did I bite that nice girl's head off?" She forced out a brittle laugh. "And I insisted on being called Dr. Graham, not Mrs. Wallace. I suppose that matters a whole lot, doesn't it? My title." Silent tears streamed down her face. "Nothing matters except that you get well." She leaned down and kissed his cheek, drying the spot where her tears had fallen with her thumb.

Slowly, she forced herself to stand and walk out to the

corridor. She spied the young nurse whom she had jumped on earlier.

"Excuse me," she said. "I want to apologize for my outburst earlier."

The nurse smiled at her with true compassion. "It's perfectly understandable. Your husband is seriously ill, and you're under a tremendous amount of stress."

Katrina shook her head. "That's still no excuse for taking it out on you when you were just trying to be kind. Please forgive me."

"There's nothing to forgive," the nurse answered. She hesitated a minute and then added, "There's a chapel on the second floor if you would like to have a quiet moment."

Katrina nodded. "Thank you. I think I just might." She forced a smile at the nurse and headed to the elevator.

The chapel sat at the end of the hall across from the business offices, which were now all closed and dark. As Katrina pushed open the heavy door, a sense of peace immediately enveloped her. In the subdued lighting, she could see four rows of small pews separated by a narrow aisle. Thick, red carpeting silenced her footsteps as she proceeded on trembling legs to the front, where a beautiful stained-glass window picturing Jesus healing the paralytic on the mat shone down. She raised her eyes to soak in the sight of the healing as tears poured from her eyes.

Then she fell to her knees, whispering, "Oh, Father God. You are the great physician." Her voice broke, then her words came out in a rush. "Oh, Lord, I know I have drifted away from you. I ask your forgiveness and pray that you will hear my prayer. Please, God, heal Adam. I don't ask this because I am worthy, but because you are a God of mercy. Help me feel your presence during this trial and help me be strong. In Jesus' name, amen."

She stayed on her knees for a long time, simply letting her heart speak to God, and straining to hear His voice in the midst of the storm. Finally, she rose, filled with supernatural peace, and made her way back to Adam's room.

A little while later, a knock sounded at the door. The young nurse stood outside, accompanied by an orderly with a roll-away cot.

"I thought you'd be more comfortable on this than that old chair, if you want to spend the night, Dr. Graham."

"Thank you," Katrina said, her voice thick.

Although she was sure she wouldn't sleep a wink, Katrina was out the moment her head hit the pillow. She awakened only when the morning nurse came in to suction Adam's endotracheal tube and change the I.V. bag.

"How is he?" she asked, feeling guilty for having failed to keep her all-night vigil.

The nurse shook her head. "The same, I'm afraid."

"Oh." Katrina's spirits plummeted. "What time will Dr. Phister be in?"

"Usually around eight o'clock."

"All right. I'll wait and talk to him."

"Would you like some coffee?"

Katrina gave her a tired smile. "Yes, thank you, that would be nice."

The nurse brought back a Danish with the coffee. "I thought you could stand a little sugar."

"You're all so kind," said Katrina, a lump forming in her throat. She attempted to sip the hot coffee, forcing it past the lump, as she gazed with despair at her husband. The sense of peace from last night threatened to dissipate.

Dr. Phister made his rounds a little before eight. After a cursory exam, he drew Katrina aside.

"Kate, we have the preliminary results of the serum titers. It looks like it's the Western Encephalitis strain. That's probably the best of the three, prognosis-wise."

"But he's not improved at all. When is he going to show some improvement?"

"Kate, you know better than to ask me that," chided the doctor. "You know I don't have any more idea than you do."

She sagged. "I know."

"We're doing everything we can."

They always said that. Especially when they didn't *know* what to do.

"And you can't do Adam any good by having a breakdown yourself. So what I want you to do is go home, take a long shower, have a nap, and don't let me see you here until dinner time. Oh, and by the way, eat something."

"But–"

"No arguments, Kate. Doctor's orders. Someone will call you

if there's any change."

"Promise?"

"Yes. Now go home."

———•●•———

Katrina had lost all track of days and time. She was surprised to see Scott at home in the morning.

"Why aren't you at school?" she asked, her tone cross.

"Mommy, it's Saturday." The child gave her a bewildered look.

"Is it? Oh my gosh, I'm totally confused." She scrubbed her face with her hand.

"Dr. Graham, you look terrible," said Lucy. "Let me make you a nice breakfast, and then you go lie down."

"I want to see Daddy," demanded Scott.

"I'm sorry, honey, but they don't allow children to visit in the hospital. Besides, Daddy's very sick."

"I don't care. I want to go!" Scott yelled and stomped his foot.

Katrina met Lucy's eyes. Lucy gave a slight nod of her head, indicating that Scott had been difficult the last couple of days.

She sighed. "Now, Scott, I explained to you how your daddy and I need for you to be a good boy right now. Daddy's very, very sick and I have to spend a lot of time at the hospital. I don't want to have to come home to your tantrums."

Scott assumed his defiant stance—legs spread, arms crossed over his small chest, and chin thrust out. "Then why *did* you come home?"

Taken aback, Katrina forced her tone to remain as calm as possible. "I came home to get some rest, Scott. I don't expect you to completely understand, but the last couple of days have been very hard on me."

"What about *me*?" yelled the child.

Once again, Katrina felt the familiar guilt. Once again, Scott had been shoved onto the back burner while more pressing matters demanded her attention. He was only a little boy. He couldn't distinguish the lack of attention due to a catastrophic illness from the lack of attention related to his selfish mother's career. And nobody had really sat down and discussed the seriousness of Adam's condition with him. Everything had happened so fast.

"Oh, sweetheart," she said, "come here." She patted her lap and he climbed into it. Katrina brushed the dark hair out of his eyes, thinking how much he needed a haircut. His hair was so like Adam's that it momentarily seized her heart. "I guess you've been feeling kind of left out of all of this, haven't you?"

Scott nodded, his eyes downcast and his lower lip protruding.

"Well, we didn't mean to, honest. Remember the other day? I told you I quit my job so that I could stay home and spend more time with you like some of the other kids' mothers do? Well, I meant it, Scotty, and when your daddy gets well, that's what I'm going to do."

He looked at her, narrowing his eyes.

"But right now, your daddy needs me. He's very sick, Scotty. Remember how sometimes when you get sick I stay up all night with you? Well, sometimes grown-ups get sick, too. And I've got to stay with your daddy as much as I can. I really need you to help me by being a good boy and minding Lucy. And I need you to keep praying very hard for Daddy."

The ringing of the telephone interrupted the conversation. "It's the hospital, Dr. Graham!" cried Lucy. "Mr. Wallace is awake!"

"Oh, thank you, God!" Katrina hopped up so fast that Scott slid to the floor. She reached down and kissed him. "I've got to go back to the hospital, sweetheart. I'll be home when I can. I love you."

Katrina broke all speed limits getting to the hospital. She raced down the corridor, nearly colliding with Adam's day nurse.

"It all happened so fast," the woman said, as they trotted along together down the corridor, Katrina's shoes clacking loudly in contrast to the nurse's muted footsteps on the linoleum. "Suddenly, he was awake and wanting to know where he was."

Katrina burst into the room, the nurse on her heels. Dr. Phister was bending over the bed, and Adam, looking disoriented, was attempting to sit up.

"Slowly now," ordered the doctor. But when Adam and Katrina saw each other, there was no "slow" for either one of them. She flew across the room, elbowing the doctor out of the way, and Adam fought his I.V. tubings to take her in his arms.

"Adam," she murmured, tears running down her cheeks. "I

was so scared." She clung to him as if her life depended on it.

"Throat hurts," Adam croaked, looking at the doctor with accusing eyes.

"That's from the endotracheal tube," explained Dr. Phister. He turned to Katrina. "He can have some ice chips and small amounts of fluids, but go slow." He let them embrace for a moment, then added, "I haven't had a chance to tell him much, Kate. Perhaps I'll leave you to it. He's a bit confused, as you might expect." The doctor exited the room, motioning for the nurse to follow him.

"Headache. It was so painful. Thought I was getting the flu." Adam coughed and tried to reach for his water cup.

"Here," said Katrina, handing the cup to him and adjusting the straw. "Go easy. And don't try to talk too much. I'll tell you everything."

The news depressed Adam terribly. "How utterly careless of me," he muttered. "Of all the stupid things . . ."

"Shh." Katrina cradled his head against her shoulder. "It's all okay now." But she wished there were some way to keep him from ever going back into that lab.

CHAPTER FIFTY-EIGHT
CHARLOTTE

Everything seemed to move in blurry slow motion. Jeff didn't even remember how he got rid of Lisa or how he got Charlotte into the apartment, but somehow, she was sitting on his sofa, her crying subsided, and he was trying to force her to drink some strong tea.

"All right, baby, can you tell me what happened now?" he prodded.

Through little chokes, she managed to get out, "They found out about us."

"Who did? What are you talking about?"

"Someone saw us together and told Miss Young." Charlotte sniffed and wiped her nose on her sleeve. Jeff pressed a tissue into her hand. "She . . . she called me into her office and said that she would put a stop to our meetings. She said a lot of horrible things about us."

"Then what happened?"

"She said I was grounded until I left the home. That I wouldn't be allowed to go anywhere except school. Until I'm eighteen."

He set the mug of tea on the coffee table and gathered her in his arms. "Charley, this will be the first place they look for you."

"I know. I'm sorry. I didn't know what else to do." She looked at him, her eyes searching his. "I thought you wanted to be with me as much as I want to be with you."

"I do!" he cried.

She lowered her eyes, unshed tears clinging to her lashes. "I thought you loved me, Jeff."

"I do. Oh my gosh, Charley, if you only knew how much."

Her lower lip began to tremble. "I shouldn't have come here. You obviously don't care about me as much as I thought you did, and I'll only get you in trouble. I'll go back to the home."

Fear seized him. He couldn't bear to lose her now. Not after they had come so far. Two years without seeing each other would destroy everything they had. And Lisa! He groaned inwardly. How could he have made such a stupid mistake? It would never happen again. If only Charlotte would believe him and trust him again.

"No," he said, his mind churning. "Here's what we have to do. First, we've got to get you out of here. Come on, we'll find you a motel for tonight." He started to pull her up.

"But—"

"Then tomorrow, after they've checked with me, and I've told them I haven't seen you, we'll get out of town. Do you still have the money in the bank?"

"Yes, but—"

"Good. Tomorrow, withdraw everything. Only be careful. They may be looking for you there."

"Nobody knows about the money except you."

Jeff's thoughts ran amok with his words. "We'll have to buy a cheap used car. Once we're out of the state, we'll have to get rid of it and get another. Then we'll go somewhere and get married and—"

"Married?" Her jaw dropped open.

"Yes, married. Now I'll go to work in the morning as usual, so as not to arouse suspicion. Then I'll pretend to get sick, come back, take all my money out of the bank, go buy a car, pack up what I've got, and come get you. Are you listening to me, Charley?"

"Married?" she echoed, raising her eyebrows. "But Jeff, what about . . ." She gulped, hard. Taking a deep breath, she blurted out, "What about that other girl? And who else is there?"

"Oh, Charley," he groaned. "There's never been anyone else, I swear. The girl tonight was a big mistake. I . . . I don't even know her. It was . . ." He paused, unable to excuse his behavior. "She gave me a ride home, that's all."

Charlotte looked so hurt. He couldn't stand the way she was looking at him. How could he ever explain it to her? He sank back down on the sofa and took her in his arms, again. "I love you and only you, Charley. Nothing like that will ever happen again. I promise. You must believe me."

—•●•—

The pain in her heart was almost too much to bear. Now she truly understood the term "broken heart." She didn't know if she could ever believe him again, not after he'd betrayed their special love. She certainly hadn't been expecting *that* reception from the one person in the world she had trusted. Her head ached with conflicting emotions. What was she going to do? Go back to the home? Run away with Jeff? Or run away without Jeff? She couldn't think.

"I'll go to the motel for tonight," she said. "Then I'll think about what I'm going to do."

—•●•—

She lay awake, tossing and turning all night. Why was it that everyone she loved betrayed her? Should she go back to the home? There she'd be a prisoner for the next two years and have no chance of working things out with Jeff. But if she ran away with Jeff, then he would have to quit school in the middle of the semester, as well as give up a good job. Besides, what if he betrayed her again? She couldn't live day by day worrying and waiting for that to happen. No, there was only one thing to do—what she had always done in the past. Rely only on herself. She felt completely empty, a huge hole in her heart where her love for Jeff had once been. A tear rolled down her cheek, as her gnawing loneliness deepened.

"What's the use?" she sobbed into her pillow. "Why even bother to go on living?" A dark idea began to form in her mind. But did she have the courage to kill herself? She sat up in bed and turned on the light. A wave of despair washed over her. There was nothing here to help her. No pills, no gun, no knife . . .

"What am I thinking?" she cried aloud.

Shaking all over, she turned on her side and, for the first time, noticed a Bible on the nightstand. She reached out and fingered the cover. Jeff had talked to her so often about his faith. She snorted. Some faith. He was no better than all the others—a liar and a cheater. She drew in a ragged breath.

She thought about the church she went to with Jeff. It was a welcoming church where she could literally see the love of Jesus in the faces of the people. She had felt the urging of the Holy Spirit tugging at her heart. After being so conflicted for so long, she was beginning to think she understood what it meant to be a Christian. Not harsh and judgmental like her grandparents, not perfect and prideful, but filled with love and peace and joy, knowing she was loved in spite of her flaws. She wanted that. She *needed* that. She opened the book and began to read. Sometime in the middle of the night, she found herself really talking to God. She poured out her heart, every broken detail of her life, and asked forgiveness for her sins. Then she asked God to take control of her life.

A huge burden lifted from her shoulders. This setback was not going to defeat her. She had lived through worse. But this time she wasn't alone. She had God with her!

But what should she do about Jeff? God hadn't exactly shouted the answer in her ear. She set her jaw and lay back down. She would get up early, go to the bank, and get on a bus to somewhere . . . anywhere, as long as it was away from here. Sometime around daybreak, she fell asleep.

She woke to bright sunlight streaming in through the blinds and rolled over to look at the clock. Noon! Now she was going to be late getting away. She threw on her clothes and left, hoping to find a branch of her bank nearby. It took a while, but she finally found a bank several blocks away. She withdrew all her savings and tucked it into her purse, looking around to make sure nobody was watching. Then she set off for the long walk to the bus station.

She arrived hot, tired, and hungry. Quickly scanning the schedule, she saw that the next bus, which went to Birmingham, didn't leave for another hour and a half. Why not? Birmingham was as good as anywhere else. With her heart in her throat, she stepped up to the window and requested a one-way ticket. She watched the clerk anxiously, looking for any obvious sign of recognition, just in case someone from the home had alerted them to be on the lookout for a runaway. But the clerk gave her no more than a bored look along with the ticket. She guessed that by now, the authorities must have already checked with Jeff. A hot stab of pain shot through her chest at the thought of Jeff. Trying to hold up her quivering chin, she told herself they were better off without each other. She would only complicate his plans for his future, and he would only break her heart—if that were possible to do more than once.

Now all she had to do was wait and hope that she could get through another ninety minutes without someone finding her here. She looked around for a coffee shop. There was nothing inside the bus terminal. Cautiously, she ventured outside and searched the street for a place to eat, but the bus station was not located in the best neighborhood. She thought about her life's savings in her purse. Even though the air was warm, she shivered. No, she couldn't risk losing her money. It was her only ticket to freedom. Discouraged, she plopped down on one of the hard benches to wait.

Then another thought struck her. In her panic to leave last night, she had left her notebook behind. For anyone's prying eyes. The memory of Jeff's midnight escapade to seize her notebook flitted uninvited through her brain. Jeff again! Oh well, there was nothing she could do about the notebook now. But she did wish she'd remembered to bring it. She'd written a lot of things about Jeff that she'd rather nobody else see. It could even get him into trouble. Maybe it would serve him right, she thought, miserably. He had just been leading her on all this time, making a fool out of her, tricking her into believing he loved her.

She wished she could stop thinking about Jeff. She had to think about what she was going to do once she got to Birmingham. She would have to find a place to live, get a job. Suddenly, all her problems seemed overwhelming. How was she going to manage alone? For the first time in years, she thought about how her mother had struggled alone and how she had ended up. No, she couldn't think about that now. She was stronger than her mother. She would never let herself end up like her mother.

Would the time never pass? Her eyes kept glancing at the big, ugly wall clock, with its seemingly broken hands. She leaned her head back against the uncomfortable bench and closed her eyes. She must have drifted off, for the next thing she knew, a blurry announcement for the departure of her bus rattled from an overhead speaker. Clutching her purse tightly to her body, she stood and joined the small line of people moving out to the loading platform.

She had just reached the door, when she heard, "Charley!" and saw Jeff running toward her.

"Oh my gosh, Charley, what are you doing?" he cried in an anguished voice, as he caught up to her, grabbing her to him. "I've looked everywhere for you. I've been out of my mind with worry."

"Just let me go, Jeff, please." She wasn't going to cry.

"Charley, they'll be here any minute looking for you."

"The bus is leaving. They won't catch me."

"Charley, if they don't catch you here, someone will be looking for you when the bus stops. Come on, I've got a car." He released her and reached for her hand.

She hesitated.

"Come on, Charley." When she stayed rooted in place, his shoulders slumped. "Look, if you don't want me to go with you, fine. I'll understand. But at least let me get you safely away. You'll never make it by bus." He grabbed her hand and pulled her after him, talking over his shoulder as they ran. "But I'm prepared to go with you. I love you, Charley. You're my life. I'd give up everything for you."

He hurried her into a dilapidated Chevy, piled high with all his worldly possessions, and started the engine.

As they drove away, a rather strange question occurred to Charlotte. "Jeff, when did you learn to drive?"

He turned and shot her a sheepish grin. "Well, actually, I'm only halfway through driver's training. I don't have my license yet."

Her eyes grew big, then she started to laugh. He glanced over, relief flooding his face, and then he began to laugh with her. "It's going to be all right, Charley. From now on, it's you and me."

CHAPTER FIFTY-NINE
ADAM

Adam showed quick improvement over the next few days. Katrina had even managed to sneak Scott past the nurse's station for a visit. The day before his discharge, Adam had a visit from his PhD supervisor, Dr. Umbach.

"Glad to see you're doing better," the wiry little professor said, as he perched on the edge of his chair, looking ready for a quick flight.

Adam could tell by the man's fidgeting that he had something on his mind. "Yes, I'll be getting out of here tomorrow. Probably be able to come back to work sometime next week."

Dr. Umbach cleared his throat and looked away. "Well, er, you see, Adam, that is something I need to discuss with you."

Adam's heart began a nervous cadence against his ribs, and his stomach clenched in trepidation of what Dr. Umbach had to say. "Go ahead."

"Well, er, you see . . ." The professor stopped, cleared his throat again, and after stalling for an excruciatingly long moment, said, "You see, what happened to you has scared a lot of people."

"Scared me, too," Adam said.

Dr. Umbach emitted a slight chuckle. Then, becoming serious again, "The department has taken the position that your project is too dangerous."

Anger rose in Adam's chest. "Now wait a minute. There are

always certain risks when you're dealing with live microbes."

"Exactly my point—"

"But I assure you I will take all the necessary precautions to ensure this doesn't happen again."

"Adam, it might not have been *you* who was careless. It could have been *anybody* in the lab." Dr. Umbach took a long, noisy breath through his nose. "We feel the risk is too great. We are simply not equipped in our lab to deal with a project like this."

Adam sat up straight and leaned forward, his anger escalating. "But doggone it, you approved the project before I even started. We are talking about a major university here, not some high school chemistry lab."

Dr. Umbach hung his head, not meeting Adam's glare. His courage seemed to have left him. "I know we approved it," he said, his voice tinged with sadness, "but, we've had to redefine our position."

"So what does that mean?" Adam's voice rose. "Scrap the whole project? Throw two years of work down the drain? Come on, George, you know this is important. You *know* we need a major breakthrough in the field of anti-viral drugs."

The professor shrugged. "Adam, I'm sorry. It wasn't only up to me. What if you had died? Or what if someone working in your lab had died? The university cannot take that kind of responsibility."

"I can't believe this." Adam's lips tightened and he shook his head.

Dr. Umbach pushed himself out of the chair. "I'm truly sorry, Adam," he repeated. "Perhaps when you feel up to it, you can come by my office, and we can discuss another project."

Adam didn't answer.

"Well," he said, "I need to be going. Get better. See you later."

Adam still didn't answer, as his supervisor hurried from the room.

Two years' work!

———•●•———

Katrina found Adam in a foul mood when she came by later. After Adam explained what Dr. Umbach had said, she had difficulty hiding her own relief.

"Don't worry about it now," she told him, knowing full well he was going to worry anyway. "You'll find another project."

"No, Kate, I don't think so," he said, his tone weary. "This one has been so time-consuming, so stressful. I don't think I can start over."

"It's all right," she assured him. "If you want to quit, that's fine with me. You can probably get your job back at Fenner."

"I've let you down. I've let myself down."

Katrina locked eyes with her husband. "You know that isn't true. It doesn't matter to me whether you have a PhD or not. All I care about is that you're alive and healthy."

"I'm a failure," he repeated.

She stood. "I'm not going to stay around and listen to this. I'll be back when you're not feeling so sorry for yourself." She started to move toward the door.

"Kate, wait," he cried. "Please don't go."

She paused, waiting to see what he would say.

"You're right. I *am* feeling sorry for myself. And I think, perhaps, I'm a little entitled to." The corners of his lips turned up in a half-hearted grin. "But I'll try to be more cheerful if you'll stay."

She moved back to her chair and sat. He took her hand and, for a long time, neither of them spoke. Finally, he broke the silence. "Kate, I was wondering."

"Yes?"

"Well, I hate the thought of going back to Fenner as a failure." Her body stiffened and she pulled her hand away. "Now wait. Hear me out."

She set her jaw in her usual stubborn manner. He had to laugh.

"What's so funny?" she demanded.

"You are. My stubborn little Kate."

Against her will, she grinned.

"Anyway," he went on, becoming serious, again, "if I go back, I'll only be making half, if that much, of what you make at Fenner. We've got a big mortgage payment and a lot of other expenses—"

"Adam, Scott needs me at home. The money isn't that important."

"But you love your job, Kate. Don't try to tell me you don't. Staying home is going to be a big sacrifice for you."

"So, it'll just have to be a sacrifice."

"But wouldn't it make more sense if the person who was the most valuable to Fenner worked and the other stayed home with Scott?"

Katrina frowned. "What are you saying, Adam? That you want to be a housewife?"

"Well, no, not exactly." He laughed. "But think about it. Why can't a father stay home with his child?"

"Wouldn't that look rather strange?"

"To whom? Just because we've been conditioned by society to think that the mother has to stay home with the children while the father works doesn't necessarily make it bound in stone. We've never followed normal convention in our family, anyway."

"I don't know," she mused, thinking how wonderful it would be to be free to pursue her career without having to feel guilty about her child.

"I know I would like it." His voice became more animated. "You know that's the one thing I always regretted with my daughters. I was never home with them. And lately, I've been making the same mistake with Scotty. It would be a great opportunity for both of us. How many kids get to be with their dads all the time?"

"Maybe it would work," she agreed. "Yes, it just might work. My mother always says, 'When God closes a door, He always opens a window.'"

THANK YOU, DEAR READER

If you enjoyed reading this book, the best thing you can do to help the author is to tell others about it. Ellen would also greatly appreciate you rating her book and leaving a brief review at amazon.com and goodreads.com. Simply type in the name of the book and the author. When the website comes up, click on the picture of the book, scroll down, and there will be a button to click to leave a rating and a review. A review doesn't have to be long—a sentence or two telling what you liked about the book. Was it interesting, informative, thought-provoking, etc? Thank you so much for your support.

Ellen would love for you to visit her website: https://ellenfannonauthor.com and subscribe to follow her weekly blog, *Good for a Laugh.*

READ ON FOR THE NEXT EPISODE OF HONOR THY FATHER

CHAPTER ONE
CHARLOTTE

They had been driving quite a while before Charlotte spoke again. "Where are we going, anyway?"

"That depends on you, Charley." His eyes darted in her direction and back to the road. "Is it going to be you and me?"

She peeked into the back seat, crammed with all his worldly possessions, and nodded. Jeff had to love her to give up everything he had worked so hard for. This semester of college was down the drain. And he would have to start job hunting again.

"I'm sorry I got you into this mess," she murmured.

Jeff's lips turned up into a half-smile. "Don't be. It was too difficult being apart and having to sneak around to see each other. Two more years would have been impossible." He cast a glance in his rear-view mirror. "We've got to be careful, though, until we get out of Florida."

"Why are we going east?"

"Because, most likely, if anyone's looking for us, they'll figure we're headed either west or north into Alabama. I don't need to tell you what would happen if we got caught."

Charlotte's heart fluttered. Probably she would be sent to juvenile detention and Jeff would go to jail.

"We'll head toward Tallahassee and then drive north. We'll get married in Tennessee."

Her heart pounded even harder. "But I'm only sixteen."

"That's okay. You can pass for eighteen. Besides, if I'm not mistaken, I don't think you have to be eighteen to get married in Tennessee."

"But I don't have a dress to wear."

He laughed. "All right. We'll stop and buy you a dress. And a ring."

Charlotte smiled. This was going to be a mighty strange wedding. But a warm glow began to fill the innermost parts of her being. She had never felt so cherished in her life.

After crossing into Georgia, they stopped while Jeff traded in their car and Charlotte shopped for a wedding dress. Now it would be more difficult for anyone to find them in a car with Georgia plates. The second car, a '63 Plymouth Valiant with a noisy muffler and several paint jobs, looked worse than the first. But it ran all right. Besides, it wasn't easy finding a car for a few hundred dollars where people didn't ask a lot of questions.

Jeff swung back by the department store to pick up Charlotte, who waited at the entrance holding a shopping bag.

As she climbed into the car, he said, "It looks like you found a dress."

"Yes. And shoes. I can't get married in *these*." She held up her feet with their worn sneakers.

"No, I guess not. Well, let's see the dress."

"You can't. It's bad luck."

"All right." He laughed. "But I don't know how we're going to get to a courthouse tomorrow without my seeing you."

They drove on for a couple more hours after the sun disappeared below the horizon. Charlotte fought to stay awake, and looking at Jeff's profile in the dim shadows of the car, she could see the fatigue settling on his face.

Finally, he let out a weary sigh and spoke. "Charley, we can't go any further tonight. There's a motel up ahead. We'll stop for the night and start out fresh in the morning after we get some sleep."

"Okay," she agreed, although her heart skittered at the thought of spending the night alone with him.

He pulled the car into the parking lot opposite the lobby and turned off the engine.

"You wait in the car while I check in. I don't want anyone

seeing us together."

Once safely inside the musty little room, they breathed a sigh of relief. Jeff turned to her and held her at arm's length, looking into her eyes. "By this time tomorrow, you'll be my wife, Charley."

She nodded, a large lump forming in her throat. Everything seemed so unreal.

"Any misgivings?" he asked.

She shook her head.

He pulled her close. "I love you so much. And I'm going to do my best to make you happy. I'll take care of you and I'll always be there for you." He tilted her chin toward him and placed a tender kiss on her lips.

The warm glow that had begun earlier continued to envelop her body, convincing her everything would be all right. Something stirred within her, and as he released her, she pulled his lips back onto hers. Time seemed to stand still as they remained locked in their passionate embrace. Then, as though in a dream, he swept her up and gently laid her on the bed, wrapping his body around hers.

She didn't know why she had been so scared before. Surely, this was the ultimate in loving someone, becoming a part of him. She felt her body transcend beyond the realm of reality as Jeff's kisses became more burning, like little needles of fire. Feelings and sensations she had never known came alive and became entwined in a harmony so perfect it defied human expression.

Then suddenly, he pulled away and sat up, his head in his hands. Confused, she sat up, too. Had she done something wrong? Although this experience was new to her, she thought things had been going pretty well. *Really* well. Her racing pulse slowed ever so slightly.

"What's wrong?" she asked, a tinge of disappointment and fear in her voice.

Jeff groaned. "Oh, Charley." His words came out breathy and full of anguish. "Nothing is wrong. It's all *too* good..." His voice trailed off, then he added, "but we're not married yet."

She looked at him, wide-eyed and expectant.

"I told you I would always protect and respect you. And this," he said, waving his hand, taking in the surroundings of the shabby room, "isn't doing either. This is taking advantage of you and letting my raging hormones run amok."

"But we're getting married tomorrow," she protested, her own hormones ablaze.

"Yes, but we're not married tonight. I want everything done right in the eyes of God." Jeff chuckled. "Although I'm not sure what He thinks about our taking matters into our own hands by running away together. I have to admit I really didn't ask His opinion."

Charlotte hung her head. Wasn't it just last night she had decided to turn her life over to the Lord? And it was her fault they were in this situation.

"Still, what's done is done. We can't go back now. But I don't want to compound things by—"

"I understand," she said, although her flesh screamed otherwise.

"I'll sleep in the car tonight, Charley." He placed one last gentle kiss on her lips and quickly walked out the door, leaving her frustrated, but grateful.